As host of *Saturday Live* and *Friday Night Live* Ben Elton has proved himself the most popular and the most controversial comedian to emerge in recent years. As well as his own stand-up routines Ben's numerous writing credits include *The Young Ones*, *Filthy Rich and Catflap*, *Happy Families* and the award-winning *Blackadder*.

STARK

STARK

Ben Elton

WARNER BOOKS

A *Warner* Book

First published in Great Britain by Sphere Books Ltd 1989
Reprinted 1989 (twenty-three times), 1990 (five times), 1991
Reprinted by Warner Books 1992, 1993

ISBN 0 7515 0700 8

Printed in England by Clays Ltd, St Ives plc

Warner Books
A Division of
Little, Brown and Company (UK) Limited
165 Great Dover Street
London SE1 4YA

CONTENTS

BREAKFAST IN CARLO

Carlton is a little coastal town some miles south of Perth in Western Australia. They're a strange contrast those two towns. Perth is home to a higher density of millionaires than any other city in the world, but just down the road in Carlton people hang kind of looser. Certainly the place has its fair share of bread-heads and hustlers, but it's still got a laid back feel. Boats and cafés and taking it easy are the things a visitor carries away in the memory.

Perth gets up in the morning and says, 'OK let's do it, let's make money, let's get on with a load of really high-powered stuff right now!'

Some mornings Carlton doesn't get up.

It's a nice place to holiday in, or retire to, so actually quite a bit of money is made there in a gentle kind of way, a lot of it by a man called Silvester (or Sly) Moorcock. Sly lived in Perth, he was one of that city's many self-made rich, smug bastards, and finding the need to get further into property for tax reasons, he had bought up all the old granny duplex's and made Carlton (or Carlo to its friends), one of his many possessions. Some of it he knocked down, some of it he rented out. Some of it looked as if he'd got half-way through knocking it down but then changed his mind and decided to rent it out. Such a place was occupied by Colin.

Yes, Sly owned Carlo, but he didn't rule the roost – not in Colin's little part of town anyway. All right, so Sly could have evicted Colin. Also, if Colin had had a job, Sly could have made him redundant. He could have impounded his possessions and done him for non-payment of rent. But so

I

what? Colin didn't really own anything anyway and when it's time to move on, it's time to move on.

No, Sly didn't bother Colin overmuch. So the guy was a billionaire, what could he *really* do to you? Nothing. In the searing heat and natural abundance of a Carlton summer, Colin had much more pressing enemies than Sly. Let's face it, Sly was unlikely to appear as if from nowhere, on Colin's bread-board and make him feel like throwing up. He wasn't going to creep into the fridge and hide in the folded spout of the milk carton so that when Colin popped back the spout wings, there he would be! all horrid and scuttley! Then, off like a bullet, but not before he'd shocked Colin into dropping the milk and ruined Colin's day.

Sly Moorcock was more powerful than God in Carlton, but Colin had never had to throw the butter away because he'd found Sly having a fuck in it – it takes a special kind of bastard to make you do that. Colin's enemies were cockroaches, he had no time to worry about billionaires.

COCKIES

Cockroaches have an extraordinary physical resilience. You can smash one to bits on your living room floor leaving it in numerous cockroachie pieces and a little later when you have steeled yourself to clearing it up, it's gone! It's cleaned *itself* up! Some say that other cockroaches have simply come and carried it away to have for their dinner but this is not true. Cockroaches are definitely bionic, they can rebuild themselves. If you put the shattered corpse of one in the bin, it will wait until you are gone and then slowly pull itself back together again, gluing on its head with its own horrid goo. Then, when it is ready, a born-again cockie, bigger, scarier and somehow managing to have more legs than it started off with, it will scuttle out, refreshed, from a mound of potato peelings making obscene gestures at you with its little cockroach fist.

Nothing is more deflating than being sneered at by a cockroach. It is said that cockroaches would survive a nuclear war better than anything. They would brush off fall-out like they brush off being smashed to bits with a shoe.

As Colin lay in bed, watching with distaste the phoenix of a new cockie rising out of the ruin of its dead self, it seemed to him eminently likely that in the barren aftermath of the final folly; when the poison winds blow cruelly over the rotting debris of us, the previous top dogs, cockroaches will inherit the earth. After all, they had clearly already inherited Carlton. Colin was thinking of charging them rent.

Perhaps, he thought, the government had been conducting secret nuclear tests and the holocaust had already come to Western Australia.

POMMIE POSEUR

Colin was a pom. He'd lived in Oz since he was thirteen but that doesn't make any difference, if you're a pom, you're a pom. The Aussies have a strange double standard when it comes to poms. For instance, they are fairly happy to cheer Lady Di and have a Union Jack on their flag, but that doesn't stop most of them calling you a whingeing pommie wanker if you happen to remark that it's hot when the mercury's pushing 40 °C.

Colin did not care. However hot it was Colin always thought he was cool – small and cool. He was one of those rare people who try to be cool and somehow manage in the process to be a bit cool – not much, but a bit. He was so unashamed about his pretensions that they kind of worked. For instance, despite living in Oz, he managed to speak in an accent that was situated somewhere in the mid-Atlantic, half-way between Britain and the USA – having arrived at this location via some pretty groovy forties movies and some equally crucial rock lyrics. By rights this should have been horrible, marking Colin down as the worst kind of poseur, but it didn't. It almost did, but it didn't.

Probably it didn't because Colin wouldn't have minded being considered a poseur, in fact he would have thought

3

being called a poseur quite an interesting pose. Everybody poses, the coolest people pose most of all, they just make it seem natural. Colin had a picture on his damp patch of Brando in *The Wild One*, dressed in leather, leaning on his Triumph with a little peaked cap on his head, tilted to one side, looking slightly off-camera with an expression on his face that seemed to be saying: 'Listen, I may be sensitive, confused and inarticulate but I could still beat seventeen types of shit out of you, OK?' Now *that* was posing, but nobody minded because it was Brando. He remained cool, even though he was an utter poseur with a damp patch behind him.

It's all a question of confidence. Colin never had any money, but he acted like he was loaded. Poverty was always a temporary problem for Colin. His present period had lasted about twenty-five years.

His clothes were piss-poor but he wore them with aplomb. He would practise things like opening and lighting his Zippo lighter with just one hand and throwing cigarettes up in the air and catching them in his mouth. Strangely this did not make him look like a total wanker – it nearly did, but not quite. There was a tiny degree of charm in the way Colin accepted his many failures with the same easy confidence that he greeted his few successes. When Colin missed his mouth with the fag he acted the same as if he'd scored a hit. When he burned his thumb with the lighter he yelped with pain in a manner that suggested that pretty soon anyone who was anyone would be burning their fingers on Zippo's and yelping with pain. Colin's surname was Dobson. Being aware that James Dean would never have been cast in '*Rebel*' if his name had been Colin Dobson, Colin called himself CD. Since the advent of compact discs this had given Colin an opportunity to do his great joke about being perfect, clear and flawless. Astonishingly he managed to deliver this without sounding like the biggest dickhead in history. He came a very close second.

BREAKFAST THOUGHTS

CD got out from under his grey duvet and lit a fag, he missed his mouth twice which delayed the evil moment of lighting up by about ten seconds. This was good, CD was trying to introduce a programme of starting later in the day and even ten seconds counted. His problem was he didn't want to give up, he really liked smoking, he was one of that ever dwindling group of people who still thought it looked cool. Like most committed smokers, he worried about it all the time. Unfortunately, whenever he found himself dwelling on the proven dangers of the weed he got so uptight he had to have a fag.

'Catch 22,' he would say, throwing one up towards his mouth. Which was ironic really because he probably hadn't caught twenty-two in his entire life.

As CD fished about in the dirty clothes bag for a pair of pants that had only been worn once, he thought his morning thoughts. He thought, as he thought every morning, that it was time to go to the launderette. He thought, as he always did, that it was time to get a new toothbrush. The bristles on his present one were flattened so far back that they were parted in the middle. He had a toothbrush that looked like the top of Oscar Wilde's head.

He hoped, as he always did, that the state of the exterior of the kettle did not reflect upon its internal cleanliness. Logic, of course, insists that the outside of a kettle is an entirely separate entity to the inside, but none the less the thick, greasy, dusty gunge that coated the whole thing was a bit disquieting.

Yet again, as CD wandered through to the kitchen, he tried to gather together the resolve to throw away all his crockery apart from one bowl and one dinner plate. It was, after all, nearly two months since he had done a proper wash-up, his life was a series of mini wash-ups. A plate in the evening for toast, a bowl in the morning for Weetabix. The rest of the pile just sat in the sink laying low his spirits whenever he looked at it. In a world crowded with tiny bummers there is little more depressing than an ancient sinkful of scummy washing-up.

Of course, CD conceded, the alternative to junking it would be to wash it all up, but what false hopes lay in that cheating dream? CD knew that doing the washing-up just meant a brief, transitory illusion. A cruel glimpse of an unattainable civilization where one plucked a mug or a plate at will from the tempting gleaming pile – squandered resources – and made each new coffee in a fresh cup. A paradise soon lost, and in an obscenely brief time, the pile is back, only this time it seems bigger, scummier, even more teetering.

CD considered himself an ecologically concerned person. And yet, like everybody else, he would sooner use a clean cup than wash up a dirty one.

There was a cocky struggling in the water, wriggling, what looked to be its last wriggle. Knowing cockies it probably had a set of scuba gear. CD stared at it in a morning trance, the dirty cockie in the dirty washing-up in the dirty little house that was owned by Sly Moorcock.

DINNER IN LOS ANGELES

Sly Moorcock himself was feeling pretty elated. It had been years since he had genuinely appreciated any of the things that his enormous success had brought him. The thrill of acquiring and consuming had long since faded for Sly. He would never recapture those early joys and he knew it. None the less, as the car left the airport he was feeling good enough to at least enjoy the memory of them.

'Welcome to Los Angeles,' the chauffeur said, 'I believe you'll find we have some gorgeous weather laid on for you.'

Sly grabbed his chance, 'If I want a disc jockey, kid, I'll buy a radio station. Drive the car.' Sly grinned to himself, he had been acting like a rich, arrogant bastard for so many years now he'd forgotten how good it could feel.

Being rude is one of the principal hobbies of the wealthy. Not very rude, just a bit rude, constantly brusque and impatient, implying that one's own life is much more important than that of the person you are talking to. This attitude is at its most satisfying when applied to pretty girls at hotel receptions. Sly remembered nostalgically the warm masculine glow and the tremendous erection that had consumed him the first time he had really flexed his muscles in this manner.

'I'm sorry, Sir, but the room isn't ready yet, perhaps you would like to . . .'

'What I'd *like*, dear, is my room, *right* now, OK lovely? I don't care how you do it poppet, but do it. *You* may have time to polish your nails young lady, but I have a business to run.'

There was something monumentally saucy about a pretty girl in a prim little outfit, with her first name pinned to her tit,

7

hating you so bad that she'd like to kill you and not being able to do a thing about it. The same game could be played with some airline hostesses.

But on the whole those thrills were history for Sly. He had had to learn the hard way that the difference between being poor and not being poor is far greater than the difference between being rich and being stupidly rich. Being able to own a swimming pool is physical pleasure, being able to own hundreds of them is just an abstract idea. Sly had only one dick, only one stomach. There was only so much he could do for them, and yet each day he worked harder to get more of what he didn't need and couldn't use.

EMPIRE-BUILDING

What fun it had been, back in the early seventies when Sly had done his first major deals. Then it had seemed to him that there was an almost frontier, empire-building spirit to his corporate battles. As if he too was using guts, balls and naked cunning to build a new Jerusalem, just like those early Aussie pioneers in their slouch hats and broken boots. How fondly he remembered the days when, with flares flapping round his ankles and kipper tie a foot across, he had lost a friend every time he picked up the phone.

Sly had been one of the very first corporate raiders. He had really been a part of developing the whole craft – or art form as Sly preferred to put it. Even twenty years later he often dwelt fondly on how amazingly clever he had been.

It had started in a pub. Sly was having a beer with an old friend from school and the old friend from school was very upset about his family pie-making business.

'We should never have moved into ham and cheese,' the old friend from school was saying, 'ham and cheese is a poof's pie. I told Dad, I said, "Dad, ham and cheese is a poof's pie. The great Australian bloke is not going to take kindly to having to build the best bloody country in the world on ham and cheese pie."'

8

'He wants meat,' sympathized Sly.

'Of course he wants meat,' the old friend from school said, 'you can't surf all day and root all night on ham and cheese.'

EASY AS PIE

The meat pie plays a significant part in Australian culture. It is far and away that country's most popular snack, it fills the same place in their hearts and tums that fish and chips used to fill for the British. It is often referred to as a 'rats coffin' and the recipe has not changed since it was first discovered being used as part of the lining for Pandora's box. Consisting of pastry so greasy if you drop one on the floor it will stop the boards creaking, and a substance called 'meat' which is made of minced string in gravy.

This horrendous creation, taken almost obligatorily with a squirt of tomato sauce, is delicious. Delicious in a way that only truly awful, stupefyingly, unhealthy food can be. Delicious in a way that vegetables (or indeed anything that is good for you) can only dream of being. Hence it has so far withstood all efforts to ponce it up.

This had been Sly's old school-friend's dad's mistake. He had tried to ponce up the great Australian pie. He did not understand the most important rule of yummy snacks. That they are not yummy *despite* being so awful, they are yummy *because* they are so awful . . .

'It's not as if we put peas or carrots in them,' the old school-friend protested. But secretly he was ashamed, he knew that he and his father were in the wrong. Ham and cheese is a poof's pie.

'Not to worry, old school-friend,' said Sly, who always had trouble with people's names. 'Your dad's company's still in great nick, you're very big in doughnuts, you dominate the mock-cream fancies market, and your apple turnover, turnover is the fastest in WA. Christ almighty, heart disease is one of the biggest killers in Australia, that's a statistic you and your dad can be proud of.'

9

'Oh sure, no worries,' said the friend, 'I'm not saying we're in trouble, I mean in real terms the company's fine, but a cock-up like that hits your share confidence. Market-wise we're at a bit of a low ebb.' And that was when Sly had his brilliant idea.

The next day he quit his job as runner for the fast-growing Tyron Organization and went to his bank to borrow a lot of money. He had stumbled upon a fascinating situation, a healthy company with extremely valuable assets, which was temporarily depressed on the market. My, my, my said the spider to the fly.

On the strength of the information he had got from his old school-friend, Sly bought a majority holding in the friend's family firm at a bargain price and took over as boss. Now a lesser maverick than Sly might have stopped there, content to be the new head of a successful bakery. Remembering the incident only as a stern warning never to chat pies with pals. But Sly was destined to be more than a baker, he wanted to be a bastard. So he smashed the company up, flogging the Cream-Horn machine to one rival, the Viennese Twirl twirler to another. Before long there was nothing left of his old friend's family firm and Sly was sitting on the foothills of what would one day become a mountain of cash.

Sly soon realized that it did not take a ham and cheese debacle to render healthy companies temporarily vulnerable. So erratic is the stock-market that at a time of depressed trading, any concern, even a very successful one, can find itself laid open. Suddenly, the mere hard assets of a company, the carpets, the typewriters, the amusing stickers that say 'you don't have to be mad to work here but it helps', if sold off separately, can add up to a considerably greater value than the sum total of the share value quoted on the index.

The fact that these companies are going concerns that make things and create jobs, is entirely immaterial to the business of asset-stripping. This is scorched earth capitalism, you buy something, smash it up, flog the bits and move on. Then the predator, faced with the question of what to do with the money he or she has made, will probably do it all over again. Cutting a swathe through jobs and dreams, growing bigger and more destructive with every deal.

GOLDEN BOY

An even more curious side to this strange way of making a living is the way in which it is regarded socially. Sly found himself lauded and held up as a role model to other young Australians. Far from being seen as a vandal whose job was destroying other people's jobs purely for personal gain, he was presented as someone who created work, bringing money into the state and helping to keep the wheels of commerce turning. His youthful good looks made him popular with all and he quickly found himself regarding women in the way he regarded companies: things to be used and discarded, he would take from them what he desired and move on. Astonishingly, this too won Sly not contempt and condemnation, but jovial respect. It seemed that not only was this man a brilliant operator, but also he was a hell of a lad to boot. Curiously, this side of things had become rather irritating for Sly. He liked power and it is quite difficult to experience power if all gives way before you. You can't push people round if they're already bending over backwards, it gets boring. Even the sex began to get on his nerves – even with people bending over backwards. Sly was a fantastically successful individual, but he could not be said to have had a fulfilling personal life.

CITY OF ANGELS

And that's why it felt so good to feel good again. As Sly glided in from LA airport, minor irritations, like deep personal discontent, were forgotten. He had the thrill again. The thrill of being, irrationally, pointlessly and idiotically rich. He felt like he'd arrived, and the reason for this childlike elation was a dinner invitation. Silvester Moorcock had been invited to dinner.

Nothing very special about that of course, he'd had dinner before, often. Admittedly, this time he would be dining with some of the richest and most powerful men in the world, but once you've eaten smoked salmon mousse out of the bottom of a Penthouse Pet you have high standards as to what makes a meal swing.

It was not the invitation, but what the invitation represented that made Sly hug himself with excitement that night (normally he would have paid someone to do this for him, but he'd been in a hurry at the airport and anyway, it was a very private moment). Sly knew that he was about to be accepted into a club. An exclusive club. So exclusive a club in fact that it had no name and no membership list. It had no premises and you could not apply to join. A person simply drifted into membership having achieved the required qualifications. These qualifications being truly enormous wealth and the social conscience of a dog caught short on a croquet lawn. It was, and is of course, rare to find the former, without the latter.

The venue for the meal was unpretentious enough. A private room in a restaurant in Los Angeles. With certain obvious exceptions, the super-rich are a fairly faceless bunch and do not feel over-paranoid about going out in society, especially a society that provides itself with its own private police force, as Beverly Hills does.

If Los Angeles ever had a town planner, all the movie stars should club together and get him a guide dog. Whoever it was he must have designed the place while his brain was in a meeting. The town is a mess, worse than the suburbs of Perth, thought Sly as he limo'd through the streets. Streets that looked as if someone had dropped a load of buildings on either side and by coincidence they had all landed the right way up.

Los Angeles, like Sly's native Western Australia, suffered from too much space and too much sunshine. For years and years developers had simply spread out, leaving one shit heap and building another a hundred metres further on, creating hundreds of square miles of depressing, low-rise sprawl.

When the oil runs out LA will be completely finished as a city, millions will starve to death. For most people the nearest shop would be five or six hours walk away and, since in areas like Beverly Hills you quite literally get picked up by the law for walking, most people have forgotten how to do it.

Sly's limo purred up outside 'California Dreaming', a restaurant which made a virtue out of what it called its 'exclusive pricing policy'. The motto was, 'If you want to eat here, be prepared to sell your house.' The idea being to keep out scum and riff-raff. It didn't keep out scum and riff-raff of course, it just kept out people who did not have a ridiculous amount of money.

Probably about a twentieth of the world's ready cash was represented round the table that night so, not surprisingly, the food was good. Not good enough, of course; it would have been the same quality if only a twenty thousandth of the world's wealth had been present, or even, horrible thought, a twenty millionth.

This must be one of the principal blights on the horizon of the super-rich: the fact that luxury and quality is finite. Paying a million pounds for a meal would not make it worth a million pounds; it would not make it ten thousand times better than one that cost a hundred pounds; it would probably not even be twice as good. The earth only has so much bounty to offer and inventing ever larger and more notional prices for that bounty does not change its real value. One day, of course, if there is any justice, heaven will prove to be a store-house of new and unimagined luxuries. The guiltless will scoff great mounds of ambrosia, washing it down with jugfuls of nectar, but it is unlikely that any of the mega-mega-rich will be invited to that particular blow-out.

One presumes that billionaires are not stupid people, they cannot be unaware of the paradox of their great wealth. 'Just what am I working for!' they must shout rhetorically at their art collections, full of art which secretly they don't like. They know the answer of course. They have long since exceeded any possibility of conventional satisfaction. They are working to fuck up the world for everyone else.

THE CLUB

And so Sly joined the club, although club is far too small a word to describe it. For the first time Sly, now a bona fide billionaire bastard, was to take his place at a cabinet meeting of the World Government of Money – or convivial dinner party of like-minded colleagues as they would have preferred to put it. In his wanderings around the upper echelons of society, Sly had often heard hints and rumours regarding a shadowy super-elite, a group wielding almost incomprehensible power who were preparing some secret and terrible purpose. Now it seemed he was being asked to take part.

Of course it was not quorate, by no means all the billionaires who were in on the conspiracy were present. They were dotted about the world, joylessly going about their business of fucking things up for everyone else. Their presence was not essential, for the Government of Money is not like a conventional government. It has no debating chamber, nor specific list of representatives. No official documents guarantee its legality. Indeed, many of the people round the table would have strenuously denied that it was a government at all and perhaps even half-believed their denials. But it is a government, as powerful as any. An invisible, amorphous, multi-headed dictatorship of money.

And it had a plan.

As Sly entered the restaurant, thrilled and excited, he had no idea what that plan was, or where it was leading to. As it happened, it was leading to hell and beyond. Sly's life was about to change utterly. That evening he was to be indoctrinated into the Stark Conspiracy.

FOR THOSE IN PERIL
FROM THE SEA

Some characters in this narrative will loom large, being directly connected, either for or against the great conspiracy which Sly was to join that night. Others must come and go for they are only indirectly connected, but are no less a part of it for that. For the influence of Sly and people like him is impossible to calculate, their tentacles spread across the globe. Sly lived in Oz, he was eating in Los Angeles, but his money was everywhere. His bucks had assumed a life of their own, they were out there doing things of which Sly knew very little and cared even less. Just as long as they went forth and multiplied it was fine by him. His bucks were animals that he had let off the leash. They ran about the world in an uncontrolled frenzy, bursting into the lives of people that Sly would never meet nor think of.

For example, as Sly entered the restaurant in Los Angeles some of his money was floating off the coast of Britain. Of course Sly was aware that a few of his bucks had found a temporary home as a majority holding in a Belgian waste disposal group, his brokers always consulted him before making a share purchase. But what did that tell Sly? nothing about reality. Certainly Sly knew about the company's collateral, its profit and loss curve, its disposable assets, its history on industrial relations and the chances of an injection of public funds should it hit the skids. But that was all he knew. He saw his investment purely and simply as a device by which to make money. What the company actually did was a matter of supreme indifference to him.

He did not know about Captain Robertson; he did not know about the great toilet irony; he did not know about the Pastel family on holiday . . .

BRASS IN MUCK

Captain Robertson was a sad and bitter man. All his life he had wanted to be master of a ship. And what sort of ship did he end up being master of? a sludger. Scarcely a dashing or romantic command.

'What do you do for a living mate?'

'I lug shit up the Thames and dump it in the North Sea.' Captain Robertson would occasionally try to cheer himself up. 'It's a rotten job but then people have to do toilet,' he would say to himself as yet another great steaming slick slid out of the bowels of his barge and began its slow journey back to Britain.

Of course he was right, people *do* have to do toilet. Even the most rabidly concerned environmentalist would be unlikely to volunteer to cork their bot. But it doesn't have to end up dumped virtually raw in the North Sea. It can in fact be processed and used as fertilizer. It could be re-eaten via a nice healthy cauliflower rather than a deformed fish. But perhaps this would be too long-winded a route by which people – like Sly's bucks – could go forth and multiply.

The situation is quite ironic really because people are normally so fastidious about their bathroom hygiene. They are happy to invest in a foaming blue-flush which, although costly, is guaranteed to produce a sparkling bowl and lemon-scented toilet freshness that the whole family will enjoy. However, anything that happens beyond the U-bend is somebody else's business.

THE PASTEL FAMILY ON HOLIDAY

The Pastels had had a lovely day wandering around in the freezing rain and the whole family were getting peckish.

'Now then, kids,' said Mr Pastel, 'I'll tell you what we're

going to have for our tea ... Mussels, that's what, just like your mother and I had on our honeymoon.'

So they did, they had mussels and the whole family got the utter and total shits, because the mussels weren't just like on the honeymoon, since then the world had changed and the mussels with it.

Mussels and oysters feed by filtering tiny particles out of the sea water. These days that includes chemical wastes, agricultural poison and heavy metals. Also an awful lot of bacteria and viruses from human excreta, which cooking and cleaning does not always remove (cooking and cleaning the mussels that is, very few people cook and clean their excreta). Poor Mummy Pastel ended up with acute viral gastroenteritis and died, but we've all got to go sometime.

Sly didn't know Mrs Pastel, she didn't know him, but they were bound together in life and death by money.

COURT, HIPPIES AND LOVE
AT FIRST SIGHT

Anyway, back to CD who had just finished his Weetabix, well, finished the part he was going to eat. He was not a very good eater, especially when he was uptight and this morning was a bummer because he had to go to court, which for sure is the kind of thing to ruin a guy's day.

He took some care in selecting what to wear. He had a pretty minimal wardrobe, but you have to make the effort if you're appearing in court. After some thought he selected a pair of pretend Levis with a designer tear on the knee (he'd actually done it on a nail but in the world of being groovy you take your luck where you find it). He also wore his metal-tipped cowboy boots, an ace shirt which had metal tips on the collar, an ecologically sound tie with a picture of a steaming whale carcass on it and the slogan 'Stop the bloody whaling', and a sports jacket. CD still turned up the lapels of his sports jacket, even though no one else had done this since 1978. To this ensemble he added his droopy, mirrored shades.

I cannot see, CD thought to himself, eyeing his reflection in the broken wardrobe door he used for a mirror, any judge trying to deny that I am looking *good*, I mean *bitching*. Perhaps he couldn't see because he had his shades on.

However, whatever the judge thought of it, and however prejudicial the mirrored shades may have been to his sentence, CD was later to thank his lucky stars that he had elected to go to court strutting like an ace king of teenage cool, because it was at the court that he met Rachel. And when a guy meets the girl of his dreams he should for def' be wearing his pretend torn Levis, metal-tipped boots and shades.

So love found CD at the Carlton Criminal Court. An unlikely location being as how the place was about as romantic as anal warts. The Old Bailey it was not, no ancient oak and dignity for the Carlo crim' processing plant, just veneered chipboard and nineteen-year-old coppers showing off.

CD hated young coppers. Getting busted by someone who could be your dad was one thing, but getting pushed around by a couple of teenage casuals was quite another. Older cops were all right on the whole. For a start they were bored with their jobs and wanted to get home for their tea. Also, their egos were sufficiently well-developed not to need massaging on every piss-poor little bust they made. The problem with some young coppers is that they're exactly the same as the blokes they're called upon to nick. Putting them in uniform doesn't make any difference.

It was CD's contempt for this type of cop, the smug, strutting, government sponsored juvenile delinquents, that got him the black eye.

'Just because you've got a big shiny uniform doesn't mean you've got a big shiny dick,' he had remarked casually to the walking zit who had collared him . . . and there he was, in the gutter going 'No, please, please, don't hit me again, please.'

CD's crime was to paint CND symbols in the middle of the road. The straight white lines were already there so it seemed silly not to complete the pattern. It wasn't the sort of thing CD was wont to do under normal circumstances. He was an intelligent bloke and he knew that this action would not reduce the nuclear arsenal by so much as one radioactive pea-shooter. What's more, he was extremely dubious as to the propaganda value of his protest. It was difficult to imagine an average punter walking along the street, seeing the symbols, slapping his forehead as if to say, how could I have been so blind and shouting 'of course, that's it! We must ban the bomb'. It just wasn't going to happen that way.

Although CD was unquestionably against the bomb, this

was not the reason for his crime. He had actually committed it because he was drunk and because he wanted to go to bed with the girl from the day-centre for peace studies, and painting tarmac was her idea of a romantic evening.

KAREN THE HIPPY

'I really think it will be a valid statement,' this insanely deluded girl had whined. 'It will prove to people that there *is* an opposition, that they don't *have* to sit down and take it.'

Looking back on the whole incident, CD was at a loss to work out why he had conceived a desire for this monumentally stupid person. Thinking about it in retrospect he wouldn't have thought it could be done.

It wasn't that Karen was unattractive, she was very attractive in a wet kind of way. She had an immense mass of highly frizzed hair and was very tactile.

'He was sad and uptight and scared so I gave him a cuddle and I think it helped,' she would say with stupefying complacency. Karen was under the erroneous impression that she had a soothing, calming personality and was therefore an immense pillar of slightly mystical womanly strength to those who knew her.

Worse than that, she was one of that large group of men and women who are convinced that they can give massages, forcing them on any acquaintance who unwisely admits to anything from a slight headache to being about to attempt suicide. This type of 'massage' consists exclusively of grabbing the subject's shoulders from behind and kneading away as if making pastry. The idea being that every muscle in the subject's body instantly dissolves into a warm fluidity, releasing years of built-up twentieth century tension.

In reality the victim sits there, gritting their teeth, suppressing their fury and probably laying the groundwork for an enormous ulcer. Karen normally spoke in a kind of highly sincere, little girly voice that made you want to kill. It was meant to imply the pure simplicity of true knowledge and self-awareness. In fact it implied grounds for justifiable homi-cide.

'I think it would be really nice and pretty to have the peace group outside, away from man-made structures because I think that would be very ironic and apt.' Why were the people who wanted the right things usually such wankers? CD had thought when he met Karen. Surely it didn't have to be that way. If it did it definitely knackered any possibility of ever gaining mass popular support for anything.

CD thought back to the lads he had been at school with. He felt fairly confident that it would take something more convincing than the offer of a massage from Karen to turn them onto an alternative culture. The appropriation of radical thinking by lazy, self-obsessed hippies is a public relations disaster that could cost the earth.

CD met Karen at a benefit concert to support a women's peace camp situated outside some mysterious US com-munications installation up in the Northern Territory. This was a pretty good cause and he was there partly because he was happy to support it, but mainly he was there because he had worked behind the bar and it was twenty-five bucks. That particular gig was the easiest money CD had made in quite a while. It had been organized and published by Karen and people like Karen, hence for the first hour there was only them, CD and the band there. The hippies had spent so much time discussing whether sausage-rolls were offensive to non-meat-eaters they had forgotten to put their poster up in the community bookshop. Karen was fairly outraged.

'I really don't understand people, right?' she whined, 'I mean, it's *their* world, too, right?'

Later on eight people turned up and the banner fell down. It was hung up behind the band, a big picture of a skeleton in a US steel helmet.

'It's brilliant, isn't it,' Karen said as she hung it back up. 'Jill did it. If only more people could see it I'm sure they would understand better what we're trying to say.'

Finally Karen started the bopping. She did this after

spending half an hour wandering round saying, 'Why aren't people bopping? God, people are so boring.'

Four people danced, and watching them CD could scarcely keep his dinner down. He himself was no great dancer, but at least, he thought, I have the decency not to flaunt it.

CD considered ageing hippy dancing to be one of the most embarrassing forms of movement in the world. The problem is that the people involved see it as a form of self-expression rather than as a jolly thing to do. They believe this so strongly that they feel honour-bound to express themselves even when there is nothing to express – which is always. The result is that they hop slowly about the dance floor gyrating and waving their arms with an expression of concentration and delight on their faces. Matched only in intensity by the horror on the faces of anyone unfortunate enough to witness the revolting display.

None the less, as CD stood behind the bar sipping a beer, for some reason he conceived a horrid little desire to try and get a bit of a feel-up off the one in the middle whom he knew to be called Karen.

Maybe it was divine intervention because, of course, if he hadn't made his move he would never have got involved in the painting expedition, he would never have found himself in court for vandalism, and so he would not have met Rachel. God works in mysterious ways.

COURT

The judge fined him a hundred and fifty bucks plus costs. This was an unexpectedly harsh blow. CD had reckoned on maybe seventy-five. Perhaps it was the tie. If you want a judge to like you, don't wear a picture of a filleted whale carcass to court. On the other hand, maybe it was CD suggesting that the judge should not come crying to him when he got nuked to bollocks and beyond. Maybe it was a combination of the two, plus the shades and the trousers and the boots. Some people would call CD plucky; most people would call him an utter pratt – either way he was undeniably prone to displays of pointless bravado which always made everything worse.

Whatever it was, the fine was a lot. Too much for CD who was, as always, terminally short of cash. He tried a desperate plea in mitigation. If all else fails, tell the truth . . .

'Your Majesty,' he said, trying to look honest, 'the truth of the matter is, I agree with you, painting symbols on the road was a pointless act of vandalism. But, can I level with you, your Highness?' CD attempted to make his tone ingratiatingly man to mannish. 'There was this chick, right? and she's a bit of a peace freak and I wanted to impress her so I could well . . . do the business, right? Anyway . . .'

CD's fine was increased to two hundred and fifty.

FALLING IN LOVE WITH RACHEL

Rachel was up for a driving offence. She had some highly credible ancient old car, bright red with white-wall tyres, jacked-up rear suspension and reflecting glass on all the windows except the front one. It was a car that almost seemed to be pleading with the cops: 'pull me over, I must be doing *something* wrong'.

On this occasion it was thirty kilometres over the limit in a built-up area, plus a baldish offside rear tyre. Three demerits on a licence that was already feeling the strain. Mind you, it would have been worse had Rachel not made careful preparations.

Rachel was most striking to look at, a natural red-head with pale skin that led her to wear huge hats for eleven months of the year. It wasn't that she was particularly beautiful but she was vivacious, and those men that did fancy her fancied her a lot. Rachel was an all or nothing type of girl in her looks, her opinions and her car.

She had come to court in a smart two-piece suit borrowed from her mother. Her hair was an elaborate coiffure and she carried a brief-case. The whole ensemble was designed to suggest a serious-minded, conservative young woman for whom driving was essential. She looked like Margaret Thatcher and it clearly worked because she got off pretty lightly. On hearing her sentence Rachel thanked the judge and took her wig off. This wasn't to show off but because it was ninety in the shade. However, not surprisingly the judge totally did his nut and considered doing her for contempt. Reason returned when he caught the amused eye of the journo from the *Carlo Times*. He decided he could do without wigs becoming the basis for another debate on civil liberties. Like all judges, secretly this one wished he had lived in some earlier age. He just bet Judge Jeffries didn't have to deal with some cub hack plastering 'COME OFF IT JEFF, WHY DON'T YA!' across the front of two thousand advertising freebies. You couldn't win any more, thought the judge. What was the betting this little bitch could come up with some damn religion where wigs were compulsory for women up on driving offences.

Rachel walked free.

Situated just behind the court was a pub called the Dancing Cockatoo. This pub has a jolly sign which inevitably led the Aussies, with their natural wit, to call it the Pissed Parrot. It was here that most of the ne'er-do-wells, shop-lifters, peace freaks and prostitutes found themselves after their encounters with the fearful majesty of the law.

And it was to the Pissed Parrot that CD had gone to drown his sorrows and to wonder where he was going to raise two hundred and fifty bucks. Shortly after which, Rachel entered and ordered a gin and tonic. She was wondering about getting a less flamboyant car. Both of them had gone to court alone, neither of them needed their hands holding, and there they sat, alone.

Except that within the space of a casual glance CD was no longer alone. He was with Rachel, far away from the Pissed Parrot, walking hand-in-hand, laughing in the rain, having their first ever row about something silly and then making up in a variety of interesting positions and locations and then not being able to remember what the row had been about in the first place. He fancied this girl like mad, he fancied her purely and spiritually. This girl clearly oozed with character, intelligence and . . . lots of other things like that. This, CD knew, was what had captured his heart so suddenly. Obviously he desperately wanted to root her as well but, CD assured himself, that wasn't the only thing.

He *had* to make a move. Never would such a conversation opener exist again. They were fellow lags, joined by that invisible fellowship that unites the criminal fraternity. Comrades, forced together against a hostile world. Normally when you go up to a strange girl and try to start up a conversation, reflected CD, it's bloody obvious that you're making a play for them. But this was different. This time he had the perfect opener, plus endless opportunities for idle chatter, casually getting to know each other through their shared experiences under the majesty of the law. One thing CD was certain of, he resolved to be himself (whatever he thought that was). His recent experience of pretending to be a committed peace-nik had led him to near financial ruin and he hadn't even got a root. CD determined that this time there would be no lying or deceit, she would have to accept him for what he was.

'So you got done for trying to ban the bomb,' said Rachel from across the pub, 'I think that's really great.'

'What? Oh yeah.' CD replied, 'I'm a pretty committed peace-nik.' He was nothing if not adaptable.

Rachel was interested. 'I've been wondering about all that stuff myself,' she said. 'I used to go out with an American sailor, he was OK but his mates were real dags. Totally war obsessed.'

'Yeah well, maybe it's not their fault, it's all indoctrination isn't it?' said CD magnanimously.

'No way!' replied Rachel. 'People have to make their own decisions.'

'Oh yeah, that's true too,' conceded CD hurriedly.

'That's why I think what you did was good,' said Rachel, 'You have to decide what you're into, and go for it . . .'

This had always been Rachel's way. During her brief punk phase she had dyed her beautiful red hair mauve and her father had cried. She hadn't even wanted to do it much but what was the point of being a punk if you didn't dye your hair? CD's crime interested Rachel because it was self-expression for a purpose. For a long time she had been uncomfortably aware that she was wasting her time and that she didn't really care about anything. She was interested in someone who did.

CD, sadly, was, to coin a phrase, interested in one thing and he was desperately trying to think of a good line to edge him towards it ... 'By the way, my name's CD. You look fantastic in that suit.' As he said it he knew it was a mistake. This girl was into peace, she was a thinker, he couldn't blagg her with cheap flattery. He might just as well have marched straight up and asked her to sleep with him.

'Sorry, what a stupid thing to say. I might just as well have marched right up and asked you to sleep with me.' What was he saying! If the suit line was a mistake, this was a disaster! Seldom had a chat-up situation been so ineptly handled. CD had to recoup the situation. Quickly he reminded himself that he was cool. He reminded himself that he was, after all, wearing cowboy boots with metal tips, pretend torn trousers and shades – a combination little short of sexual dynamite. He had started badly but all he needed to do was to stay cool and let his trousers do the talking.

'OK it's like this, I have just taken a pretty heavy rap for defending world peace and I'm confused. Now if you don't let me start again, swearing that you have forgotten all that has passed between us so far, I'm going to kill myself. The choice is yours.'

'It's a free country,' she said.

'Got her!!' thought CD, 'torn jeans, they can't resist it.'

MORE DINNER IN LOS ANGELES

As Sly took his seat his sense of satisfaction had not left him, how could it? Now he was really at the very centre of everything that mattered. He had been accepted, accepted as a colleague – a colleague in a great conspiracy. But what was the plan? Sly had no idea for what secret and shadowy purpose the group had come together. Certainly to make money; colossal, unimaginable, utterly meaningless sums of money, of that he was certain. They were there to make money.

He was wrong.

But he had to wait to find out. For these slavering corporate predators prided themselves on being civilized. Business must wait until after dinner.

There were no menus at 'California Dreaming'. You ordered what you wanted. Sly, in a mood of jolly bravado, ordered swan. It had always intrigued him that in England apparently only royalty are allowed to eat swan. On this very special night Sly felt like a king himself and reckoned he deserved a slab of Her Maj's exclusive tucker.

The *maître d'* – a svelte figure who gracefully exuded that peculiarly Californian air of superiority that made one embarrassed that one was not oneself a homosexual – accepted Sly's order with a rather deflating matter-of-factness. His manner suggested that he rarely took orders for anything *but* swan. That tiny flick of his eyebrows seemed to say 'if just one more person asks me for swan I shall go and work for Col. Saunders'.

It's a strange thing about waiters, because while Sly could happily have faced down a corporate takeover bid from

Ghengis Khan, that one bloke's offhand acceptance of his magnificent self-indulgence made Sly feel like a piece of shit.

In the kitchen, the *maître d'* hastily consulted with the cook. They decided against pigeon because there was a good chance he'd recognize it. The same reason ruled out grouse. Eventually the chef had a brain-wave and slaughtered the cat. Poor Tiddles yielded a goodish portion of tough, light brown meat which the chef pan-fried in garlic butter and mushrooms. A lady guest in the public section of the restaurant had arrived in a beautiful coat layered with hundreds of ostrich feathers. A couple of these discreetly pruned, plus a duck's beak, completed the picture and Sly was duly served his swan.

'To tell you the truth it tastes worse than a dead cat,' said Sly in reply to the polite enquiry from his neighbour.

As it happened, the talk about the table was far too interesting for Sly to worry overmuch about what he was eating. Conversation normally bored Sly, he always felt like he knew what people were going to say. This made him very irritating to talk to as he never let anyone finish a sentence. He would normally say 'Yeah, yeah, yeah, yeah, yeah' at machine gun speed within five seconds of anybody saying anything. This, of course, meant that Sly never learnt anything. If somebody were to shout at Sly, 'Sly, the building we are standing in is on fire' Sly would probably say, 'Yeah, yeah, yeah' and burn to death.

That evening, however, Sly did not feel his usual need to forcibly stamp his personality on the gathering. He did not do his normal thing of wriggling with discomfort until he was able to prise open an opportunity to say something wry, witty, pithy or tough, just to show everyone what an impressive bloke he was. For instance, he never felt happy at major political dinners until he had contradicted the Prime Minister. It didn't matter what he said, just as long as he scored a point. His proudest moment to date had come at a dinner party in Canberra, when the Prime Minister, commenting on the primitive Australian economy, had said: 'Us Aussies are still riding on the sheep's back.'

Quick as a flash Sly responded, 'You stick it in what you like Bob, just leaves more birds for the rest of us.' This had got a huge laugh and firmly established in Sly's mind the idea that he should go into politics. He was, in his own opinion, a top-class racon-fucking-teur.

But that night at 'California Dreaming' Sly was definitely prepared to sit quiet and listen. After all, these were not politicos – vain little scumbags with a small talent for middle management. The men Sly was facing (for there were no women at the dinner) were men of real power: power that would last. What did they want? What were they doing dining together? When would he learn of the great plan, whatever it might be? Perhaps the unofficial chair of the evening sensed Sly's tension for, as the coffee came round, he made the introductions.

ATTILA THE HAMBURGER SALESMAN

'Gentlemen, few of you have had the opportunity to meet our Australian friend socially,' said the fat, affable American who had recently sold his eighty billionth hamburger. 'Although,' he added chuckling, 'he's burnt a few of your asses in the futures market.'

Sly flushed with pride, it is very rare that the mega-rich receive genuine praise. If you crap on people for a living you can't really expect a great many heart-felt tributes to come your way. So it was particularly gratifying that this important and brilliant man should treat him with such friendly esteem.

And Tex Slampacker *was* a brilliant man. His insight into the human soul had made his hamburger marketing uncannily successful. He had elevated the manipulation of people through retail outlets into an art form. It was said of Slampacker that he could sell shit if he wanted to, which was, of course, exactly what he did.

His outlets are the same all across the world, identical in

every detail. Frontier forts of an occupying army riding rough-shod over the myriad ancient cultures that they have colonized; sneering at the quirky individualism of their subject races; laughing at those who waste time considering choice and variety when they could be making money. From the deepest depths of Islam to the heart of Christendom, the Slampacker invasion is complete. Napoleon couldn't hold Moscow but Slampacker could and did.

Richard the Lionheart was halted long before he saw the gates of Jerusalem; Slampacker just walked right in without a fight. Life-styles and customs that had stood for centuries, fiercely resisting the attempts of foreign powers to subvert them, had fallen to Slampacker in a decade.

Tex Slampacker knew no French (except of course the words franc and centime) but had he known any, the phrase *vive la différence* would have completely mystified him.

COMING TO THE POINT

'Let me fill Mr Moorcock in on our principal concerns at this point in time, gentlemen,' said the burger king, 'because, as you are all well aware, the day is fast approaching when action must be taken and we are very much hoping that Mr Moorcock will be joining us in our endeavours.' As Tex Slampacker rose to speak Sly felt an incredible expectant thrill. More than ever now, the enormous potential of the evening hit him. Here he was amongst the very biggest players in the world, the Yanks, the Japs, the Arabs ... Clearly something was afoot and he, Sly Moorcock, the Aussie street kid made good, was to be a part of it. Countless billions must be involved, the power and influence that sort of money represented was mind-boggling. It must be global, that was obvious thought Sly feverishly as Slampacker wiped his brow. God knew what ... What the hell were they planning to do ...? Buy the Society Union, maybe that was it!! Christ this lot could afford it, *and* make it pay.

Suddenly Sly was sweating. Brief-cases and computer

terminals had appeared on the table. Shadowy figures materialized from nowhere to guard the doors ... The situation was colossal, the potential for profit beyond computation ... Slampacker, the first man ever to make a million dollars in under five seconds was addressing them all for *his* benefit! The utter strangeness of the situation almost enveloped Sly. All these predators, all these mavericks, men dedicated to personal and individual gain, joined together in one room! Conspiring! What could it possibly be about?

'Gentlemen,' said Slampacker. 'Fourteen individual species of butterfly have become extinct since this meal began.'

There was a significant pause during which Sly tried to work out what he presumed was some tortuous Yankee metaphor. It wasn't. Sly could scarcely believe his ears but Slampacker, a gung-ho, hard as nails mega-cynic, began to talk like some kind of damn hippy. He spoke of the ozone layer. He spoke of the greenhouse effect. He dwelt at great, and what Sly considered unnecessary, length on the various types of waste that are floating about in the world's water system. He seemed particularly concerned about trees. Slampacker, a man whose never-ending need for beef pasture had made him responsible for cutting down more trees than all the shipbuilders, furniture-makers and carpenters in history put together, spoke with dull passion on the subject of the destruction of the forests.

Sly itched to shout 'who gives a fuck' at him, but the atmosphere was wrong, people were listening and, to Sly's astonishment, they looked scared. Eventually, to Sly's relief, one or two around the table began to shift about a bit and fidget.

'Good,' thought Sly, 'somebody's going to tell the fat old bastard to save his hang-ups for his shrink.'

But, to Sly's further aggravation, those who wished to chip in clearly wished to do so because they felt that Slampacker was not pitching the case strongly enough. Various world-class money men, men who Sly would have bet a chain of breweries cared more about hair restoration than reforestation, started to

31

LOVE AND CONFUSION

Of course, if Sly thought he was experiencing frustration, he should have tried sitting in CD's trousers.

CD was definitely surprised. He had thought he'd been in love before but clearly he hadn't. Nothing he had experienced so far in life had prepared him for the gutful of emotions he had been at the mercy of since that moment at the Pissed Parrot. It was extraordinary. At first he thought he must be ill.

CD could not understand it, all that stuff that claims to be about love; mushy stories; wet songs; unpleasant childlike cartoon figures holding hands and saying, 'Love is doing the washing-up even when it's not your turn'. These things CD now discovered had absolutely nothing whatsoever to do with love as he was currently experiencing it. In the world of pulp publishing, pop charts and greeting cards, even when love hurts it usually hurts in a nice and tasteful way; yearning glances; attractive anguish and broken hearts. The truth is, it's a pain in the guts.

And that was another thing. Why is it that the heart has been singled out as the seat of all emotions? OK so it occasionally misses a beat, but what's that compared to the long sleepless hours of dull stomach ache? The guts are unquestionably the seat of the emotions, that's where CD felt the pain. But of course it wouldn't look so good on the Valentine cards; eight feet of small intestine with an arrow through it or a cute little cartoon figure feeling queasy and saying 'Love is wanting to go to the lavatory'.

CD had been prepared by countless juke boxes to feel exhilarated, tearful, turned on by love, he certainly had not

33

expected to feel sick. It was as if he had gone mad. He was acting in a way that he despised himself for. It was fifteen years since he had tried his hand at poetry. He had thought that shameful, inexcusable episode in his life was over and forgotten forever. There is absolutely no excuse for amateur poetry writing, it should be against the law. Teenagers, CD reluctantly accepted, should be allowed a brief foray into this repulsive, self-indulgent activity. After all, every kid in the world goes through a period when they are under the impression that they are the only person who has ever suffered, the only person who has ever really truly understood confusion and rejection, and exam revision and acne. Obviously this horrid time needs an outlet other than vandalism and hence, while it lasts, every kid is clearly entitled to pen the occasional teen-anguished epic. But these should be decently burnt within a year and the habit soon dropped. At the age of fifteen CD had decided to ditch poetry to leave more time for masturbation and had never had cause to regret the decision.

But now what had happened? Here he was trying to find a rhyme for 'Rachel' and coming up with 'bagel'. Sitting there, alone, his eyes prickling, his guts churning, trying to write something that should it ever get out would force him to commit suicide out of sheer embarrassment.

And this was not the only alarming symptom. Everything was changing, CD was definitely not the same person he had been a week before. Conversations had become a means to bring the subject round to how much he loved this girl. He didn't want to do it, it just seemed to happen.

'Are you going to watch the footie then, CD?'

'Yeah, maybe, you know I've met this girl called Rachel. I think she'd like footie. She's an extraordinary girl, you know I really think I'm in love and I don't know whether to be happy or sad or what.'

He felt an absurd affection, even loyalty, for Carlo Criminal Court, where he had first set eyes on her. He had bought a copy of 'Money for Nothing' which had been on the juke box in the Pissed Parrot when he had tried to make conversation. It was ridiculous but when he played it, which was often, he always felt he had to listen to the very end or somehow he was letting her down. She would never know, and she certainly wouldn't care, but he still had to listen to every bloody note.

It was so weird he had only met her on a couple of occasions and yet now he thought about her literally all the time, constructing little fantasies to himself as he wandered about. Lacking almost any knowledge of Rachel at all he filled in the gaps himself. Sometimes she was Doris Day, a happy little housewife with whom CD would share the domestic chores and construct a normal life. In this dream he even had a proper job and kids were on the way. She was chirpy, devoted and, of course, insatiably saucy. Other times she was a tough, committed alternative woman intellectually brilliant, artistically innovative, courageous, combative and, of course, insatiably saucy.

These fantasy characters bore no relation to the real Rachel and, of course, they did not need to for CD had fallen in love with her whatever she was really like and it only remained to discover what he had let himself in for. This was one thing CD did know about love: it can happen regardless of personality. How often had he noticed couples who seemed totally mismatched struggling through their lives together. Couples that made you say 'I never would have thought he was her type', and yet there they were, a Zen Buddhist and a female mud-wrestler applying for a mortgage and looking at curtain material. CD was discovering now for himself that love is not logical. He didn't know anything about Rachel, why was he so certain that she was perfect? And why when, as he knew he must, he discovered that she was not perfect, did he know he would forgive her? Clearly because love hates logic, it cannot be planned, it cannot be created and it cannot be stopped. It will, at all times, do its own thing like a hippy on the dance floor or a back-packer's bottom when it gets to India. One thing was clear, if there's a part of the body less involved with love than the heart, it is the head.

This is why CD was in such a state of disarray. He was a cleverish, cynical person, and he was out of control. Captain Love had taken command of the ship and CD was heading for the rocks.

Clearly it was time to form a plan. CD could not go on listening to 'Money for Nothing' and having trouble with his bowels for ever. He had seen Rachel once since the encounter at the Pissed Parrot and it had not been a conspicuous success. All he had done was crack jokes and try to catch another tantalizing glimpse through the tiny gap that gaped between the second and third buttons of her blouse. One of the great male delusions is the belief that girls are unaware when they are being ogled. No one has ever managed to discreetly eye a cleavage. You might as well put out bunting saying 'I am getting a stiffy'. On the other hand taking a sneak peak doesn't necessarily mean that the peeker is falling in love. Blokes do it on instinct. So despite being acutely conscious of his staring, Rachel remained unaware of the immense turmoil that she was causing in CD's stomach and in his trousers.

Poor CD. Most girls suffer the subliminal harrassment of being ogled in silence but Rachel was made of sterner stuff. She could handle the embarrassment of confrontation.

'Stop staring at my boobs!' she had snapped and CD had never felt so mortified in all his life. For the rest of the evening he had been in danger of cricking his neck in his efforts to demonstrate that he was staring at the ceiling.

But, CD was an optimist, he reckoned that there were grounds for hope, after all, they already had quite an intense relationship. So far Rachel had embarrassed him, made him feel sick and turned him into a bore, there was certainly an emotional bond developing which he felt he could build on. What he needed was a plan.

A PLAN(ISH)

CD decided to pull himself together and concentrate. It was clear to him that a degree of serendipity was going to be required to nudge along the essential process of wooing the gorgeous Rachel. This was obvious from one glance at the differentials. She was a love goddess; she was the font from which all beauty flowed; she was a sexual weapons system waiting for a crazy man to push her button – and he was a pratt.

Playing an honest hand CD was destined for disaster on the courtship front, so he was going to have to lie. He recalled that at their first meeting at the Pissed Parrot, Rachel had expressed interest in his bullshit about peace freak connections. So a committed 'citizen of the world' approach seemed to be the clearest route up her dress. This was fine as far as CD was concerned. He did not care who he pretended to be. He was so obsessively hot for Rachel's action that he would have gone on a diet and claimed to be Mother Theresa if it had promised even the chance of a feel-up.

As it happened there would be no element of hypocrisy in the little charade CD was planning that could besmirch the purity of his horrendous horniness. CD was hip to all the principles held dear by the peace lot, he just felt that clothes-wise a small thermonuclear blast would definitely improve their appearance. After all, there isn't really much you can do with a tie-dye T-shirt except atomize it into oblivion so that it may never return to offend the eye.

Reflecting on these reflections, CD determined that if he had to play a bit of a hippy, it would at least be a tastily dressed one. He would show Rachel that a concern for the future of the planet and crucial threads were not mutually exclusive. It was possible to desire peace on earth and not look like you'd been dragged through a puddle on the way to a jumble sale. Who could tell, maybe besides making Rachel his own for all eternity he would do those hippies some good!

As he dressed, CD stared out of the window to the place where Dave used to play when CD had first come to live in his little duplex. CD didn't know Dave. Dave was not destined to play any part in the story of Stark. In fact he was already dead. But his story is connected, as all stories are. He

DAVE AND BILL: AN
INVOLUNTARY KILLING

Dave was killed by Bill.

They never even met, but Bill killed Dave as surely as if he'd shot him in the skull. Obviously Bill never meant to do it, but few of the terrible things done in the world are meant.

DULL

It happened this way. Bill had given his life to nylon – he was very into nylon. Some people are into leather or PVC, Bill was into nylon. Not wearing it, you understand, or stretching it tight across the buttocks of a close friend and popping his thumb through at the point of least resistance. It was the structure of nylon which fascinated Bill. It needs a special type of person to be seriously into hydrocarbons. Basically you need to be very dull. Not dull in the way that is normally classed as dull, the sports bore or the person who reads the books about the SAS that you can buy reduced at station bookstalls . . .

'Oh yes, it's the most rigorous training in the world. Apparently they were put on full standby red-alert mode maximum kill facility alert, the moment the Home Secretary got the news.'

Much duller than that, dull to the point where it is almost a creative act. Those who met Bill often wondered if they were missing something . . . 'I suppose I'm very stupid,' they would say, 'but I really don't see the fascination.'

Any single-mindedness is obviously in danger of being dull.

Single-mindedness about something that is already dull is clearly double dull. The problem is that a dull person remorselessly pursuing a dull idea can appear a bit like a clever and inspired person who can see something that others can not. The well-adjusted observer begins to doubt his or her critical faculties and asks if perhaps there might not be something in it after all. This can be a bit worrying in the case of the various political and religious maniacs who want everyone to think the way they do. But in Bill's case, it was not worrying, just very very dull.

If you went for a drink with Bill he would somehow work the conversation round to carbon research. His only other skill besides carbon research was working the conversation round to carbon research and, it has to be said, he was pretty good at it.

'Fancy a drink, Bill?'

'I'd rather do a bit of carbon research.'

But Bill was all right, he bored people but he didn't eat them. The world and its spouse had no reason to regret Bill's birth. Not, that is, until he killed Dave.

The chain of events that put Bill on the path to murder started right back when he was at school. He was a total and utter fart as a kid, thin, farty and dull, dull, dull. The sort of kid who was 'really incredibly into science' and used this as a substitute for a personality. Every class has a couple. They take great pride in carrying sciencey things in the pockets of their blazers. Electrical screwdrivers, conversion tables, bits of wire. Their conversation is monumentally dull because they feel the need to announce their scientific obsessions in even the most commonplace sentences. If they did not do this they would cease to exist and be marked absent on the register.

'Is that your chair, Jenkins?'

'Specifically and fundamentally,' replies Jenkins, 'you would not be a hundred and eighty degrees off in presuming the affirmative.' And then Jenkins would look pleased and slightly embarrassed as if having delivered rather a good joke.

Bill and his ilk are awkward kids; always grinning and

getting taller. They go around at break-time offering to prove by equation that one and one equals three, but then get it all wrong.

As they grow older these people get into Deep Purple and Bowie and grow their hair in greasy mops. They start drinking cider and blackcurrant and go to university and say things like: 'Last night we got what I believe is technically described as rat-arsed.'

Inevitably, as a recreational subsection of their dullness, they become Real Ale bores and they are the most boring of all Real Ale bores because they can tell you the specific gravity of the beer they are drinking. Worse, they know what specific gravity is.

Such a fellow killed Dave.

Dave, who was not remotely boring and, were you lucky enough to meet him, would keep you enthralled for hours. Not that that makes any difference to the crime. If Dave had killed Bill it would have been just as wrong, but he didn't. Bill killed Dave.

THE SUBLIME AND THE RIDICULOUS

Bill was actually pretty bright. Whereas most science farties end up as computer programmers, he was destined for bigger things. He took three pure science 'A' levels and went to university determined to get into nylon. It was in the middle of Bill's second year – during his brief dissolute phase, when he seemed to be paying more attention to the Silly Buggers Society than to nylon – that Dave was born.

On the same night that Bill tried gamely to walk the length of the student union bar with a full half-pint of Real Ale balanced on his head and a radish up his arse, at the same moment, far away, Dave drew his first breath. Talk about the sublime and the ridiculous.

Ironically it was also that evening, the evening bloody murder began to creep slowly into Bill's life, that he found love. The killer met his moll. He met her upstairs at the student union, in the smaller Bistro Bar – so called because you could buy wine there. Her name was Jane and Bill boldly asked to sit beside her, remembering too late to remove the radish. Jane had witnessed his earlier cavortings and pretended to be totally contemptuous of them, but really she thought the whole thing pretty exciting stuff. This was because Jane was nearly as dull as Bill – her idea of a rave was a Cadbury's Creme Egg. She thought Bill sophisticated and a proper hoot. So worldly and romantic with his extensive knowledge of early Bowie and nylon and the future calendar of the Silly Buggers Soc': 'We're going to dress up in girls' nighties and push a double bed up the High Street to raise money for cancer.'

And so it was that on the night Bill got his first ever girlfriend – a night of fumbling and snogging and that triumphant feeling of having grown up – on that night of all nights, Dave was born and Dave was doomed. Bill the nice, dull, git with the brand new, dull, bossy girlfriend, was to be his nemesis. There would be a terrible bloody murder; a frenzy of panic, agony and desperate violence, a moment's shocked disbelief and it would be over. Dave was twenty-one years younger than Bill. It's hard to say why but somehow this made what happened all the sadder.

MODERN BIRTH

These days giving birth underwater is very fashionable, middle-class mums will travel to France and spend a fortune so that some hippy French doctor can grab them by the tits in the shallow end of a school swimming pool. The theory seems to be that the warm water is highly reminiscent of the womb, so you drop your sprog in the pool to comfort it. Of course, your average womb hasn't normally had a class full of little boys pissing in it a few hours earlier and the acoustics of a cold meat storehouse. Also few wombs are lined with luminous white tiles and administered by a bloke who's a dead spit of Adolf Hitler, except for the mop and bucket.

None the less, apparently the awesome transition from Mum's tum to big bad world is less traumatic if done via the local baths.

Dave's family had been giving birth underwater for generations. But not for them the sanitized safety of a whirlpool bath and a French quack with a degree in being groovy. There were no doctors present at this birth, just two midwives, not professionals, friends, but friends who had done it before lots of times. There wouldn't be a problem. No birth is easy but as they go this one wasn't too bad. Dave's mum heaved and strained, the midwives coaxed and prodded about a bit to help ease him out and eventually he came, breech born, head last, but in perfect nick. The umbilical cord was broken pretty sharpish, as is necessary, and the midwives swam Dave to the surface in order that he might take his first breath. This is how dolphins are born.

DEATH OF A STRANGER

Very little is known about dolphins – by humans that is, probably dolphins themselves know a little more. However, enough can certainly be guessed at for them to be raised far above the level of 'dumb animal'. Their intelligence, ability to communicate and social interaction are so clear that it seems reasonable to assume that they also possess personalities, feelings and emotions. Despite the genocide that has been wreaked upon them, they still seem to bear humanity no ill will. In fact, there are countless stories of dolphins aiding humans in distress. Documented instances of them warding off sharks at their own personal risk and also of nudging the unconscious survivors of shipwrecks to the shore. These, like the practise of midwifery, are not fanciful human inventions but the facts regarding another race of beings.

One day Dave was swimming about minding his own business, when he was caught in a fishing net which, despite possessing a phenomenally sophisticated sonar system, he had not noticed. After a brief and desperate period of thrashing about helplessly, Dave drowned, unable to get to the surface for the oxygen he required.

The net was made of a revolutionary new nylon that is lighter and stronger than previous nets. It is also undetectable by dolphin radar. Bill had been pleased with the development. He had been a crucial cog in the research team that had come up with a very slightly more efficient and profitable way of going fishing. You can't stop progress and, after all, it's only a few dolphins.

THE PURSUIT OF LOVE.
THE DINNER GOES ON

DREAM DATE

He picked Rachel up in a cab. CD did not drive and Rachel wanted to drink. The memory of her recent bust and straining licence was fresh in her mind and she was taking no risks.

CD was wearing a cream three-piece suit, wide lapels and slightly flared trousers. Flares keep threatening to make a comeback and so to CD's mind he looked five minutes ahead of the next fashion, rather than ten years behind the last one. CD was a true optimist.

He had added a CND stud earring for style, also to confirm his character as a committed activist and finally because he believed it made him look swarthy and romantic. His aftershave was seriously whiffy and the cowboy boots, newly polished (right round to the heels as well) were a walking dream.

'CD,' he said to himself as he contemplated his reflection in the broken wardrobe door, 'you are a love rocket, primed, charged and already requesting flight clearance from mission control.' He was, indeed, a true optimist.

When Rachel opened the door CD nearly lost his cool and blasted off there and then. She was orgasmic! Sauciness beyond his wildest dreams! – and CD had had some pretty wild dreams. She had on a little black cocktail number and the baddest suede, pointy, red shoes you ever saw. CD nearly flipped when he noticed they too had metal tips. Was this a sign? Of course it was; they were as one. Rachel wore nothing else, no jacket, no tights, it was a real hot night and it was getting hotter by degrees as CD's mercury threatened to burst out of the top of his tube.

'No rush, the guy's meter's running,' said CD who was in much the same position himself.

'I'm ready,' replied Rachel.

CD nearly fell over – down boy, down! This was more than he had dared hope for! What sort of phrase was that to use at eight-thirty! The temptress, the teasing, taunting, tempting sauce bucket! Clearly she wanted him, that much was obvious, wanted him badly. 'I'm ready,' she had said . . . God that was fast work, this lady wanted it *all* and she wanted it *now*. Why else would she put it that way? She could have said anything . . . she could have said . . . uhm 'we can leave immediately' or . . . well anything, but no, she said 'I'm ready.' Said it? she *breathed* it. If that wasn't the old green light to oblivion thought CD, he was a stupid wanker. And, of course, he was right. It wasn't and he was.

TURNING GREEN IN LA

It was, without doubt, the longest dinner it had ever been Sly's misfortune to attend.

Festel had begun to speak, the head of a Norwegian chemical consortium. Here was a man with a monumental contempt for the common good. A man proud of his record that despite the numerous compensation claims that resulted from him putting poorly tested drugs on the market he had never paid out a single penny. He remained oblivious to the anguish of gangs of mothers holding up babies with no legs or torsos.

It was widely believed that Festel had personally arranged the framing and imprisonment of an employee who had threatened to expose the way his company rushed drugs onto the market. And yet, to Sly's astonishment and anger, this same man suddenly seemed to have turned into a sort of wood-nymph, Pan-like figure, desperately concerned for the

46

pastoral balance of the planet. He pointed out that fifteen million trees were felled every twenty-four hours in India alone. The resulting soil erosion was almost visibly creating deserts. What was more, without the forests there was a terrible danger of catastrophic flash-flooding.

India? Sly was at a loss to understand why he had flown all the way to LA to whine on about trees in India ... Bastard probably owns property in Delhi, he thought.

Trunk spoke next. Trunk was a car man. He had been a colossus in motoring for over thirty years. Hence few had been closer to the vanguard in the battle against legislation on lead-free motoring than he. Trunk had fought it tooth and nail, lobbying politicians, obstructing research, deliberately encouraging his own technicians to distort their findings in order to produce ambiguous results. This, despite being well aware all along of the terrible toll that lead emissions take on growing bodies and minds. Trunk's motive in all this had been the fear that other manufacturers might not take on the cost of the retooling required and of the slightly more sophisticated engines. He could be left on his own with the other bastards selling slightly cheaper cars. Rather than risk this, he had tried to stop the whole idea. This was the metal of the man Sly now heard bleating on about sneezing seals and how some damn mammal or other was choking on its own phlegm.

Sly knew all this, he read his Sunday colour supplements, everybody knew about pollution, so what? One thing was for sure, if he had come half-way round the world to be asked to join some damn top-snob, green charity whinge for tax loss purposes, he would tell them to stuff it up their arseholes.

Lord Playing, the British tobacco giant, spoke up. Here was a man who was presently denying, on his mother's grave, that his company had been sure about the connection between tobacco and lung cancer since the mid-fifties. Denying that he had personally suppressed the findings and harrassed independent researchers. But now this same cynical man was shouting down Festel claiming that it was the salination caused by the rise in the water-tables that was the most terrifying aspect of the death of the forests.

'And where is the oxygen to come from, without trees?' the tobacco king added.

The whole evening sounded more like a gaggle of green Euro MPs having a whinge than a cabinet meeting of the World Government of Money. It wasn't that Sly disapproved of worrying about the environment – he didn't like having to swim round clusters of old rubber johnnies when he went for a dip in the sea, any more than the next fellow. But what had it got to do with *them*? Jesus, if they wanted a donation why hadn't they written to him? Sly was no longer simply disappointed, he was angry. If there was one thing Sly couldn't stand it was whingers.

A QUESTION OF PRINCIPLE

In the cab Rachel had asked if CD was a vegetarian. It was a very tricky moment. What to reply? CD loved meat, his idea of vegetables was tomato ketchup. He was the sort of bloke who reckons not fishing out the bit of gherkin in your hamburger counts as eating your greens. But what did Rachel think? Was she a veggie? She was into peace, but that wasn't conclusive. Jesus had been into peace but he never said anything about having to eat rabbit food or multi-grain when you fancied a hot dog. What should he say? People were very touchy on this subject. If he said no would she throw red paint over him and say she refused to share the same cab as a murderer? Those animal rights activists did not mess around. He didn't want the first time Rachel visited his place to be when she came round to put dog shit through his letter box. CD knew these people. Once, at a folk concert, he left his jacket on a seat and some bastard had written on it in lipstick: 'There used to be a dumb animal inside this leather jacket. There still is.' The annoying thing had been it was only imitation leather. Served him right for going to a folk concert of course.

But, how to answer? Maybe she wasn't a true fanatic, maybe she was a conscience-stricken would-be veg, that was worse. That would mean a mind-numbing, tedious six-hour discussion on degrees of personal responsibility.

'Well, I'm prepared to wear leather shoes but I wouldn't personally harpoon a whale.'

'I'm *basically* a vegetarian, it's just I get this *craving* for half a pound of bacon every morning.'

There were so many opinions on the subject, so many chasmic pitfalls to be circumnavigated. It's all a question of degrees. Some people are quite happy to eat a raw chicken stuffed with a couple of shoals of fish but consider it an offence against God to toy with a chop. Others would eat anything, great steaks dripping with blood, raw suchi, sausages, bloater, black pudding, haggis, unwary family pets, anything, and yet would call the police if they caught you even considering veal.

'You know how they make it don't you? They tear the baby cow foetus from the mother then artificially fatten it by feeding it napalm and electrocute its testicles to make the meat whiter, then cut its head off and stuff it up its arsehole *while it's still alive*!!!!'

People just take their pick on the subject of vegginess, draw their line where they feel like it. It's not about conventional morals. Hitler, after all was a veggie, but he didn't mind cooking Jews. There is absolutely no logic on the subject, but you cross people at your peril.

'Are you a vegetarian?' she had said it so simply, so casually, as if it was of no consequence.

No consequence! Ha! As CD squirmed and writhed and desperately tried to compute the chances of various answers being acceptable, he knew that his entire sex life could be hanging on his reply.

'Because I fancy a hamburger,' Rachel continued.

He could have kissed her.

Neither of them had much money and there was only an hour until the film and so they decided to dine at

Slampackers. They did this knowing that it would probably make them feel sick, knowing that the stuff had much the same effect on the complexion as napalm had on North Vietnam and also knowing that it was absolutely delicious and they could just fancy one.

CRUSHED IGUANA

They studied the enticing menu, with its dazzling array of choices. Cheeseburger, cheeseburger with salad and sauce, double cheeseburger with twice the salad and twice the sauce. Curiously there was no Iguana or fruit-fly on the menu. No open-ended list of as yet undiscovered life forms but, indirectly, that was what CD and Rachel were consuming.

Thousands of miles from where Rachel and CD stood there had once lived an Iguana. Had that Iguana still been alive it would have wept to see that facile menu (obviously being alive wouldn't have been enough, it would have had to have been able to read, and speak English . . . and Iguana probably don't cry anyway, but whatever . . .).

The Iguana, and millions like it, and millions more unlike it, for a tropical rain forest contains a wider variety of life forms than any other environment – with the possible exception of a sleeping bag at a rock festival – all these life forms had died in the service of Slampacker. They had been consumed along with the slice of gherkin smothered in secret recipe sauce.

Iggy had been chewing a fly when he first felt a tremendous rumbling. At first he thought that the fly must have disagreed with him and that he himself was responsible. But then the rumbling got louder and more terrible and Iggy realized in his little lizardy brain, that something was wrong. He knew his own bottom and no way was it capable of producing flatulence that was clearly going to feature on the Richter scale. This, Iggy sensed, was an approaching disaster, and of course he was right, which was no comfort at all. Being right is not as good as being alive. Suddenly Iggy found himself surrounded by plummeting species. Species which he had never seen before. Shaken from the various life levels that the forest houses were many creatures as yet undiscovered by humankind. Creatures that never would be.

They don't cut down trees anymore, it's too slow. They blow them up, or push them over with bulldozers. This was how Iggy and his host of little forest pals – whom Beatrix Potter would probably have called things like Simon and Jemima – met their ends, under bulldozers. For such is the demand for beef that the global hamburger addiction has fuelled that the rain-forests, which provide oxygen and change the weather, are being bulldozed down to create short-life pastures.

Besides the obvious undesirous side-effects, can be added the fact that much of science and medicine is derived from plant and animal research. It's just possible that the undiscovered cure for cancer went splat the day Slampacker sent Iggy to join Dave the dolphin and Mrs Pastel.

IDENTIFYING THE ENEMY

Sly's mind was in a spin. He wanted to punch their faces and shout: 'Shut the fuck up about the environment!!'

Tex Slampacker could see that Sly was irritated by the discussion. 'Look here, boy,' he barked, 'you know my burgers?'

Sly did indeed know them for although he could have afforded to eat an elephant full of caviar every lunch-time without going to the cash machine, he still secretly craved Slampackers and scoffed plenty.

'Well, hell, we all know what the damn boxes are doing to the ozone layer, Christ I wish we'd never developed the damn things,' he continued. 'But we *did* and those boxes mean I don't have to pay anyone to wash up dirty plates. I am faced with a cruel choice, gentlemen. Voluntarily cut my profits by re-introducing crockery, or subject the world to the risk of skin cancer.'

Tex Slampacker was deeply affected by this awesome moral confusion. Just framing the phrase 'voluntarily cut my profits' had felt like swearing in church. He was a hard man, not easily upset, but some things offended his conscience.

CASE FOR THE DEFENCE

That was it for Sly, he'd heard enough. He jumped to his feet. He was angry now. To think he had respected this man. 'Cruel choice, Mr Slampacker? Cruel choice?' he snapped, surveying the assembled company with that famous Aussie squint. This was his money-making look and with it Sly could have sheared the wool off a sheep's scrotum if he'd thought there was enough on it for an egg cosy. 'Forgive me, mates,' he said, fist in hand, the good old boy, teaching the highbrows horse sense, 'but I see no choice here, I see no dilemma. Clearly we have a question of morality to face, gentlemen, and I hope we're men enough to take it on.'

It would be a brave bookmaker who would have taken odds on that one but Sly wasn't leaving room for hecklers. 'Look we're all bloody sorry about the trees, of course we are, but people want the wood for Christ's sake! What can we do? You don't force them to buy your damn burgers!! The laws of a free market economy are sacred and we are guardians of those laws. Strewth, mates, you can't bugger about with market forces, that's social engineering, gentlemen, Brave New 1984 and all that. Your average bloke doesn't want some little Hitler from the ministry telling him what he can and can't buy! What he can and can't make! For sure it's a shame about the sneezing seals, and the birds with mouldy armpits, and the ozone layer, a bloody shame, and Christ if anyone's passing the hat round I'm in for 10K towards cancer research, no worries, but you can't stop progress and progress is marketing . . .'

The faces around the table remained inscrutable, Sly had no idea how they were taking his little lecture but he didn't care. He wasn't closing *his* aerosol factory until it stopped making a profit. 'Listen, Mr Slampacker,' he continued, 'if you didn't use those boxes some other bugger would and then where would you be? I'll tell you, mate, hanging out in the sun to dry with the wombats using your hat for a toilet. Meantime the ozone layer's still fucked and the other bastard's building a private dermatological ward to get the malignant melanomas chopped out of his arse. Gentlemen, we can't weaken, it would be a crime to interfere with the sacred laws of free enterprise simply to protect the environment. Do that and what do you get for an encore? I'll tell you, some green cop telling you you can't take a piss in your back garden because it upsets the ants.'

Sly would have continued but to his astonishment he found himself interrupted by warm applause. He had thought that he was speaking against the mood of the meeting. Now he discovered that he had captured it perfectly.

'Young man, you speak for all of us here and also those who attend in spirit,' said Slampacker. 'We are all of us engaged in one activity or another that is destroying the environment, we don't like it, we wish we weren't, but in the long run, what can we do?'

There was a brief silence during which around the world the acid rain fell, the nitrates seeped through the soil into the rivers, the greenhouse effect melted the ice caps and the kids breathed the lead from the leaded petrol. Sly realized that he was amongst friends. They weren't wimping on the problem they were merely recognizing it. What next? he wondered.

CONNECTIONS

And well Sly might have wondered for the problem was so clear, so terrible. The earth was dying. To be more specific, the earth was being killed. Done to death by its fond owners. Killed by the pursuit of money. For the men gathered around the table it was so utterly frustrating to have inherited the earth and then have the damn thing die on you. And, of course, its death would mean their death, everybody's death.

Like it or not, the human race, powerful though it is, remains only a part of the astonishingly complex chain of beings that makes up life on earth. It is not an island and cannot survive without the other life forces; the life forces that create the oxygen and food, that clean the water and protect us from the sun, the forces that bind the soil together and prevent the deserts spreading across the whole globe; the forces that keep the ice caps from melting and drowning us all.

It's all connections. If dung beetles didn't eat cow shit, we'd be knee-deep in flies by now. Eating cow shit is a dirty job, but somebody's got to do it. Luckily, either by divine plan or cosmic coincidence, at the dawn of creation the dung beetle said, 'Oh, for God's sake, *I'll* eat the cow shit, if no one else will.' But the dung beetle, like all other forms of life, depends on all other forms of life. From micro-organisms to Great White whales, it's a chain. Break that chain and all the money in the world will not save you from the ecological Armageddon that will engulf us all. So, what was to be done?

They were coming to that, they had a solution. They'd been working on it for a while. Everyone had a part to play, including Sly.

'Mr Moorcock,' said Slampacker, leaning back in his chair, 'I'd like to tell you, if I may, about the Stark Conspiracy.'

LOVE AMONG THE
RADICALS

During the meal at Slampackers, such as it was, CD told Rachel about the film he had thought they might go and see. As a preliminary to establishing his character as an active peace campaigner, he had chosen a movie he'd read about recently in a groovy-ish mag. At the time he had marked it down as the sort of film which he would rather be forced to eat than watch, but in the present circumstances it suited his purpose . . .

'It's about the parallels between the way men run countries and the way they run their personal lives. I mean, the parallel between pricks and missiles is a bit laboured these days but I suppose maybe that's because it's true.' CD was desperately hoping that Rachel had not read the review he'd read. She hadn't, and he would have been gratified to know that she was thinking that he seemed an interesting sort of bloke, a bit intense maybe, but a cut above the usual dag.

In this respect at least, CD's plan was working. Rachel had always been a bit of a closet radical – she liked the feeling of talking about something that mattered. And so they finished their delicious Slampackers, except for the horrible bit of gherkin which they had both fished out, and went to the movie. As they had both suspected, it was well meaning but bloody awful. Its principles were presented with such horrible monolithic certainty that it would have turned Ghandi pro nuke. Afterwards the director gave a short speech. He did this after every performance of the two-week run at the little arts cinema.

'Some people,' the director said with what he believed to be a knowing smile, 'can't see that missiles are penis extensions. Oh yeah? Well I don't know what's going to come flying towards us when some man pushes the button but it certainly won't be a fifty-foot flying cunt.' This, the director considered, was not only a brilliant and conclusive point but also a hilarious joke and his personal favourite. Although, in fact, he would not have known a joke if he had found one hanging off his earring.

'I think he was being cynical. You know, talking like an idiot in order to make an astute point,' said CD putting on a brave face. He would have put pink icing and a cherry on it if he had thought it would get him any closer to Rachel's affections.

'I think he was talking like an idiot because he is an idiot,' replied Rachel. And CD, who agreed with her entirely, had to think about cold porridge and vinegar for five minutes to stop his monumental desire becoming too obvious.

RADICALLY INEFFECTUAL

In the weeks that followed they went to a benefit concert together, and a discussion group, and looked around the community bookshop and generally became a recognized feature of alternative haunts. All the time with CD anxiously impressing on Rachel what a committed, worthwhile individual he was. He need not have tried so hard. She liked him, it was his mates that annoyed her. Limpish, tired individuals, endlessly discussing how screwed up the world is, without apparently having very much intention of doing anything about it.

'They're dull, Colin,' CD could not get her to call him CD. 'Your friends are dull. They're not going to save the world.'

CD could only shrug, beginning to wonder whether in constructing the fiction that the people from the community bookshop and local theatre collective were his soul mates, he might not have made a mistake. Right from the beginning he had pretended that he knew them all much better than he did.

'Hi, Todd,' he had said, casually to the bloke at the peace bookshop the first time he had taken Rachel down there. CD had checked out the name beforehand, he knew that if you address someone with sufficient familiarity the chances are very good that they will presume that they know you, especially if the person is a hippy. The plan had worked perfectly, except for the fact that Todd had turned out to be a bit of a boring wanker and CD now had to live with the fact that Rachel thought he was Todd's mate. CD, sensing his tactical error, had decided to try and distance himself from the wet types he had pretended to be so close to. There would be no more 'Hi Todds'. He intended to remodel himself as a hard, practical man, looking for hard, practical solutions. He was even considering buying a pen-knife. That was his plan anyway, unfortunately the whole thing was ruined by the return of the dreadful Karen.

THE RETURN OF THE DREADFUL KAREN

CD had been innocently sitting in a café with Rachel when suddenly and without warning he and his cappuccino were enveloped by a mass of frizzy hair.

'Hi-i-i-i,' Karen cooed, and then demanded, 'Hug please.'

It made him ill to do it but CD was obliged to provide a weak little squeeze. Uninvited Karen plonked herself down, bags and hair everywhere. She liked to effect the attitude of always being in a slightly scatty rush, as if a great many people depended on her.

'Can't stop,' she said, stopping. 'Christ CD haven't seen you since we got busted painting the road, what a night, man!'

'Since *I* got busted,' replied CD, his heart sinking. He desperately hoped that Rachel had forgotten that he had slightly exaggerated his crime when they had first met, claiming that he had been arrested for trying to break into a US naval installation to prove that any terrorist could steal an atom bomb.

'Was that the same night you tried to break into the naval installation?' asked Rachel.

'Is this your new lady?' said Karen, giving Rachel what was intended to be a smile of radiant sisterly love.

If there was one thing that Rachel hated it was the term 'lady'. 'Why don't you bring your lady?: May I introduce my lady. Rachel would almost have preferred anything; girlfriend, bird, she would rather have been someone's casual fuck than their 'lady'. May I introduce my casual fuck . . .

'No,' answered CD, 'this is Rachel, a friend of mine.'

'I *see*,' said Karen with a touch of girlish innuendo, as if to suggest that CD was concealing all sorts of delicious secrets but that she wouldn't pry. 'CD and I were nearly an item ourselves, weren't we?' she confided in a nauseating frank manner which was designed to suggest a modern woman who combined independence and vulnerability in equal measures. Karen stared at people when she spoke to them, at least they thought she was staring at them. She thought she had a disarmingly frank and open countenance.

CD wished that the floor would open up and swallow him, even if it had been eating garlic and hadn't brushed its teeth for three days.

'You look a bit uptight, love. You need a hug,' Karen said. Then she delivered her knockout punch. 'I know, I'll give you a massage.' It was a vicious blow and she delivered it below the belt. CD was down, the umpire was counting him out. He dragged himself back from the brink and hit back.

'Uhm, listen uhm . . . Oh yeah, Karen isn't it? We really have to go, maybe catch you, whenever, OK?' It was good, but not good enough. As he rose the waiter brought the food they had ordered.

'Now, you're really untogether, CD, are you sure you're OK . . . Oh wow, no you're *not*, I mean are these shoulders tense or what? . . .' The claws descended on his shoulders and began to knead away like he was tomorrow's croissant.

At that moment CD discovered what Rachel and most

women learn young, that if someone forceful decides they want to touch you, and they present it as an act of friendship, it is almost impossible to stop them. CD and Rachel had been enjoying Sunday brunch at a café, it was a lovely jolly morning despite the heat. CD had been contented, basking in the light of Rachel's radiant sauciness and now the dark shadow of a wet hippy had fallen upon his happy idyll.

His food sneered up at him – it's extremely difficult to tackle waffles and maple syrup when someone is trying to wring your neck. CD did not know it but the solution to his problem was very close. Not the problem of Karen, of course, she was insoluble, like the hairs she had left in his coffee. Nor indeed the problem of how to persuade Rachel to let him have a go at her, that was a toughie too. Just the problem of how to deal with maple syrup. Because thousands of miles away, a highly-trained team of specialists were working to make problems with maple syrup a thing of the past. Working, in fact to make maple syrup a thing of the past.

DIE BACK DIPLOMACY

The crack unit was headed up by Wayne Strongman, a tough, two-fisted career diplomat who carried a personal phone like it was a side arm, and wore a laminated I D on his pyjamas.

His job at present was stone-walling the Canadians on the problem of US acid rain destroying the Canadian maple trees. Negative diplomacy it was called – a job he knew well. He had been a top trouble-shooter in the Republican Party Damage Control Group for the last two elections. What Wayne Strongman didn't know about twisting a statistic could be written on the back of a stockbroker's tax return.

'The point is,' he said with the quiet assurance that had made him such a feared prosecuting attorney and such a deeply loathed dinner party guest, 'that your people have not been able to establish a *direct* and *proven* correlation.'

Henri Le Conte, Strongman's opposite number, lost his rag.

'I *beg* your bugger-up pardon!!' he said.

Got him, thought Strongman ... An angry man at a conference table is a wide open target, he is a man saying, 'here is my ass, kick it'. Le Conte rose to the bait, shouting:

'And when every fuck maple tree in Quebec is bastard dead! Then you won't need damn all bugger correlation! Is that it!' (It is a strange thing about second languages, no matter how well the foreigner learns them, perhaps to the point where technically they speak better than a native, no one is ever capable of swearing properly in any language other than their own. Le Conte was a French-Canadian and, as he himself often lamented in his strong French accent ... 'I never know when I need a bugger, or where to put my bollocks.')

Now Strongman was staring at him passively. It enraged Le Conte ...

'How much proof is required hell bloody! Do the owners of your factories and power stations have to come to Canada and chop down the fuck trees themselves!!'

There was an embarrassed silence which Strongman allowed to linger one beat into being seriously uncomfortable. His team knew well enough not to break an embarrassed silence. 'Sometimes it's what you *don't* say,' he often told them. Strongman had sent innocent men to the electric chair with a well-timed theatrical pause.

'Henri,' he said dispassionately to the red-faced French-Canadian. 'I can understand you being upset. Clearly it's not just a matter of lost revenue, to you guys the maple tree is your national symbol.' That was the way, play it soft for a moment ... but just a moment, just long enough for them to register that you're being conciliatory – then hit them. 'But frankly, I find the implications of your outburst deeply offensive. I can only presume you feel that we on the US team are a bunch of dumb and unprincipled ecological vandals.' He continued quickly, before Le Conte could agree with this. 'Well, let me tell you Mister, you're barking up the wrong damn maple tree! Do you think we don't have maples in

Ontario? New England? US kids got a sweet-tooth too! If we can verify for *certain* what's killing the damn things, well you may rest assured, Sir, that the United States government will pursue it to hell and beyond and nail it to the wall, by crikey! But before I start closing factories; before I start putting men out of work and forcing their families onto welfare, by Heaven, I'm going to be as sure of my ground as an old pig and that's *hog* sure!!'

He had just made up the 'old pig' metaphor. Strongman liked inventing pretend colloquialisms, it confused foreigners.

'Mr Strongman,' said Le Conte, badly wanting to kill him. '82 per cent of the trees in the Beauce-Megantic region are showing signs of pollution. It's sulphur dioxide from *your* factories. Ten years from now we will have no trees left. This is a world emergency . . . Quebec produces over two-thirds of the world's maple syrup. We've cut our acid rain, you've got to cut yours.'

'We can't be sure. The connection isn't proven,' said Strongman, reasonable again. 'Believe me, our top men, the best, are on this thing. We're chasing it Henri, oh yeah, we're chasing it like a pan-fried Tennessee whore with the clap, and that's *finger licking* chasing.' That was a good one, thought Strongman, they'd laugh about that tonight. He couldn't help but notice the secretary's admiring glance. Who knows, maybe . . . Anyway he'd certainly waffled that dumb French kayak's maple syrup right up his sweet backside, you bet he had.

Le Conte, a native of Quebec, wanted to cry. With great sadness he called upon his science officer to present the Canadian argument yet again.

The negotiation machine would continue to produce bullshit at a comparable rate to the industrial production of acid rain. The US/Canadian dialogue had been going on for so long it would certainly outlive the trees. It takes a maple tree about five years to perish from a phenomenon known as 'die back'. They die from the top down. Like a balding man, their branches recede. The syrup farmer taps his trees each

61

year and watches them die by inches, becoming poor, sad, shabby shadows of their once mighty selves. This disaster is, of course, not confined to maple trees but is beginning to affect the majority of all the trees in the world.

THE FHAGWASH

The waffles had gone cold and CD's shoulders were numb. Finally, Karen released him.

'Anyway, I really have got to get my act together,' said Karen, turning down a non-existent invitation to hang around. 'Boogaloo and Rhumtitty are probably coming round for supper tonight or some other time. It's so difficult to cook for Yanyaroos.' Karen had a habit common to many people who pride themselves on possessing approachable and open personalities. She referred to people that she knew as if everyone knew them. Ostensibly this was because Karen believed that the world is actually full of love and that there are quite enough artificial barriers created between people without constructing extra ones.

'Karen, I don't know any of the people you're talking about,' CD had remarked on their one night together.

'Just because you don't know someone,' Karen replied, 'doesn't mean you can't be a friend of theirs.' She spoke with the same tone of happy confidence that Einstein must have used the first time he said $E = MC^2$. In actual fact, her habit of trumpeting the names of her acquaintances was her way of reassuring herself that she had friends. Unfortunately the effect of this habit, on someone who did not know better, would clearly be to presume that CD and Karen were not only mates, but that they shared much the same circle of friends.

Obviously this was distastrous for CD. After all he had only just made his decision that he must quickly disassociate himself from Karen's type and suddenly, up pops Karen, blithely speaking as if she and CD balanced at the hub of the same social wheel. Worse still, it was a wheel which appeared to include Yanyaroos. CD was right to feel concern on this last point. There are a lot of Yanyaroos in WA and Rachel, like many, found it extremely difficult to understand the fascination. She could not, for the life of her, see how wearing a picture of a bearded, multimillionaire guru around your neck and dressing only in blue clothes could lead to spiritual enlightenment.

Strangely, another person who found Yanyarooism a pretty surprising phenomenon was Yoga Fhagwash, Chief Guru of the Yanyaroo cult, whose picture it was that hung on Karen's friends', Boogaloo's and Rhumtitty's, chests.

'I just don't understand it,' he would say to his aides and girlfriends, 'I tell all these middle-class white people to wear blue clothes and send me half their money . . . and they do!!!'

At first, the Yoga Fhagwash, unable to believe his luck, had tried to keep up appearances. Playing it all very spiritual, issuing poems and thoughts and mantras about enlightenment through denial. After a while, though, his confidence began to grow. He began to experiment with the credulity of his followers, suggesting for instance, that possessing twenty-five Rolls Royces was an intensely religious statement and what's more, not letting anyone else have a go in them maintained their purity and integrity.

To Fhagwash's relief and astonishment, there was no reaction. 'They don't seem to care,' he remarked in astonishment, while writhing in warm cocoa-butter on a water-bed full of champagne.

Rachel was convinced that originally the popularity of the cult had been based on its advocacy of free love. Fhagwash was a monumental root-rat himself and encouraged his disciples to go for it like a pack of rabbits on a weekend in Amsterdam. Yanyaroos were practically ordered to have it off willy nilly. This was what annoyed Rachel.

'I mean, it's like a never-ending adolescent fantasy with God saying how great you are for snogging. Well *yuk*!'

CD wasn't sure. He couldn't help thinking that if scripture

lessons at his school had been one long feel-up session there would have been a lot more converts to the Bible.

Since the advent of AIDS, of course, everything had changed. The Yoga Fhagwash had swung to the other extreme and gone completely ape mega-moral. The arch wick-dipper had become the arch party-pooper – possibly because he didn't want his source of income dying off. Fhagwash went rubber-glove mad. He had people putting a dustbin-liner over their heads before they washed their own faces. It wasn't long before his disciples were having to wrap themselves in cling film before making a telephone call. Soon, if they wanted to go out, they'd probably have to have themselves laminated.

The future of Yanyarooism lies in the balance. It is questionable whether people will want to give money to someone who says they can't have it off. Rachel was entirely indifferent to the future of the cult but one thing was for sure. If CD was thinking of going to dinner at Karen's, with Boogaloo and Rhumtitty, then he was going on his own.

DENIAL

Karen was finally going. She got up and kissed CD.

For one appalling moment Rachel thought she was going to kiss her. Thankfully Karen confined herself to a squeeze of the shoulder which was still over-familiar considering it was based on an acquaintance of about fifteen minutes.

'Come round to dinner sometime, you must,' was her parting shot. 'Rash and Basil and Tish and Blossom said they might probably come round one evening or, if they don't, some other time.'

Another big, sloppy smacker delivered on the lips through a cloud of frizziness and she was gone.

There was a pause. Then CD spoke.

'I have never met that woman before in my life.'

STARK CONSPIRATOR

MAN WITH A MISSION

Sly had left the dinner in L A a changed man. Changed for ever. He flew home to Oz a fully committed member of the Stark Conspiracy.

THE PROBLEM WITH ABORIGINALS

Unfortunately with trust came responsibilities. Sly had a specific role to play, a role which he knew would not be an easy one. He had been charged with acquiring the land. The consortium had done their homework and Western Australia was certainly far and away the best bet for the very detailed specifications necessary for their purposes – no doubt that was why Sly had been brought into the group at all. The clever bastards had already roughly picked out the bit of scrub that they wanted, which was almost convenient. Except, of course, for the Abs.

In his efforts to ingratiate himself with his new partners, Sly had spoken glibly of simply persuading the Abs to move on to greener pastures but in the back of his mind he knew it would be tougher than getting red wine chunder out of a duck down duvet. To say that Abs were a strange crew would, in Sly's opinion, be stretching the well-known Aussie talent for understatement to its limits. He knew kangaroos with more horse sense than an Ab. They were stubborn too, strange and stubborn, that was Abs, and on no subject were they stranger and stubborner than on the subject of land.

Land was an obsession with Aborigines. Of course, no one

could argue with a man being attached to the place he hung his hat. Sly himself had a little spread on the Swan River that was his pride and joy. It had a swimming pool the shape of Western Australia, an outdoor cocktail bar made of glass, with real fish inside it, and a genuine Henry Moore which Sly had bought unseen and had hastily had to plant a bunch of gum trees to hide the bloody monstrosity.

Beautiful land, beautifully appointed, but unlike some Abs he'd happily move on if he was paid enough. What was their problem? What were they protecting? Nothing, just a load of dust and rocks and empty bottles. It wasn't what was on the land, it was the land itself. For some reason specific bits of land had specific spiritual relevance. Sly thanked God he wasn't religious, he'd have bulldozed down Notre Dame if he'd thought there was half a barrel of oil underneath it.

Maybe the Abs have grown up, thought Sly in a brief moment of hope. Maybe they'd move after all! He'd give them good grazing country, access to a river, their own pub! But deep in his heart (which was not awfully deep), Sly knew they wouldn't. He could just see some bastard head man, standing leaning on his stick, staring straight through him – chewing his gums, through a huge, stupid, white beard that made him look like he was frenching a sheep. He wouldn't budge an inch. The bloody-minded old goat would fuck Sly off like he was Lord Muck with a million in his jeans, instead of some broke old derelict with a headful of lice.

These were Sly's bitter reflections as he sat in his first-class seat the morning after the dinner. It wouldn't have been so difficult a few years before but land rights had become a real big issue in the last decade or so. You couldn't just push people around anymore. You'd get every government sponsored bleeding-heart in the country down on your back. It was ridiculous, how were you supposed to run a country for the good of all if you kept worrying about people's damn rights?

Sly looked at the middle-aged hostess who was serving his champagne. Steel-grey crew cut, clearly a lesso, thought Sly.

That was equal rights for you! Sly could remember when air hostesses were a bunch of little spunks, every one. They'd lean over to pour your fizz in their cute white blouses and you'd get a tiny, tantalizing glimpse of the tops of their frilly little bras. Sexier than any full-on strip show that glimpse, thought Sly, because you knew the girl had class. They'd get sacked at twenty-eight of course, and why not? Why should people get a meal ticket for life at the expense of the consumer, he asked himself? What was a hostess *for* he'd like to know? Jesus, a machine could serve the fucking drinks and microwave the chops. A hostess was there to make the flight more bearable.

But *now* of course, that was called sex discrimination. No sackings on grounds of sex or age. These days you either got served by some boy faggot or a middle-aged hag who never married a captain because she was a muff-tucker. The only way to get a decent floor show was to fly a Far Eastern airline like Malaya or Singapore. Beautiful girls but could you trust the pilot? It wasn't that he was an ogler or anything like that, Sly assured himself, he'd never been a perv, *no way*!! It was just nice to look at pretty young girls, everyone knew that, so why couldn't these damn do-gooders admit it?

He wished he'd used his private jet.

Sly was getting pissed and working himself into a frenzy because he knew that what he had promised in Los Angeles would be very difficult to deliver. He just fervently hoped that when he headed north to scout around, the Aboriginals he would have to deal with would not be the spiritual type and would like a drink.

THE COLLAPSE OF A DREAM

Sly may have been feeling bitter, but CD thought he was going to die. He was discovering that there are worse feelings than just being in love. There is something horribly worse, much worse than he could ever have imagined. Unrequited love. Two of the saddest words in the English language had laid CD as low as sure as if they'd been written on a brick and he'd been hit over the head with it.

The shock of learning how much he was capable of feeling made him scared and angry. He had always presumed that he was a fairly shallow sort of person, not wont to feel either joy or sorrow to any great degree, and now he discovered that he was at the mercy of feelings way way beyond his control. It was very confusing, he felt impotent, awash with emotions so palpable they seemed to have an actual physical form. The feeling that had dwelt in his guts for the last few weeks now seemed feather-light and gentle compared to the large piece of lead that somehow had managed to insert itself into his abdomen whilst he wasn't looking. Because . . .

She wasn't interested!

No, it wasn't anything to do with that Karen woman, Rachel had assured him in answer to his desperate protests . . . or any of the other people he had introduced her to. It was simply that she didn't feel that way about CD. Also she had had no idea that he felt that way about her either. She felt that they had just become very good friends, which was great. That was the way she wanted it. There was certainly no question of anything else. Just friends, that was all.

'I'm sorry, Rachel, I can't deal with that. It would be too much,' CD had said with dignity. Just friends! What a suggestion! What an insult to the strength of his feelings. Didn't she understand how much he loved her? Just friends! What did she think he was! You can't feel the things he was feeling and settle for 'just friends'!

'I'm an all or nothing sort of person,' he had said, looking at her with what he thought was an expression of boundless sorrow. 'Me and half-measures never did get along.' The eyes misty now, staring at hers with unrelenting frankness. In his anguish CD failed to recall that this trick did not work for Karen the hippy, and was unlikely to work for him. 'I have to have it all,' he added, switching his look to lean and handsome.

Rachel said, 'That's a shame, Colin. Oh well, I suppose that's it then.'

This was a surprise. One of the most irritating features of unrequited love is that hope springs eternal. CD had rather been hoping that Rachel would say, 'oh well, in that case, do you want me now or shall we wait till we can find a bed?'

Summoning up all of his dignity, which at that point took about a picosecond, CD rose to leave. 'I'm history Rachel. I'm outa here, yesterday's news. Maybe I'll travel, don't look for me tomorrow baby, because I'll be gone.'

'What about the casserole dish?'

'Keep it.' He slung his pretend leather jacket over his shoulder.

'It's mine. You've got it at your house.'

In a magnificent gesture CD walked out without a word, returning a few minutes later with a brand new casserole dish.

'See you,' said Rachel.

'Yeah, maybe,' CD replied with another portion of boundless sorrow. This time he really did leave. Walked out magnificently. Stood on the pavement in his torn jeans and burst into tears.

HERO

He had no right to resent Rachel for not falling in love with him. He knew that but, by God, he did and as he walked home his anguish assumed ever more heroic proportions. He was magnificent in his loneliness. He could do anything now because he no longer cared. There was no greater force than a man with nothing to lose, CD told himself. He could achieve great things because all his achievements would mean nothing to him. Nothing because he was nothing and nothing comes of nothing. And when he had done all these great things, and returned, tired or dead, the fruits of his terrible solitude spread about him for all to see, then she would be sorry, then she would realize what she had passed up. Then she would weep and wish that things had been different. But he would just smile at her – presuming he was still alive that is – smile at her with infinite weariness etched in the lines of his lean, craggy face and then turn away without a word . . . No wait, maybe he would say . . . maybe he would say . . . well, something brilliant about fucking casserole dishes anyway.

But for now it was definitely over. He had told her, that was it, he had walked out of her life for ever and he was going to stick to that. He would never speak to her again, that was the only way. He knew it was the only way . . .

HOPE SPRINGS ETERNAL

'Hi, Rachel, your friend and main man CD here, Colin to you.'

It was evening, hours after he had left her at the café with the casserole dish. Not that he had held out that long. He'd been trying since about three minutes after he got home but she had been out.

'Oh, hi Colin, I wondered if you'd phone. I had to go to Mum's. Promised to help her with the garden.'

This was scarcely the hours of anguished pacing along pavements made strangely unfamiliar by her new isolation, which was what CD had rather hoped Rachel had been up to but, there you go. He wasn't quibbling, he'd recovered slightly. Hope springs eternal.

'Listen, I was just wondering if we could still be, you know, what we are at the moment, you know, just that,' he said.

'But of course, that's what I want, Colin,' replied Rachel, 'as long as you know that I meant what I said, I really did, and I do.'

'Oh yeah, of course, forget it, no problem, won't mention it again,' said CD. 'It'll be exactly the same as it was.'

'Great,' said Rachel, knowing that it would never be the same again.

Actually, although neither Rachel nor CD knew it, nothing was ever going to be the same again. Nothing in the whole world.

It was only early on in the southern summer but already it was very very hot, much hotter than usual. The times were definitely a-changing. It was definitely very very hot.

ON THE BUSINESS OF STARK

Sly piloted his own four-seater light aircraft out of Perth and headed north east, up towards the Territory. It was a flight he normally enjoyed hugely, the place was so utterly enormous. It was what flying must have been like in the very early days, when you had the whole sky to yourself and could dodge and weave as you felt like it.

These days it was like playing space invaders with air traffic control. That wasn't flying, circling high in the stack, waiting in line to put down in a blanket of smog so thick you couldn't see the landing lights. Petrified to drop or rise by the width of a credit card because you'd probably get a jumbo in the face..

'Those passengers on the right of the plane should get a good view of the mountains and those on the left should just be able to make out a 747 full of terrified people pointing at you and screaming "get the fuck out of the way".'

Sly would not personally fly himself anywhere these days except over Oz. Maybe Africa would be all right but Sly wasn't going to go to Africa if he could help it. As far as he could see, the Third World was getting Thirder, soon they would have to start calling it the Fourth World, maybe even the Fifth. A continent full of poverty. What would be the point of going there?

POOR BASTARDS

Actually, as he sat at the controls of his little plane, Sly was on a journey into poverty on the business of Stark. He was going to chat with some Abs, and you don't get much poorer than your average Ab'. That's why most people hate them, thought

72

Sly, they're so horribly poor. It gets on your nerves. Why do they have to hang around all the time being so poor? Why don't they fuck off and be poor somewhere else?

Lots of Aboriginals end up as piss-heads, causing people to say 'no wonder they're so poor, half of them are piss-heads'. It would, of course, make much more sense to say 'no wonder half of them are piss-heads, they're so poor'.

Australia is guilt-ridden by Aboriginal history and people get nasty when they feel guilty, they seek to find a scapegoat and often end up blaming the victims themselves . . .

'Jesus, mate, they're fucking rolling in it. Christ the government's so fucking wet it just spoon feeds them handouts and they piss the lot up against the wall.'

This, of course, is the way people deal with degradation the whole world over. Sympathy for victims is always counter-balanced by an equal and opposite feeling of resentment towards them. How often had Sly said:

'See that tramp. Wanted money for a meal. I gave him a buck of course . . . Ha, probably earns more than I do, probably got a fortune stuffed under his mattress.'

Sly never asked himself why someone with a fortune stuffed under his mattress would choose to sit in a gutter all day.

PARADISE LOST

Sly was flying over Kalgoorkatta. They dug uranium there, Sly had a lot of money in it. It had been a hell of a battle to get the government to give the go-ahead. People were such a bunch of old women when it came to nuclear energy. It had cost the earth to prove how safe it was. Dinners, party donations, all expenses paid fact-finding luxury trips. Those high-minded political types did not sell themselves cheaply.

All Sly and his colleagues wanted was a tiny, tiny relaxation in the frankly impractical laws on how much uranium was produced. Also, it would be nice if there were less restrictions on who they were allowed to sell it to and, finally, it would make life easier if they did not have to ask so many embarrassing and impertinent questions as to what the buyer wanted it for. Just a small rationalization of these absurdly restrictive laws would net ten billion a year, which would of course generate some very juicy corporate tax, not to mention the jobs.

Besides this, the consortium argued, you can't stop progress. If they didn't do it someone else would. The Canadians were already doing it in fact. Yes, that had shocked those bastard greenies. Canada, land of the maple leaf and the acid rain protest was flogging uranium off the back of a barrow to just about any piss-poor, potential terrorist base of a country that could afford it.

Sly's mining consortium hadn't got everything it had wanted but they had got enough and Kalgoorkatta was by way of being a bit of a boom town. It was dangerous work and it certainly-screwed up the land a bit, but you can't make an omelette without breaking eggs.

Lots of eggs. What a mess it was! Until he flew over it Sly had never realized just how hellish a few hundred hectares of virtually unrestricted mining could look. It was a couple of years since he and the other members of the consortium had stood on the pretty hillside with the champagne and photographers, bleating on about it being a great day for Australia. Since then a good approximation of Hades had been produced. The land was scarred and smashed and poisoned. Soon it would also be empty. When that happened Sly and his friends would fence it in and move on. Land was there to be used.

THE DESERT OAK

A couple of hundred years before the mines were laid, an Aboriginal man had used the land himself. He was on walkabout and thirsty. Aboriginals were often thirsty. This came from living in an enormous desert. The fellow in question was thirsty but he was cool. He was cool because he knew that all he needed to do was find a desert oak tree. It wasn't called a desert oak tree in those days of course, what the Aboriginal in question called it one can only guess at. Possibly, 'Sir' or perhaps 'darling', something appreciative certainly because this tree was going to save his life. You wouldn't have thought of it as a life-saver, not to look at certainly. No one, not even its mother, could have called it an inspiring or handsome tree. The desert oak was, and in fact still is, as a breed, a hugely unimpressive scrappy, crappy little tree. Its best friends would say so.

'Tree,' they would say, realizing that you have to be cruel to be kind, 'do not go entering yourself in any horticultural shows. You will only embarrass us all.'

But the desert oak can smile knowingly to itself, it has a secret. Because although on the surface it may be just a six-foot skinny streak of fibre with about ten leaves to its name, beneath the desert floor it is a very different story. For the desert oak can put down roots as deep as three hundred feet. In fact, as far as need be to reach water. Let there be no question about it, ugly as fuck though it is, root-wise the desert oak does not mess around. Still waters run deep and so do desert oaks. Other factors that make this tree remarkably together, as far as living in the desert goes, include its ability to 'die' at will. When times are hard, and let's face it they almost always are, for a tree in a desert, the top bit of the tree just switches off. Drops its leaves, shrivels up and pretends to be dead.

You wouldn't notice the change to look at it, of course. So unimpressive is the desert oak in full bloom that the difference between it stretching its branches and saying, 'God it's good to be alive and a tree today' and it pretending to be dead, is not marked. In fact, the two states are almost identical. None the less, that is what it does, on the surface the tree 'dies'. Underneath though, the search for water goes on and when that water is found, after what could be as much as fifteen or twenty years, the top bit comes back to life and blossoms into its full patheticness.

Possibly conscious of the trouble it has gone to to find

water, once found, the desert oak makes the most of it. It stores it, sucking up as much as it can up through its three hundred foot roots, and storing a few pints in its horrid, spindly little trunk.

And this is where the thirsty Aborigine comes in. Because the Aborigines have always known about these trees. They had worked out a way to get at that water without the tedious necessity of having to put down three hundred foot roots and pretend to be dead for twenty years themselves. What they used to do was this. They would make a little hole in the bark of the tree and put a twig in. Then they would sit under the twig with their mouths open and wait for the water to drip in.

This is what our man did, hundreds of years ago, on the site of what was to become the over-mined, useless uranium plant. And once he had drunk enough, he didn't just get up and piss off, leaving the tree to drip till it died. No, he removed the twig, got a bit of gum from the bark of a nearby eucalyptus, and bunged up the hole he'd made. This was the way it was done. You plugged up your hole.

The Aborigines were a Stone-Age society, one of the most primitive on earth. They had not even developed a simple television game show. But they knew that if you looked after the environment there was a good chance it would look after you.

Now Sly and his friends had taken what they wanted from the land just as the Aboriginal had done. But they had no intention of bunging up their hole. Too expensive, too much trouble.

The term 'primitive' is clearly a highly subjective one.

PROTEST AND SURVIVE

CD had intended to change his entire policy regarding his pursuit of Rachel but he was not in a position to do so. Rachel liked the things they had been doing together just the way they were. The peace and ecology bit had really got in amongst her and she wanted to get more involved. As far as she was concerned, CD was inexorably linked with all this growing interest. That was what their relationship was based on and she liked it that way. After all, she knew plenty of blokes to drink and play pool with but there weren't many who'd schlepp 20K to a meeting about how much raw sewage was getting pumped into Perth's swimming waters.

AUSSIE ADS

Today's schlepp was to a kind of protest bazaar at the naval installation thirty kilometres north of Carlton. For the previous six years there had been a permanent women's protest encamped close to the public jetty and this was a day of support. The US South Pacific fleet was coming in, which was always an occasion for excitement, horror or indifference, according to individual attitudes to US fleets.

CD and Rachel arrived a little late and the party was in full swing. The hippies were painting their children's faces, the police were pretending to be friendly and a small group of strippers and hostesses were waving their boobs about.

This was because the arrival of the fleet was a very special time for the clubs and strip joints of Perth. The owners would send down their dancing girls to hang adverts off the quay and bare their breasts as the ships came in. 'Come to the 301 Club and see bonza Aussie tits' the signs would say. The girls jumped up and down, jiggling their bonza Aussie tits as a kind of foretaste of what the lucky sailors could expect if they visited one of the clubs.

This, incidentally, is an example of classic Australian advertising. It tends to be abrupt and to the point. For instance, if a manufacturer has produced a sausage that he (or she) considers to be long and meaty, he will call the produce 'Long 'N' Meaty Saussies' and advertise it thus: '"Long 'N' Meaty Saussies", they're long and meaty (and they're saussies).'

Half-way to the printers with the advertising copy, the manufacturer will realize that he has not pointed out that the saussies are Australian. He will immediately rename them 'Long 'N' Meaty Aussie Saussies' and proudly boast: '"Long 'N' Meaty Aussie Saussies", they're long and meaty, and they're saussies, pure Aussie . . .'

After some thought he might add, 'eat 'em!' just to make the situation absolutely clear. It makes a change from the sort of ad where a picture of a lizard on a pyramid, basking in the sun, is supposed to make you desperate for a fag.

THE ONE WORLD FESTIVAL

Anyway, the poor cold girls jiggled and the poor cold US sailors whooped and hollered from the decks of their ships, no doubt thinking that if the girls did this at the docks, what fabulous and exotic pleasures could be expected on paying twenty bucks to get into a club. None, sadly. Just more tit jiggling, minus the goose-pimples.

CD and Rachel arrived rather late.

'Look at those girls,' said CD, looking. 'Pretty gross, eh?' he added looking some more. 'I mean, just totally out of order,' he said as he took another long, hard look just to make sure it really was as offensive as he thought it was.

Rachel wasn't interested in the girls, gross or not. She was taking in the scene as a whole and experiencing a gutful of frustration and doubt. There, floating out on the high seas, was the US South Pacific fleet, looking, it had to be admitted, pretty hard. On the dock in opposition to this bay full of death-tech, stood the protesters, looking (it could not be denied) rather pathetic. Balloons, painted children's faces, acoustic guitars . . . 'I mean, for God's sake,' thought Rachel.

Anyone faced by a battle fleet is going to feel a sharp sense of scale. It can only add to the inadequacy to be surrounded by street theatre and kids with T-shirts saying 'I want to grow up, not blow up'.

'I hate the way people always feel they have to justify their principles by linking them to their snotty kids,' she said.

Rachel didn't like most kids very much. She found them selfish and demanding and socially inept. She certainly did not feel any need to lend substance to her hopes for a better world by harping mawkishly on the fate of the poor innocent kiddies. As far as she was concerned she was a poor innocent kiddie herself and would be till the day she died.

'It's so utterly yuk, bunging your own ideas on the chest of some revolting little sprog . . . We don't know what a kid wants anyway,' she moaned to CD, who was eating a vegetable samosa from a stall.

'Any one of these kids could be in the navy itself in fifteen years,' she continued, warming to her theme. 'I'm at this protest because *I* don't want to blow up. At least we know I haven't grown up to be an axe murderer. This lot might. They're probably more likely to actually. They reckon kids react against their parents' beliefs, and I'm not surprised,' said Rachel, staring around at the hippy throng. 'Wouldn't you turn into an axe murderer if your mother's idea of sweets was carrot cake?'

'Don't be so hard on everybody all the time,' said CD, who was enjoying his samosa and feeling benign. 'These people are cool. It's not their fault they've got poor dress sense . . .'

'Jesus, will you look at that fellah I just served,' said Rick the samosa maker, 'what *does* he look like!'

As it happened, CD believed himself to be effecting the casual elegance of an English gent abroad, strolling about on an early summer day. He was wearing a perfect linen suit and was the epitome of taste. Unfortunately he didn't have a perfect linen suit and certainly the old cricket trousers and chef's jacket were not an exact imitation.

Rick and his live-in friend, Judy, were convinced that CD must be drug squad.

'It's all so bloody pointless and *dull*,' Rachel moaned, 'nobody's *doing* anything.'

'Well, what the hell are you doing?' asked CD, who was vaguely experimenting with an idea that it might turn Rachel on if he was more butch and dominant. He toyed with the thought of adding, 'bitch', but mercifully reason prevailed.

'Nothing,' shouted Rachel, 'that's what makes me so angry. I'm not doing anything. I'm hanging around with a bunch of hippies, and hippies bore me shitless.'

'Hippies bore everybody shitless, Rachel, it's their job,' replied CD. 'Hippies even bore hippies shitless. That's why they take so many drugs, just to avoid having to talk to each other. They say it's to change their heads but it's not.'

'Well, it ought to be. If my head was as dull as that I'd want to change it,' said Rachel.

CD and Rachel stood in silence. CD trying to think of something dominant to say and Rachel reading a huge sign on one of the dock walls that said 'Perth Premium Gold – A regular drinking beer for a regular beer drinker'. Anyone who scorns Australian copywriting would scorn no further if they could have seen the effect that this advert was having on Rachel. Her whole soul cried out for a beer. Then somebody began to sing 'Blowing in the Wind'.

'Right, that's it,' she said. 'I'm going to the pub.'

But, just then there was a stirring in the crowd. Something interesting was happening on one of the ships. Rachel stayed to watch.

THE *USS ENORMOUS*

The US Navy, in a monumentally optimistic bit of public relations, had opened up one of the warships to public inspection. The people of Carlo were to be allowed to take a look at the hardware to which they were hosts. What the thinking was behind the American decision is hard to say. Why people, nervous that their little town was being made into a prime nuclear target, should be less nervous for getting a closer look at the cause of their fears is a question not easily answered.

'And what you are standing on here, folks, is a United States warship, yes sirree. It's this little mother them Ruskis are going to be aiming at when they miss and hit your town.'

CD would have quite liked to have gone and had a look, although he wouldn't have admitted it. Actually, if he had gone, he would have been rather bored. The US Navy did not intend to give much away.

Second Lieutenant Kowalski was detailed to welcome the tourists aboard and escort them around those few sections of the ship that were not classified. He had been carefully chosen. Tall and splendid in his pure white uniform, he had an easy, open face and manner that made you just know he would defend democracy until his sabre broke. He dazzled his smitten audience of love-struck young women and death mad little boys, with a whirlwind of technology.

'This here is a US Naval 8.2 litre unload and distribution facility, manually operated by a single crewman.'

Moving on from the toilet the awestruck group were privileged to inspect an On-site Perimeter Confinement Safety Unit, or ship's rail. It was here that the excitement Rachel had observed from the shore occurred.

Through CD's second-hand binoculars she could see that two men had somehow managed to detach themselves from the group of sightseers and were scaling one of the sort of conning tower affairs that these ships seem to bristle with. One stopped only a few feet up but the other was tremendously nimble. He almost seemed to be running vertically. If he had been wearing a red and blue body stocking Rachel would have thought it was Spiderman. Having climbed as far as he could go – a good thirty feet above the shouting sailors – he attached himself to a satellite dish, managing to almost sit in it as if he was about to be stir-fried in an enormous wok. He raised his fist in a triumphant salute towards the protesters on the shore and then unfurled a twenty-five foot long banner that slashed about like a scythe in the strong wind. It was inscribed with the legend 'Nuclear Target'.

That was by no means the end of the entertainment, for suddenly there was a flash and a bang and all the shouting sailors dived for cover. It took another three bangs before they realized that these were not SS2os but simply fireworks let off by the other man, who had not climbed so far, to draw attention to the protest. The sailors, furious for having been duped, soon hauled the firework fellow down but it took twenty minutes for them to reach the one with the banner and bring him and his banner back to the deck. The protest was sufficiently dramatic for it to be shown on the news that evening. It wasn't much but it was something, and it was also undeniably exciting.

Watching from the shore, Rachel and CD did not know it but this was their first encounter with Walter and Zimmerman. They were soon to become comrades-in-arms against Stark.

ZIMMERMAN AND WALTER

ZIMMERMAN

Zimmerman's intense dislike of weapons of war had come upon him quite suddenly – literally in a flash. One moment he was walking through the jungle not decided on the subject either way, the next moment his private parts were hanging off a nearby tree and he knew he didn't like bombs. The doctors had done wonders, they fixed his legs, sewed his guts back together, but, sad to say, all the wonders of micro-surgery could not get his tackle down out of the tree.

A few months later Gough Whitlam brought the Australian Army home but it is said that for those who experienced the horrors, each one left a little piece of themselves out in Vietnam. In Zimmerman's case it was his lunch-box. Ever since then he had never felt himself a whole member of society and, of course, he wasn't, because he no longer had a whole member with which to be social. He had not felt himself a part of what governments decided. He had not felt himself bound by their rules – basically, he hadn't felt himself.

Why had Zimmerman joined up in the first place? It was a question he often asked himself whilst contemplating the wreckage that lay inside his trousers. He could remember things quite clearly up until when he was about eighteen. It was about then that he had dropped a couple of tabs of acid and gone to see John Wayne in *The Green Berets*. He remembered that. But from then on it all got very confused. There were bangs and flashes and a series of very unpleasant experiences. Suddenly, it was three years later and he was being carried off an Army Medical Corps Hercules air transport. Sadly minus his hand luggage.

Since then Zimmerman had learnt that during the vague period of lights and bangs, he had turned into an exceptional soldier. Eventually becoming a commando. The army, it seemed, had trained him to do unspeakably horrid things very well indeed. They trained him diligently and his skills served them well. Zimmerman knew they had been pleased because they had given him a top combat medal of which he was proud.

Zimm had been very popular with his comrades. There was a good reason for this. They said he had guts. They were right, certainly he had guts and normally they were full of drugs. This made him very amenable. When someone was needed to creep down a suspicious looking hole, a hole which probably contained half the Vietcong Army, the others would shuffle their feet self-consciously and look shyly at Zimm.

'Zimm'll do it,' they would say to each other reassuringly.

'He's a real regular guy.'

By 'regular guy' they of course meant raving lunatic but were being tactful. When someone is stupid enough to risk his arse continually while others hide behind it, you let them.

Sad to say, by the time Zimm got back to Australia, his brain was fried. One thought was clear in his head though. One thought had sustained him throughout the long years since 'Nam. Zimmerman was going to save the world. That was what he spent his time doing, saving the world. That was what he was doing when he scaled the conning tower of the USS *Enormous* and unfurled his banner. He was saving the world.

He had been saving the world when he had broken into the tobacco company's laboratories and set all the dogs free. Certainly, the net result had been a bunch of Beagles wandering around half-starved and desperate for a ciggie but Zimm never thought his actions through very clearly. He just wanted to save the world, which seemed simple enough to him.

84

WALTER

It was lucky then that Zimm's constant companion was Walter, a very together guy indeed. Extraordinarily together considering he was a hippy and hippies are not on the whole known for their togetherness. It was Walter who was with Zimm on the USS *Enormous* telling Zimm to cool it as they were led away by the military police. Walter always knew when Zimm was in danger of flying off the handle and exercising some of those terrible skills that the army had taken such pains to teach him. There were little tell-tale signs like veins bulging on his forehead, tiny codes in the things Zimm would say, like, 'I'm going to kill the dickhead in the white uniform.' Walter knew to pick up these hints and act on them.

Walter had a genuinely calming presence. When talking to him one really did get the impression that things were all right.

'Tell me things are all right, Walter.'

'They're all right.'

And, somehow, for a little while at least, they were. Of course, after a while Walter's cool could begin to irritate because there are times in every person's life when they want to fly off the handle. If the car explodes for instance, or you turn out to have an uncanny resemblance to an escaped psychopath and get wrongly sent to prison for a thousand years. Walter's response to disasters like that would be to say:

'It's OK, it's cool, try not to become uptight about it.'

This obviously could be pretty aggravating. But often Walter's calm, almost spiritual demeanour was a comfort to those who met him. Not the judges and police officers and representatives of chemical waste disposal firms, obviously. Nor the hire-purchase people to whom Walter would patiently explain that money exists only in their heads. But most people . . . well some people, found him calming – for a while anyway.

You needed to be calm to do the sort of things Walter was in the habit of doing. When you've sat in a tiny motorized dinghy with a shit scared Blue whale on one side of you, a seriously pissed off whaling fleet on the other side, ten foot waves underneath you and an explosive harpoon sailing over your head, you either learn to be cool or you go through a lot of pairs of trousers.

For Walter was green. He was as green as the contents of an Eskimo's hanky. He loved animals and plants and everything. (There was one plant that Walter particularly loved, although rolling it up and setting it on fire and sucking it to death was a funny way of showing it.) Walter also had a selfish motive for his green-ness, he firmly believed that peaceful co-existence with other life forms on the planet was the only way that the human race itself would survive.

A lot of people took the piss out of the sort of things Walter did. 'Oh wow, man,' they would say, 'Save the whale, yeah, and black lesbian disabled dwarfs for a nuclear free health food shop.' In fact, both Rachel and CD had been guilty of this type of comment in their time. But Walter knew that these people were wankers. Whales are the largest creatures left living on earth, the heart of a Blue whale is higher than a tall man and it weighs half a ton. The creature itself grows to a hundred feet and weighs a hundred and sixty tons. Everything pales in comparison to a creation of this awesome magnitude. What is the Taj Mahal or the Golden Gate Bridge to a living force with arteries so huge a child could crawl along them? Yet they were being wiped off the face of the earth to make soap.

'Listen, man, would you unpick the Bayeux Tapestry to get a reel of cotton?' Walter said at his trial. He got a thousand dollar fine.

WALTER AND ZIMMERMAN

It was Walter who turned Zimmerman on to Eco stuff. He suggested to Zimm that he needed to channel his energies.

'Listen, man,' Walter would say, 'like, one day you're freeing Beagles, the next you're riding the bus all night defending old ladies . . . I mean, cool, don't get me wrong, very cool. I just feel, like, we should, like ... you know, formalize our avenues of protest, right ...? Or does that sound a bit too much like heavy fascist mind control, and, like, pretty soon we'll be as bad as the people we're protesting against?'

'Well, it does a bit, man,' Zimmerman would reply.

None the less, despite the organizational pitfall of not wishing to get into any kind of fascist mind control thing, Walter and Zimmerman had sort of come to a conclusion as to what they were. They were Green Commandos. When they bothered to get up, and were straight, Zimm's horrifying military skills combined with Walter's ability to keep them in check, made them quite a team. They had saved animals, destroyed logging equipment, blocked up chemical waste pipes. Once they even burnt down a factory full of polystyrene packing bobbles. The little action of flying the peace banner over the ship was just a minor diversion for them.

Not so for Lieutenant Kowalski. He was a crazy man. He had never felt so insulted in his life. After all, here was the US Navy extending the hand of friendship and these two hippies had put a turd in it.

In fact, as the police escorted Walter and Zimm from the ship, a lot of people involved with the peace protest shook their heads critically. They strongly disapproved of confrontation, especially if it involved law-breaking.

'That's just silly,' they said, 'making people angry won't help.'

But Rachel felt it might help more than painting CND symbols on children's faces.

BULLENS CREEK

Sly was flying much further north than Kalgoorkatta. He was heading up over the Great Sandy Desert. It was in this vast area of almost empty wilderness that he had been asked to secure the land required for the astonishing and immoral project that he was now a part of. He felt then, as he had felt on the jumbo the morning after his dinner, that this was going to be a lot more difficult than his fellow conspirators thought. The land requirements for the project were very specific, unfortunately they were also very contradictory. The two main points, ranking above all other considerations, were firstly that it had to be utterly remote and secondly, that good communications were essential. Great, thought Sly, a most ingenious paradox.

STARK REQUIREMENTS

The need for isolation was obvious. The less people knew about what was going on the better. Mineral exploration and leisure development were to be the cover story and they would do at a casual glance. However, if someone started delving deeper and the real purpose of the site was discovered, well, Sly just hoped he had a convenient top-floor window to jump out of. Secrecy was the key, therefore, not only did the place have to be remote, but a contoured landscape was also considered essential – it is easier to undertake massive construction projects discreetly if you can hide behind a few hills. Also, an uneven terrain made electronic surveillance more difficult. Luckily most of the US spy satellites were pointing at the Soviet Union. The Americans were unlikely to bother the team Sly was now a member of. After all, Americans like multimillionaires. Their whole scene was hassling commies. Sly hoped so anyway because if some over zealous under-dog at the CIA or in the Pentagon did get on to them, no politico on earth would, or could, defend their actions. For the first time they would not be able to buy themselves out of trouble.

It was a salutary thought. Despite the enormous political clout that multimillionaires wielded, especially when organized in groups, so dark was their present purpose that were it to be revealed, even the most bent politicians in the world would be forced to turn and bite the hand that had fed it for so long. This was why privacy was essential. As has been said though, unfortunately, so were communications. The leisure cover story would not last long once things really got going. When the consortium moved it would have to move very fast indeed. Surprise would be the essence of success. If the world had more than a moment's warning, all might be lost. Hence they had to be able to assemble the personnel, the technology and the huge mass of hardware quickly. This could not be achieved with restricted access.

Anyway, the upshot of it all was that they were not actually spoilt for choice as to locations. The optimum spot seemed to be an area west of a place called Bullens Creek. It was hilly-ish, which is about as hilly as it gets in Western Australia, and it was utterly isolated apart from one road to Bullens. Bullens Creek itself, on the other hand, had just about sufficient communications for Stark's purposes. It had been fully integrated into the Telecom system five years previously. It was on the interstate highway and it had an airstrip. Also, it was only about five hundred miles north-west of Perth so what lines of communication there were would not be too stretched.

DULLSVILLE WA

After a long dull flight, Sly landed at Bullens Creek airport.

Topol Bullen had been the first white man to find the creek, back in 1867. If at the time he had entertained any hopes that one day a thriving metropolis would grow up about the place, thus ensuring him and his name a kind of immortality, he had had it. Bullens Creek had started off tiny and tedious and gone downhill from there. Being the person after whom Bullens Creek was named is actually a slightly more anonymous thing than not having a place named after you at all. Even the people who live there have only half heard of it.

'Bullens Creek? Oh yeah, I think it's a little tiny town somewhere up towards the Territory. Come to think of it, buggered if I don't live there myself.'

Bullen himself never lived to discover that his name was to become a place that almost everybody in Australia had never heard of. He was killed by a camel whilst looking for his shorts, having had a dip in the creek he had just found. He had ridden the camel all the way from the coast and was under the impression that they had become friends. So had the camel, who was, therefore, rather surprised that on arriving at their first water for weeks, a meagre puddle dried almost completely in the appalling heat, Bullen had tethered it to a gum tree in order to get first slurp. Bullen's reasons for doing this were actually very sound. Camels can suck up literally gallons of water in a matter of seconds and Bullen, understandably, wanted to get in quick before the camel drained the puddle. The camel did not realize this however, and, thinking itself betrayed, broke its bindings in an anger of thirst and kicked Bullen out of the way, killing him in the process.

In fact, for quite a while, the place was called Camel Kick Creek, but eventually Bullens Creek prevailed – which is a shame because Camel Kick Creek is a much better name. The reason the name got changed was that there was a rather boring habit amongst the early white settlers of Australia. They liked to name places after very dull Victorians. During the same period, people in the USA were giving places terrifically exciting names like Tombstone, Deadwood,

Hangman's Tree and Death Gulch, but the old Aussies preferred things less colourful. For instance, there lies, almost bang in the middle of Australia, one of the largest monoliths in the world. An unfractured mass of glorious red sandstone that rises one and a half kilometres up from the flat desert floor and descends four kilometres beneath it. It has an astonishing, almost symmetrical shape and, according to the light, it changes colour from burning orange through fierce red to deep, cool purple. It is, of course, regarded with mystical awe by all who see it. The early Australians chose to call this wonder of the world 'Ayers Rock' after a dull Victorian administrator in a stupid hat – who happened to be chief secretary of South Australia.

It is, of course, a little unfair to make a comparison between Ayers Rock and Bullens Creek. In fact, the name of Bullens Creek was really rather apt because Bullens Creek is very boring and Bullen had been a very boring man. This was actually why he set out to stride across the Great Gibson and the Great Sandy Desert in the first place, he had got sick of people yawning at him when he talked about his theory. All the other explorers who set off on similar quests had great theories that people loved to listen to. Fascinating stuff about vast inland seas or a continent-sized oasis full of lush vegetation, fabulous rivers and endless free sex. Bullen's theory on the other hand was very dull indeed. He claimed that the vast hinterland of Australia was nothing but a dry, hot, flat desert with some dingos and a few broken bits of rock. He was right of course, but it was still a very boring theory. Had he ever made it back, people would have still yawned at him. After all, the only thing more boring than being dull is being dull and right.

Even the camel that got him was bored. 'What a dull drink,' it thought, and sauntered off, becoming one of the earliest of the domestic camels imported into Australia to return to the wild. Today, of course, there are herds of wild camels in the deserts of Oz but then it was quite a novelty – certainly more interesting than Bullen's Creek, anyway.

It was well over a hundred years since the camel had killed Bullen and that still ranked as the most exciting thing that had ever happened in the area.

What people do for diversion in isolated country towns is a bit of a mystery all over the world, although the physical similarities, hair-lips, low foreheads and high instance of mental disorder may go some way to solving the mystery. It used to be said that the best way to stop a girl getting pregnant in Bullens Creek was to castrate her brother.

Things definitely improved after they put in the airstrip and metalled the roads but once you've looked at the war memorial and said, 'Christ it's hot' a couple of times, you're still a bit stuck for raucous amusement.

One of the things they do in places like Bullens Creek is form dinner clubs. Sly was aware of this country habit and was relying on it to provide him with a medium whereby to ingratiate himself with the white locals. He felt that this would be a sensible preliminary to trying to negotiate with the aboriginal community.

Having parked his little plane, he strolled into the old shed, grandly titled the Airport Terminal, to get his paperwork sorted. Here, as he expected, he found a sign announcing the regular events which the town was looking forward to.

Royal Rotary Mouse – 2nd and 4th Mondays, venue – Queen Victoria Pub.
Grand Order Mason Sheep Shearers – Wednesday, venue – Queen Victoria Pub.
Lion Club Elks – 1st and 3rd Thursdays, venue – Queen Victoria . . . etc.

The fun went on and on. Scanning the lists of officers, Sly was struck by the number of times each name occurred, but in a different post. For instance, John Timpkiss might be the treasurer of the Elks and the secretary of the Mouses, whilst Phil Barcle was the opposite. Either lots of people in Bullens

Creek had the same name, or else all the clubs had the same members. The latter was, of course, the case. They could have just formed one big club but of course that wouldn't have been any fun. The variety provided endless diversion. It was a job sometimes for a bloke to figure out which stupid hat he was supposed to be wearing that night. Sly knew that since he was probably the most prominent visitor to Bullens Creek since the camel that got Bullen, he would be approached to address one of these institutions. That was fine by him. The sooner he started getting his story straight, the better.

THE NERVE CENTRE OF ECOACTION

The place was real dark. Rachel wasn't scared of the dark, no, it wasn't the dark that she was scared of. It was not being able to see anything that she hated. She had already gone arse-over-tit twice, tripping on some form of creeper. The garden of Zimm and Walter's place definitely needed tending.

'We should tend that garden sometime,' Walter would observe.

'Man, it would take a Napalm strike to even make a dent in it,' Zimm replied. 'Doctor Livingstone is still in there looking for the source of the Nile.'

And so they let it go. It was getting increasingly difficult to get to the front door, as Rachel was discovering.

Country music was drifting through the darkness, whining, mournful music, straight-forward music. That was the great thing about country music, it did not mince words. The word 'obscure' is not in the country dictionary, foot-notes are not required. For instance, the country ballad writer wishing to suggest that he is low and blue because his baby is gone, would probably write something like. 'I'm low and blue because my baby is gone'.

This was how Zimm liked his music. Plain speaking was important to him, he hated hypocrisy. 'I want you out of my head and back in my bed before the morning comes', sang Lorreta Lynn as Rachel struggled up the path in the blackness, vegetation brushing her cheeks and deeply suspect substances underfoot. Just about every cat in Carlo shat in Walt and Zimm's garden. Walter thought it was OK because cats are clean shitters. They are always very careful to dig a shallow toilet and fill it in again afterwards. The problem obviously comes when the land has been so overcrapped that the surface is 100 per cent cat crap, which means the cat digs a hole in the crap, craps in it and then carefully pushes crap on top of it. A soul-destroying activity and one calculated to make any cat lower its personal standards.

There was no light inside the shack save the glow of a cigarette brightening with every draw and then dulling almost back into the blackness.

'Whoever you're looking for, they don't live here,' said a voice located just behind the cigarette.

'I'm looking for eighty-two King Edward the Seventh Empire Terrace. Have I got the right address?'

Whoever did the road naming in Australia was a serious empire freak. You'd be walking down some street in Sydney, half-Greek, half-Italian, half God knows what and the place is named after Queen Victoria. Zimm and Walter tried to get their street renamed Dead Abo Terrace and the local Freedom Association pushed a burning rag through their letter-box.

'You're here,' said the cigarette end, 'but you've got the wrong address. Like I said, whoever you want don't live here.'

'I'm looking for the two guys who got busted on the USS *Enormous* this morning.'

What happened next was an object lesson in why it was a bad idea to send confused young men off in a haze of drugs to fight a war that no one understands and can not be won, then bring them back, trained killers with fried brains and no bollocks. There was a split second of confusing movement. The cigarette end shot to within an inch of Rachel's face and she found herself pinned to a tree with her arms firmly clamped behind it. Her head was pushed right far back exposing her neck and although she could not be sure, she was conscious of the possibility that there might be a knife at her throat.

When her assailant spoke he sounded almost offended,

which struck Rachel as strange since she appeared to be the injured party. In fact Zimm was offended. He had a genuine persecution complex. He felt people did not respect him as a person. He felt they just saw him as a terrifying space case to be humoured, patronized and, if at all possible, avoided. He was, of course, right about this. It was a paradox of Zimm's sad mental condition that despite being pretty much a complete nutter, he could, on occasion, come up with an analysis as breathtakingly astute as this one.

'Oh man, I mean, what is the point, right?' he demanded, 'I mean, just what is the point? I mean, what am I, a non-person or something? Did they leave me out of the constitution, is that it? . . . Uhm, yeah, every guy and chick has a right not to be hassled in their own space, except Zimmerman . . . Like, if a dude was in court, right? The judge would say to him, "You are convicted of pulling someone's head off and eating it, have you anything to say before I bang you up in the slammer for ever? . . ." And the dude says, "It was only Zimmerman's head, your honour . . ." "Oh in that case you get a ten bucks reward and a new hat." *I said we weren't home!*'

Rachel sensed that with the last line her attacker had returned to the planet earth and some response was in order. However, even if her head hadn't been thrust right back, making speech pretty difficult, she would still probably have been at a loss for an appropriate remark.

Many people put Zimm's erratic speech patterns down to his terrible experiences in 'Nam, but in fact he had always been weird as anything speech-wise.

'I'll never understand you, son,' Mrs Zimmerman used to sigh – and she was right, she never did.

Just as Rachel was trying to decide whether kicking her assailant's shins would be a good or a bad idea, Walter turned on a lamp. It was a sixty watt bulb but after the darkness it made everyone blink. The light flooded out through the open French windows to the tree against which Rachel was pinned. She heard a gentle movement and then the light was gone. This was because Walter was now standing in the doorway and it fitted him perfectly. It was almost as if the doorway had been built around him, and what's more, by a carpenter who liked his doorways figure hugging. For Walter was huge, terrifyingly so – far bigger than he had looked at the docks. Rachel commended her soul to God. Zimmerman, at six foot two with his lean and wiry frame had been worrying enough, but his companion was the proverbial brick shithouse. A municipal version with fifteen sitters and a thirty yard trough. He was not fat, although the years had lent a certain dignity to his midriff, he was just huge. A shaggy bearded bear of a man in a smock and khaki shorts.

As it happened, Rachel need not have been afraid (of Walter, that is – she was still in the vice-like grip of a lunatic), because Walter was the gentlest of souls, Rachel could tell from his voice.

'Zimm, what are you doing, man?' Walter said. 'I mean, really, what are you doing? You have to cool it, you know? I mean, this is a terrible thing, pushing people around like that is a terrible thing. I just don't know what you think you're doing. If you do these terrible things, Zimm, you know I'm going to have to start thinking that you and I are on totally different wave-lengths. Like me on one wave-length and you on another wave-length, but a different one, not the same as mine at all. That's what I'm going to have to start thinking if you don't cool it.'

Despite her difficult situation, Rachel could not help but be impressed by the extraordinarily mellow quality of Walter's voice. It was a lovely calming voice. It made you think that things were going to be OK and she felt this despite the fact that Walter seemed to be talking almost complete drivel. She couldn't help but wonder what the effect would be if he ever said anything worth listening to.

Zimmerman, releasing Rachel, stepped back and was caught in what few rays of light managed to squeeze past Walter's huge frame by holding their breath and thinking thin. Rachel could now see that even without the voice, and despite his quite absurd size, Walter was definitely the one she'd prefer to meet on a dark night. Zimmerman looked like a piece of human granite. He wore the traditional Ozzie singlet, which is a baggy vest with very low cut armholes and his muscles looked like they had been painted on by Leonardo da Vinci. There wasn't sufficient fat on him to fry an egg (although the grease in his hair would have tempted Slampacker to open a franchise on his head). When you've been blown to bits, as Zimmerman had, you either train hard or you don't get better. Zimm had got better and then gone on getting better. From his shiny, greasy, biker-looking jeans to his short, greying beard, he was muscle and bone. Above the beard was a different story. He looked out to lunch – Mr and Mrs Sanity were clearly not at home to callers. His temples were quivering with riotous indignation and his deep-set eyes flashed about behind the long, sweaty strands of hair that fell forward from his centre parting. He was still mightily aggrieved.

'She said she's come about us getting busted on the boat this morning . . . I mean what *is* the point? All the cops are down at the Pig Pen thinking what shall we do this evening to justify the extortionate amount of bread the public pays us to be pigs? Shall we, like, go and catch a rapist or something? No, let's go hassle Zimmerman, that'll really make the streets safe for the kids to play in.'

'I'm not a police officer,' said Rachel. She could not bring herself to use such a monumentally dated and unfashionable expression as 'pig'. The fact that Zimmerman's mind had closed down in 1972 was his problem, not hers.

'So, what's the story, lady, where is it at?' said the mellow one.

Rachel was seriously beginning to regret having come. Not because of being half assaulted but because she seemed to have fallen in with yet more hippies. It was expressions like 'where's it at' that made Rachel suspicious. But she decided that she would have to persevere.

'I wished I'd been on the boat with you,' she said. 'I was one of the people on the quay waving a sign.'

'Man,' said Walter with what, for him, was a tone of excitement – which meant it would have anaesthetized an epileptic trapped in a stroboscope. 'You were one of the girls with their tits out? *I* wish you'd been on the boat with us.'

Rachel put Walter right. Walter admitted that although he abhorred sexism in every form, if it had to have a form, the form of a load of chicks waving their tits around didn't seem such a bad option to him. Rachel said she didn't think that Walter had thought this one through properly. Walter admitted that this might be true and promised to think about it really hard later in bed. Zimm said it was all one to him because he didn't have any bollocks anyway. Rachel thought this a pity, kind of like finding an E-Type in perfect condition, except the gear stick had been broken off. Introductions thus affected, Rachel went and got CD from the car and Zimm volunteered to make some tea.

SPYING OUT THE LAND

DINNER AND BULLSHIT

The sun had been down for hours but that didn't seem to make much difference in that baking summer of Stark. The Queen Victoria Pub's upstairs room was like the inside of a microwave. Dinner was over. What had started out as a summer salad had been reduced by heat and humidity to a sort of vegetable stew. The royal toast had been made and the beer was flowing, served in the curious Australian glass known as a pony, which is about the size of an egg cup. The point being that you drink in small units because if you leave your beer in the glass too long it will evaporate. Due to the climate, beer is served at almost zero degrees. A person freezes to the glass. In other countries you might complain about a bit of lipstick on the rim of your beer, in Australia you might find someone's lips.

'Gentlemen,' said the chief dingo, rising to his feet and calling order. 'The Royal Hatch of the Old, Stupid and Contemptible Dingo's (Bullens Creek chapel) have great pleasure in welcoming a self-made multimillionaire and good old all round Ozzie bloke, Silvester Moorcock.'

Sly rose to his feet amidst admiring applause. It did not disconcert Sly that he found himself addressing an audience who were all wearing false dingo ears. He considered himself lucky that it was not a Tuesday, in which case he would have been talking to the Chapel of the Charitable Chickens, which would have meant beaks, feathers and singing the 'Honourable cluck cluck song' on the stroke of each hour. Sly chose his words carefully, he wanted to win them over, to make them like and trust him so they would not start asking questions when he came to make his purchases. He gave them his best shot, his trusty 'Road to Success, I made it, you could make it too' speech:

'Listen, I'm pure Aussie, right? This is a great country and the honeypot is open to all. Christ, if a stupid bastard like me can get a pawful, anyone can,' – they loved the self-deprecatory stuff – 'I mean, any old pie-brained dickhead with no teeth and a wallet full of condoms way past the sell-by date can make it in the lucky country.' The older blokes were ecstatic.

'Sure, you need some talent and application,' he added, 'people who are not prepared to put the hours in need not expect to travel club-class . . .' Some of the audience attempted to nod intelligently at this – not a very advisable thing to do when you are wearing false dingo ears.

'You also need luck, of course you do,' Sly granted magnanimously. 'Christ, you got to be in the right place at the right time. The fellah with the goldmine isn't necessarily the best miner around but he's the fellah who found the gold, and good luck to him. Mind you, I don't say you can't *make* luck sometimes. Oh yes. That fellah who found the gold, well, chances are he was *looking* for that gold. Maybe he was the fellah who was prepared to go looking for gold in the hills that the mine expert said weren't worth touching. Maybe he just thought hell, maybe I'll get lucky . . .'

This meaningless tripe was slipping down pretty well with the fourth or fifth beer. The audience knew they weren't exactly listening to Abraham Lincoln but it was pleasant enough stuff. They liked the rugged frontier side of it and redneck anti-intellectualism. Actually it was a much cleverer speech than it sounded because Sly was getting around to a point. 'Listen, mates. There's more than one way to bite the tail off a kangaroo. Are you with me?'

They weren't but they didn't mind pretending. It was too hot to argue.

'What I'm saying is, if there ain't no gold to be found then dig for something else. I'm telling you, there isn't a hill in Australia that a profit can't be wrung out of if you think hard enough.'

Here, Sly lost his audience somewhat. Everyone in the room knew that their scrappy little hills had been surveyed to death and the only things ever found were a few old Ab' relics that a couple of archaeologists had got excited about for half an hour. But Sly pursued his theme of nothing ventured; nothing gained, with his usual force and charm so that when, just before he sat down, he announced his intention of taking another look at the whole area, he almost had people believing that he had a chance. After all, it was his time and money and if he *did* find something! Bullens Creek would become, figuratively speaking, a goldmine. Perhaps even literally! After all, look what this same man, Sly Moorcock, had done to Kalgoorkatta! Who could tell, maybe he would work the same magic in Bullens Creek.

By next morning reason had regained its throne. Nobody was planning swimming pools or European holidays, but Sly had laid a firm foundation for his story. They believed that he was going to take another look at the hills. Who cared? He was just a crazy bloke with more money than sense.

A TRICKY PROBLEM

Sly headed towards the Yalurah community, peering over the top of the enormous cage-like steel 'roo bars that jutted out in front of his car. The land was owned by the Aboriginals that lived there. It had been granted back to them during the great land rights debate of the early eighties. Sly would have to play this negotiation very carefully. He could not be sure whether there were spiritual connotations to the place. He could not just say that there was an equally unattractive bit of useless scrub, just like the one the government had kindly granted them, fifty miles up the road and he'd give them a crate of scotch to piss off. The point was that the bit of scrub up the road might not have the same Dreamtime connections that the one they were on did.

Besides this, for all the fact that Sly claimed they were, Aboriginals were not stupid. If he wanted to get them out they were certain to ask themselves why he wanted them out. The conclusion that they were bound to come to was that the land was worth something. Now a few years ago that might have made them up-the-price but, no more than that. These days however, they were getting a touch more sophisticated. It was not unknown for Aboriginals to actually take an interest in mining themselves. Sly smiled as he remembered the awful crisis of principles that had beset the do-gooders and bleeding-hearts during the great uranium debate. For years these people had bleated on and on about Aboriginal self-determination; about giving them back control of their lives etc., etc. As if they wanted to do anything but drink anyway, thought Sly. Then along came the possibility of uranium on Aboriginal land and of course the same do-gooders were totally against more uranium mining but, unfortunately, some of their darling Abs weren't. The Aboriginals saw that finally they had a chance of grabbing some white man's money. It had been a delicious irony really. The do-gooders suddenly found themselves in the role of trying to tell the Abs what was good for them. The very thing they had been screaming about for donkeys years.

Anyway, Sly knew that if he gave the impression that he was desperate to acquire their land, the present occupants were bound to presume that he knew something that they didn't and hang on in until they found out what it was. It was a tricky little balancing act. He had to get the land off them while making them think that he didn't particularly want it.

Still, as Sly reflected, they *were* only Abs and he had ridden rough-shod through half the boardrooms in WA. He reckoned he could handle it.

MAKING AN OFFER

The negotiations were not going well.

'Drink?' he said to the representatives of the community

that he sat facing – he had brought a splendid supply of the very best beers and spirits.

'We're dry here, mate,' said the old guy with a tone that directly translated as 'so fuck you'.

This was a big setback for Sly. If the place was dry it was going to be a damn sight tougher to manipulate them. Sly took a swig himself, not because he wanted any at all but because it was obvious that he was dealing with some fairly together people and he did not want them to think he had just been hoping to get them pissed.

'So it's no good hoping to get us pissed, mate,' the old bloke continued and Sly realized that although he did not particularly hate Abs in general, he sure as hell was starting to hate this wily old bastard.

'It's like this, Mr Culboon,' he said, forcing a smile. Sly explained that he was looking at a number of locations in Western Australia, of which this was only one, in an effort to find a suitable location for a business venture that he had in mind.

'Business venture, here? What are you going to do, sell white art to us Aboriginals?'

This was all Sly needed – a fucking comedian. He waited while the old boy got his laugh and then paused a little longer, eyeing the bare formica table, the rickety walls, the fat bellied children. Poverty hung about the place like they'd framed it and nailed it to the walls. These people did not have much to lose, it was time to assert himself.

'Listen, *mate*, you can sit and take the piss if you like, but while you're sodding me off, some other guy's walking off with a fat bank roll the size you wouldn't dream of.'

'I don't dream about bank rolls, big or small, mate. You do, I don't. Which I suppose is why you've got a brand new Toyoki and I've got a 1967 Holden, but, you're in my house so you'll watch your manners or you'll fuck off, OK?' The man was clearly a philosopher as well.

Sly was having to quickly revise all expectations of Mr Culboon, the head man who sat before him. He had looked such a clown to Sly but clearly he wasn't a clown at all.

'What do you want our land for, mate?' Mr Culboon asked.

'I don't want your land *particularly*,' Sly replied.

'Well, what are you doing here, then,' said Mr Culboon leaping on the point like a prosecution counsel, 'has my house suddenly become an in place for Perth money men?'

This wasn't getting Sly anywhere. He was in severe danger of wanting to strangle this Culboon fellah — which would certainly have soured future negotiations.

'I need some land, and as I say, this is one of the sites we're considering.'

'So, it's nothing to do with mining then?'

'Of course it's nothing to do with mining, Mr Culboon. Your scrappy little hills are a pile of shit and you know it. There's more minerals in a bottle of Perrier. You could dig for ever and you wouldn't come up with enough gold to fill your front teeth in. They're worthless, of course they are, or else why do you think the state government let you have them. You can be damn sure they weren't going to give you an oil-well.'

'So why do you want them then?'

Sly had to admit it was a fair question.

'Well, Mr Culboon, I'll tell you. Myself and my associates have formed a consortium called "Oasis" and we are investigating the possibility of setting up a desert vacation re-treat.'

There was an incredulous pause. Mr Culboon looked at the others in the room, they looked at him. Then they all looked out of the open doorway. They looked at the flies, the 'roo shit, the flat, shimmering boredom of a featureless bit of desert ringed by piss-poor, reddish little hills too steep to walk, too boring to climb. They looked at the one road — the road that ran from them to Bullens Creek and back again — a road that ran from nowhere to nowhere. Then they all looked at Sly.

'Vacation!!' spluttered Mr Culboon, and nearly wet himself.

Sly had to undergo the distinctly uncomfortable sensation

of a group of people from an alien culture – a culture towards which he had always felt massively superior – pissing themselves laughing at him. The noise of the laughter attracted some women from outside. They put their heads around the door and asked what the gag was.

'This fellah says he wants to turn our shithole into a vacation oasis!' said one of the men with tears in his eyes. The women howled.

'Ha, ha, so the beautiful people are coming are they?' a woman grinned. 'I can just see them getting off the plane saying, "mmm nice smell of dingo piss".'

They all howled some more, and more, and more. Sly felt that he was losing control of the conversation.

'Look!' he said, 'I'm perfectly serious and so's my money, so if you want to hear me out, fair enough, otherwise I'll fuck off now.'

'Fuck off now if you like,' said Mr Culboon, still laughing. Sly ignored him and continued.

'All we need is sunshine and you will agree that you've got plenty of that. We can't get planning permission on the coast anymore so we're looking inland. I'm talking a totally man-made environment here, pools, tennis courts, a theatre, discos, and, get this, a gambling licence. We are talking Las Vegas! Have you ever been to Ayers Rock? That's a totally self-contained holiday complex built out of the desert, what's the difference?'

'Ayers Rock,' said Mr Culboon who, one hopes, had resigned himself to the fact that he and Sly would never be friends.

'Well, exactly, the last thing your dedicated pleasure-seeker wants is a bloody great area of natural beauty that he's going to feel obliged to traipse all over. He wants to have fun! . . .' said Sly, getting down to business, 'we have various options of which, I repeat, this is only one. Now we have a one million dollar relocation budget for whoever happens to be living where we decide to build. There are ninety-seven of you, which works out at ten thousand dollars each to piss off. What do you say?'

People were taking him more seriously but Mr Culboon was very doubtful.

'A million bucks for a bunch of Abs? You must like this place mate.'

'We'd have to pay someone off wherever we went. And, besides,' Sly added piously, 'the consortium I represent are not unaware of the spiritual value of the land and wish you to be aware that this will be thematically integrated into the overall design of the complex.'

'How touching, a Dreamtime Cocktail bar, I reckon – and this folks is the very place where the dumb Abs drew their stupid pictures – that'll be your thematic integration, mate.'

'Look, *mate*, I'm not here to fight a race war. I'm here to do some business, and if you don't like it I'll take it elsewhere, all right?' Sly could see that a few of the faces did not look so anxious to laugh at him anymore.

'We'll think about it,' said Mr Culboon, 'give us a number where I can contact you.'

This was all Sly had hoped for and it was good enough. He reckoned that once he had gone they'd come round in the end. He was prepared to up the money, if necessary, but that Culboon was a clever bastard and he didn't want to appear over anxious.

JUDGING A BOOK BY ITS COVER

Appearances are so deceptive especially when they cross a cultural divide. To Sly's white eyes, Mr Culboon had looked like a semi-savage. He had the traditional scars across his chest, deep and fearful. Plenty of ash got rubbed in them Sly had thought looking at the great welts that bubbled out of the old man's brown skin like surf in a sea of gravy. Also he had had his two front teeth removed, a practice which was utterly beyond Sly, it made the man look idiotic.

But really it's all a question of what you're used to. For instance, Mr Culboon and his wife both had big old floppy pot bellies. They were not a young couple and his especially hung like an enormous tea-bag across his belt. Neither he nor his wife were remotely self-conscious about this. Now the wife of one of Sly's principal business rivals in Perth, a woman called Dixie Tyron, had also been developing a gut like that, plus thighs with saddle-bags on them that flapped around like soft, quilted fins. She, unlike the Culboons, was not happy with them and had undergone a form of surgery recently developed in America, which involved injecting the fatty regions with some chemical which actually dissolves the fat, making it possible to suck it out. In comparison with this phenomenal self-mutilation, knocking out a tooth or two seemed merely eccentric.

When the whites first encountered the blacks in Australia, they were horrified to observe that they didn't seem to wash. This led them to conclude that they were uncouth, filthy creatures who barely knew how to look after themselves. In fact the exact opposite was the case. Their not washing, or rather not washing in the conventional Western manner, was a very sensible thing indeed. To a desert Aboriginal, water is used for one thing and one thing only, drinking. It is simply too scarce to get into the habit of using it for any other reason. They knew where it was, they protected it, they conserved it. Sometimes they worshipped it. What they did not do was put a rubber duck in it and splash it all over the place. Aborigines did wash, of course. They washed in smoke and heat, rubbing themselves down in their own sweat. All peoples adapt themselves to their environment. In the days before easily available heating fuel, the ancestors of those first Australian settlers had sewn themselves into their clothes for the winter.

A CALL FROM OCKER TYRON

The morning Sly returned from Bullens Creek he was awakened by the phone ringing. Actually, 'ringing' is too dignified a word for the wet, simpering trill that was oozing listlessly round the room. It sounded like a small marsupial sitting in the bath and farting through a descant recorder. Sly hated the new phone tones. He could remember when a phone had sounded like a phone. 'Ring, ring,' that was something a man could answer with vigour and purpose. These days he felt like saying, 'I'm not picking you up until you ring properly'.

On this occasion he could not even find the phone – he did not actually know what it looked like. The apartment, as with all of Sly's properties, had been done out for him by an interior design team. Sly had told them he wanted a one-off shag den and so they had set out to create a relaxing atmosphere, free of tension, comfortingly co-ordinated throughout, with everything blending in. The result had achieved just that and hence Sly could never find the phone. He stared about himself wildly for a moment and then, not for the first time in this situation, ran out to his car.

The interior of the car had not been designed by someone who wanted to be subtle and relaxing with everything blending perfectly. No, it had been designed by someone who wanted to suggest a rich, powerful man with no time to waste. 'Your quartz quadrophonic personal communication and data processing unit is located in your fully computerized, digitally automized, central console unit,' the salesman had said.

This meant the phone was between the seats and Sly was grateful for this simple arrangement. He jumped in, barking his shin on the car door. Somehow it is even more galling to knacker your leg on an Aston Martin that cost a hundred and fifty thousand dollars. This was a car that could withstand the impact of a two joint articulated road train, fully loaded with cans of lager. It had a roll cage a fat elephant could have used as a trampoline. It was so safe you could have used it as a nuclear fall-out shelter for Christ's sake and yet you could still bark your shin on it like the car was a Ford fucking Escort.

He picked up the quartz quadrophonic personal communication and data processing unit.

'Yeah.'

Sly was looking at his leg. For a moment there was nothing then, suddenly, as if by magic, a great glistening puddle of blood materialized. Quickly he hung the offending leg out of the window. Even multimillionaires don't like getting blood all over their soft, beige leather bucket seats. So, there he was, draped across the passenger seat, dripping leg hanging out of the window, gear stick trying to force its way through his back, about to have a phone call that was relevant to all life on the planet. If there is indeed a God, and if he really did make man in his own image, he must look a right dildo.

'Who's that?' said a rather unpleasant, gruff voice. Mind you, in fairness, the way Sly was feeling he would have found the voice unpleasant if Kiri Te Kanawa had rung him up.

'What do you mean, "who's that" arsehole? You rang me,' Sly replied, suddenly feeling nervous. He didn't like enigmatic calls. Sly hit the various telephonic security switches that had started flashing on the dashboard. He wanted the call taped, just in case it was blackmail. After all, he had had a creative and athletic evening with the Malaysian hostess on his last stop-over from the UK. Mind you, there was no law against peanut butter, or where you put it for that matter – it certainly tasted better than on Satay.

Sly also activated a signal distorter so no one could locate him from the position of his phone, a signal search so that later on, if desired, Sly could discover the location of the caller, a scrambler, in case a third party was listening in and finally, a frequency blocker on the off chance that someone had put a bomb under the car and the phone was the trigger. Sly had no reason whatsoever to presume that he needed any of these things but they advertised them in the magazines you get on airlines and Sly, as always, had been bored.

Of course, some people got off on this sort of thing because it made them feel like men. Sly was not this big an idiot. Ocker Tyron was though, and it was him on the other end of the line. He too had activated all his blocking, mixing, tracing and scrambling gear – consequently what was left of the line was pretty poor. Fifty grand each so that they could say 'pardon' at each other.

Without the 'pardons' the conversation went like this:

'Don't call me an arsehole, it's Ocker Tyron.'

'Oh no,' said Sly.

'Don't say, oh no, like that. What's the problem.'

'What do you mean, what's the problem? You're the problem, Ocker. We hate each other. You know it and I know it.'

Tyron was genuinely taken aback.

'Well, just because we hate each other doesn't mean we can't be friendly,' he said.

'What do you want, Ocker?'

'How did you get on with the Abs and the rednecks?' Ocker asked, knowing full well that Sly had got on crap and enjoying the knowledge.

Sly nearly fell off his seat, except that it's almost impossible to fall off a bucket seat in a car when you are leaning across it with one leg out of the window. He convulsively jerked though. Sadly he convulsively jerked with sufficient violence to release the handbrake – always put your car in gear on a slope. Sly spun round, or tried to, he had little room to manoeuvre. As it happens, he had little time either, in seconds the car had rolled into the gate post at the foot of the drive. All he succeeded in doing was agonizingly adding to the mess on his leg as the injured part dragged across the lock button on the door. One knackered leg, one knackered wing – the leg was worth slightly less.

'Shit!!'

'Yes, I rather thought that would surprise you,' Ocker Tyron sneered down the phone.

'Look, fuck off, Tyron. I'll phone you back.' Sly put the phone back in the fully computerized, digitally automized, central console unit. Jesus! What had happened? Five minutes earlier he had been asleep. Now he had a bleeding leg, a dented Aston, and worst of all he seemed to have breached the confidence and trust of the Stark consortium.

He went inside and had a cup of coffee. There was no point trying to avoid it, Ocker Tyron was on to him in some way and he had better find out what he knew and what he wanted.

Ocker Tyron was an old rival of Sly's. Sly had worked for Tyron years back, before he had pulled off his great pie scam. Ocker was a cliché-style Ozzie multimillionaire. A tough, boorish maverick. He and his exuberant wife, Dixie, styled themselves virtually as Australian royalty. He as the tough, powerful, elder statesman of national commerce and politics; she as a charity dispensing ambassador of goodwill.

Dixie had a peculiar talent for making many thousands of dollars worth of clothes look like she had bought them at Woolworths. This was her famous common touch (famous because it was often mentioned in her husband's newspapers) which she firmly believed endeared her to the honest folk of WA. In fact, of course, they would have liked to see her fry.

Sly hated them both.

'Tyron, it's Moorcock.'

Sly was struggling to keep his temper. Tyron had taken his revenge for the previous conversation by having his secretary leave Sly on hold for five minutes.

'Ah, Silvester, ready to have a civilized conversation now are we? Because I really don't have time for personal abuse.'

'Well, shut up then you stupid dickhead and get on with whatever it was you phoned me for.'

'The land project. You screwed it didn't you?'

'What do you know about the land project?' Sly turned on the lie detector and watched the blips on the screen. They weren't foolproof but it made Sly feel slightly better to flip it on. It was a bit like making an obscene gesture at the bastard behind his back.

'Oh, come off it, Sly, I know everything about Stark. You don't think I'm not involved do you? I'm worth twice as much as you.'

'They never mentioned it to me.'

Sly didn't know what to make of this. Had Tyron found out about the project and was he trying to muscle his way in on Sly's back? Perhaps he really was a member. Tyron was certainly richer than he – if differentials still meant anything at their exalted level.

'Of course they didn't mention it, we talk about this as little as possible. Slampacker called me to say that you were on board and that they'd asked you to find the land, and of course bung in your bucks . . .'

'Yeah, well, I'm finding the land aren't I? So why don't you stay out of it?' Sly was most disconcerted to learn that Ocker Tyron was a colleague in the project.

'I can't stay out of it, can I, old son? I'm assembling a great deal of the equipment, that's my job. Pretty soon I'm going to need somewhere to put it.' Ocker Tyron switched to scramble and dropped his voice. 'All this paraphernalia is rather difficult to pass off as harmless mining gear, you know. People notice things.'

Just talking about it made Sly's head swim.

'Are you sitting on the stuff now?'

'No, but it won't be long, fuel, power, control systems, the hardwear itself. I am going to need somewhere to put it. The stuff is scattered all over the world, but it's coming. Soon you and I are going to be nominal proprietors of a rather sophisticated installation. And so . . . we need the real estate.'

'Look, I'm getting on with it, OK? It isn't easy. What we're planning here is a disgustingly and immoral –'

'So what's new, love?' said Tyron. 'You just got Oz Businessman of the Year for being disgusting and immoral morning, noon and night . . .'

'Come off it, you know damn well that this is different. There's not a politician in the world we could buy off if they got a whiff of it. That's why I have to tread carefully. People own the land, I don't want to cause a stir.'

'Yes, well, if you can't do it, tell me and I'll do it, OK? Stay in touch,' and with that Ocker Tyron put down the phone.

Sly was left feeling absolutely livid. Tyron knew it and leant back in his huge chair happily. The voice of his secretary piped up.

'I have Mr Nagasyu on a secure line for you, sir . . .'

NAGASYU, THE JOKE AND THE WHALES

Mr Nagasyu had got incomprehensibly rich with a very simple idea. He had noticed the huge Japanese success in making things smaller. People seemed to like their high-tech titchy. Determining to take advantage of this curious quirk, he had set about making things so small that they kept getting lost. Radios that you had to leave on, or you wouldn't be able to find them again, state of the art speakers and electric toothbrushes that could easily slip down between the cushions on a sofa. As Mr Nagasyu had guessed, Nagasyu products had constantly to be replaced and he became quite stupidly rich.

'Hullo, Mr Tyron,' he said, 'Slampacker tells me we have decided on the optimum location.'

'That's right, Mr Nagasyu,' Tyron replied. 'It only remains to acquire it, there are one or two small obstacles to be kicked aside.'

'Well, please to hurry up. I am sitting on some extremely embarrassing equipment.'

'Oh, I'm sure not,' said Tyron, trying to lighten things up. 'I heard a Jap's bollocks were his best feature.'

Luckily Nagasyu did not understand Western slang. Even if Tyron's joke had been funny, Nagasyu would not have got it. He did not possess a sense of humour nor did he aspire to one, which made him slightly better company than Ocker Tyron, who also did not possess a sense of humour but cracked gags all the time. Tyron did not do this because he was under the impression that he was any great hoot, he was a pretty realistic man and realized that his sense of humour was facile and uncouth. Tyron cracked gags as an exercise in power. Normally when he cracked one, he was surrounded by people who had to laugh, and they always did. Ocker was always struck by how silly people looked, simpering nervously at his childish comments. It was this kind of personal therapy that fortified Ocker Tyron's private contempt for the human race. A contempt that made him capable of doing the things he did. Unlike Tyron, Mr Nagasyu was possessed of a degree of style and sophistication. Nonetheless, despite their different personalities, Nagasyu was every bit as hard a man as Ocker Tyron and Nagasyu had wrought an easily comparable amount of damage on the fragile planet.

HULLO YOUNG LOVERS

As it happened, Walter and Zimmerman had cause to know a little of Nagasyu's brutality. It was one of his ships that they had been shouting at when the harpoon had sailed over their heads and into the whale that they had been trying to protect.

They shouldn't really have had to be in such a dangerous position, because commercial whaling has finally been outlawed by international agreement. The task now is to restock the species and, of course, only the whales can do that. Unfortunately, there are so few of them left that it will require a level of whale sauciness liable to melt the ice caps. These are hot-blooded creatures and at one hundred and sixty tons they certainly know how to make the earth move. Still it has at least given the horny young whale a new and telling chat up line. 'Come on darling, we have a duty to restock the species.' Certainly beats, 'Look I just think it would be really beautiful, OK? Because I actually love you as a whale, you know? Not just as a sex object.'

Whales are quite shy and secretive about their love-making, which is no mean achievement when one considers that a

Blue whale gets to be about one hundred feet long. Anyone who has tried to keep things quiet with parents in the next room will sympathize with two shy young lovers trying to keep the noise down when their combined weight is over three hundred tons.

Unfortunately, despite the commercial ban, whales are not being politely left alone to do the business. Sad to say, Japan, Korea, Norway and Iceland still hunt and kill the tiny whale population that remains, bypassing the law by claiming that the cull continues for 'scientific' purposes. The real truth is that so spectacularly huge are these beasts and so efficient have hunting methods become, that despite the appallingly depleted numbers, it remains profitable to go after them.

Nothing kills passion faster than an exploding harpoon in the guts.

MASTERMINDS

There is, of course, one truly intriguing whale question which it would be lovely to get an answer to. Whales have the largest brains on earth. What do they do with them? Let's face it, you don't need a brain that would get stuck in a lift in order to open your mouth and swim towards a load of stupid plankton.

What do whales do with their brains? Are they philosophers, struggling with the thorny questions of existence? saying to themselves, 'I know I think, therefore I am, but plankton do not think, therefore they are not, in which case, what have I been living off all these years?'

One of the things they certainly do with their brains is survive. They have survived for millions of years – or at least they did until people started sticking spears into them. The fact that they are not intellectually equipped to deal with this threat does not reflect adversely upon their intelligence. After all, if Albert Einstein had been mugged by Silvester Stallone, he would probably have got his head kicked in. It is to be profoundly hoped that Silvester Stallone is not, at the end of the day, able to claim intellectual superiority over Einstein.

Whales have been lounging about and eating plankton for

some fifty million years. Not a bad achievement, especially when compared to humankind's rather pathetic four hundred thousand. Maybe that's what whales do with their huge brains – they don't fuck things up.

It takes the human race to the very limits of its intellectual ability to fuck things up in the way it does. The brain-crunching effort that has gone into developing the technology to kill, destroy, poison and pollute, pushes our greatest minds to the very limits of their potential. Perhaps if they had been just a little bit cleverer they wouldn't have done any of those things in the first place.

Maybe you have to be really clever simply not to fuck things up. Perhaps Mummy and Daddy whale shake their heads sadly over little Timmy, saying in screechy whale talk:

'Poor Timmy is severely retarded, we'd better send him to a special school. He's working on a way to pollute the sea with high-level radioactive waste, and he's too thick to realize that this is stupid.'

Of course, not all creatures who have survived billenium have big brains. The Sea Cucumber, for instance, is nothing more than a machine for sucking sand – so no chance of 'O' levels there. Everyone has their way of getting by as age gives way to age. Ways that worked perfectly well, until the bad kid moved in on the block.

TIME IS SHORT

Nagasyu didn't care how many whales he killed. He had bigger fish to fry.

'Time is short,' he barked down the phone at Tyron. 'Amongst other things I have assembled several square miles worth of solar energy panelling. I am anxious to unload, Mr Tyron. Are preparations for the Stark site going ahead smoothly?'

'Don't worry,' said Tyron with easy confidence.

He knew that if Sly Moorcock could not sort out those Abs, he damn well could.

THE FIRST ENEMY
OF STARK

At the offices of the *Financial Telegraph* in London, Linda Reeve was on the phone as well. You wouldn't really have thought it to look at her but Linda Reeve and the Great Blue whale had something in common. Something even more basic than that they were both mammals. More immediate than that, Linda, like the Blue whale, was largish with nice eyes. The most fundamental thing that Linda Reeve had in common with the Blue whale was that she too was in serious danger of becoming extinct.

Linda was talking to a colleague on the *Wall Street Examiner* in New York.

'Have you noticed, Chrissy? It's happened again, this time with Nagasyu?'

'What's happened again?' the voice crackled back irritably. It was still early in New York and Chrissy was trying to deal with the twin blows of a total smoking ban in her office plus it was de-caf' day for the coffee making thing. One of the strange things about life – which one day Chrissy intended to write a brilliant article about – was that despite the fact that she knew that caffeine and de-caf' day were strictly alternated, it always seemed to be de-caf' day. This, she presumed, was life.

The whole thing made Chrissy fume. Journalists giving up nicotine and caffeine! What price tradition? They'd start telling the truth next. Chrissy was a tough, independent New Yorker, totally unlike her rather stodgy English colleague. Small and dark and energetic, from a big New York Jewish family, she referred to herself as the runt of the litter. 'Not because I'm small,' she would say, 'but because I'm a girl . . . seven brothers. I think my father wanted his own platoon in the Israeli army.'

Linda knew Chrissy could be a little abrupt at times and so she was not put off by Chrissy's manner.

'What I was telling you about,' continued Linda, patiently – she was a quiet, persevering soul – 'another liquidation – a pretty big one. What are these people doing with the money they create?'

'Who knows,' said Chrissy, biting her nails and finding them a poor drug substitute. 'Home improvements. Mistresses. This is the free world remember, Linda. People are allowed to do what they like with their money.' The New Yorker thought Linda's observations interesting but nothing to get excited about. Certainly not on de-caf' day. 'You've got to get this thing out of your hair,' she continued, 'it's becoming a drag.'

'Home improvements, Chrissy? What is he doing? . . . uhm' Linda struggled to think of a witty illustration. 'Uhm . . . installing, something . . . uhm very very . . . expensive . . . in his home.' Poor Linda never had been a gagger. She returned to safer, drier territory. 'He's realized over ten billion yen and as far as I can see, he hasn't put it back in the market. Either he's sitting on it or he's bought something absolutely coloss'. Christmas, Chrissy! What can you buy for ten billion yen?'

'Look, Linda, he's worth fifty. Maybe he got religion and put it in the poor box.'

'Well I think it's worth a story.'

'Oh yeah,' replied Chrissy sarcastically. 'Real riveting stuff, Linda, "Man Spends His Money", sounds like a hell of a scoop. You go with it, pal, but I don't promise that the *Examiner* will pick up on the syndication.'

'Yes, I suppose it is a bit vague. Listen, I'll get back to you if I come up with anything else,' said Linda, brightly.

'I'll be holding my breath,' said Chrissy.

As Linda put the phone down on her friend she couldn't

help thinking that maybe Chrissy had a point. Chrissy was normally a pretty clear thinker. Linda had known her for a couple of years, although they had never actually managed to meet. There are not many women in financial journalism and each had noticed the other's articles. It had been Chrissy who had made contact, Linda would have been far too shy. Chrissy suggested that they might loosely stay in touch and swap ideas. Linda, who had few friends, had jumped at the idea. It had been fun, a real friendly chemistry had developed between dull Linda and the American live-wire.

Linda could not blame Chrissy for her dismissive attitude. After all, what did she have? Nothing, just some people choosing to get hold of a chunk of their own money. But there *were* a lot of them doing it and it *was* so much money. Linda just felt that something was going on. Maybe nothing bad, almost certainly nothing criminal, but something.

She thought it might be worth a piece on a new puritanism in the financial community. People wanting to return to a less speculative market; wanting their money close to them – almost under the mattress, so to speak. She searched the desk for her tiny Nagasyu word processor, finding it under a book. It certainly was an astonishing bit of technology, slim and beautifully designed. The only problem was you kept losing it.

'They probably want you to lose it', Linda and her colleagues would say to each other, but then laugh at the very idea.

She found the screen and began to write.

'One crash too many,' she headed it. 'Why is Tex Slampacker, the Tsar of all the burgers, pulling out of car production? Why has Ocker Tyron, the West Australian high-flyer, sold out of the Snowy River irrigation project? At home, the Duke of Cumberminster is no longer a major investor in the Channel Tunnel, he has taken his money and run, why? Today we learn that Mr Nagasyu, the Japanese microelectronics mogul, has realized yet another percentage of his enormous wealth. What has he done with it?' Linda was pleased, this was beginning to sound good.

'Of course,' the article continued, 'within the vast network of deals and counter-deals, none of these are world shattering questions, but none the less, in all of the above sell-offs, no other major player has stepped in to pick up the dumped assets and the national government has ended up making up the shortfall with public money. It is almost as if there is an orchestrated campaign to take hard currency out of the market-place. Almost as if the very people who built and benefit most from the absurd complications of super-capitalism have lost faith in it. Do they want their money in their pockets where it's safe? Perhaps the last crash was one too many. Maybe the monster bit its keepers just a little too hard this time.'

There was a fair bit more along these lines, detailing other interesting cases. Linda thought it was a nice, light, magazine type article.

Her editor didn't.

'This is little short of prying, Linda. Good Lord, a man's personal finances are his own affair,' he spoke as if she had disappointed him.

'I can take Tyron out of it, if you like,' Linda replied.

'The fact that we are published by Ocker Tyron is entirely irrelevant.' Now the editor was angry. 'I control editorial policy on this paper, and none other.' He spoke as if he almost believed it. Perhaps he actually did. There are, after all, none so blind as those who will not see. He continued in a more reasonable, almost placatory tone – perhaps he realized he was protesting a touch too much.

'Let me ask you this. If you go to the bank and empty your account, say you just walk out of that bank with a couple of thousand or whatever in your pocket, well, surely that's your business isn't it? You wouldn't thank me for prying into it would you? asking you what you wanted the money for and what you were going to do with it? It might be private – you might be having plastic surgery or something. Well, it's the same with your article. Not one of your people is pulling out of his own industry, they merely appear to be rationalizing the fringes of their operations.'

SUPPING WITH THE DEVIL

ARISTOS

Ocker Tyron sent for his half-brother, Aristos. He had been saving Aristos for something like this. Aristos was the classic talentless little brother, hanger-on, dickhead. He was twenty-eight and had either dropped out of or fucked up everything he had ever attempted. He smashed up expensive cars, spilt booze on expensive clothes, showed off at night clubs and apart from having access to a lot of cash was a complete and utter drag to be with. Dixie, Ocker's wife, perhaps recognizing a grosser version of herself, loathed him and constantly lobbied Ocker to drop the embarrassing little freeloader. But Ocker couldn't – his mother would not hear of it.

Aristos was the result of a brief second marriage that Mrs Tyron had leapt into with a Greek baker about a year after her first husband, Ocker's father, died.

Ocker's father's death loomed large in his legend. He always claimed that his father died of 'being decent'. This was Ocker's moral justification for being a professional bastard. He said that his dad had been an honest, friendly, fair-minded man, who knew nothing of the law of the jungle. This was why he had died poor, because he was taken advantage of, an innocent amongst the wolves.

This was all in fact complete rubbish. Old Mr Tyron had been a bitter, vicious, small-minded bigot who died poor because he was crap at his job. None the less, Ocker had used his father's untimely death to leave school and begin, with almost religious zeal, what was to be a life-long career of shitting on people.

Hence, by the time Aristos could talk, his big brother was already well on his way to building one of the largest business empires in Australia. This was Aristos' problem, old Mrs Tyron claimed, and Ocker had to take note because he idolized his mother. Not because he loved her, deep down he didn't, he didn't even particularly respect her. He idolized her because he thought it right and fitting that tough, self-made men such as himself should idolize their mothers – also, it drove his wife, Dixie, crazy. The problem for Ocker was that along with Mum came Aristos. Mrs Tyron believed that Aristos' stupendous lack of distinction was due to his being intimidated from an early age by Ocker's equally stupendous abilities and success. She contended that Ocker was indirectly responsible for his brother's condition.

'You were always there,' she would say, in defence of her baby, 'succeeding, winning. How could little Aristos be himself while he was standing in the big man's shadow?'

'I suppose I should apologize that we live in a two million buck house, is that it? That you can give twenty grand to the Methodists and make all those tight-arsed matrons green? Do you wish I had dropped dead lugging crates of lemonade for the Popso Brothers, like Dad? Then maybe little Aristos could be a well-balanced personality. Would you have preferred it that way!!'

'You leave your father's memory be!' Mrs Tyron would say, crocodile tears welling in her eyes. 'If he was here now he wouldn't let you talk to me like that, big as you are he'd belt you.'

If Dixie was around during one of these carbon-copy conversations she could never resist the opportunity to have a dig at Mother under the guise of standing up for her man.

'You shouldn't speak like that to Ocker,' she would declaim, false eyelashes flapping in time with her false loyalty, 'he works terribly hard for us. We all owe him a great deal.'

'Some of us more than others,' old Mrs Tyron would sneer significantly. It is a strange thing, but those who are linked to a person by ties of blood always feel that they have a greater claim over them than those that the person has chosen to share their lives with of their own free will. Hence Mrs Tyron firmly believed that she had more right to be in Ocker Tyron's life than had Dixie Tyron, despite the fact that Ocker had chosen to be with Dixie and, of course, he had not chosen his mother.

'Why, you're not even family,' old Mrs Tyron would say to the woman whom Ocker had pledged his life to in the sight of Jesus.

During these confrontations, the cause of all the trouble would normally be still snoring in his bed upstairs and this was bitter gall for Ocker. Aristos' very physical proximity filled Ocker with barely suppressed fury. There was something so utterly unmanly about a twenty-eight-year-old, healthy man living in his brother's house, hiding behind their mother. Most irritatingly pathetic of all was the fact that Aristos had even begun to learn his mother's excuses.

'I know I'm a passenger, Ocker,' he would whine in what he imagined was an ingratiating tone. 'But you know ... you've done so much, I just don't know where to begin. I suppose it would be different if you were an ordinary bloke, then maybe I wouldn't feel so bad. Then maybe I could get something together, you know?'

It would be impossible to exaggerate the feeling of impotent contempt that this kind of grim effort provoked in Ocker. It made him want to kill. That Aristos should be so witless as to believe that he could hoodwink Ocker with this poorly performed second-hand mix of pathos and flattery, somehow it was almost an insult. It was like when children try and manipulate you and their efforts are so transparent it makes you hate them.

To be fair to Aristos, it wasn't that he hadn't tried to take a place in the business, he had, a bit, but he was just a very untalented person.

But now Ocker had a little job which seemed tailor-made for Aristos. He needed someone who had a known connection with the Tyron organization and therefore could

125

invoke its power and mystique, but who was also totally disownable.

His mother aside, Ocker could easily drop Aristos if he had to. Everyone knew that Aristos was a frustrated dead loss, so if the shit did hit the fan it would be simple for Ocker to disclaim all knowledge of Aristos' actions. What's more, Aristos would be dealing with and seeking to manipulate people of perhaps even less talent and originality than he had. The set-up seemed perfect. Who could guess? Perhaps he would emerge from the experience a better and less irritating person.

ARISTOS GETS A JOB

Aristos entered, trying to assume an air of brisk efficiency. He had on a beautiful Italian suit. Unfortunately he shared with his sister-in-law an inability to wear clothes so it looked like a bloody awful Australian suit. He wore shades. Aristos wore shades most of the time. He did this for anonymity. After all, as a major figure in society he needed to maintain some privacy. Actually, of course, the only time wearing shades is anonymous is in bright sunlight. Wearing sunglasses indoors is pretty much guaranteed to draw attention to you. Aristos knew this really, that was why he wore them.

'Yeah, I got the message to get my ass over here, on the car phone,' Aristos said pointlessly. But he liked people to know things like he had a car phone. Ocker knew already, all the company cars had car phones.

'I was actually en route, but you know, when you buzzed I just did a U-eee and burned straight back. So what goes down?'

Aristos was trying to be casual, but really he was very excited, touchingly thrilled to have been summoned to Ocker's office. Even if it was just for a bollocking it had still given him the chance to swish purposefully through the outer office with all the pretty girls saying, 'Hullo, Mr Tyron.'

'Can't stop, girls. Ocker buzzed me on the car phone, got to get my ass in there pronto.'

For a moment Aristos was the young dynamic trouble-shooter of the Tyron empire. He pictured himself as a daringly unconventional Mr Fixit. Gotta problem? Call Aristos. Sure he breaks rules but he gets results. It was a delicious fantasy and whatever Ocker actually wanted him for would not spoil it. What's more, he would be able to swish out again through all the outer offices with a look of gutsy concentration on his tanned, boyish features, giving the clear impression that he had been charged with some tough make or break assignment. Aristos just bet that any one of those pretty secretaries would give anything to be the first Mrs Aristos Tyron. No, it didn't really matter what Ocker wanted, he had been summoned, that was enough.

To Aristos' delight and astonishment Ocker did have a job for him. He was actually going to be given an important assignment. Aristos was so grateful he could have cried. Instead, as he always did when excited, he got carried away.

'Look this is terrific Ocko, really terrific. I mean, OK, I'm not saying I haven't got plenty on my plate at the moment, because for sure right? I have. But hey, pressure is something I'm used to handling right? I mean, you know that. Listen, Ocko, I've been thinking, we don't see enough of each other, what say we do some clubs, right? Just us guys, we could drink beer, talk . . .'

'Shut up, Aristos.'

'Sure. No problem.'

'There's a difficult and slightly unpleasant job I want doing,' Ocker said.

'So you need a difficult and slightly unpleasant guy,' Aristos replied, purposefully, not realizing what he was saying.

'The firm can't touch it directly, it's not entirely legitimate, so I want to sub-contract. You're going to be the liaison, OK?'

Liaison! Aristos could not believe it, he was going to be Ocker's liaison! And people said he was a dickhead! Yes, well, they were going to have to change their tunes a bit now, weren't they? now that he was a liaison. Maybe he could even have some cards and letterheads done.

'Aristos Tyron: Liaison'.

Ocker looked at his half-brother, wondering whether he could trust him and decided that even Aristos couldn't fuck up such a simple little assignment. It is strange that Ocker, who understood most things, especially regarding human weakness, actually did not fully understand just how stupid his little half-brother was. Sometimes he suspected it, but it just didn't seem possible.

As it happened, Ocker did not have much choice, he could not use any of his regular employees. In the unlikely event of trouble they would understandably not want to carry the can alone. Aristos had just the right combination of stupidity and family loyalty that meant he would probably even take a custodial sentence if he thought it looked cool and gained him his brother's respect.

'Officially, I and the Board know nothing whatsoever about it, right?'

'Right,' said Aristos, as if he knew everything about it.

Ocker handed Aristos an unpleasant leaflet with a flaming torch and a cross on the front and explained what he wanted his brother to do.

ARISTOS' MISSION

It was an extremely hot morning. It was extremely hot every morning that summer, abnormally hot in fact. But Aristos had no time to consider the weather, he was busy liaising.

The shiny black Porsche purred through the slightly shabby suburb. Whenever it had to stop at the lights the occupant seemed to be rather impressively on the car phone. Clearly a high-flyer.

'At the third stroke the time will be . . .'

Aristos nodded thoughtfully as if receiving important news. After a few red lights he reckoned he had had enough of the speaking clock and decided to phone his mother.

'Mum, it's Arry. Guess what, I'm Ocker's liaison! Yeah, it's very hush hush, I'm on an important job. What do you think of that, eh?'

Mrs Tyron was delighted and immediately rang Ocker to express her approval.

'You're a good boy, Ocker, making your mother happy, giving Aristos such an important job. A liaison and all, it must be a very big responsibility.'

'Mum, I'm just using the little prick as a messenger, he has a company car he might as well make himself useful,' Ocker explained, beginning to wonder if enlisting Aristos' services had been such a good idea.

'Oh, Ocker,' chuckled Mother, 'you hate us to see your soft side, don't you? But underneath you're just a big sloppy teddy bear, aren't you?'

It took ten minutes of this infuriating gunk before Ocker could get his mother off the phone. Finally, with ill-concealed fury, the big sloppy teddy bear managed to get the receiver down.

IN SEARCH OF THE NORSEMAN

'Mrs Gordon?' enquired Aristos with a winning smile – he could be quite personable when he wanted to.

'Uhm, well, yes,' she replied nervously, because the man was carrying a personal telephone and had sunglasses on. Obviously he was a policeman. Gordon was in trouble again. She *hated* it when Gordon was in trouble. There would be policemen, the local reporter, tearful Aboriginal women screaming abuse at her at the bus stop.

'Might I enquire, is your son Gordon Gordon in?'

Aristos could see the woman found him fairly awesome. He casually allowed his jacket to fall open revealing the bleeper and the computerized personal memo on his belt. Mrs Gordon thought one of these must be a new sort of weapon, which, had he known, would have made Aristos very happy, because that's what he always pretended they were. When he clipped his bleeper on in the morning he normally spent a moment or two zapping Klingons with it.

'Gordon Gordon, is he in?'

Mrs Gordon was no good at lying, especially when she was nervous.

'Uhm . . . I don't know . . . perhaps . . . no he's not. Is he in trouble? Those Aboriginals make up a lot of that stuff, you know, there's two sides to every story.'

'He's not in trouble. I just want to see him, I have an appointment, I phoned him yesterday.' He paused for a moment and then added, 'from my car phone.'

'Oh, I see, an appointment. Well, he's still in bed actually, it was Friday yesterday. Friday's his night. You'd better come in.'

Aristos entered making a tiny gesture to an imaginary minder that he should stay by the Porsche and watch the street. The hall was neat and tidy although there were jarring notes. A collection of baseball bats and night sticks for instance, two air pistols and a shot gun, an immaculate pair of red-brown sixteen hole Doc Martens, with red laces. Aristos had clearly come to the right place.

Upstairs, still sleeping, was the man that Aristos had come to see, Gordon Gordon, living proof that there is no God.

BLOOD RELATIONS

There are actually quite a few skinheads in Perth and Gordon Gordon was one of the more prominent ones. Anyone unfortunate enough to have seen him lying there asleep, under his swastika bedspread, would have been surprised to learn that one of his principal creeds was a thing he called racial superiority. It is strange that Gordon, who had ready access to several mirrors, should be so enamoured of this idea. Because, if somewhere in the universe there does exist a race of tattooed, crop-headed Neanderthals, looking anything like Gordon, whoever they are superior to must be a pretty sad bunch indeed. Gordon Gordon was definitely no great advert for anything, least of all a master race. Looking at his thick neck and brutish forehead the term that sprung to mind was not so much 'racial purity' as 'in-breeding'.

So, where did Gordon come from? What was his 'race'? The one that he dreamt of fighting and dying for?

Well he'd be horrified to learn that recently scientists seem to have reached a consensus on where Gordon came from. They believe his earliest relatives lived in North Africa.

'That's rubbish, I am a fucking Norseman,' Gordon would no doubt claim, pointing to the crossed axes that hung on the wall above his bed.

But, sadly for Gordon, it's beginning to look as if we all came out of Africa. The new science of genetics has revealed that the differences between the various supposed human 'races' are truly only skin deep. Our lips may be slightly different, but our DNA is virtually identical. This points towards a common root for us all. Gordon Gordon, white supremacist and all round idiot, is a nigger.

What was it that turned Gordon Gordon into a Nazi? Surely not the fact that his first name is the same as his second? This could make a person a bit bitter, but surely is not justification for wanting to kill all the Jews and blacks and gays and commies in the world.

When people feel put upon or inadequate they search for someone to blame.

'It isn't my fault.'

It is a cliché, but none the less true, that Nazis are the most inadequate people of all. The proof of this is that they don't just blame other people for single worries in a moment of pique or angst, they blame other people for their entire lives. Everything bar nothing that is wrong in the life of a Nazi is someone else's fault.

Pissed off at work? Fucking Jews have got the best jobs, haven't they? Crowded pub? They let too many queers and scruffs in. Bus is late? Bastard blacks too lazy to drive properly aren't they?

In literally every area of a Nazi's life there is a seething, jealous, resentment. An obsessive, corrosive belief that they are not getting what is rightfully theirs, and not getting it because of all the other bastards in the world.

PROPOSITION

Gordon came downstairs to the sitting-room where Mrs Gordon was giving Aristos a cup of tea. Gordon thought Aristos looked like a wop and a poof. Aristos thought Gordon looked completely alarming. Gordon had on a Union Jack T-shirt, from which protruded brawny tattooed arms and a neck as thick as the head it supported. He looked like a dangerous thug and of course he was.

'Yeah?' said Gordon.

'Er, Mr Gordon,' said Aristos, trying to be casual and commanding. He held his portable telephone like a shield, it proved his power and superiority. Why didn't it ring? Why didn't it ring?

It rang. With a monumental effort Aristos managed not to jump.

'Excuse me,' he said casually, and turned on the phone, holding it to his ear.

'This is your Australian Telecom alarm call,' the computerized voice said.

'Listen,' Aristos snapped back at the machine, 'I told you to hold all calls. I am taking an important meeting ... I don't care how many million ... Sit on it till I can get to the computer in the Porsche. Just do it!!!' He finished with a flourish, adding as an inspired afterthought, 'You're all sacked.' He put the phone down and apologized to Gordon. Astonishingly the ploy had worked, Gordon was impressed.

'Get my breakfast on, Mum. I want to talk to this bloke.'

Mrs Gordon left and Gordon gave Aristos the look that he used when wishing to imply that he was listening but none the less he remained a hugely violent and unpredictable wild man so he was not to be messed with. Aristos wondered whether Gordon was ill. He seemed to be squinting and grimacing in a slightly alarming manner.

132

'I'm listening,' said Gordon.

Aristos explained that he had read Gordon's leaflet entitled 'Why The Norseman is The Superior Race' with interest and had found it, on the whole, a rattling good read. Gordon was not above the natural pride that any author feels when he hears his work well spoken of and made a tiny gesture as if to say that it was just a little thing he had thrown together. Unfortunately Gordon was a large and unco-ordinated man, so much so that even tiny gestures were unwise. When they had cleared up the tea cup, Aristos continued.

'Yes, I found your argument that the white man is naturally superior because he invented everything . . . uhm, very succinct.'

'Of course it's succinct. I wouldn't have had it printed if it wasn't succinct, would I?' said Gordon. 'I mean, your car, right? Who invented it?'

'Uhm . . .' replied Aristos.

'A white man of the Nordic race, that's who,' continued Gordon who, like all great orators, was given to asking rhetorical questions. 'It's the same with the airplane, and . . .' he glanced about for inspiration '. . . the electric fire. All invented by white men of the Nordic race, which proves his superiority over all other races.'

'Well, exactly,' agreed Aristos. 'Now, it said in your leaflet that you have formed a party, the . . .' he referred to the unpleasant leaflet that Ocker had given him, 'White Supremacy People's Fair Deal Party. It also suggests that your organization is not averse to a degree of direct action, is that the case?'

Gordon agreed that it was and Aristos got down to business. He explained that he personally was in sympathy with a great deal of what Gordon stood for and was, in fact, prepared to supply a certain amount of funding in return for . . .

'Who do you want thumped, Mr Tyron?' asked Gordon, who was not as thick as he looked, which was a shame really because if he had been as thick as he looked his system probably would have broken down under the intellectual strain of having to breathe. In which case, the world would be that one bit nicer a place to live in.

Aristos explained the delicate mission that Ocker had instructed him to explain. Assuring Gordon that all expenses would be taken care of, plus a handsome donation to the White Supremacy People's Fair Deal Party. Gordon thought the proposition sounded very tasty. However, he prided himself on being a fair-minded fellow and felt obliged to point out that the rich and powerful elite of Germany had thought that they could buy and use Hitler and that Hitler had ended up using and controlling them. Hence Gordon wished to make it quite clear from the outset that there was to be no whingeing if he, Gordon, ended up using and controlling Aristos plus all Aristos' Jewish capitalist friends.

Aristos agreed to risk it.

TYRON'S METHODS

Enlisting the help of Gordon Gordon was not to be the only method Ocker Tyron was to employ to interfere with Sly's business. A week after Sly had visited Bullens Creek, Ocker started to turn the screw.

All day long the wasp-like little plane whizzed and buzzed about over the Aboriginal community. The pilot was good. He'd learnt his trade crop spraying. Now he was on a more obviously antisocial mission. He could get in real low before throttling back, so low that no matter how many times he did it, the people on the ground always felt that this time he really would crash into them. This form of harrassment was an old Tyron trick, and he wasn't the only one to have used it.

When the Northern Territory was discovered to be mineral rich, aerial buzzing had proved useful on more than one occasion. The reason it was required was that the territory had been developed much later and much more sparsely than the rest of the country and the Aboriginals had managed to hang on to their traditional life style in the bush. Getting them out was becoming increasingly difficult. It wasn't like the pioneer days when they could have been shot down. Even in Queensland hunting Aboriginals for sport had been illegal since 1927. These days they had some rights, so people like Tyron had to 'persuade' them to get off any decent land.

As the tatty shacks shook and rattled with the vibrations from the plane, the occupants cursed Sly.

'That bastard, Moorcock, wants us out right enough, he's not even waiting for an answer,' said Mr Culboon. 'Bastard.'

'Bastard.' His wife agreed.

Neither of them could understand the rush. What had they done to deserve this?

'Christ, who the hell would want to come to this dump on holiday anyway. Even the flies only come because there's plenty of shit.'

'Maybe he's got another reason for wanting us out,' said his wife.

'But there *can't* be anything. I mean, what could it be? The place has been surveyed. Like he said, if there was anything here they would never have given it to us. No, I reckon this is just his way of warning us not to think about raising the price.'

As it happened, the community had already taken the decision to accept Sly's offer. It was, after all, a great deal of money and there was nothing particularly wonderful about the hole they were living in.

Sly had made a big hit with the rednecks of Bullens Creek on his first visit. He would not be so popular the next time – not once it was realized that it was him who had provided the cash for a bunch of Abs to move to town and put down mortgages on some fairly decent properties.

Mr Culboon would have phoned Sly earlier but, as often happened, the fragile telephone link that existed between their community and the outside world, was knackered. Therefore, late in the afternoon, Mr Culboon set off for Bullens Creek to make the call.

He arrived in town at about the same time as Gordon and his legion. In the gathering dusk Mr Culboon did not notice the hired mini-bus full of unpleasant young men, and had he done, he would have avoided it. Mr Culboon had encountered enough racist thugs in his time not to wish to seek their company.

Gordon sat in the front seat of the van, resplendent in a combat jacket, camouflage trousers and tightly laced-up Doc Martens, sixteen holes, red laces, just like proper British skinheads wore. He was briefing his legions on the details of the operation.

'Storm-troopers, we are undertaking this operation in defence of race, culture and . . . uhm . . . well race and culture are good enough reasons to undertake an operation, in my opinion,' he said decisively.

The assembled storm-troopers agreed with this, although they would not have recognized culture if it sat on their faces and wiggled.

'Australia is a white man's continent, it is ours by right of conquest and we intend to have it all, which is what tonight's battle is all about.'

Gordon cut a ridiculous figure. A stupid, dull thug attempting to look like the leader of a crack fighting unit. On the other hand, he was no more ridiculous than the little gang he was addressing; stupid, dull thugs attempting to look like a crack fighting unit.

Unfortunately for the people of the little Bullens Creek community, they may have been a pretty pathetic bunch but they were a pretty pathetic bunch who had clubs, knives, petrol, darkness and cowardice on their side.

Mr Culboon got through to Sly.

'Listen, you bastard, Moorcock. You can have the place OK? I don't know what you want with our land and I don't care. It's yours, so you can call off your stupid plane, all right?'

'What plane?' said Sly, slightly surprised at Mr Culboon's aggressive tone. He did not deceive himself that he and Mr Culboon would ever be soul mates or bosom buddies but he felt naked abuse was unnecessary and said so.

'Oh yeah, mate. I suppose your fellah's just spending his day trying to piss us off for the fun of it,' Mr Culboon replied.

Sly was mystified but clearly Mr Culboon did not want to discuss it.

'Just get us the money, mate, all right? Then we'll be gone and I won't need to talk to you again.'

Mr Culboon slammed down the phone and went to get himself a beer. The community may have been dry but he was in town now and it wasn't every day that a fellow and his wife got ten grand each for a useless bit of dirt.

As he entered the pub, Gordon and his gang were leaving, having consumed a certain degree of courage. They pushed past him contemptuously, forcing him to flatten himself against the wall or get trampled underfoot.

'Sorry about them, Mr Culboon,' said the bar person, who was a mate. 'Never seen such a bunch of wankers in my life.'

The bunch of wankers had spent their time in the pub being just loud enough to make everyone else in the pub feel uncomfortable. Mr Culboon was not surprised. If there was one thing he could not stand it was groups of young men. They didn't have to be as horrible as the lot that had just left. Any gang of young men made Mr Culboon want to spit. In his opinion, there should be a law stating that no more than three men between the ages of fifteen and thirty should be allowed to assemble together in a public place.

There is something strange and horrid which happens to even the most reasonable blokes when they go out with the 'the lads'. They rejoice in their collective strength. No longer are they scared, farty little sad acts who don't know who they are or what they are doing on earth. Suddenly they are cocks of the roost, they are unassailable, they have power and influence. On a train, in a pub, there they are, loud and arrogant. Lads. Confident in their numbers. Noisily flexing their muscles, making everyone around them feel small and impotent, causing normally liberal-minded people to bitterly wish a policeman would come along and put them all in the army for a hundred years.

Gordon, and his fellow members of the White Supremacy People's Fair Deal Party, got back into their van. They studied the map. There was only one road between Bullens Creek and the Aboriginal community, so even they were able to plan the route.

'Now all of you, watch it! All right?' said Gordon. 'We're going in to scare them, don't get carried away and do the business properly, OK? There'll be a right time for that when ... uhm when the time is right ... Yes ...' he continued, well pleased with this powerful and stirring phrase, 'when the time is right. When will there be a right time for that!!' He shouted into the darkened mini-bus and his fellow crusaders dutifully and slightly drunkenly shouted back:

'When the time is right!'

'Exactly, mates, exactly.' Gordon did not really like referring to party members as 'mates'. It lent nothing to a speech and was scarcely calculated to inspire martial ardour but he had long been stuck for a suitable effective collective noun. The usual ones were 'comrades' or 'brothers' but they were both out. 'Comrades' sounded too fucking commie, and if there was one thing Gordon hated more than blacks it was commies. It will be remembered that Gordon considered himself a fair-minded soul and he realized that a black could not help being black. But a commie, well, a commie was a traitor to his race. The other option, 'brothers', Gordon had been forced to disregard as well. It sounded too fucking queer and if there was one thing Gordon hated more than commies, it was queers. The upshot of this linguistic puzzler was that he was obliged to try to stir his troops by addressing them as 'mates'.

In fact there was no need to stir the assembled gang, they were quite stirred enough already. The prospect of a quick, safe, vicious bit of brutality was really making their pulses race. This, plus a gutful of lager would have stirred a concrete cuppa.

SCREAMS IN THE NIGHT

The bus pulled into the centre of the little cluster of buildings and the heralds of a new dawn all piled out and attacked a group of total strangers for no reason whatsoever.

They threw two petrol bombs at the general store and when the first people ran out to check out the commotion, they hit them with baseball bats. They shouted some things about killing niggers and they threw some anonymous leaflets about that said 'slavery or death, it's your choice'.

There were about three minutes of horrible shouting and screaming, running feet, calls for arms and torches, scurrying silhouettes in the flickering light of the burning store – then it was all over. Having managed to give one man a serious kicking, and before the people they were attacking could get organized, the Nordic knights all rushed back to their van and drove away.

'We did it! We did it!' shouted a jubilant Gordon Gordon. 'We really did the business.'

He did not know it, but they had been doing the business of Stark.

A STEP TOWARDS
EXTINCTION

UNLOADING THE EMPIRE

That same night, Sly was also labouring over the business of
Stark. It had been soul-destroying work, dismantling even
relatively small sections of all that he had worked so hard to
create and make secure. But, he had no choice, he had his part
to play in the big scheme, like all the others. Quite apart from
acquiring the land, he had been charged with getting hold of
large quantities of uranium. This required a lot of money —
and a lot of money by Sly's standards was plenty.

The uranium was definitely a problem. He couldn't just
take it out of his own mines. His entire output was strictly
monitored. If the government got one whiff that he was
creaming any off they'd take him apart bit by bit and the game
would be up, for sure. It was so ridiculous, he was allowed by
law to flog the stuff to the French, yes, that was fine, no
problem there. And what did the French do with it? Blow it
up in the Pacific, that's what! Thus causing the Federal
Government endless embarrassment from cancer-ridden
environmentalists and luminous Aboriginals. It was so
frustrating, the Labour Party seemed to have no objection at
all to Sly putting the naughty bit in Froggy Exocets and yet he
wasn't allowed to hang on to a few tons of his *own* uranium for
his *own* personal use. The world was going mad.

All it meant was that Sly, who personally dug good, top-
grade Australian uranium, would have all the trouble of
acquiring the stuff on the world black market – probably

buying his own stuff back at ten times the price. Still, at least by getting the stuff off some shady character whose address was a portable fax machine, Sly was guaranteed discretion. The dealer Sly was using wanted ten million dollars in two dollar bills, this was not the kind of fellow likely to publish his memoirs. Anyway, the guy wasn't likely to live long, he positively glowed in the dark.

Sitting in front of a video screen as the dawn came up, unloading cash assets into the market, had been a strange experience. Some of the stuff he sold he didn't even know he had. Who would have thought he had a shit-dumping operation in the North Sea?

A couple of blips on the screen and he didn't anymore. Captain Robertson got himself a new invisible boss. It didn't make any difference, he still hated his job.

He was looking for smallish, easy to dispose of assets, stuff to chip away at. He did not want to unload any major conglomerates, it would be bound to attract attention. Stark had been very clear on that score. In fact he had been trying to discreetly break up his empire into more manageable chunks ever since he got back from the dinner in LA. His people had been pretty surprised.

'Sly,' his whole upper-management team had wailed, as if they were but one upper manager, 'you're laying us wide open. Putting out the cream and waiting for the cats. We're gonna get picked off bit by bit.' Of course they were right. According to every accepted business practice, Sly was inviting major losses. But he wasn't fighting for profits any more, he was fighting for his life. Unfortunately he could not confide this knowledge to his upper-management team and so he had to allow his upper-management team to think he was losing his grip.

One advantage of this piecemeal sell-off was that it made it much easier to unload assets discreetly. After all, if even Sly did not know that he owned half the stuff he was now selling, no one else would.

CURIOSITY KILLED THE CAT

Actually, somebody else did. As a matter of fact somebody knew Sly's business better than he did; poor, dullish Linda Reeve of the London *Financial Telegraph*.

She had long been researching a book called *An Analysis of the Social Roots and Financial Strategies Pertaining to the Most Prominent Fifty Business Empires Constructed Since the Second World War* or *Megabuck: the Lives and Loves of the Top Half Hundred*, as her publishers wished to call the book.

It had been the detailed knowledge that this research afforded her that had enabled Linda to make the connections she had made regarding Nagasyu's diverse sell-offs and Slampacker's and the others that she had noticed.

It was eight o'clock in the evening in London and she was working late, nibbling a chocolate, staring with a puzzled frown at her VDU. It had been luck that she caught the first of Sly's dumps. The Prince of Wales had recently made a series of major speeches on the state of the North Sea. The death of Mrs Pastel from viral gastroenteritis, after eating a dodgy mussel, had given him the springboard he needed to try, yet again, to force environmental action on pollution. It was beginning to look as if local councils were going to have to pay far more to waste disposal contractors.

Clearly it was a situation from which an unscrupulous but legal killing could be made by any shit-dumper who wanted to double his prices for a 10 per cent improvement in the service he offered.

Hence the *Financial Telegraph* presumed that trading in waste companies would be fairly fierce. It was while putting together a small piece based on this assumption that a colleague of Linda's had remarked with surprise that a big player like Silvester Moorcock had elected to buck the trend and pull out of the business altogether. That very evening he had dumped every single share of the Belgian waste disposal conglomerate that he had been so heavily into.

Linda nearly missed it when her colleague made the

observation – her mind had been elsewhere. Linda had just been given a small box of chocolates by a cleaner whom Linda had helped with her accounts. It was the end of the day – choccy time so to speak – and there were four people in the room. The problem with chocolates is that they operate on a loss curve of massively diminishing returns. The first one out of the box, the strawberry cream say, is of far greater value than the last few left, the despised cracknels and nougats and such like. In fact, these chocolate lepers are often never eaten at all and are left forever, unable to be thrown away because they're still there, and yet never eaten because they're so horrid. Linda knew if she offered the chocs around the loss of the four best ones would halve the value of her box.

Of course she knew what she had to do, but she didn't like it. As Linda's colleague was telling her about Sly's sell-offs, Linda was watching both strawberry creams, a turkish delight and a soft caramel disappear. Luckily, neither of the lime barrels were touched or Linda seriously wouldn't have heard the momentous snippet. But, she did hear it and, still pursuing the half-formed theories that her editor had rejected so dismissively, Linda decided to take a little look at Sly. She rummaged through the huge mounds of books and papers that habitually covered her desk, finally locating her tiny Nagasyu keyboard.

Now, of course, there are tens of thousands of transactions going on at any one moment in the world markets and Sly's interests were so diverse that normally trying to pick up his trail would take months of painstaking research just to get a clear view of a single half-hour period. But, Linda had already done the research for her book. She had a computer program that detailed over 80 per cent of known Moorcock investments. She knew where most of his money was hiding. All she had to do was to instruct the computer to keep scanning the ever-shifting market until anything connected with Moorcock made a move.

She did not have to wait long.

It was extraordinary. Moorcock was undressing like a born

again naturist, selling off anything from ouija boards to weapons systems. All for ready cash too. Linda searched in vain for any corresponding reinvestment but found nothing.

She told herself not to get excited. She realized that the fact that she had gone looking for this, and had found it, would make her all the more anxious to prove that there was something in it. But there *must* be something in it. So much money was leaving the market but only through the big individual players. Middle-range investors, pension schemes, banks, etc., were not moving.

Something *had* to be going on amongst the big men but Linda did not believe that it was co-ordinated. Above all else, she knew that people like Slampacker, Moorcock, Tyron and Nagasyu would die before they would co-operate with each other.

But something was definitely going on, she thought, trying to clean her great big green glasses and getting chocolate on them. Had all the big men got the willies together? Had they all seen something coming that most people were too small to spot? Were we heading for the biggest crash ever and were the rats deserting the sinking ship? leaving small investors, pension funds and governments holding soon-to-be-worthless stock?

Selecting a horrid hard centre, she attempted to bite the chocolate off without eating the bit in the middle. No chance of course, she soon had half a Brazil nut in her mouth, which she hated.

Hero fantasies flicked across Linda's mind. Would she be the woman to predict the great crash? Would she ring the warning bell that cushioned the little fellow from the worst of it? She pictured silver-haired grannies thanking her brokenly for rescuing at least part of their pathetic savings and honest young lovers who would still be able to send the tots to good schools because of her prompt action. An MBE! . . . If she was right . . . But of course she wasn't. Linda pulled herself together. She had an interesting little anomaly that was all. There would be, without a doubt, some perfectly ordinary explanation. Still, she might as well ask. Linda reached for the phone.

The telephones in Sly's office complex did not trill, they rang. His whole body had jerked, he had nearly hit buy rather than sell mid-deal. He'd been trying to unload a plant that produced condensers for fridges and driers, instead he near as damn it purchased half a million ex-US Army condoms. Sly could think of literally nothing more revolting than a second-hand condom.

Sly, of course, never answered the phone in his office but at that time of night he was the only person there and the thing kept ringing. Eventually he walked through about three secretaries' offices to where incoming calls were intercepted and picked up the phone.

'Sly Moorcock speaking.'

He was pretty surprised to find himself doing this but not half as surprised as Linda Reeve was to find herself speaking to the billionaire himself. She had known that somebody would be about because of the heavy trading, but she was astonished to find Sly running his own market stall.

'Uhm . . . Oh, right, Mr Moorcock, ahem, excuse me phoning like this . . .'

Sly didn't mind. He was in a kind of mischievous mood what with selling off all his stuff. 'That's OK. It's pretty late to call, but that's OK. Are you in bed?' Messing around with all his money had made Sly feel powerful and randy. It was very late, he just presumed the woman was a drunk gold-digger chancing her arm.

'What!!' said a shocked voice, to Sly's satisfaction.

'I said, are you in . . .'

'I'm phoning from London.'

Linda did not like his tone. She put on her firm voice. This was the voice that she always dreamt of using to the horrible young men whose job it was to hang off scaffolding all over London and make women feel uptight. Linda, although by no means particularly attractive, had a big bust. This one quirk of fate had meant that for her entire life, since the age of thirteen, the mere sight of scaffolding or road works had made her tense up and scurry along, blushing with anger and looking at her feet. Of course you don't need to have big tits to get intimidated, all women are scrutinized. All over any city, at any time of the day, there are women crossing roads to avoid the men hanging off scaffolding. They should add a bit to the road work warnings on the radio, 'and a lot of building in the High Street today so delays for motorists, and, of course, female pedestrians can expect to be biting their lips with anger and embarrassment as their bodies are assessed and commented on.'

On the phone Linda would be the toughie she would love to have been in the streets.

'I am not in bed, I am working, Mr Moorcock. My name is Linda Reeve, I'm with the *Financial Telegraph*.'

All Sly's smugness evaporated instantly. It wasn't that he was doing anything guilty, he just felt guilty and who could blame him? After all, he was personally involved in attempting to perpetrate one of the greatest moral outrages in history, including the invention of Pot Noodles. Anyone would feel guilty.

'Oh yeah, what do you want?'

Sly was making no further effort at flirtatious charm. He didn't care if it was Marilyn Monroe on the other end of the line, she was a journo and the last thing on earth he wanted right now was interest from journos.

'Uhm-uhm, we-we at-at the-the FT-FT,' Linda said, the line had suddenly got worse and she was trying to ignore the off-putting echo of her own voice coming back at her as it bounced around the globe.

'We were wondering why you're selling so much of your stuff-stuff.' She had not meant to put it as frankly as that, she had meant to speak briskly of 'asset stripping' and 'large scale dumps', but the echo, and the fact that she was actually talking to the man himself, had pretty much thrown her. Not half as much as she had thrown Sly though.

What the fuck did she have on him?

He was sufficiently shaken to make a big mistake. He started to deny something that clearly she had already established.

'Selling my stuff? Come on, what are you talking about?' Sly realized as he spoke that with this tack he would hang himself. The bitch wouldn't have phoned him if she didn't have something. Sly turned mid-sentence, 'Listen lady, I don't know who you are, or even why I'm talking to you, but you'd better get back to the woman's page, OK? Do some fashion stuff or something. Selling? I'm rationalizing, OK? Dodging and weaving, pulling out, putting in. Nobody hits a moving target and you can quote me. Now I've really got to . . .'

Sly's second mistake was trying to patronize Linda. He guessed it as he was doing it. People who got to work for the *Financial Telegraph*, especially women, couldn't be bullshitted as easily as that.

'Mr Moorcock,' replied Linda, now feeling a lot better, 'Mr Moorcock, you have dumped a ouija board factory, two local newspapers, a pharmaceutical lab, part of an oil-well, a chain of sweetshops, a TV station in Papua New Guinea, electronics, fertilizer, weapons, do I have to go on? And yet I cannot detect a single reinvestment. You must have over a hundred and fifty million Australian dollars in your wallet now.'

'Woah! Hang on a minute here, Ms Reeve,' snapped Sly, shaken. 'What is this? Snooping? We have laws you know . . .'

'The information is there for anyone who cares to look,' Linda interrupted, thrilled that she seemed to have got to him. 'I've done nothing wrong.'

Sly wanted to finish the conversation before he put his foot in it any further.

'The information is there, my dear, now it's up to you to interpret it. Let me give you a hint. I am a very rich man while you probably make no more than 20K sterling per annum. This is because I have ideas. I have ideas and you

148

snoop. If I told you my ideas, maybe you'd be as rich as me, which is why I'm not going to tell you them. So far your facts are correct, I've flogged a few of my small holdings. But any peeping Tom could come up with that. Ring me back when you've figured out what I'm up to, baby. G'day from WA.'

He put the phone down and he was shaking.

His last shot had been good, Linda thought he sounded like a confident man with an idea to make money . . . maybe he was. On the other hand, she had definitely got to him at first, and there were the others . . . Her search would continue, to discover what, if anything, was going on and if there was one last edible choccy in the box.

FACEFULL'S

It had been an unpleasant jolt but Sly wasn't over worried. He reckoned he had handled the situation pretty well and, after all, it was only a dumb pom journo. For the remainder of the night he carried on the lonely task of unloading his assets and by mid-morning on the following day he was close to fulfilling his financial obligations to Stark.

He decided he deserved a treat and so he went out for a burger. A burger in a public eatery. Sometimes he got like that, fed up with top-class food and top-class poncey people. Sometimes he liked to eat plain grub in lively, real places, served by spunky students in mini-skirts, working their way through college.

He liked to sit alone, away from the hundreds of people whose lives were in his hands. Anonymous, watching the world go by for a moment. He especially liked to watch the girls. Real girls. Girls who ignored him, girls who wore clothes rather than bait. Girls who had their own stuff to do. He was watching a group now, three of them, maybe they were from an office, they were so lively and unaffected. Why shouldn't they be? They got three hundred bucks at the end of each week and spent it. What was there to be affected about?

Sly had never really got used to mega-wealth. He was a bobby sox and apple pie man at heart. But, you can't fake it, you can't live a simple life when you've got a complex and enormous income, no matter how much you want to.

And so, occasionally, Sly would sneak out of the office just for a look at the real world – the one he had left behind when he first stitched up his friend's pie factory. He would sneak out to look at real girls and eat real food.

Actually, finding real food was becoming more and more difficult as Sly was about to discover. The yuppy decade had ruined simple food. Now every bank clerk thought he was a gourmet. Burger cuisine had arrived. Facefull's was the sort of place that would not let food alone, they had to ponce it up in some way or other. Sly could only presume that the reason for this was so that they could charge more for it.

'Ten bucks for a bit of fried chicken!'

'Well you're paying for the Chinese lettuce and the little miniature tomatoes, aren't you?'

Looking around him, Sly made a mental note to move into burger franchises and designer vegetables, but then he remembered that Stark was soon to make that part of his life a thing of the past.

He accepted a menu from a waitress in a huge T-shirt, belted at the waist to make a dress. In Sly's jaded mood she seemed to be a living embodiment of freshness and vitality. He smiled his winning smile. She thought, shit, the leerers never tip.

The menu was three square feet of laminated plastic. The thing flapped around like a sail in a transatlantic yacht race, you could have gone surfing on it.

The reason for the menu's great size was not because the selection was fabulously extensive. On the contrary, the choice was minimal, burgers, steaks, ribs, chicken and a thing called seafood, which was white and covered in breadcrumbs. The problem was that each dish apparently required a stomach turnling trite description, presumably so that the diner was left in no doubt about just how horrible the meal was going to be.

'Facefull's saucy prawns between the sheets. Gorgeous juicy prawns stretched temptingly between luscious layered squirts of the chef's own sauce! – Irresistible!'

Sly had never met the chef but he was damn sure that he could do without a squirt of his sauce.

Sly wanted a burger, so with incisive intuition he ordered a thing called 'The Facefull Burger: Just a plain facefull looking for a home! Juicy ground beef on sesame, a touch of mayo', a little exotic salad and oh, by the way, our fries are the best.'

This description was off-putting enough, but it sounded like gastronomic heaven compared with what Sly got. They had not mentioned Kiwi fruit, nor the avocado and they definitely hadn't warned him about the pine kernels. These were not the things a person wanted to have to scrape off his food when he fancies a plain burger. The touch of mayo' had become about a pint of sickly sweet slime. There were *currants* in the salad and the fries were thick cut and done in their jackets!

With sinking heart Sly realized that he was in a burger joint that was too trendy to peel its potatoes.

Sly went back to staring at the waitresses.

THE ECOACTION TEAM

Linda Reeve, the dumb pom journo, was not going to be the only ripple in Sly's pond that day. Another one was drawing up outside the brasserie in a beautiful old red Holden with white-wall tyres.

The red-head in the huge hat, who was driving, turned to her companions.

'Colin, you stay here with Zimm, OK. Me and Walter will go in and talk to him,' said Rachel.

'Cool,' said CD, who clearly thought it wasn't. His idea of a great day out was not sitting in a car minding a half-mad bollockless psycho with a chip on his shoulder. On the other hand, CD was a reasonable guy and he realized that Zimmerman might be rather a liability in a fashionable eatery. Since Zimm's terrible injury he had developed a considerable empathy for bullocks and with it a deep hatred for anyone who served or ate veal. He didn't often go to restaurants, but when he did, there would be big trouble if he found veal on the menu.

'OK, I'll stay with Zimm,' he said.

'You stay where you like, kid,' said Zimm, 'I want a burger.'

So all four of them trooped in. The manager did not like the look of them, but the man in the shorts was so huge he decided to let discretion be the better part of valour. Had he looked a little closer he would have been more concerned about the tall, thin guy in the singlet.

Zimm's mind was racing and the place was liberally stuffed with large potted plants, and he was trying hard to hang on to himself. If he wasn't careful he would be back in the jungle once more and go for the nearest Asian businessman.

CD saw the signs and hustled him through, noting to his horror a couple of thick jowled arsehole young execs tucking into veal schnitzel and talking very loudly to show how cool and confident they were. Luckily Zimm did not notice the veal. The restaurant, pursuing their unswerving policy of fucking up food, had elected to put tinned apricots on top of it so Zimm thought they were eating ice cream sundaes.

Rachel and Walt spotted Sly at his corner table. They went over and stood in front of him.

'Yes,' said Sly, looking up, glad of the excuse to stop struggling with the crappy food. Sly was a cool hand and was not to be phased by a group of strange looking hippies approaching him, even if one of them was blocking out the sun. He presumed that they were there to persuade him to join a new religion. Besides, not fifteen feet away was a table full of his goons, sipping mineral water and just itching to kill someone.

'We got to talk to you about Bullens Creek, man,' Walter drawled. 'They hit the kids as well, you know, your thugs just hit whatever. How do you sleep, man?'

Sly felt he didn't deserve this. Twice in ten hours it had happened, first the journo bitch onto his sell-offs and now, strange giant hippies talking about Bullens Creek. The goons were getting up from their table but Sly waved them back, he needed to know what was going down.

Sly had not heard about the terrible racist attack on the Bullens Creek community – not many people had. The reason for this being that Ocker Tyron owned both local papers plus one of the TV channels. News tends to be rather selectively reported when the people who are making it own the means of telling it.

'What's Bullens Creek to you, Mister?' said Sly.

There was something about Walter that made Sly take him seriously. It wasn't his size, not entirely anyway . . . there was a sort of monkish sincerity about him. Sly was always suspicious of true believers, you couldn't bribe them and hitting them didn't help. You had to talk to them. The lean one was even more disconcerting. Sly was a very practised judge of character and strength and this guy looked off the scale. Maybe he was just a very well-formed hippy but he looked kind of like a killer to Sly. And then . . . then there was the girl. She had something too, Sly couldn't put his finger on it. But he would have liked to.

He did not notice CD.

'Mr Culboon and his people were going to pay you, bastard, but you had to make sure didn't you? You're fucking scum, man, that's what you are.' Sly nearly fell off his seat! What the hell did this bunch of penniless looking hippies know about Culboon? Surely they weren't a group of eccentric billionaires who were in on Stark as well?

'You'd better sit down and explain what your problem is,' he said tersely. It was a corner table for four so there was only room for Walter. Zimm, Rachel and CD hovered . . .

'Your goons want to know whether you want them to take us,' Zimmerman said, eyeing the table around which Sly's men were sat. Zimm's arms hung loosely by his sides, the fingers alternately stretching and relaxing.

'Business associates,' said Sly, again waving his security back. 'Drink?'

'I don't drink with vicious, violent scum,' said Walter.

'Yeah, well me neither, normally,' said CD, 'but I'll have a Facefull Forcefield.'

He had always wanted to have a really enormous, extravagantly expensive cocktail and he wasn't going to miss the opportunity now one had presented itself. Faced with this collapse of solidarity, the other three said they'd have beers. Sly gave the order and behind the bar the Facefull Forcefield was prepared. This, like all the other cocktails, consisted of whisking up a load of fruit juice and cream, adding about one measure of mixed spirits, putting six straws and a small fruit salad on top and charging fifteen dollars for it. CD thought it was fantastic.

'What do you know about the Culboon business?' Sly asked.

'I know one thing, man. I know that although I am a completely committed man of peace, my friend Zimmerman is a war-crazed loon and he wants to kill you for what you did.'

Sly looked at Zimmerman. Zimmerman looked back and said:

'If you're not eating that can I finish your food?'

Sly gladly offered him the plate and prevailed upon Walter to explain himself. He learnt that Walter and Culboon were old friends and that he, Walter, had been distressed to get a call to say that a gang of Nazis had attacked the community.

'I mean, man, you know you guys are just utter pigs, right? The dude was coming round, he was cool to take your bread and split.'

Rachel squirmed in silent embarrassment at this awesome lexicon of completely unfashionable terms. CD thought it sounded great. Zimmerman wasn't listening, he was trying to decide whether there really was a tinned pear with cloves on top of his burger or whether he was suffering from LSD flashback.

Walter continued in the same aggrieved terms:

'I mean, why can't people just be cool? First the plane all day, freaking all the kids out, then the fascists. I mean, just what is in your head, man? I'll tell you, bad shit, that's what. You have a head full of bad shit. You should see a doctor, yeah and what's more, you're going to need one when Zimmerman's finished with you.'

Walter turned to Zimm for confirmation but Zimm had his own problems. Were those tomatoes really only the size of grapes? They seemed to be, they certainly looked that way.

Then again, Zimmerman had once seen a huge pink dragon in a bikini emerge from the top of his commanding officer's head, so he was aware that appearances could be deceptive. But man, if they were real, those two little balls were just about the smallest tomatoes he had ever seen. After a while they started to remind him of something, and his eyes filled with tears.

Sly was very worried. What did they know? What were they talking about? Who the fuck were they? And why did the tough one look so homicidally upset?

'Look,' he said, 'I don't know what this is about. Sure I have an interest in Bullens but this is the first I've heard of any attack.'

This was too much for Rachel.

'Oh come on, Moorcock. First you offer a huge amount of money for their land, God knows why, then when they hesitate for one second they get beaten up. What do you take us for, a bunch of airheads?'

Sly decided not to answer that one. He was still confused but he was also relieved. They didn't know why he wanted the land, they didn't even seem interested.

'I mean, why the hell do you even want the land?' said Rachel.

For the first time, Sly found himself disliking the girl. Also, the tough hippy was beginning to look alarmingly volatile, he sure looked angry. Sly decided to try and take control.

'Look, I can see that it's going to be difficult to prove that I had nothing to do with this, but I didn't,' said Sly truthfully and firmly – although he was beginning to form a pretty sound theory about who had. Christ, Ocker Tyron was a vicious, stupid bastard. Why couldn't he have left things up to Sly?

The situation was tricky. Sly shot a glance at Zimmerman, who was obviously getting ready to explode. Sly had to allay their suspicions and stop them probing any further. He had to try and get the proof they needed to show that he had not been involved. The restaurant was nearly empty now. He produced a portable telephone and offered it to Rachel.

'Dial the Bullens Creek police station, here's the number.'

Rachel took the phone. CD was green with envy. He would have loved to have had a go on one of those phones.

'Ask for the chief, say it's Sly Moorcock calling.'

Rachel did this and having thus established that it really was the chief of Bullens Creek police, Sly took back the phone, motioning Rachel and Walter to lean in and listen close. He turned the volume on the phone up a little, but not too much. He definitely fancied Rachel and liked the idea of getting closer to her, Walter he would have to put up with.

'Hi Brad, Sly ... Oh yeah, thanks, I enjoyed it too, the Dingo's sure know how to throw a rage. Listen, you know I'm taking an interest in land purchase round your way, lot of action, high investment, good for the town and all that. But, I heard you had some trouble out at the community. I don't like that Brad, what's the story?'

Rachel and Walter could hear the police chief's reply quite clearly. He was the exuberant, shouty, friendly type, if you were a white land-owner that is.

'Oh, no worries, Sly, definitely a one-off. Perth have picked up the ringleader, a known skinhead trouble-maker called Gordon Gordon. He'll do some time, no question. This is his umpteenth bust on similar charges, the little shit. I mean, Christ no one's in love with the Abs, but this guy's pathological. He just can't stop bashing them. They do over the odd country town, it's happened before. They put up posters and stuff about white Australia. Pathetic really, the fucking Japs own the place anyway. But don't you worry, Mr Moorcock, when he gets out, if he shows his face around here I'll hand him over to the Ab' women, they'll fucking eat him.'

Sly thanked the policeman, turned off the phone and put it away.

'Well,' said Sly, 'that's the story. Pretty disgusting stuff, in my opinion. Quite frankly I deeply resent you implying that I would be involved with a thug like that. Apart from anything else, what do you think it would do for my reputation?'

Walter and Rachel had to admit he had a point. He really

did seem to be genuinely surprised about the whole thing, which was hardly surprising really, since he was. Maybe it really had been a coincidence.

Sly reckoned he had convinced the girl and the huge hippy but the tough one was obviously still furious. Sly hoped they got him out before he blew. They didn't.

Zimmerman could bear it no longer. He had finally decided that what was on his plate was real and he did not like it.

'I mean, what's the point!' he shouted. 'I mean, what *is* the *point*!! You know, I mean, is it me or what? I rarely get a chance at decent food . . .'

Walter was a little hurt at this since he did most of the cooking at their place, but Zimmerman was too upset to worry about Walter's sensibilities.

'So when I do right? When I do get a stab at some groovy chow, what's happened to it, man? I mean, what has happened to it? I'll tell you, it has been *fucked up* man! That's what! You know, I mean, shit, like, tinned pears and sweet mayonnaise and skins on the chips!! I mean, man, what is the point? Can't anything be normal any more? Can't a groover just have a burger without having to scrape eight tons of shit out of it!! And what's with the tomatoes that remind me of my bollocks! Very tactful, man, I must say. Fuck you!'

Zimmerman walked out to polite applause from the few remaining guests. On the whole they agreed with every word he had said, although they had found the bit about his bollocks confusing.

'I'm glad somebody finally *said* something,' they all whispered to each other.

DINNER NEAR SINGAPORE

Sly and Tyron shared a private plane to Nagasyu's private island off the coast of Singapore. They barely spoke for the whole journey, that is until five minutes before touch-down when Sly noticed an ominous grey frigate hanging around in the little harbour.

'Jesus,' he said, pointing, 'what the hell are the navy doing here?'

Tyron looked.

'That's not the navy,' he said, 'that's Nagasyu's.'

'He owns his own warship?' asked Sly in surprise.

'Four of them, and four MI6s. He's a very big player, Silvester,' was the patronizing reply.

On landing, Sly was shown to his chalet by a uniformed and armed guard. This was a distinct change from the gay *maître d'* at 'California Dreaming'. Sly felt uncomfortable, he wished he'd brought a gun himself. Dinner was held under a beautiful South-East Asian sky, with the lights of Singapore City turning the vast canopy a fabulous dappled orange.

'Well, there's one thing I'll say for pollution,' said Tyron bluntly as they took their seats, 'it's certainly improved the views. The damn stuff's so thick the light just bounces back at us . . . and the heat,' he added more morosely. The terribly unnatural heat of that southern summer was scarcely relieved at all by the coming of night.

Even in the time that had elapsed between the dinner in Los Angeles and this, Sly's second session of the World Government of Money in Singapore, he could sense a gathering urgency in the proceedings. There was less preliminary chatter, people wanted to discuss the project and nothing else. Despite the fabulous tropical spread that Nagasyu had laid on, nobody felt like eating much. They picked at the odd irradiated bit of fruit but the atmosphere was too tense and edgy to really hop into it. Besides, a starlit picnic loses some of its charm when the waiters are packing machine guns and there's an armed warship in the bay. A lot of this security was, of course, to do with Nagasyu's own private operations and nothing to do with Stark but it all contributed to the general air of fatalistic doom.

'See about that sludge slick in the Eastern Atlantic?' Slampacker observed gloomily. 'Jesus, we weren't expecting those for years.'

Slampacker was still in the chair. He seemed to be the unofficial president of the board. Many of the other faces had changed though. Understandably, due to the location, there was a larger contingent of Asian billionaires. As with Los Angeles though, it didn't really matter who attended because any conclusion that the discussion produced would be instantly beamed to all interested parties.

'I've seen pictures,' Slampacker continued, 'yeuk! Green and yellow and red bubbling goo. The damn thing looked like one of my burgers with the lid taken off.' Slampacker spoke in English. Much to Sly's relief English remained the lingua franca despite the majority of the group being Asian. Tex Slampacker was referring to yet another man-made ecological disaster. A horrible, stinking, messy disaster – but that wasn't what worried him. It was the timing. It had come too early. He felt like a man who conscientiously plans his dental appointments and suddenly an unwise toffee pulls half a pound of metal out of his teeth.

GOD'S SPIT AND THE DOMESDAY GROUP

In order to provide some parameters to their desperate rear-guard action some twenty years before, the Stark consortium (which Sly was discovering was much older than he had first thought) had set up a top secret research team to predict the point at which world eco-balance would become critical, and drastic final action would have to be taken. For example, they had known about the connection between aerosols and ozone a decade before public research reached the same conclusion. This was partly because the Domesday Group, as the research team was called, were far better funded than government research, and partly because with the edge that their extra knowledge gave them, Stark were able to perpetrate a highly effective disinformation campaign. Hence, holding back aerosol bans for ten years, causing countless cancers and making an awful lot of money.

The Domesday Group had also predicted the terrible slime slick to which Slampacker was referring. They had informed their masters that in the not-too-distant future, the pointless over-farming of the industrial world would cause large quantities of nitrates and phosphates to gather in the sea, caused by agricultural run-offs. These would eventually turn the sea into a kind of nutritional soup for the ever present microscopic algae which thrive on these elements. Having been given such a good free meal, these oxygen consuming algae would multiply rapidly and gel into a vast floating, slimy glob, doubling in mass every twenty-four hours and continuing to do so until they had used up all the available nutrients. The problem with this glob, apart from the obvious bummer of having two feet of scum covering part of the eastern Atlantic, is that these algae use up so much oxygen in their phenomenal reproduction that they stifle everything else in their bit of sea. A level of three million algae to a litre of water is fatal to marine life. Underneath the slime slick that had so upset Slampacker, levels were running at ten million a litre. That is a very overcrowded jug of water.

'God's Spit' as the Domesday Group had called their prediction, for obvious reasons, was one of thousands of documents that they had submitted to Stark over the years, and now, yet again, they had been proved right. God had spat on the ocean. But what was worrying Slampacker and his companions so much that night was the timing. This particular disaster had not been predicted for at least another five years – it had happened too early. As an isolated incident this would be acceptable but the Domesday Group were having to constantly revise their predictions backwards as events overtook them. Species of animals that were not meant to die out until mid-twenty-first century were already extinct. Trees were proving far less resilient against acid 'die back' than had been hoped.

This meant that the bottom line, Vanishing Point, the moment at which the world will cease to be able to sustain balanced life, was approaching much faster than had been expected.

'It is coming towards us quicker than we are going towards it,' Slampacker explained, unnecessarily.

The original Vanishing Point scenarios arrived at by the Domesday Group had been really quite optimistic. They reckoned we had three generations at least. They did not see a total breakdown happening until at least the second half of the twenty-first century. At the time the fledgling group that was to become the Stark consortium had taken great comfort from this, hoping that perhaps technology might come up with eco solutions that did not require them to take a drop in profit. Thus relieving them of the terrible necessity of having to intervene directly.

It should be remembered that the first article of the unwritten constitution of the notional World Government of Money is that under no circumstances should anyone be expected to take action that would reduce their profits, whatever the consequences of not taking action. Stark's central assumption being that there is no point in curtailing antisocial activities, because if you don't do it someone else will.

Unfortunately, ever since those heady, optimistic days, Armageddon had been getting closer. The consortium had already decided that the time had come to take drastic action even before Sly joined, now some alarmists in the group were beginning to wonder if they had made their move too late.

'That kind of speculation is quite pointless,' snapped Mai Wo, a small South-East Asian bloke who Sly knew well by reputation. He was much admired for managing to employ more labour for less cash than anyone else since the Pharaohs built the pyramids. Mai Wo brought the same calm logic to his assessment of the Armageddon plan.

'Whether we are too late or not is a non-variable, we cannot affect it,' he said, accepting a cheesy nibble from a waiter in a steel helmet with a small howitzer under his arm. 'We must presume that vanishing point is upon us and that we must act immediately. This we have done. So, let us put panic from our hearts, our shoulders to the wheel, and act as swiftly and as efficiently as we are capable of.'

He spoke as if they were embarking on some great public work, rather than the cruellest and most selfish plan imaginable. He made the others feel good about themselves. Possibly this was how he managed to persuade his enormous workforce to labour so philanthropically on his behalf – maybe it was because in his country trade unions were virtually illegal and the opposition were all in prison.

'Mr Mai Wo is, of course, absolutely right,' Slampacker said, 'and hence I have asked Professor Durf of our Armageddon Co-ordinating Group, to say a few words on what measures we are going to have to employ in order to accelerate our preparations to meet Vanishing Point when it hits us. Professor Durf . . .'

PROFESSOR DURF AND THE AVALANCHE EFFECT

There was a smattering of polite applause as the dynamic young South African rose to his feet and fixed them with his one eye, the other one having been lost doing his national service. He claimed that he had lost it at the hands of a black soldier, which was true in a way. It had been a black orderly who had over-polished the floor of the officers' mess on which

Durf had skidded stabbing himself with a cocktail stick and thus fixing a small sausage to his left eye.

Durf was present at the dinner because, obviously, a group of people whose talents are centred around making money, could not operate the sort of project that they were planning on their own. Hence, over the years, a carefully selected and heavily controlled group of experts had been recruited to the team. All were shadowed and monitored, day and night, by a vast army of agents who had no idea what they were watching for. Just as most of those being watched, like the Domesday Group for instance, were completely in the dark as to the nature of the ultimate plan that they were unwitting parts of. Sad to say, science is no longer pure: commerce pays for it and commerce calls the tune. Domesday Group scientists produced results for their corporate masters just as they produced aerosols, defoliants and new methods of sticking sugar frosting to cereals. Professor Durf, head of the Armageddon Co-ordinating Group, was one of the handful of people outside the actual World Government of Money who knew the true nature of the plan; he was a part of it. Since the death of his predecessor, Professor Blakely, he was one of its principal architects.

Despite his central role in the Stark Conspiracy, there had been nothing sinister about Blakely's death. He had not been on the verge of spilling the beans – people just die, that's all. Although, with hindsight, the more thoughtful members of Stark realized that the cause of his death was chillingly ironic. He had been on a skiing holiday at Klosters in Switzerland and had been killed by an avalanche. Killed directly by an avalanche that is, but at one remove he was killed by the fires on the Mersey and the Thames and the Tyne.

Klosters used to be pretty safe, it still is, relatively, but none the less all over Europe the ski resorts are becoming ever more plagued by avalanches. In fact so bad has the problem become that whole Alpine villages are being forced to evacuate themselves when the warnings sound. Now one might say: more fool them, how stupid to build their Alpine villages in the paths of potential avalanches. The point is, of course, that for hundreds of years the villages have been perfectly safe. The thick tree cover on the mountain sides had anchored the snow to the ground, and that which did slip away was soon stopped and dispersed by the tough little high-flying forests. Not so anymore, unfortunately. Acid rain sweeping across Europe for a hundred years or more has dissipated the forests. The mountains are going bald. It is possible to filter the factories and power stations that produce the sulphur that turns the water to acid, but it's expensive, so of course it is not done. Little fir trees on frozen mountain tops do not carry a lot of weight when it comes to balancing market forces – but they carry a fuck of a lot of weight when an avalanche lands on your head.

Professor Durf was addressing the assembled party.

'Gentlemen, as you have been discussing, the Domesday Group no longer feel able to make a prediction as to when the world's chain of being will collapse under the pressure of having to generate capital. We may have two decades: we may have two minutes. The avalanche factor teaches us that we are simply not sophisticated enough to compute the myriad possible knock-on effects that could result from any one of the millions of environment shifting activities in which you and your colleagues are engaged.'

The 'avalanche factor' was a term coined in honour of Professor Blakely, whose death graphically demonstrated the fact that it is relatively easy to deduce a cause from an effect, but a mental nightmare to predict effects from causes. Who could possibly have figured out that a factory in Manchester would cause an avalanche? You'd need a brain the size of Heathrow airport. But, once it's happened, then it's comparatively easy to work backwards to the cause through a process of deduction. Causes do not become identified as causes until they have taken their effect. Meanwhile you've got a mountain on your head or an ocean completely covered in smokers' phlegm.

This was what the World Government of Money feared

most, the rogue eco-catastrophe, so unexpected, so obvious – after the event. The unpredictable disaster that would cheat them of their prize in the race for a solution to their predicament. The avalanche factor.

'It is because of this terrible uncertainty,' continued Professor Durf, 'that we have decided to reassess our timetable. It would be most regrettable, I think you'll agree, to achieve all that we have planned and then to die of skin cancer or suffocation on the morning that we had decided to push the button.'

This was a joke. Professor Durf was a smug fact-head. The sort of idiot who would annoy a whole cinema full of people by sighing and laughing loudly at the very scariest bits of a horror film, then come out at the end saying, so that everyone can hear, 'But it was absurd. It is a bio-physical impossibility for anti-matter to transpose itself in that manner.'

One of the reasons that Professor Durf had been selected for the project was that he had no friends and hence was less likely to breach security in idle chatter.

CRASH, BANG, WALLOP

Professor Durf continued:

'And so we have a problem, gentlemen, a very big problem. Out of the blue – or perhaps these days I should say out of the smog – the summer of Stark is upon us. It appears that we have to act *now*. Unfortunately the astronomical costing of the final stages of our project has always been computed as taking place over a number of years, leaving time to slowly accumulate spending capital and negotiate the prices of what we need from strength. Each one of you have slowly begun breaking up your resources and had intended to continue doing so for the foreseeable future. Unfortunately, the predictions of the Domesday Group and the fear of avalanches, has made it a necessity that the final assemblage takes place *immediately*, within months. No one in the consortium makes the hardware required for Stark, only governments do that. When we suddenly attempt to buy everything at once, we will force the prices sky high. We will create a sellers' market for the things we are trying to buy. In short, gentlemen, we won't be able to afford it.'

There was a nervous silence as the assembled company struggled with the meaning of the words 'can't afford'.

Durf was loving every minute of his brisk, bossy monologue. If he hadn't been an incredibly brainy person he would have been an officious one-eyed council clerk or something. Sly hated him. All right, Sly had decided to go along with the monstrous project because he could see the logic in it but Christ, you didn't have to enjoy it!

'Now hang on a minute,' interjected Tyron. 'What the hell is this "can't afford"? Why, if the Stark consortium were to liquify all its assets we could afford anything.'

'But of course, Mr Tyron,' replied the aggravating Durf, 'and, over years, it might even be possible for all of the members to do so, by bleeding small sections into the market piecemeal, as you have all been doing. But, let me ask you, Mr Tyron, if you wished to unload *all* of your holdings tomorrow, who would you sell to?'

'Well . . .' replied Tyron. But of course Durf, as usual, was only asking a rhetorical question.

'Mr Moorcock? Mr Slampacker? Mr Nagasyu? Lord Playing? Perhaps of course. But unfortunately at the same time *they* are trying to sell *their* companies to you. We all swap companies and no one comes out with a penny.'

The logic of Durf's point was beginning to sink in. He continued.

'Sure, a few of the Consortium would find buyers outside of Stark. Not all the money is in the conspiracy. But, a lot of the maverick, moveable, ready cash is. Basically, if we wanted to sell all the assets committed to Stark immediately – as we must, according to the Domesday Group – only Stark can afford to buy it. *Ipso facto*, we have an empasse.'

Well, there wasn't much anyone could say. This was, without a doubt, a bit of a blow.

'So, is that it?' said Sly. 'Nice meeting you all. Forget the whole thing?'

'Gentlemen,' said Durf, who was absolutely getting an erection from all this tension and attention, 'we have a solution to suggest to you. Mr Mai Wo, perhaps you would kindly explain.'

'Thank you, Professor Durf,' said the sanitized slave-owner, who was received warmly at the White House, Downing Street and any other centre of the civilized world he cared to visit.

'Gentlemen. We need to bring about a situation where the hardware we wish to purchase costs less than the capital that we are able to generate. The present market is buoyant, nobody can afford to buy us out and the things we need are hugely expensive.

'This, then, gentlemen is my suggestion. We *engineer* a crash. All together we begin to unload the very cream of our assets, creating a massive bear market. With the kind of mega-stock that we can load the shelf with, other lesser stock will become worthless. Who will buy John Citizen's meagre assets for a dollar when the mighty Slampacker group stocks are up for ten cents? Overnight a panic spiral of previously unknown proportions will develop. A vortex of selling will consume all the notional capital in the world. Small businesses, dependent on credit, will collapse. Little investors will go to the wall. As in previous crashes, only the very biggest will survive. Those with real assets, those who own the actual means of production will actually emerge even stronger because they will be all that's left. Us, gentlemen. Oh sure, on paper our fortunes will be cut by 90 per cent, but in *relative* terms, compared to the carnage around us, we will be richer than ever. Add to this the fact that the prices of the commodities that we wish to buy will also collapse in the general crash: governments will lose huge tax revenues as businesses go bankrupt and men are laid off: millions will turn to welfare, the politicians will be desperate to raise money. Then, gentlemen, it will be a *buyers'* market and *we* will be buying.

In the months following the collapse, which will be our site construction period, governments will be counting their pennies to buy food. I should imagine everything from solar panelling to orbital guidance satellites will be in the bargain bazaar.'

DEATH WARRANT

Nobody could deny that deliberately creating a great depression was a pretty huge concept.

'Well, it's never been done before,' said Ocker.

'Exciting, isn't it?' said Slampacker.

'You mean,' interjected Sly, 'that the average bloke's last experience before the ecological vanishing point will be one of crippling world slump?'

'Exactly,' said Mr Mai Wo.

'No final party; nothing like that?'

'We have to create the right financial conditions for our purposes.'

Well, you learn something every day. Sly had thought he was a hard bastard. You couldn't help but be impressed though – the little git had it all worked out.

'Nobody likes this, Moorcock,' said Slampacker, his tone, for the first time, something other than cosy and benign. 'You got a better suggestion? The world's fucked, somebody has to do something. I didn't notice any of your "average blokes" refusing to buy my burgers, or aerosols or use the electricity from the acid power stations. We're all in this together, everyone in the world, right? We just happen to be in a position to do something about it. Let me tell you, son, when the time comes to stand before God, I shan't hang my head in shame, no sir! Not unless every other body and soul on this planet does likewise!'

Sly noticed that the assembled company were all glaring at him with some hostility. He realized that his compatriots were very sensitive to the moral issues of what they were involved in, which was hardly surprising since they were in the process of organizing the most bastard trick in history.

'Listen, Mr Slampacker. I'm just catching up here, OK? Just getting the parameters. You won't find me wanting, and frankly I resent the implication that you might. I was told that all our discussions were to be frank and open, that's all I'm trying to be. I'm getting the land aren't I?'

'We hope,' added Tyron.

'Acquiring thousands of acres of Aboriginal sacred sites, discreetly, is not easy, especially when people stick their noses in where –'

'Now hold on boys, hold on,' interrupted Slampacker, back to his old soapy tones. 'I'm sure you're doing a wonderful job, Sly, wonderful. Let's not fall out over silly things, after all, we have a long way to go together. Now then, I believe we were discussing all this financial wheeler-dealing, right?'

'Yes, and I have something to say on the subject,' said Sly. He hadn't been going to bring it up but he felt the need to say something more to prove he was a dedicated part of things. 'It may be nothing, but there's a stupid journo on my back. She's probably just fishing around but she's got all my withdrawals and rationalizations noted down in her damn filofax like a shopping list. Now I'm sure that –'

'What's her name?' Slampacker snapped, again losing his teddy bear quality.

'I don't know, I got rid of her as soon as I could. Linda something.'

'Linda Reeve?' interjected Mai Wo, a note of surprise in his voice.

Sly turned to Mai Wo in surprise. 'She's tailing your deals too?'

'Just a call. She'd noticed I was pulling out and not putting back. She has a theory that the big players are losing their nerve, but she thinks it's all unilateral action. She's not looking for a conspiracy.'

'Oh yeah and how long's that going to last?' Slampacker now looked a lot more like the sort of man who would order the destruction of an entire rain-forest. 'This bitch has phoned my people too.'

'This is a serious irritation.' Mai Wo used the word 'irritation' with a chilly detachment that would have made anyone who cared for Linda Reeve very nervous indeed. 'If any hint that we are working together were to emerge before we create our crash, it's just possible that the powers that be could act against us. Close the banks, suspend trading, etc. That would be most inconvenient.' Mai Wo's language was always mild. 'Irritation', 'inconvenient', he might have been discussing a parking fine, but he wasn't. And if any insurance broker who heard him had been asked to provide cover for Linda Reeve, even Stark wouldn't have been able to afford the premiums.

'We need to know what she knows, what she thinks and what she's said.' Slampacker clearly wanted to end discussions on the subject. 'She works for the *London Financial Telegraph*. You own that don't you, Ocker?'

'Yes, I own it. I own her boss and I own her. This situation is simply not a problem, we shouldn't even be discussing it. Tomorrow I will have my people look into it and deal with it. There'll be no need for anything drastic but you won't be hearing from her again.'

With that the discussion moved on to the other business at hand – Durf's plans for assembling and distributing the required hardware. It all hinged on Tyron and Sly as the consortium members closest to the centre of things. Sly was to carry on with the business of acquiring the land and having done so was to start with all haste, to prepare it. Meanwhile, Tyron would provide a dumping-off point for the equipment that must soon now begin flowing into Western Australia. He had a massive mining consideration which was all played out. It should be possible to store pretty limitless stuff there and pass it off as a consolidation point for Tyron Mining paraphernalia . . .

A MAN WITH A FUTURE

Finally, the meeting ended. Sly decided not to stay. He

wanted a change of company. Nagasyu's people took him across to the city in a launch and he walked out into the hot streets in order to collect his thoughts. He needed to reconnect with reality. And yet, as he looked about himself; the buildings; the history; the milling crowds, he realized that Stark would soon become the new reality and all this would be a memory.

It was so difficult to comprehend. Sly tried to make himself grasp it. Make himself really take it seriously. As he wandered about he kept telling himself that he was looking at the past, like an old film. It was time to consider the future.

Who would he save? Who did he love enough? Who could he tell? Anyone? Who would he confide in and protect, and love for ever? No one, that was who. Sly didn't love anyone, that was the truth of it. He didn't love anyone and nobody loved him.

By God though, he could make somebody love him. Couldn't he just? With what he knew, with what he had to offer, he could make somebody love him till the end of time. But who?

THE POST

Chrissy sat back on the sofa in her apartment and prepared to luxuriate over her letter. She loved getting mail and a letter was something to be savoured. Not work stuff obviously, although such is the instinctive pleasure of getting anything through the post that even that is better than nothing.

Perhaps it is something to do with the fact that when you're a kid, the only things you could ever get through the post were utterly exciting. Strange how childhood impressions linger, often remaining more pervasive than the experiences of later life. It's a pretty safe bet that 90 per cent of the mail any particular individual gets will be either dull, depressing or downright disastrous. The bills, the summonses, the junk . . .

But, very occasionally, comes that rare delight; a personal letter. And the remote possibility of that happy event is enough to make every trip to the mat to pick up the post a potential thrill, despite the near statistical certainty of disappointment. It seems that the distant echo of those childhood birthday cards, some containing book tokens and even postal orders, can still call to us from across the years. Old auntie what's-her-name would be pleased to know that her small, kind gesture so long ago had such a lifelong resonance.

STUFF TO DO

Chrissy put the bill in the 'stuff to do' pile. She was very together about bills. At least she was very together about putting bills in the 'stuff to do' pile. After that things got a little looser. The 'stuff to do' pile was rarely less than an inch thick. It had a presence, that pile; a spirit of its own. Sometimes it seemed to be staring at Chrissy like some evil priest, gleefully reminding her of her inadequacy. It would mither her whenever she felt good, deliberately deflating her. After she'd finished an overdue article or done some research, she would glance across the room and there the pile would be, shouting, 'All right, fair enough, you've done that but what about me! You've *still* got loads of stuff to do in the "stuff to do" pile.'

The strange thing is that when she finally did attack the pile, it was so easy. Cheque-book, envelopes, stamps and in an hour it was over. The relief of an empty 'stuff to do' pile was one of the most lovely sights in the world. But, despite this knowledge – the knowledge that if she just got on with it it would be over in an instant – the pile always grew again. No matter how often she swore to deal with the bills more regularly, it always took a final reminder to make her tackle the pile. And so, for the want of a few minutes self-discipline, she allowed a terrible malignant beastie with fifteen envelope-shaped heads to live in the corner of her apartment.

JUNK

Chrissy wasn't too bothered about the 'stuff to do' pile on the evening that she got the letter. Why, it was barely teetering yet, the venom that the monster spat was of little consequence whilst it had no final reminder to reproach her with. The pile could wait.

She tossed the junk mail in the bin, unopened. And in doing so, Chrissy unwittingly made a joke and a mockery of the lives, loves and endeavours of countless people whom she would never know. In that casual gesture she trampled upon an awesome human achievement and upon great sacrifices contributed by the natural world. Why didn't she stop to think? Why didn't she dare to care? What a bitch.

If only she could have seen them, seen their disappointment as she hurled their creation back in their honest faces. The person who cleared the land to plant the fir trees; the persons who planted and tore up the fir trees every second or third year; the drivers and the ships' captains who got the trees to the mill; the thousands who work in the mills and in the huge pulping plants and paper factories – if only Chrissy could have seen them she would have wept bitter tears of self reproach to have dismissed their lives so casually.

The copywriter? Did Chrissy not care that he had spent so many lonely hours trying to think of a tempting way to get her to accept ten days free home perusal of a fifteen volume history of the Wild West? The printer and the four colour offset litho process of which he was so proud – was his life to be just a pointless joke because of Chrissy? The animals and insects that were wiped out when billions of acres of forest and moorland were turned over to single crop, factory, fir tree farming. Did they give their lives in vain?

One can only hope and pray that those involved never discover that after the monumental worldwide effort and the truly awesome consumption of natural resources that went into bringing a piece of junk mail to Chrissy's door, she simply threw it away. Gone, gone, gone; all their hopes and dreams and sacrifices, rejected in that one contemptuous gesture. They must never know, for they would put up their arms in horror (or spindly leggy things in the case of the insects) and say, as Zimmerman would say, 'What *is* the point!? No, I mean really, what *is* the point?'

Over a year, as a moderately high-earner in the US – the country which wrote the original handbook on pointless consumption – Chrissy would receive between five hundred and a thousand bits of junk mail. Plus over a hundred 'free' newspapers, perhaps fifty cab firm cards and fifty offers from local estate agents to dispose of her property. She, like most people, threw the lot away unopened.

LETTER FROM LONDON

Her letter was from Linda Reeve in London. Linda did not

often write but when she did it was normally something pretty good.

On glancing at the opening paragraph however, Chrissy felt a momentary irritation because it was immediately clear that Linda was still harping on about this business about Nagasyu and Tyron and Slampacker, and all the other assorted billionaires she was putting in her book. However, as Chrissy read on, despite herself, she began to wonder whether there might not be something in it. Linda had included a copy of the article which her editor had rejected, plus a series of less specific examples detailing withdrawals of smaller sums of money, or where some reinvestment had resulted. Chrissy had to admit that it read pretty well. Somewhere, somehow, in recent months, thirty billion US dollars worth of stock had been converted into cash by a smallish group of individuals and simply disappeared.

In her article, Linda seemed to be suggesting that perhaps a collective fear was sweeping the upper echelons of the financial world and that some of the big men wanted their money where they could see it. But could they see it? Linda couldn't, and nor could Chrissy. It was unthinkable that they had simply put it in the bank. People used to watching their bucks divide and grow like amoeba were not going to put up with 7 per cent a year in a deposit account. And yet, none of those concerned had any major, high-profile project underway that would require heavy cash flow. Where had it gone?

Unlike Linda, who was deeply conservative, Chrissy was a bit of a radical. She did not have a very high opinion of the people she regularly studied and wrote about. Therefore, Chrissy did not have much time for Linda's theory about paranoia. These guys' religion was chasing money, they weren't just going to pull out. They'd screw everyone else in the world before they'd do that. So what was it? It would be wonderful if there was something illegal going on. Drugs would be terrific, but reason told her that this was out of the question. The people Linda mentioned were too big to bother to take risks like that. Arms seemed a possibility.

Perhaps it was a huge global arms syndicate! Linda had produced twenty-three names, that would be very big indeed for a syndicate, especially since all the people involved were big enough to play a lone hand.

It did look interesting, Chrissy couldn't deny it . . . Maybe she should take a look? On the other hand, maybe she should finish the article that she was writing about the aftermath of the unprecedently hot northern summer (suntan lotion and ice-cream futures were very big). Then again, she was long overdue to write to her sister in Wisconsin. Maybe she should do that . . . And she hadn't done her aerobic home workout in *seven months* – God she was definitely going to have a heart attack. Also, the toilet needed cleaning in the corner. The 'stuff to do' pile seemed to have grown, nothing had been added in the few minutes since she had last looked but it had definitely got bigger . . .

'OK,' it hissed at her maliciously, fluttering its papery arms, 'So there ain't no final bills, so what? How about that insurance form? Huh? And the new cheque card application? You still have that to do don't ya? And the register of voters, that's two weeks old already, do you want to get disenfranchised? You will be, if you don't do it! Come on, Chrissy, look at me! There is so much *stuff to do* in the "stuff to do" pile'.

THE HONEST, DEDICATED JOURNO IS A RARE AND ENDANGERED SPECIES

The next day, during her first cup of coffee, Chrissy thought she'd ring Linda to apologize for being so dismissive on the phone before and say that having read the letter she now thought that perhaps there might be something in it.

Chrissy was hoping that she could persuade Linda to send the programs she had used for her book on the rich guys, down the line so that Chrissy too could pick up quickly on their movements wherever they were dealing. This would be stretching a pen-pal friendship quite a long way. After all, it would have taken Linda a very long time to put those programs together. Still, if Linda wanted Chrissy's help . . .

'Hello, Linda Reeve's phone,' the voice said.

'Hi, is Linda around?'

Looking back, Chrissy was sure that she had sensed something wrong even in that moment.

'Uhm, might I ask your business?'

'My name's Chrissy Waldorf, I'm on the *Wall Street Examiner*, we're friends.'

'Uhm . . . well, she's unavailable at the moment,' the man replied.

'Well, can you get her to call me?'

'Look, I'm awfully sorry, we're rather upset at this end, I'm afraid Linda's dead . . .'

Chrissy ran cold. Maybe there is something in sixth-sense, she felt like she'd known even before she picked up the phone. She did not reply, her mind was racing. The man on the other end clearly felt obliged to offer some further explanation – he had been doing it all morning.

'Dreadful business. It seems that she surprised a burglar and, well, uhm, he killed her . . .'

'A burglar?' said Chrissy, 'in her apartment?'

'Yes, that's right.'

'Did he get away with anything?'

The man at the other end was slightly put off that this was the American woman's first consideration. But, there you go, that was Yanks for you.

'I believe it was a very professional job. A great deal was –'

'Listen, are you at her desk?' Chrissy spoke urgently. Maybe poor Linda had been murdered coincidentally. First the letter, now this . . .

'Well, as a matter of fact I am but –'

'Will you do me a favour? Lock it, put everything inside and lock it right now and keep the key.'

The man at the other end explained that he would be happy to but that he saw no point as it had already been emptied and the top had been completely cleared. All that remained was a half-empty box of chocolates and he didn't suppose that she wanted that. No, he didn't know who had done it. It had certainly been done when he arrived that morning. Perhaps the police . . .

Chrissy checked with the police. Then, posing as a relative, she checked with the editor. Neither knew who had emptied the desk. The editor thought perhaps relatives or one of Linda's colleagues, really he was very busy and everybody was very upset.

After that it was evening in Britain and Chrissy had to wait out the rest of the day and until early the next morning for London to wake up again. When it did she checked as best she could with the relatives, managing to contact Linda's mother. Mrs Reeve was clearly strung-out but hanging on. She believed that it was important that one contained oneself. Refusing to break down she dealt politely and clearly with Chrissy, who claimed to be a closer friend than she was. Unfortunately, Mrs Reeve knew nothing of who had emptied the desk, nor did any of Linda's colleagues that Chrissy managed to speak to. None of them were particularly interested either. It appeared that as far as anyone knew, Linda did not keep much of interest in her desk.

This was not the point as far as Chrissy was concerned. The point was that it had been emptied and nobody knew who had done it. Clearly a stranger had emptied it, hence obviously they thought she *might* have something of interest in it. Interesting enough to risk a search. Interesting enough, it seemed, to kill her.

The police report made it clear that the burglar was a professional. There had been a highly accomplished, no-nonsense entry, a swift, silent clear out, the lot. If that was the case, thought Chrissy, why had he killed her? Professional burglars are rarely murderers. You don't last long in a job if you start killing people. It's the one-off thug who normally panics and lashes out. The conviction was firmly growing in Chrissy's mind that this fellow had killed first and burgled afterwards.

PRIVATE INVESTIGATIONS

DISCOVERING MURDER

Linda's last letter to Chrissy, those few pieces of paper that Chrissy held in her hand, was, it seemed, the single and only piece of Linda's work left in existence. Chrissy felt cold even to think about it.

It had not been difficult to work this out. Chrissy had spoken a number of times to Linda's parents who were kind, helpful people. They had found out what she asked them to. Linda's flat, it seemed, still contained an awful lot of paper, love letters from Linda's one affair, bills, her attempts at poetry, but there were no papers relating to any aspect of Linda's work left whatsoever. Nothing, not a note, not an old article, not a floppy disc. Her entire career had disappeared.

'But I really can't see that it's at all sinister,' Linda's father, a quiet, sad voiced, ex-army officer, said. 'The police assure us that the burglars were very thorough. They really gutted and filleted the place. Even took the clocks, anything of value, the food mixer, the more expensive clothes, everything.'

Of course they did, Chrissy thought to herself. The only way to avoid arousing police suspicion was to make what was in fact a premeditated murder, appear to have been committed absolutely and indisputably for reasons of professional burglary.

Any burglar together enough to remove only the expensive clothes, is together enough to know that a girl's journalistic research is worthless to him . . . Unless, of course, it isn't.

That had been their mistake, that was what made Chrissy absolutely certain that something terribly wrong was going on.

They had constructed the façade of a serious, tidy, professional burglary in order that the police would presume that they could see at a glance what had been stolen. There was no ransacking here, no shadowy motive. It was all very clear, the police would not think to start looking for scraps of paper and note books that they did not even know existed. But Chrissy knew they existed. They must do, Linda was a very conscientious journalist. It was unthinkable that she would not have research data at home. Therefore, this supposedly pragmatic and professional burglar had taken the trouble to sort out and steal something he could not possibly want. The burglary *must* be a front, and what's more, a front based on the assumption that only the people who took out the contract on Linda were aware that her research was in some way compromising. This meant that Chrissy had a short start on the killers. Clearly they could not know that Linda had passed on the body of her research to Chrissy, or, Chrissy presumed, she would already be dead too. For the moment at least, although 'they' remained invisible to Chrissy, at least she was invisible to them.

Poor Colonel (retired) and Mrs Reeve were bewildered by Chrissy's questions, but it was obvious to them that this strange American girl thought that something was wrong.

'Look, if there's anything we can do . . .' the Colonel said, having to make an effort to keep his voice steady. 'Linda really was a marvellous sort, you know . . . terrific . . . really terrific. What I'm saying is, if you think that there's something, well, uhm, fishy in all this . . .?'

Chrissy reminded herself that the enemy had already killed once, killed a girl for reading a computer screen. She did not wish to provoke further tragedy.

'No, really, please forget it, Colonel. It's nothing, just a little project Linda and I were working on . . . about beetroot,' she added for some unknown reason. 'I suppose it's selfish of me, I just didn't want to have to re-do her work, that's all. Sorry . . .'

'Beetroot you say?' said Colonel Reeve absently, '. . . Linda never liked beetroot, but nobody does really, do they? I mean, not honestly. Stains the lettuce and puts you off . . .'

Chrissy excused herself as gently as she could and put the phone down, leaving the old Colonel thinking about beetroot and his dead daughter and trying not to cry.

FOR THE LOVE OF A GOOD WOMAN

CD was also puzzled. He reckoned he understood Silvester Moorcock. He had more in common with him than the same taste in women. CD could spot a smooth operator when he saw one. After all, it took one to know one. Of course, CD acknowledged that there were differences between the two of them. For instance, Sly was worth several billion and CD had about forty bucks —but CD did not believe in getting hung up on minor details, they obscure the broader view.

Rachel and Walter had pretty much accepted Sly's protestations of innocence regarding the Nazi attack. After all, there was no reason for the Bullens Creek police chief to lie about it. But CD wondered why Sly had bothered to go to the extent of trying to prove it. After all, what were they to him?

CD pondered this question in the week or so after their meeting at Facefulls and the only explanation he could come up with was that Sly had something to hide. How, CD asked himself, would an entirely innocent multimillionaire react to being confronted by four penniless scruffs accusing him of promoting fascist race attacks for personal gain? Well, CD reckoned that there was a pretty strong chance that he would sue them. He might have them beaten up, he would certainly tell them to fuck off, what seemed unlikely was that he would ask them to join him for a drink and give the craziest one his hamburger. And yet this was exactly what had happened. The man had positively cooed at them, going to quite a bit of trouble to prove that he had not been involved in the attack. More than that, he had exposed to them what was clearly a rather dubious relationship with a police chief, purely in order to show some strange hippy that he had nothing to do with something. In CD's mind this suggested extremely strongly indeed that Sly *did* have something to do with it.

Love is a great motivator. CD still loved Rachel, truly and achingly. If only the strength of the love that people feel when it is reciprocated could be as intense and obsessive as the love we feel when it is not: then marriages would truly be made in heaven.

With every day it hurt more. The longing, the frustration; the frustration was definitely the worst. He absolutely ached to make love to Rachel, he would have done anything to see her naked. He would sit up long into the night tearfully whining to Zimm about it and drinking Zimm's home-brewed beer. CD was lucky to have such a willing confidante. Normally the ridiculously over-in-love are an utter and total drag to their friends and intimates, but Zimm loved hearing about CD's problems – it made him feel better about not having any balls.

Anyway, suffice it to say, CD had only got involved with the whole protest thing in order to endear himself to Rachel, first as a hippy and then following into association with Zimm and Walter and becoming an activist. He reckoned now he was in, he might as well go the whole hog. In for a penny, in for a pound, so to speak. If he could find something out, come up with something interesting, then maybe he would be worthy of her. Then maybe she would love him and let him up her dress.

She wouldn't, of course, the world doesn't work like that, but love is blind and hope springs eternal.

CD could not think what it was he might find out. Whether Silvester Moorcock was involved with Nazis perhaps? Why he wanted the land so much? Maybe nothing at all, but for the love of a good woman he was at least prepared to have a bash. He only had one lead; this skinhead bloke, therefore he would have to follow that.

CONNECTIONS

Even before the terrible news of her death, Chrissy had been dubious about Linda's naïve contention that the various financial dealings that she had pinpointed were unconnected. Linda's theory that a kind of atmospheric change was occurring in the money markets and hence causing a bunch of people to act in exactly the same way, but independently, was far too airy-fairy an idea for Chrissy to give any credence to at all. In her mind, Linda could not have it both ways. If the various deals *were* unconnected, then they were of no significance. Conversely, if they were of significance then they *had* to be connected. Therefore, since, due to the manner of Linda's death Chrissy had already satisfied herself that something significant was going on, it had to follow that the various billionaires isolated in Linda's reserarch were, in fact, all in cahoots with one another. If this was the case then Linda had clearly stumbled on something enormous, which was why she had been killed.

A quick bit of mental arithmetic was enough to make Chrissy weak at the knees. A significant percentage of all the money in the world appeared to be working together. What's more, it was doing it in secret and it was prepared to kill to keep that secret. What the hell was going on? Chrissy's mind reeled at the possibilities. So far they had only released a tiny potential of their spending power. If they wanted to, collectively, these men had the power to purchase entire countries. Christ Almighty! Capitalist predators working together. It was contrary to the whole system. But what power they would have! They could buy out national debts, hold governments to ransom, close down whole economies if they wanted to. Had these people got bored with making cars and stereos and aerosols? were they going to start making history?

Clearly speculating as to what they were up to was fairly pointless. First of all she needed to firmly establish the connections. She did not have remotely enough at the moment to make any kind of case. And what if she did?

putting the murder aside, people were legally allowed to move their money about if they liked. It was what they were planning to do with it that she had to discover.

She knew that she could not say a word until she had something. Once you put your head above the parapet these people clearly shot at it. Maybe what they were planning would count as some kind of insurgency, treason perhaps? They were international figures – could one be treasonous against the whole world? Maybe the C I A were already on the case, it was certainly their territory, but these people were so enormous perhaps they owned the C I A? Maybe they owned the President? they certainly paid to get him elected. Chrissy realized that she had nothing and could trust no one. She was on her own.

She quit her job – she was freelance anyway – cashed in her stocks and shares and began to dig – to dig as secretively and as anonymously as she possibly could. She had no desire to share Linda's fate.

Using the names in Linda's letter, Chrissy began to try to trace the movements of the super-rich over the past few months, trying to establish that connection. It was tough, tough work, but not impossible. These were very high profile people. One useful source was the huge number of glossy magazines about money that had proliferated as the yuppy decade ran its course. They were basically gossip pretending to be theory and criticism, hence they chronicled peoples' movements when they could just to fill up the hundreds of useless shit pages that they published every month.

Hotels were another good source. It was comparatively simple for Chrissy, posing as a reporter from one of these appalling mags, to persuade publicity-minded managers to discreetly confide the names of the more illustrious members of the business community who saw fit to patronize their establishments. Also, Chrissy had a friend in American Diner. It was a big favour, but she managed to persuade him to divulge one or two details concerning where various Platinum cards had been active over short periods of time.

Eventually, hollow-eyed and a half a stone lighter, she pinpointed the evening in Los Angeles.

She was in a position to prove that at least fourteen of the names mentioned in Linda's letter had been in Los Angeles for less than ten hours on the same evening. Obviously this was not conclusive, LA is a pretty vital business centre, you would expect millionaires to congregate there. But it was all she had. Praying that they had not met at a private house, Chrissy started to contact all the major hotels and restaurants in LA. She chose Silvester Moorcock's name, they probably wouldn't bother phoning Australia to check him out.

'Hallo, my name is Patty, I am the personal assistant in the US to Mr Silvester Moorcock, the Australian industrialist. I believe he dined at your establishment on the —th of the —th this year. We cannot locate a solid gold watch that was inscribed 'to Sly, stay real, Jimmy Carter'. It is of considerable sentimental value and Mr Moorcock wonders if he lost it that night and if you had found it. Obviously, if you had you would not have known who to send it on to.'

'I'm sorry Patty,' (this was LA remember), 'but we know of no watch.'

'Oh well, in that case I wonder if I have the correct establishment. Could you possibly check with the manager whether Mr Moorcock dined with you that night.'

Chrissy reckoned it was a pretty fair bet that you did not get to be manager of a top LA restaurant without remembering your billionaires. Time and again Chrissy stuck out. Many apologies but Mr Moorcock did not dine at so and so's that night . . .

'I would definitely have remembered, Patty, because that was the night King Hussein of Jordan took the upper-lounge room.'

Finally, to Chrissy's delight, her perseverance paid off. She dialled 'California Dreaming' and found herself speaking to a very superior *maître d'*, who remembered the night clearly.

'Yes, Ms, Mr Moorcock certainly dined with us that night. I recall Sir chose swan, a very wise choice for Sir to make, if I might opine. However, I'm afraid we have no record of Sir's watch and may I assure you that our staff are utterly trustworthy.'

Chrissy grabbed her chance.

'But of course. Mr Moorcock wanted me to make a point of mentioning the quality of the staff and the excellence of the swan. It's difficult these days to find an establishment that can properly accommodate such an important group of men.'

Chrissy was terrified that he would reply that Moorcock had dined alone, or with a lady friend or whatever. He didn't, she wanted to hug him.

'We do our very best, Ms, and I'm happy to say that our very best *is* the best. Mr Slampacker always honours us with his patronage when he entertains.'

She had it! A connection . . . Very gently Chrissy tried for more, she didn't want to be greedy but she had to get as much as she could.

'Catering must be hell I should think. So many cultures. I'll bet Mr Nagasyu wanted raw fish or something . . .'

'I do not recall what Mr Nagasyu ordered,' the *maître d'* said coldly. Clearly his suspicions had finally been aroused. He was wondering whether Chrissy was a gossip journalist, she would get no more out of him. But that was fine, she had got enough.

A VISIT TO THE MASTER RACE

Chrissy's research had not been much fun but CD would have happily swapped it for the task that he had set himself. Taking a bus to Perth and then walking out to the suburbs to find a brutal thug who was on bail for criminal assault, was not CD's idea of a great evening.

He had taken great care to prepare himself for the part he had to play because he was well aware that if this Gordon Gordon fellow smelt a fraud, he would be in serious trouble. Getting your head kicked in type of trouble.

It had not taken him long to find out where the White

Supremacy People's Fair Deal Party hung out. A trip to the library to look up some old newspaper reports of Gordon's previous escapades had informed him that this unpleasant group of people frequented the Old Sydney Hotel. So that was where he was going. He had had his hair cut short – not a crop, more like a soldier would have it – and he wore a suit with a union jack tie left over from his brief mod-revival period.

His plan was to play a pom, and boldly approach Gordon, masquerading as a representative of British fascism.

He entered the pub, effecting an arrogant sneer that he hoped would suggest that he did not want trouble but if that was the way anyone wanted it, they could have it. CD was a small man but he knew how to walk tall. He needed to walking into a pub like the Old Sydney. It was what is called a 'Lingerie' pub, this being a place where you watch a semi-strip show which goes only as far as sexy lingerie. This prudish reticence does not indicate any fledgling moral principles on the part of the management, rather the local by-laws that forbid full on strips in the pubs. Apparently the strip club owners were threatening to put in dart boards and pool tables.

There were flags on the walls and various weapons, also a few sporting trophies and framed photos of long forgotten footie teams. The owner or brewer involved had clearly asked himself the question: 'What do men like?'

Basing his assumptions principally on his own tastes, the landlord had come up with the answers; wanking, war and sport. Hence it was along these lines that he had decided to theme his pub. Of course very soon his pub was full of war-mad wankers talking about sport. The boss often congratulated himself on his astute target marketing. It did make for a pretty unpleasant atmosphere, of course. If you stood at the bar you could almost feel the bitter and unfulfilled macho pretensions of the clientele – every one of whom by rights should have been a top mercenary in Angola or a football star.

CD spotted Gordon Gordon easily. He sat alone, watching the lingerie girl wear her lingerie. He was wearing his lingerie too, in a way. Inevitably it was a hot night and he was sat in his vest. He sat there with his muscles permanently flexed. He did not want people to know this of course, the idea being that the rippling state of his arms actually represented Gordon in a state of relaxation. His tattoos were a fairly comprehensive collection of daggers, eagles, flags and guns. He had a bunch of empty glasses in front of him. He didn't let them clear any away; he liked people to know how much he had drunk, which was plenty. His near-bald pate gleamed in the dullness as it reflected the changing coloured lights – they were the only bright thing in his head.

The management had thoughtfully provided these lights in order to add a touch of theatricality and glamour to a show which, when all was said and done, consisted of a girl walking around a stage in her underwear.

CD ordered a glass of water. This was a calculated part of his pose. Despite appearances to the contrary, he had to presume that Gordon was not a total imbecile. Organizing a political party, even a small and stupid one, must take at least a degree of native cunning. Therefore CD had determined to create a slightly more subtle persona than might be expected. There have, in the past, been police efforts to infiltrate organizations such as Gordon Gordon's. CD had to presume that Gordon would be ready for the obvious.

'Gordon Gordon?' He stood slightly behind the big thug, not a very convivial position from which to affect an introduction. At the very least it was extremely rude; at worst, deliberately putting Gordon at such a disadvantage hinted at potential violence. This was what CD wanted, it was nerve-racking and took a lot of bottle, but in the long run CD reckoned that it would be safer than trying to arse-lick the guy.

'You obviously know who I am, or you wouldn't be asking,' Gordon answered without turning around. He could occasionally play quite a cool hand and if he had had a completely different personality he might have been quite an acceptable member of society.

'So why don't you tell me what you want or fuck off,' he added.

CD moved around from behind, but Gordon did not look at him. He kept staring with bored detachment at the girl in the knickers. He was pretending to chew gum.

'I've come a long way to see you, Mr Gordon,' said CD, affecting his best laid-back cockney accent, hoping that Gordon would presume he was a cop.

'If you're going to do me, do me, mate. But watch your back when I get out, all right? If you're here for a chat, go and stuff it up your arse.'

Lots of Perth cops were ex-poms, and that, along with the suit and the studied arrogance, had done the trick.

'I'm not the filth, Mr Gordon, although I've done for a couple in my time. I represent the British race-warrior, white rock band 'Skrew, Fuk, Die and Kill'. I presume you've heard of them.'

Gordon turned for the first time to look at CD. He was suddenly very interested. He had all three of Skrew, Fuk, Die and Kill's albums, a tasteful little hat trick of two chord thrash-metal turkeys entitled respectively 'Final Solution', 'Blood on the Club' and 'JuFuker'. CD, of course, could not have known how much Gordon was into this band but he had presumed that Gordon would at least have heard of them. 'The Skrew', as their few fans referred to them, were four deeply violent and utterly talentless individuals whom the gutter-press had managed to raise from total obscurity to some vague international renown, without anyone hearing a note they played. A number of months previously there had been terrible scenes of violence in Europe when England had been playing in the Cup. The British press had gone bananas claiming that civilization would end immediately if the birch, the stocks, and death by stoning were not instantly re-introduced. In the midst of this, Skrew, Fuk, Die and Kill, who had not even been in Europe at the time, were delighted to find themselves picked up by sensation-hungry hacks as an example of the terrible spectre of resurgent fascism. Thus it was that a band, who until then could draw no more than a couple of hundred punters on their best night, suddenly found themselves instantly feared and famous, with questions being asked about them in parliament.

'What have you got to do with The Skrew?' asked Gordon eagerly. He was a true fan, he had even listened to both sides of the albums and had spent hours trying to decipher the lyrics.

'You're probably aware that they're fairly closely associated with the White British National Movement. I'm the party's international co-ordinator. May I join you, Mr Gordon?'

'All right, yeah, fine. The name's Gordon.'

'I'm aware of that, Mr Gordon,' said CD, happy of the chance to muddy their initial contact with a bit of confusion.

'No, call me Gordon, my first name's Gordon.'

'Oh, I'm sorry Mr . . .? uhm?'

'Gordon. Mr Gordon. My surname's Gordon too. Look my name's Gordon Gordon, all right, so call me Gordon, just Gordon, got it. Look, do you want a drink?' Gordon had been through this many times before and it was a source of deep annoyance to him.

'No thank you, I don't drink. We're under a lot of pressure at home, yids, reds, filth. I'm a prime target. I find it safer to stay completely in control. It is my belief that each pint knocks two dan off my black belt.' This was pushing the bullshit needle close to critical but CD believed rightly that Gordon was excited and wanted to believe in him.

'I'll come straight to the point, Gordon. The White British National Movement are anxious to start setting up some form of loose International. We see no reason why the Trotskyists should have a monopoly on co-operation.' It did not matter whether Gordon had heard of the Fourth International or not, CD knew it would sound convincing and it did. Gordon was thrilled, this was the sort of thing he dreamed of; being part of something big and strong and dignified, instead of just the dickhead who kept getting put in prison for hitting black people.

'Yes, well, the white race is racially . . .' Gordon would have liked to have spoken with the same confidence and articulacy as the pom but he wasn't up to it . . . 'the white race is racially . . . white . . . isn't it? I mean, that's what it's about, isn't it?'

'Exactly,' said CD, beginning to relax. 'Australia is very important to us. Europe's OK but, let's be honest, when all is said and done, they're a bunch of wops. Apart from the Germans, they're poor quality stuff, worse than the yanks in a ruck. Australia, on the other hand, produces the best fighting men in the world. Everyone knows that.'

Gordon swelled with pride. This was the sort of thing he could listen to all night. CD sipped his water, his eyes narrowed and he glanced about meaninglessly. He was attempting to give the impression that he was the sort of person who found it wise always to be aware of who was standing close by. It didn't work, Gordon thought perhaps the flashing coloured lights were bothering him. CD continued . . .

'Now then, the first move we are considering is some kind of cultural link. The Skrew have agreed to do an Australian tour as part of a recruitment drive. What we need is a man on this end. A man we can trust. A man who knows the local filth, who knows the top lefties, the wogs, everything. A bloke who can contain things if there's any real trouble, and of course provoke things if there isn't enough. You see, Gordon, most bands only require security but we also require provocation. Let's face it, if there's no trouble, nobody will know we were there.'

'I've got your drift, mate, no worries.' This was one of the most thrilling conversations Gordon Gordon had ever had.

'So we were wondering, Mr Gordon, if with all your extensive experience and local knowledge, whether it would be possible for you . . .'

Gordon's little piggy eyes were bright. He couldn't believe it, The Skrew . . . links with top pom Nazis . . . it was all his fantasies come true. CD was about to drop his bombshell.

'. . . to recommend someone for the job. We can't think of a single person who would be up to it.'

Even though he was dealing with a thug, CD almost felt sorry for Gordon, whose jaw dropped, increasing his already Neanderthal appearance, he was so disappointed he could have cried.

CD's tactics were clever. He knew that this fellow had told the police nothing of the attack on Bullens Creek other than that he had done it on principle. If there was any more to it than that, for instance if Silvester Moorcock was involved, Gordon Gordon wasn't telling, at the moment. CD had to get him to want CD's trust and goodwill more than any previous liaisons he had made. Gordon Gordon had to desperately want something that CD had.

CD wiggled the carrot.

'To tell you the truth, Mr Gordon,' he said, trying to sound hard and icy. 'We had originally considered asking you.'

Gordon started like a puppy, his eyes were pleading.

'Oh yes, the Grand Fascist Co-ordinating Counsel of the White National British Movement, Foreign Penetration Section,' in for a penny, in for a pound thought CD, 'and the band themselves, were very interested in asking you to take on this highly responsible job. A job which might eventually be seen as having played a small part in the inevitable world triumph of the Norse Peoples. A job, I might add, that would carry a not insignificant wage plus travel with the band and full expenses.' Gordon's tongue was nearly hanging out. 'But then there was the incident, wasn't there?'

'Incident? What incident! Who's been bad-mouthing me? I will fucking kill any man, woman or . . . man that has been bad-mouthing me!'

'Bullens Creek Abo' bash, Gordon. Bit of a mess, wasn't it? Bit of a cock-up don't you think? Can't afford cock-ups in this game, Gordon. You only get the one chance. What were you thinking of? Getting yourself busted over some meaningless, piss-poor little bunch of blacks. We thought you had plans, Gordon, we thought you were a bigger operator than that.'

'It wasn't my idea!' Gordon blurted. 'I was doing a job.'

CD had it! He *knew* there had been something more.

'Oh yes, Gordon? Well, that might change things considerably. Might. What's your story?'

CD was very surprised at what he heard. He would have bet money that Gordon would tell him that the multimillionaire Silvester Moorcock had employed Gordon and his thugs in order to try and intimidate the Aboriginals away from Bullens Creek. Instead he learnt that Aristos Tyron, the brother of a completely different multimillionaire, had put Gordon up to it, paid for the transport and made a very generous donation to party funds.

This was an exciting but confusing discovery. Gordon could help him no further; he did not know why Aristos Tyron should be interested in Bullens Creek; he did not know whether Tyron's important elder brother, Ocker, was involved. He had not, at any time, heard Silvester Moorcock mentioned in connection with Bullens Creek. All Gordon knew was that he had been asked to do the job, take the heat, and keep quiet about it – of course it didn't matter telling CD about it.

So that was it! CD took his leave, promising that the question of the job with the band would be reconsidered in the light of what Gordon had told him.

Outside CD hurried away as quickly as he could. It had been a pretty horrible experience but he was very pleased with himself. His next move would be much more pleasant and a lot more expensive. He would have to talk to Aristos Tyron.

CRASH

Chrissy had now assembled what could perhaps be called the beginnings of a case. She was in a position to prove that some of the richest people in the world appeared to be slowly dumping their shares and pulling out of traditional areas of investment. As a financial analyst she could demonstrate that this was very strange behaviour and contrary to the interests of those involved. She was also able to prove that this same group of individuals, who were rivals in business and had no particular record of friendship, had all met together for dinner in Los Angeles. What's more, there were firm indications that a similar but partially different group had met later in Singapore. Finally, she could point out that her colleague, Linda Reeve, who had first picked up on the issue, and perhaps unwisely had allowed those she was trailing to know of her interest, had been murdered. No one knew by whom but the circumstantial evidence seemed to be mounting up.

That was her case, something and nothing. What to do next?

Chrissy was sitting speculating on this question, trying to come up with even one course of action apart from confronting those involved, which she firmly believed would mean her death. The only idea she could think of was taking her story to the C I A or the F B I. But who could be trusted? Anyone? And would they be interested? After all, even she didn't have the faintest idea what was behind it all. What's more, even though the sums involved were colossal, they had not yet reached the level for real mischief. It was the *potential* in this unholy alliance that she feared.

The morning that Chrissy was thinking about this, all over New York people began to fly. They began to fly downwards, because they had lost everything.

For this was the morning that the bottom dropped out of the market. This was the morning on which were recorded the largest single price drops in history. It was a Thursday. A Thursday that came to be known as 'Oh my God we're all going to starve to death Thursday'.

All over the world prices were plummeting and so were distraught financiers. The Stark consortium had made its move.

WELCOME TO THE
PLEASURE DOME

CD could feel it two streets away, coming up through his trouser legs even through the floor of the car, like someone was playing bass drum on the soles of his feet.

He shifted his position with what he believed to be a funky little movement. He clicked his fingers and the Zippo came alive in his hand. He lit up as if the world was watching him. Shielding the smoke against an imaginary wind, he pulled at it with an expression that suggested here was a man who was only really at home doing his stuff in bed, or doing his stuff on the dance floor. Another snap of the fingers and the Zip was dead. CD pocketed it. He knew he was looking good. Very good.

The reason for this excess of *joie de vivre* was that CD was filled with a delicious confidence. He knew where he was going and he knew what to expect when he got there. This time he would be hunting in a jungle he knew. At the Old Sydney he had penetrated a strange and dangerous world. A world filled with people whose dreams and expectations were very different to his own. War, pain and inflicting degradation were not CD's ideas of good fantasy fodder. Gordon Gordon's little world had been one that CD had entered with fear and reluctance. He had done it purely for the love of Rachel, that she would be proud of him and that maybe, just maybe, she would grant him access to her body; the single thing on earth which fascinated him most and was yet totally and entirely out of reach. An unknown country from which any traveller who returned would, in CD's opinion, be out of their minds.

Tonight, though, was different. He was on the same mission; to discover why a bunch of Perth Nazis had travelled five hundred miles to beat up black people. He was doing it for the same reason; in an attempt to prove worthy of and hence to win the love of the exquisite Rachel. But besides all that, CD reckoned it should be fun. He was strutting up town to shake his booty down to the ground and get down on it like the bitchin' motivatin' groove machine he knew himself to be.

DICKHEADS ARE NEWS

It had not taken a very great deal of painstaking research for CD to pick up on the trail of Aristos Tyron. He was the kind of tedious git who turned up regularly in the gossip columns in sad identikit photos of the week's 'top parties'. CD found seven in just three weeks' worth of back numbers of the *Perth Daily News*. On close examination the pictures were definitely of different functions but, in fact, the editor might just as well have saved on the reporter's taxi fare and published the same photograph over and over, so similar were they. There he was, that gormless face, crushed in amongst other gormless faces. Bow ties and necklaces, arms about each others shoulders, huge fat mouths agape, apparently roaring with laughter at some fab elite gag that the poor, dull reader could never be a part of. All the photos suggested the same thing, that there exists somewhere a world where people are having the wildest sort of time pretty much constantly.

People have a tendency to presume that they are missing out on something. That they are missing out on some sort of key. A key to providing a better time than they are capable of providing for themselves. The other man's grass is astro-turf and it's *better*.

This is what gossip pages in newspapers depend on. They suggest that there is a mystical, club-centred world of pop stars and society beauties where a *better* time is being had. It is a strange theory, after all, there is no reason to presume that you will have a better time simply because you are standing about with a bunch of wankers and paying ten bucks for an orange juice.

But the photos suggest that there is. Those screaming faces that CD had looked at in the Carlo library; fat men, anorexic looking women. Those faces were saying, 'look at us, you'll never enjoy yourself this much'.

The photos do not record the event, they *are* the event. The photo is what matters, all that matters. As long as the photos are published, it's irrelevant what it was actually like in whichever pathetically fashionable disco they were taken.

Of course, those gormless, screaming fashion clones didn't actually have a better time than is had down at the local pub. But they *pretended* that they did, because that way, despite all the bordeom and the expense, there is a certain satisfaction, the satisfaction of being envied, of believing oneself to be special.

Getting your photo in the paper justifies any mind-numbingly stupid occupation. Ask a football thug.

DISCO DOWN

CD loved it and he was really looking forward to his visit to The Shelter. The previous year, The Shelter had been called Hobo's and had been decorated with images of the great depression, tramps, breadlines, unemployed marchers, etc. Now it had been radically redesigned to represent nuclear Armageddon; huge mushroom clouds; flights of missiles; mock-ups of newspapers announcing World War Three, that kind of thing. The girls wore little costumes that glowed and banged on fluorescent tambourines.

'Party like there's no tomorrow' was written over the bar, which translated as 'please spend all of your money as quickly as you possibly can'.

CD had prepared his entrance carefully. He knew enough to know that, despite the efforts clubs like The Shelter make at exclusivity, they are there to make money. That is what the bouncers are trained to watch out for: money, or more importantly, the lack of it.

'Let the money in,' the manager would say to a new cave-man in a bow tie. 'Let the money in and let the tit in, because tit attracts money, all right? No paupers, and no dogs.'

But, looking like money is actually only a question of confidence. You can hire what is termed a 'luxury car' from a cab hire firm, for much the same price as an ordinary car. An extra 30 per cent gets you a nice Mercedes and a bloke with a hat.

CD had insisted on pre-paying for the journey which added a touch to the price, but it meant when he pulled up outside the club he could jump out immediately, shouting over his shoulder, 'Listen, Frank, take some time out, I'll get Janine to bleep you if I need wheels.'

CD turned to the bruiser in the bow tie.

'Hi, I'm here to meet Aristos, Aristos Tyron. Is he in yet? Hey, who cares? I hear this is the sort of place it's fun to wait around in.'

As it happens, CD needn't have tried quite so hard. There are about fifteen 'top' night-clubs competing for the city's night-clubbing business, and despite the manager's efforts, exclusivity was a bit of a myth really. Most places would let you in if you could afford a plastic bomber jacket, and, of course, are happy to pay the entrance fee.

CD paid it, but he wasn't happy. Twenty-five dollars was considerably more than he expected, they must have been charging by the decibel. As he walked into the flickering darkness, the sound hit him like a sweat-soaked brick. The lights flashed and scurried about the floor, walls and ceiling. An epileptic would not have made it through the door.

The SAS in Northern Ireland have long been working on a non-violent interrogation technique called sensory depriva-tion. The idea is that they subject the suspect to blinding lights and a confusion of high volume 'white' noise that so disorientates them they will divulge anything. As CD felt his way around the Shelter, he could not help feeling that the SAS could have just paid the twenty-five dollars admission and sat the suspect at the cocktail bar.

CD had been nursing a mineral water for about half an hour when Aristos arrived. CD introduced himself immediately as a journo from a London based trend mag called *Groovy Trousers*, which had recently won an award for the best laid out feature on whether Elvis is dead or not to be published that month. Aristos, being of course a complete media and fashion victim, had heard of it and ordered champagne. One of the signs of a club dickhead is somebody who does not say 'would you like a drink?' but asks 'would you like a glass of champagne?'

This is rendered even sadder in Australia because their superb wine-making industry has come up with many excellent champagnes that are similar to the French stuff in all but two vital areas. They do not come from Champagne, and they cost about the same as an ordinary bottle of wine. Hence an Aussie club dickhead wishing to gain the same effect (for what it's worth) that his European dickhead brother gets by asking 'would you like a glass of champagne?' has to ask, 'would you like a glass of *French* champagne?' Which of course translates as:

'I want you to know that I am quite deliberately paying forty bucks for something I could get for eight and which we will both swill down like we don't know we're drinking it.'

The French have long been involved in expensive legislation in order to stop the Aussies calling their wine 'champagne' and getting them to call it a 'champagne type fizzy wine' which, legally, they have a right to insist upon. So far, however, the Australian attitude seems to have been, 'OK, so invade us'. Hence, at the time of writing, it was possible to purchase an entire twelve bottle case of Great Western champagne for the price of a bottle of Moet and Chandon. Not surprisingly, people get quite pissed at Australian weddings.

As it turned out though, all the French efforts at a 'fair go' were soon to become irrelevant and the Australians and Californians were going to get the whole shooting match to themselves. The reason for this was that as Aristos Tyron was offering CD French champagne, thirteen thousand miles away in France in a little place about equidistance between the areas of Champagne and Cognac – two tiny districts that have given the world so much pleasure – in one of the numerous French nuclear power stations, a small, unseen hairline fracture was beginning to grow and was soon to render not one drop of French wine drinkable for at least a decade. Nor most of German wine, and Spanish and a great deal of Italian – British wine of course had never been drinkable in the first place.

So Aristos and CD sat in the mindless noise and light, shouting at the top of their voices to make themselves heard, swigging on a drink that was about to become a real world rarity. Both of them would have preferred a beer.

Screaming himself hoarse, CD bullshitted for half an hour or so about the celebs he was lined up to meet in Sydney and those he had just left in London. It is not difficult to convince somebody who wants to believe and, of course, Aristos desperately wanted to believe that an important and trendy journo was going to do an 'in depth' on him.

'Can we go somewhere a little more private, Mr Tyron?' CD suggested when he realized that his eye was wandering onto the dance floor where gangs of girls, rendered infinitely beautiful by the near darkness, were doing their funky stuff.

'Hey,' said Aristos, 'how many times do I have to say. It's Aristos, OK?'

'Oh yeah, sorry Aristos.' CD lit his cigarette like he was in a high wind and stared at Aristos through the smoke. 'You have a great attitude, you know that? Most of the big guys treat us media punks like shit. Oh, sure, they want the copy, they want the column inches. Yeah, they want all that. But, the guy putting the hours in, the man with the pen, he can go fuck himself. It's *Mr* Jagger, and *Mr* Bowie, even the politicians won't unwind, and who needs them.'

'Well, you know, Colin, I like you,' a delighted Aristos replied with massive condescension. 'Sure Mick and David can be brusque, but it's tough for them too you know?'

Aristos had done it again. No matter how much a person heard about Aristos, until they met him, they could never fully comprehend just how big a pratt he was.

'Yeah, I know it's tough being a tall poppy like Jagger or Bowie,' said CD, sucking his cigarette and talking as if they were discussing a couple of war veterans deserving of very special consideration, instead of two immensely rich and hugely envied people. Affecting sympathy for the super-fortunate and their goldfish bowl life-styles is one way of dealing with the horrendous jealousy everyone feels for them.

'Hey, let's get up the celebrity bar, and have some more French champagne. It's OK, I can get you in,' said Aristos.

Most large discos have a thing they call a celebrity bar. This is where local models, local football players and the managers' girlfriends go.

Aristos walked in casually, nodding towards CD 'Friend of mine,' he said to a waitress in a tutu who had not been going to ask. The music was about ten decibels quieter and they were able to talk, just.

'Listen,' said CD deciding he had better get the job done before his ears started bleeding. 'My editor wants me to get right behind the enigma that is Aristos Tyron. Your brother is a hugely successful man. Now we've been searching around, playing a hunch that you have a little bit more to do with that success than either of you lets on. Is that right?'

'Well . . .' said Aristos, because he didn't know what else to say.

'You know, I'm getting a picture here,' CD continued. 'Not the one that you and your brother want the world to see, but the picture *behind* the picture. Suppose Ocker Tyron needed a man to deal for him when he couldn't be personally involved. A man he had complete confidence in. Who better than the guy everybody thought was just a good time boy? A ladies' man? The fellah they all wrote off as just another fascinating, hard drinking, good lookin' sexual animal? Who better than Aristos Tyron, to be the liaison?'

Aristos could hardly believe his ears, this journalist was a genius. CD had lucked out in a big way. His casual use of the word 'liaison' had convinced Aristos that he deserved the description that CD was constructing – it was just what Ocker had called him.

'That's it. I'm his liaison, the silent right hand.'

CD flattered him some more and allowed him to order more French champagne. 'What kind of situation would you liaise in, then, Aristos? I mean, no names, no pack drill, but just an idea.'

'Woah! Woah there!' said Aristos with jolly, patronizing good nature. 'You don't think I'm going to spill me and my brother's business moves to the press, do you? Ha ha, I'm no fool, Colin. Have another drink.'

'Hey,' CD assured him, 'listen, you start doing that and I'm outta here anyway. Wow, that is big league stuff. I'll leave it to you, Aristos. What I don't know won't hurt me, right?'

'Right,' said Aristos with enthusiasm. He absolutely loved CD by this time.

'Besides,' continued CD soothingly, 'this is a fashion spread, remember. The sheep reading this, all the good-looking girls and that, they don't want to know the details, they wouldn't understand them . . . What they need is a kind of broad example, just a vague hint of what the big men get up to.' CD was gambling that Aristos would not have the wit to invent an example and would, instead, merely describe a real one and try to be non-specific. He was right.

'Well, you know,' said a drunken Aristos, 'supposing somebody wanted some people leant on, not hard you understand, but persuaded, and he didn't want to get involved. Well then, his liaison might find some people to help out.'

CD was so close he decided to take a calculated risk.

'But what on earth would he want in Bullens Creek?' he asked.

'Well, you know, it could be –' Aristos was suddenly nervous. 'What do you mean? What about Bullens Creek?'

'I said we'd been scratching around, Aristos,' CD decided to go for it, 'and after I talked to the White Supremacy lot . . .'

Finally Aristos began to wonder about this total stranger whom he had been buying drinks for. 'Look, what's going on? I don't know what you're talking about. What do you want to know?'

'Nothing.' CD was having one last chance at being soothing but he guessed the game was up. 'I just want to know why Tyron got you to send those Nazis to beat up the Aboriginals.'

'He didn't! He just asked me to —' suddenly, from some unknown part of Aristos' brain, a smidgeon of native cunning forced its way through his cotton wool brain. He called the manager and demanded a security guard while he hissed at CD, 'I never said a thing to you, mate, and if you say I did, even in the *Sheep Breeders' Gazette*, I'll sue you into oblivion.'

Aristos could not have found a better way of confirming absolutely everything that CD had come to find out. The guard arrived.

'I think this man has my wallet,' Aristos said. 'I don't want a scene, just turn out his pockets.'

The man did as he was told. CD didn't mind, his mission had been a complete success.

'No wallet, sir,' said the guard.

'And no tape recorder,' Aristos said in triumph. 'You've got nothing, mate. Throw him out.'

HOUSE OF CARDS

And so the house of cards came tumbling down. That fragile global structure behind which we all shelter. A castle, built on shifting sands from little more than faith, hope and greed, came tumbling down with a crash that shook the world. A mighty crash indeed, considering that the castle was not made of anything of any substance. In fact, it was a castle that existed only in the minds of men. Constructed from nothing more solid than the financial pages in newspapers and the blips on a million computer screens. It was not a castle built from iron, or steel, nor cotton, oil or food. It did not fall because there was no more coal left or because all the cows and sheep had died. There was no physical reason for its collapse, because it was made of nothing at all. You couldn't touch it, smell it or climb it, but without its shelter, despite the appalling heat of the southern summer and the mildest ever winter in the north, the world turned suddenly cold.

GOBBLEDEGOOK

Nobody really understood what was happening. Why should they, the global money industry is so phenomenally complex that it is doubtful whether anyone really follows it. When they do the financial bit on the television news it's normally at the end, just before the little jokesy item about a panda who can't get a hard on. The reason for this is probably because, as far as the average viewer is concerned, both items appear to be about equally relevant to them.

Nobody who lives in the real world, the world where things are made, and money is earned, has anything but the vaguest understanding of the utter gobbledegook they spout just before the panda gets his thirty seconds of fame. In fact it would probably make no less sense if they combined the items together . . .

'And now financial and zoological news. In New York, on the 100 point share market index, the panda's penis fell by six points to a record low, the Dow Jones rallied late in the day to raise some interest from Poo Poo, the gorgeous two-year-old lady panda who's causing all the excitement.'

Maybe the reason that the financial 'news' is delivered in such a deliberately incomprehensible manner is that what they are talking about is, in any real sense, meaningless. We are being brought an urgent daily update, a blow-by-blow account of something that exists only because people choose to believe in it. Entirely theoretical wealth.

At the beginning of the day a factory full of jars of jam might be worth a thousand pounds. At the end of the day; a day of 'good trading'; a day of 'rallies' and 'confidence', we might be told that the same factory is worth two thousand pounds.

What has happened? Only a few hours have passed. The factory has not changed. There is no more jam in it than there was. There has been no time for the new slogan 'Let him dip his finger into something fruity, Mum' to take effect. The slimmers' version still tastes bloody awful. Nothing has happened and yet the factory is 'worth' twice as much. Where has the extra cash come from? Nowhere, that's where. It doesn't exist. It is entirely theoretical and if people choose to dispute the theory, if they all choose at once to say 'but that's impossible. All right then, give me the cash . . .', the money would instantly disappear, like the puff of smoke it is.

This, of course, is how crashes occur.

The crash that Professor Durf set in motion was a whopper. People weren't even bothering to look at the paper before they jumped out of the window. They were plummeting like hailstones. In New York City it rained investors – the only things selling were concrete umbrellas. Financial news leapt up to be top story of the day. The panda with no stiffy got left on his own at the end of the programme.

More swiftly than ever before the repercussions spread. The dole queues began to lengthen as the factory gates began to close. The last puréed city gent had scarcely been scraped up when the first suicides due to mortgage foreclosure were reported.

STRATEGIC DECISIONS

The morning after his visit to The Shelter CD's breakfast was even more cursory than usual. He'd run out of Wheaties so there was no need to wash up a plate. The papers were full of nothing but financial news so it wasn't worth lingering with a second coffee. CD liked a bit of popularism in his morning read and it was weeks since there had been a real good article about Joan Collins still having great tits despite being about seventy-five. Anyway, CD was in a hurry. He was anxious to tell Rachel and the others about what he had discovered. Mustn't hang about, he thought, could be very very important information he said to himself. But actually the main thing was he wanted them to know how clever he had been.

PLANNING MEETING

'It seems to me,' said Walter, in his usual manner, i.e. as if he were about to explain the meaning of the universe, and what's more, he was going to be right. 'It seems to me, that we have to go and have a look. I mean we have a definite duty to try to dig what goes down, right? And, apart from anything else, right, it would be a trip. We could maybe take in some desert, cook up some lizard or something. It would be a vibe.'

As far as Rachel was concerned, Walter was not making too great a case for the journey. For a start, when it came to cooking up some lizard or something, she would definitely take something.

'It's hundreds and hundreds of miles, Walter. Your Aboriginal friends have sold up anyway, what's the point?

Whatever Moorcock wants it for, he's got it now. There's nothing we can do about it.'

CD was extremely brought down by Rachel's negative attitude. He considered that he had pulled off a pretty crucial piece of intelligence gathering. He realized now that a full-on sauce session with her whispering, 'my hero' in his ear and 'do it to me again, big boy' had perhaps been a touch over optimistic, but she might at least have said well done.

'You know, Rachel, you don't find things out without taking long shots. I mean, if anything *is* going on, they aren't exactly going to take an advert out in the paper,' he said, trying not to sound hurt but hoping that she would realize that he was.

'Well don't sulk about it, Colin,' she snapped, which was not the reaction he had been trying to provoke. Sometimes CD seriously wondered whether he was losing his touch.

'All I am saying is that it's a very long way to go in order to find out something we know already,' Rachel continued.

'Which is?' asked Walter.

'Well, that some bloody appalling thing is being done to another bit of land by a bunch of rich shits. I mean, it's obvious that whatever it is they're up to, it will be awful. But what are we supposed to do about it? Mount a picket in the desert? I mean, of course Colin's right, it's significant that Tyron is involved . . .'

'That is a mean combination, baby,' interrupted Walter. And even his phenomenally mellow tones could not reconcile Rachel to being called 'baby' especially when she was feeling defensive.

'Please don't call me "baby", Walter. I'm not going to discuss it any more if you call me baby.'

'Cool. No problem,' said Walter, effecting an aura of almost religious tolerance that made Rachel want to strangle him. 'Except, like, you know, it's only a word, but cool. If you don't like "baby" I have no hang up with that. I mean, really, no hang up at all. In fact, it's great. I'll just call you like, you know, something else, because –'

Rachel was about to give up but luckily Zimm had just returned to earth and was momentarily and uncharacteristically lucid.

'Hey, Walter, man, we were discussing the desert trip.'

'I know that, Zimm, but it's important that Rachel should feel relaxed about the language parameters we're employing here,' Walter replied.

'Well great but, you know, I think we should discuss the desert now, OK?'

'OK, Zimm, that's what we'll do.'

'Good.'

'I was just about to say to Rachel,' Walter resumed, 'that what CD had got here is kind of interesting, you know? I mean, Tyron and Moorcock together could fuck up the whole of Australia. They are very bad shit. But you know, like, if it was just another planetary rape, with full legal cover and state government backing, why the secrecy man? You know, why not just do what they normally do, you know. Like boast about it. Why don't they just shout "hey man, we're fucking up the world for its own good, so fuck you". I mean, they don't normally, like hide their light under a bushel, you know? Like, when they're going to give the world cancer, they want to get the credit, dig?'

'Yeah,' agreed Zimmerman. 'But this time. This time CD had to get down on the whole spy infiltration, James Bond bit.'

'Well, I'm glad somebody noticed,' interjected CD.

Zimmerman ignored him.

'Whatever they're hiding, I guess it's bad shit.'

'OK, OK,' said Rachel, 'maybe we should check it out. But your truck's off the road, right guys? Colin can't drive, which leaves my 1964 FC Holden volunteering for a five hundred mile drive. So before I sentence it to death I'm going to at least have one more try at confronting them to find out what they're up to.'

'Man, if he's hiding something all he has to do is bullshit you, I mean, these guys bullshit for a hobby. They like being investigated because they get to do some more bullshitting.'

'Yeah, well maybe he won't bother with me. After all, who am I? Nothing for him to worry about. Maybe he'll just say, "Oh yeah, I'm grinding up asbestos and throwing it in the wind, but I have government permission lady, so fuck you." In which case, we can protest about it here in Perth without totalling my car to find out.'

'You know, Rachel,' said Walter, 'I hope you're not turning into a possession head, that would be a bummer.'

Rachel managed to keep her temper, just. People who get through life dependent on other people's possessions are always the first to lecture you on how little possessions count. Walter was, in many ways, a lovely fellow, but he was also the sort who would finish off the last of your milk and when you complained, say 'oh come on man, it was only milk'.

Rachel decided to stick to the job in hand. 'I'll ask Moorcock rather than Tyron. At least we've met him. Better the devil you know . . .' And on such tiny decisions does the thread of life hang. Had she decided to go and see Tyron, he would, of course, have had her killed.

FLIRTING WITH DEATH

Sly recognized Rachel immediately. It had been three weeks since their encounter at Facefulls. Three very busy weeks indeed for Sly. Like all members of the Consortium, he had played a large part in the terrible crash that Professor Durf had precipitated. First selling as quickly as he possibly could; then beginning to make the purchases that the group had designated as his responsibility. It had been a frantic time.

Besides this, Tyron was now beginning to report that the trickle of equipment and hardware that he was having to handle, looked like it was shortly to become a flood. On-site storage, even installation, was going to become an issue in a very short time and Sly had only just got rid of the last of the previous inhabitants. One vaguely satisfying thing was that, even in the short time since the crash, the money he had promised the Aboriginals had risen in value by over 20 per cent. Hard cash was appreciating fast as more and more people who had been rich on paper discovered that they didn't have a cent. Sly did not have a conscience as such but he didn't mind that old bastard Mr Colboon and his mates putting one over on the red-necks.

However, despite all these immediate considerations and the monumental size of the task in front of him, Sly recognized Rachel immediately. It was an inexplicable thing, but when Sly had been informed that a young woman was in reception without an appointment and wishing to discuss Bullens Creek, instead of feeling a little nervous, perhaps even scared, he had felt a twinge of excitement.

And there she was, and Sly knew that he was pleased to see her.

This was, of course, ridiculous. The last thing on earth he wanted at that moment was anyone taking any interest whatsoever in Bullens Creek. But none the less, he couldn't help it. He was pleased to see her. He walked round his desk and stood leaning against the front. 'So what's the story then, Miss . . .?' he said, trying to be commanding and sexy.

'Kelly, my name is Rachel Kelly, Mr Moorcock. I represent EcoAction. We are a group of environmentally concerned activists,' she replied, trying to be brusque and efficient, and maybe just a little bit sexy. After all, it never hurts to put out a bit.

'Environmental? I thought you were a Nazi hunter.'

'We'd like to know something of your intentions regarding the land that you have bought around Bullens Creek.'

'I'll tell you if you have dinner with me,' Sly surprised himself. He knew he was a smooth operator but even he had not expected that he would have the cool to try making a pass whilst being questioned about Bullens Creek. After all, Bullens Creek was a life and death project. Everything in the world was riding on it. On the other hand, Sly could not believe that this girl was onto anything. After all, it was understandable that environmentalists would be interested in any land purchases that he had made. Sly could not deny that now and then he had been personally responsible for fucking up some pretty large sections of Australia.

He thought all this in the time that it took Rachel to decide to say, 'Dinner? Love to. I'll call you next time I'm one hour away from death by starvation,' which she considered was a pretty good line. Rachel did not like being patronized or taken for granted, especially by someone whom, she was disgusted to discover, she found rather saucy.

'Great, that's all I need, a radical fem' greeny,' replied Sly.

'If your definition of a feminist is someone who doesn't go to dinner with creeps, there's a lot of us around.'

They were both enjoying the conversation.

'Go on, let me buy you dinner,' said Sly, trying a touch of innocent sincerity.

Rachel reminded herself that she was talking to Silvester Moorcock, one of the world's great vandals.

'No. Are you going to tell me what you're doing out in the desert or not? And I think I should warn you, we're a pretty sizeable organization. We have the funds and personnel to find out what we need to know.'

'Which is why last time you turned up with two burnt out hippies and a small bloke who wears his sunglasses indoors.'

Poor Rachel felt embarrassed for her friends, which is something that would weaken anyone's position in a power juggling conversation like this one. But she rallied strongly.

'Don't judge a book by its cover, Mr Moorcock. For instance, I've read that you're a powerful, self-assured, dominant man. I wouldn't have thought you were the sort who couldn't talk to a girl without getting a hard on . . .'

Sly looked! He didn't have one – but he looked! Just a twitch before checking himself, but it was enough; enough to make him look insecure; enough to make him look foolish. It was an extremely unfair gambit and Rachel knew it. A shocking thing to say, but then Rachel could be a shocking girl. Sly was angry, who wouldn't be. He tried to muster some cold dignity.

'All right, young lady. Thank you very much for the

cabaret, I am an extremely busy man, and don't have a lot of time to talk to foul-mouthed green freaks who –'

'Oh? You wanted to take me to dinner a minute ago.'

Sly was entirely unused to this. He knew hundreds of girls of Rachel's age, none of them cheeked him like she did. The difference of course was that all the other girls worked for him. Sly remembered why she had come to see him in the first place. He did not at all like the idea of a girl this intelligent, and with that much bottle, taking an interest in Bullens Creek. He decided to put masculine pride aside for a moment, and concentrate on allaying her suspicions.

'Before you go. You expressed an interest in Bullens Creek.' Sly spoke calmly as if they had just been exchanging comments about the weather, rather than exchanging insults.

'Well, my plans will shortly be made public, but I see no reason why I shouldn't share them with you first . . .'

Producing some carefully prepared mock plans and brochures, the same ones he had fobbed the planning people off with, he explained to Rachel the concept of the Oasis leisure complex. 'The central hotel will be entirely under-ground, and will be called 'The Ark'. This is because it will be a complete escape from the world. A place to recharge your batteries; a place for a new beginning.'

It all looked very convincing.

'Why all the secrecy then, for a hotel?'

'My dear, this isn't just a hotel,' said Sly, recovering his easy charm. 'This whole project is conceptually unique, a top security, totally safe, no hassle wind-down for the mega-rich. You can't call it just a hotel. That's like calling Elvis just a singer . . . I'm putting hundreds of millions into this scheme, you don't think I'm going to tell the world about it until I'm ready, do you?'

'You're telling me.'

'Rather that than have you demanding enquiries and sitting about with placards, getting the place a bad name before it starts.'

Rachel wondered. The brochures were all very glossy,

maybe . . . But then she remembered the Nazi attack; the obvious fact that it was a dumb place to build a hotel . . . Ocker Tyron's involvement.

'So this is just your little baby, is it?' she asked, fondling the brochures casually.

'Just mine. My risk, my profit.'

'No one else involved then? Nobody sharing the risks?'

Sly felt a slight chill, what was she getting at? She couldn't know anything, what could she possibly know? She was so young and poo looking. Christ he couldn't be scared of her. It was a perfectly reasonable question for an environmentalist to ask. His uranium interests, after all, were as part of a consortium.

'No, just me, I take my own risks love. It's the way I got rich.'

And Rachel knew he was lying. Even without the things that CD had found out, she would have known. Now they would have to go to the desert after all.

After Rachel had gone Sly sat thinking about her for a long time. He soon stopped worrying about her. He was certain that she couldn't possibly suspect anything. And if she did, how would she find out more, and who would she tell? He reminded himself that he was acting on behalf of an organization that represented a significant proportion of all the available wealth in the world, and she was a penniless greeny. But, insignificant or not, he couldn't get her out of his mind. She was so . . . well, so pretty, and so tough as well, and clever.

Sly's mind went back to the night of the dinner in Singapore when he had wandered about looking at that which was soon to be history. Suddenly he desperately wanted to tell the strange girl who had just left, all the terrible things that he knew. He longed to share the burden of the present with her; maybe even share the hope of a future. He didn't know her, but then he didn't really know any girl, not real ones, not ones he could love. Should he tell her? Should he make her love him by offering her a future? Sly pulled himself together. All this was just idle fantasy, time to worry about companions later, the job had to be done first. Besides, she was a green activist for God's sake. The last person on earth Sly was going to share his huge and terrible secret with was a green activist . . .

The phone rang. It was Tyron. Great, thought Sly, sexual frustration and humiliation, followed by a chat with a fat, arrogant bastard. What a perfect day.

'Hello, Silvester. Are we on a secure line?' His tone was strangely conciliatory.

'We are now,' said Sly, flipping his scramble switch. 'What do you want?'

If Tyron noticed Sly's unfriendliness, he chose to ignore it, it was, after all, par for the course.

'Listen, Silvester, about the land you bought for us. Now you know at the time I was a little concerned that you might have problems?'

'I recall it very clearly,' said Sly, with open hostility.

'Well, I said nothing at the time, thought you might take it the wrong way, but I decided to uhm . . . help you, you know, just as a mate.'

'No, I don't know. What the fuck are you talking about, Tyron,' Sly barked, all the tension built up in the conversation with Rachel, beginning to come out.

'Look, I didn't realize those Abs would give in so quickly, so on the night that they decided to sell up –'

Sly interrupted him furiously.

'You organized a fucking program! You stupid bastard, you stuck a bunch of Neanderthals into the frame. Nazis for Christ sake! Couldn't you have used the mafia or something!!'

'Listen!' Tyron shouted back, he knew he was in the wrong, but you could take contrition only so far. 'I did it with them because there's no way it could ever get back to me. Everyone knows that lot are mad. If I'd used anybody else the law would have wanted a motive, but with them bashing blacks is a reason in itself!! You didn't seem to be getting any results,

216

time is essential. Anyway, it hasn't rebounded has it? We got the land, the Nazi's in the slammer, and no one's any the wiser are they?'

'So why are you telling me?' said Sly, leaping on the obvious point.

Tyron's tone softened again slightly. 'Listen, I used that pig ignorant half-brother of mine. Everyone knows he's a law unto himself, so I thought even if the Nazi spills, no one will put it on me. Why should they? What motive do I have?'

'Get on with it.'

'Well it seems some reporter's been probing him and the silly bastard's admitted that he hinted that he was working as my liaison. Now it doesn't mean anything,' Tyron added quickly, 'after all, it's your land, nothing to do with me. All I wanted to know was whether anyone had been asking you questions about the deal, and that night in particular.'

Sly thought for a moment. He thought of the girl who had just left his office. He thought about the confidence with which Tyron had promised to deal with the business of the London journalist. He had never heard from her again.

'No,' he replied, 'no one's been asking me any questions.'

THE SALT OF THE EARTH

Rachel apologized to CD and he nearly had to take a cold shower. None of them knew what was going on out in the desert, but it had to be something pretty bad. Either intimidation or deceit had marked every move in the game.

'Like I said,' said Walter, 'we might as well go and have a look.'

'All right, don't rub it in,' replied Rachel.

So they loaded up the Holden in preparation for the trip. Sleeping bags, food, cassettes – you cannot after all, drive five hundred miles without vibes – and they headed on up the highway.

There is an old expression, 'the salt of the earth'. This expression has always implied approval and goodwill.

Someone who is the salt of the earth is considered honest and trustworthy, even noble, in a rough and ready sort of way. They are always good company, reasonable, kind and considerate. They are unpretentious, quick to see the other person's point of view . . . in fact 'maddening bastard' would probably sum them up just as well.

Probably the reason the term 'salt of the earth' is used is because salt is an honest, wholesome, natural thing, traditionally in short supply. And this is the point; you could not want too much of it, just as one would not want to get caught in a room full of 'salt of the earth' type people. Such an abundance of hearty, straight-talkers, saying things like 'I'm a simple man, and I don't know much, but I do know this . . .' would drive anyone to the vom bucket.

As the little red Holden headed up through WA, its passengers could not help noticing that salt was no longer in short supply and was certainly no longer being viewed with such friendly eyes. There was salt all over the place, and wherever it was, it meant barren, parched and useless land. Land where no crop can grow and no animal can feed. Salt of the earth had come to mean complete ecological and economic breakdown.

The problem is called salinization and it means that too much salt is concentrated in the top-soil, attacking the vegetation that grows there. It occurs when the water-table rises, bringing more and more salt to the surface. The water then evaporates, leaving the minerals behind and the land becomes useless. Why is it that the water-table rises? The answer is simple; because all the trees have been cut down. The trees, with their deep roots, used to absorb the water before it could rise, leaving the salt far down below and allowing the water to continue its cycle harmlessly through their leaves hanging high above the ground. Now the trees are gone and Western Australia – like many hot parts of the world where surface evaporation is speedy and the forests have been cleared – faces a terrible problem with the salt of the earth.

This is the avalanche factor. Who would have thought that

cutting down trees to create agricultural land, would render that land terminally poisoned by salt within a few short years? These days, of course, the cause and effect are well-established, but the trees keep falling.

ENCOUNTER AND DISCOVERY
IN THE DESERT

On the afternoon that Rachel, CD, Walter and Zimmerman reached Bullens Creek, the crash was only a few weeks old. But, during that time, the whole world seemed to have grown a little poorer. It had been shocking how quickly the depression took a grip. The Social Welfare became the only growth industry. Well-heeled philanthropists were beginning to think about making soup.

Not in Bullens Creek though. Here it was boom time. The whole town was buzzing, there was work and money everywhere. This was because only a few miles away a vast new development was under construction – a development that was going to bring wealth and prosperity to the town, for time immemorial. The Silvester Moorcock Group, it seemed, was building the ultimate space-age leisure complex. The Oasis, an enormous and completely self-contained city haven, constructed around six massive underground hotels called the Arks. All to be made ready in treble-quick time, because when the depression ended, as at sometime it surely must, people were going to want a holiday.

No townsfolk were actually directly employed on the project but what with the hundreds of foreign workers, living in hastily constructed dormitories, plus the endless flow of traffic up and down the one highway, there were plenty of spin-offs.

'Well, if he is building hotels,' said Rachel, sitting stoically at the wheel, 'they're extremely big ones.'

They had hit the traffic jam at least ten kilometres out of

Bullens. Earth movers, mobile drills, articulated road trains; it was as if somebody was going to rebuild the world from scratch, and had decided to start the operation in Western Australia.

'Whoever heard of a traffic jam in the middle of the desert?' moaned CD. Tempers inside the car were beginning to fray, as indeed they would, stuck in a jam with knackered air-conditioning and a relentless, blazing sun turning up the heat degree by degree.

'Man, we have to accept the situation,' said Walter, 'that is the only way to deal with it. We are stuck, and we are hot. You know man? I mean, that's the way it is, all we have to do is educate ourselves to dig it. It's a Zen thing really.'

For a minute or two Rachel and CD tried to educate themselves to dig it. At least that is what Walter thought they were doing. In fact they were wondering whether they had the energy to tell Walter to go fuck himself or not. They both knew it was utterly unreasonable to blame him for his size but it was galling for the person taking up at least half the room to start preaching tolerance.

Zimmerman was thinking about something else. He got out of the car and stared about him, blackened into a silhouette by the blazing sun. The desert seemed to make him look taller and stronger. He was wearing his usual singlet and shorts and both Rachel and CD found themselves thinking more than ever that he looked extremely impressive. Such was Walter's ridiculous size that it was easy to ignore how well set-up crazy Zimm was. He was muscular and tanned. There were scars on his shoulders but they did not disfigure him. He had an expression of intense concentration on his lean, creased face. The beard, flecked with grey, was neatly trimmed – a contrast to his straggly hair and headband. Gone was his bored lope, now he moved amongst the stationary cars with an athletic grace that suggested a tremendous latent strength. Of course, Walter had told them that Zimm was a black belt Akido, a weapons and survival expert, but what can you tell sitting in a coffee bar? With a distant horizon stretching out all round them, and a huge empty sky overhead, Zimm grew more than ever to look like what he really was. Trouble.

CD thought to himself that it was a shame that Zimm was out of his mind. Rachel thought that it was a shame that he hadn't got any love tackle.

'Yo, Zimm,' called Walter, 'keep it together, you dig? Don't go eating any cars, we're on a mission here man. The last thing we want is to draw the heat.'

Zimmerman ignored him. He knew he was on a mission, he did not need reminding. That was why he was standing in the middle of a snarled highway in the burning sun, sniffing intently. It was so difficult to be sure. If you want to get a bearing on a trace smell it's best not to do it on a flat windless plain along with a thousand belching pipes.

'Do you think you should be shouting about us being on a mission then?' CD gently rebuked Walter.

'Oh yeah, man, that's true, you're right. Yeah.' CD had clearly given Walter cause for thought. He leant out of the window again and shouted at Zimm. 'Yo, Zimm man, like what I said about the mission, that was just a gas, OK? Like, as you know, we are not actually on a mission but just hanging out and digging things, right?' Walter turned to CD. 'I guess that pretty much makes things cool,' he said and CD could not work out whether he was taking the piss or not.

CONFRONTATION

Zimmerman walked about fifty feet up between the two rows of huge, idling engines. The truckies stared down at him from their cabs. Zimmerman sniffed at the cargo of a lorry. He strolled on and sniffed at the back of a tanker.

'Hey, long-hair. Get your dumb face out of my cargo,' drawled a huge, mean-looking truckie through teeth clenched on a nasty, thin, little roll-up – a black one, made with liquorice papers. Zimmerman looked up at him. The man was driving a huge articulated double-fuel tanker, carrying the Murdoch Petroleum logo. His cab was about ten feet off the ground.

'You know something, fat man?' Zimm replied. He wasn't particularly anxious to be rude but this fellow appeared to address people by a single distinguishing characteristic so Zimm was simply falling into line. 'You know something, fat man –' he was about to continue with what he had intended to say but events overtook him.

'All right boy, don't say another word, just you keep quiet because you're going to need what breath you got.'

The big driver was very bored and he was very pleased indeed that this hippy had provided him with such a clear justification for some diversion. He climbed down from his cab. Unquestionably he was a big chap; as big as Walter but without the benign aura.

'I guess the best thing you could do is to give up smoking.' This had been what Zimm wanted to say, and he said it. He was a person who had dedicated himself to the preservation of life on earth and, within limits, this included enormous violent looking truckies. Therefore, he felt obliged to issue this warning. 'Because that ain't petrol you've got in the second tanker.'

But the truckie wasn't listening. He jumped down onto the tarmac, slightly denting it. 'How much money you got on you boy?' he asked, flexing his great heavy arms. 'Because these are your options, you hear? You've been sniffing round my load like some kind of damn thief, right? Then you march up and call me fat man, OK? Now you can't deny it, because I heard you. On top of that you start giving me that lung cancer shit –'

'It's got nothing to do with lung cancer,' replied Zimm.

'Don't you interrupt me, boy! Don't you fucking talk back on me!!' This fellow just loved being a bully. He smiled and continued. 'Now, the way I see it, all the things you done kind of makes you my property boy. You belong to me. Now, I'll tell you what I'm going to do. I am the top man, main moose-head charity organizer to raise money for the truck drivers' orphanage.'

'That's nice,' said Zimmerman, quickly treading on the cigarette butt end that the man dropped.

'Well, long-hair?' the truckie continued, clearly feeling the need to explain the softer side of his nature. 'Me and the boys reckon we leave so many fucking kids behind us on the road the least we can do is get them somewhere to stay.' He laughed coarsely at this.

Zimmerman's eyes narrowed with loathing. If there was one thing which bored and irritated Zimmerman, it was crude comments about sexual prowess.

'So, Mister,' the truckie continued, prodding Zimm hard. 'Either you hand over all you got, so's I can give it to the kids. Or, I'm afraid I shall be forced to flatten you.'

'I hates dudes who are like, terminal bastards, but lay some token charity trip on you because that makes it all right being pigs the rest of the time,' said Zimmerman.

The truckie reminded Zimm of the landlord of a pub in Carlo, who wouldn't serve Aboriginals. This same fellow proudly had a huge whiskey bottle on his bar which his customers were supposed to fill with money. Then he would have himself photographed handing it over to the local hospital. This guy had chucked out Zimm because of his hair and jeans. He had a sign up demanding 'smart dress' which means he would have served Hitler, but Jesus would have been barred for wearing sandals and a dress. The truckie didn't know of Zimm's aversion to self-serving charity, but he knew he had been called a bastard and a pig. He grabbed his Citizens Band radio.

'Ten four, brown bear, rubber duck, twice as nice, sex dog calling all rigs,' he barked into it, by way of an introduction. 'I got a long-hair here wants a pounding. I'd say six foot two, maybe twelve and a half, thirteen stone. There's a hundred bucks says I can knock him cold in under half a minute.' The traffic had been completely stationary for about an hour and so the prospect of a little diversion was most welcome. Word spread fast and pretty soon there were over a hundred hard-looking sports lovers crammed in amongst the trucks, waving money around.

Rachel, CD and Walter had also hurried along. They had

had a suspicion that the commotion might be something to do with Zimmerman and were most disconcerted to discover that they were right. Despite their earlier reflections on how hard Zimmerman had been looking, CD and Rachel had only to take one look at his opponent for their hearts to sink.

This was also the consensus attitude of the crowd. Nobody was offering money on the long-hair to win. The best CD heard was an offer to back Zimm to last forty-five seconds.

Then Walter spoke up. 'I'll take any bets on the hippy to win!' he shouted and was nearly crushed in the rush.

When everyone had finished their betting, a space was cleared, for what everyone expected to be a short fight. As the two opponents squared up to each other, Walter shouted to Zimm that Zimm was to forget for a moment that he was into love and a peace freak because it was important for him to win the fight. This was because if he didn't they would be over four hundred dollars in debt.

'OK,' said Zimm, 'but I want you to know that I don't really approve of this type of profiteering, Walter.'

Everyone had expected a short fight, but not as short as it turned out to be.

An old fellow who had been elected referee, informed the protagonists that he expected a clean fight and then Zimmerman hit the truck driver and the truck driver sat on the ground with a surprised expression and rolled over dead to the world.

There was a momentary pause and then pandemonium broke out. The crowd was convinced that the whole thing was a set up and that the big truckie had taken a fall. CD and Rachel could understand this. Zimm's victory had been so complete and so unlikely that even though they knew that it wasn't a set up, they almost believed that it was.

Walter stood on the bonnet of a cab, a disappointed expression on his face, and addressed the crowd.

'You know, man, like, uhm, I am speechless, I am just like totally, like . . . lost for words man. That anybody should feel, like that they have the right to lay this unbelievably heavy scene on us. I mean, you guys must all have some very bad shit in your heads, you know that? Very bad shit indeed. I think maybe you should look at your diets, maybe it's a diet thing and you should all go macrobiotic. Too much Ying, not enough Yang . . . or sometimes it's the other way around. Either way, it is one bad mother-fucker of a heavy trip, you dig?'

For the first time in his life, Walter found himself in the fairly unique position of having over one hundred truck drivers hating him all at once. They had not the faintest idea what he had been talking about, but some of them vaguely thought that he might have been suggesting that they go fuck their mothers, which was unacceptable. Truckies love their mothers. Mother-love, like some charity, is another of those catch-all excuses for unpleasant attitudes and behaviour.

'All right, so he shoots his business rivals and beats his wife . . . but he's wonderful to his mother.'

'Of course he is, and gives the earth to charity.'

Anyway, what with apparently trying to cheat them, and topping it with making improper and incestuous suggestions, Walter's life expectancy was now being computed in seconds . . Zimmerman spoke up:

'I didn't do any fucking cheating, you red-neck slimes!' he barked. And even with their sensibilities dulled by spending twelve hours a day staring at a completely straight road through a desert, the assembled drivers could see that Zimmerman's feelings were hurt.

'So pick your best man!' he shouted. 'Pick your best *three* men,' he corrected himself, 'and let's do the thing again. Ref', shift the debris.' Zimm kicked the prostrate form of his defeated opponent. 'Start a pile.'

It would have taken about sixteen ref's to shift the sleeping beauty, but it wasn't necessary because Zimmerman's speech had succeeded where Walter's had failed. Nobody felt like picking up Zimmerman's challenge and so Walter started to pick up the winnings.

Back in the car, as the traffic started to move, Walter announced that they now had over a thousand dollars.

They crawled past the stricken double tanker which someone had driven to the side of the road. The still unconscious form of the driver had been propped up in the cab. He woke up in the middle of the night and started trying to think up a story that would cover the facts as he remembered them. How do you explain being beaten up by a hippy in front of a hundred of your peers?

MISSILE FUEL

As they drove slowly towards town, Zimmerman was in a reflective mood.

'It just goes to show,' he remarked, 'that sometimes it ain't worth trying to do a guy a good turn.'

'You were trying to do him a good turn?' enquired CD, who remembered the whole thing rather differently.

'Sure, I was trying to tell him that I reckon one of the tubes he's hauling is carrying high octane rocket or missile fuel. You know, military grade stuff.' Zimmerman was rolling a cigarette and he was talking like he smelt missile fuel most days.

'Missile fuel?' asked CD, trying to adopt the same casual tone. 'You mean, the stuff they fuel missiles with?'

'Yeah.' Zimmerman borrowed CD's Zippo and lit his cigarette with one hand, producing that casual snap of the fingers which CD practised so diligently and which had so far eluded him. Zimmerman was sensing adventure and it was almost as if he was changing himself in order to meet it.

'What the hell is Silvester Moorcock doing shipping in missile fuel?' said Rachel, feeling a little scared.

'Well,' said Walter. 'You know, like it could be this, and like, it could be that, but I guess we have to entertain at least the possibility that you know man, it's . . . to fuel missiles.'

'It ain't to fill his lighter, man,' said Zimmerman, handing back CD his Zippo. 'Maybe I'm wrong, you know,' he continued, 'I haven't smelt it since 'Nam, but if that stuff's what I think it is, man, it burns like the sun. About a thimbleful would put this car into fucking orbit.'

There was a nervous pause.

'And it says petrol on the tank?' Rachel asked, breaking the silence. 'I mean, it doesn't say, "missile fuel for entirely innocent purposes" or anything like that?'

'It says petrol. And it isn't petrol,' said Zimmerman. And they drove on in silence.

BOOM TOWN

Walter had already arranged for somewhere for them to stay in Bullens Creek. This was fortunate because absolutely everywhere was packed to the gunnels. It was a boom town. Excited, lively and full of pricks. Money was coming in fast and nobody was asking any questions. People didn't seem to mind if Moorcock blasted and dug their little part of the world to fuck and beyond. It is strange, but no matter how many millions of times in human history hindsight has revealed the most terminally appalling human errors, we still refuse to even attempt to develop foresight.

Walter had arranged for them to stay at Mr and Mrs Culboon's little place which they had bought a month previously for eight and half thousand, and was already worth fifty.

There was no way they could find a park so they left the Holden on the edge of town, along with the thousands of Toyota Nissan Landcruiser wankmobiles, and walked in.

It was like a gold rush town must have been back in the days of the old West. Everybody out on the street, half of them very very drunk.

'Maybe they're drinking the missile fuel,' remarked CD.

'I think we should maybe keep, like, kind of quiet about the missile fuel,' suggested Walter. And everybody agreed that this would be a sensible thing to do.

It was night now and on the horizon, towards what had recently been a tiny Aboriginal village, there was a tremendous ghostly glow that lit up the whole of the sky. Work on Oasis went on day and night. At present Moorcock's builders were working off huge mobile generators flown in bit by bit. However, work was already under way to install enough cabling to buy in power from the eastern states.

Moorcock had been able to negotiate considerable federal co-operation. He was creating jobs and, like the people of Bullens, the legislature was anxious to see no evil. In fact, Australia was very proud that while the whole world staggered under the impact of a huge depression, her own home-grown entrepreneurs were rising to the challenge and risking their all instituting massive new projects.

The little self-appointed EcoAction team went into a pub, to get a better gauge of local opinion. It was just like outside in the streets, everybody was apeshit about the whole thing.

'It certainly is going to be a very big hotel,' remarked Rachel thoughtfully to the barperson, who was enthusing about the present and future prospects of the town.

'Bet it will still take an hour to get anything on room service,' said CD coolly, even though he had personally never ordered anything on room service in his life.

'Aw, c'mon, this ain't just a hotel! This is ultimate leisure,' the barman quoted. 'Like Disneyland times fifty plus the Gold Coast, this town is on the map. Yeah, we sure showed 'em. For a hundred years we were just a piss-poor bit of outback and now we're the only town in the world that ain't depressed.'

HOSPITALITY

Mrs Culboon answered the door and invited them in.

'Nice to see you, Walt,' she said and clearly meant it. 'We've gone up in the world since you last came visiting.'

'Lovely, Maud,' replied Walter, looking around the sparsely furnished little duplex.

'All thanks to that bastard Moorcock, mate,' Mr Culboon entered with the beers.

'I still think building a bunch of hotels here is one of the dumbest ideas anybody ever had, but there you go. It's his funeral,' he added philosophically.

'We think maybe he isn't building hotels, Johnny,' Walter replied, quietly sucking his beer. He then proceeded to explain to the Culboons the whole process of how their suspicions had grown, from lunch at Facefulls to the business with the suspected rocket fuel. When he had finished Mrs Culboon burst out laughing.

'By Christ, he nearly had even us believing in his Hotel Dingo piss, didn't he, Johnny? Don't it just go to show there's none so blind as those who will not see.' She wiped tears of amusement from her eyes. Nobody could really see what she found so funny. Mrs Culboon liked a good laugh.

'Walt don't know for sure it ain't hotels, he just reckons,' said Mr Culboon. 'Could be this way, could be that. Zimm hasn't smelt this fuel stuff in nearly God knows how many years. I mean, Christ, what else would the Moorcock bastard be doing in the desert? Fixing to start World War Three?'

'Well, we don't know, do we, Mr Culboon?' said Rachel. 'We just think that maybe we should try and check it out.'

'Ain't no harm I suppose,' Mr Culboon concluded after a pause for thought. 'Can only get done for trespassing I suppose. But I still say that the hotel business is the most likely explanation.'

Mrs Culboon shrieked again. CD wished she wouldn't do that.

'Johnny, what are you babbling about, you old fool. I guess the hotel business is the *least* likely explanation. Let me ask you this. Suppose we sold up and went travelling? Where would we go? I guess we ain't too likely to stretch and say to ourselves "my *my*, what I need is a few weeks relaxing in a huge hole in the ground in the middle of the desert". I guess that would really recharge our batteries, wouldn't it just.' Sarcasm was one of the principal weapons in Mrs Culboon's armoury, she liked it heavy. On the other hand, she undeniably made a strong case. Mr Culboon looked positively deflated.

And so, the next night, they all piled into the Culboon's pick-up to drive out to the old community and take a closer look at what was going down.

THE HEAT IS ON

The little EcoAction Direct Intervention/Urban Terrorist/
Green Commando/Whatthefuckarewedoinghere Unit, headed
out into a velvet night. A night that was for all the world
like an upturned pint of Guinness, with the creamy glow
of Moorcock's floodlights hovering eerily on the horizon and
the darkness above.

The sun was long gone and yet it was still hot. It had been
hot for days, months, in fact the weather was second only to
the crash as main news topic. The two combined made for a
strange feeling that something was coming to an end. There
had been a lot more religious nuts hanging out than usual.
People's minds were turning to Apocalypse. The weather has
always been a source of endless conversation but now the
mantra had changed. The song did not remain the same.
Whereas previously the comment had always been along the
lines of 'bloody awful weather . . .'

Now people constantly moaned that it was 'funny' weather;
it was not like it had been when they were young; it was no
longer 'proper' weather. The strange thing was that even
teenagers spoke in this manner.

In the Culboon's old pick-up they were sweating, the heat
was making them nervous.

'Christ it's hot,' observed Mrs Culboon, without sarcasm.

HOT HOUSE HUMANS

Professor Durf felt the same way. He and the Domesday Group
had been watching the weather with increasing alarm, for some
months. The speed of the deterioration had shocked them all.

The greenhouse effect, as every politician knows, is caused by the build-up of pollutants, which are held, floating at the top of the atmosphere, with no reason to disperse. This airborne shit slick provides no shade from the sun. The clear, pure, short-wave, solar rays pour through without a moment's pause. But once these rays have done their thing, heating up the earth's surface, the trouble starts, because the heat that then radiates upwards from the surface has changed. It is long-wave and it cannot, for some sad reason, get through the shit slick.

'The earth had a pretty good central heating system,' was the conclusion of the head of the Domesday Group, when he met Durf in New York. He was there in order to present Durf with yet more revised predictions as to the time the world had left to put its house in order. 'But we had to close the damn windows.'

'You're telling me what I already know,' snapped Durf. 'Jesus, kids in school know about the greenhouse effect. We've had heat waves before too. Maybe this is just a natural thing.'

'Yes, maybe,' the scientist replied, 'we can't be sure exactly what's going on but it's very hot isn't it, Professor Durf.'

'Listen. I know it's hot, tell me what's going to happen. Is this it? Are the damn ice-caps going to melt!' Durf was a planner, an organizer, he needed hard information, and he wasn't getting it.

'Yes, they're going to melt. Damn it they've been melting for years. I've been telling your people for years. I don't know how quickly but if something isn't done they'll go, Professor Durf, by God they'll go, like the ice in your damn drink!'

He was a worried and frustrated man, the head of the Domesday Group. He, like all those involved in Armageddon scenario research, was under the impression that the world's industrialists employed him that they might act upon the information that he gave them. And yet he saw no action; he saw no efforts at change. He might as well not have said a word. Actually, of course, action was being taken on his grim warnings, but not the kind of action that would have made him happy. He did not know about the divine pre-eminence of the profit motive. He did not know that a moral decision had been taken that market forces must come before the safety of the earth, no matter what the cost. He did not know about the grim rocket silos that were under construction ten thousand miles away in the deserts of Western Australia.

He tried again to impress upon Durf the urgency with which somebody had to start the process of depollution.

'Listen, Durf, you have influence, God knows I've written papers screaming blue murder, but it's the producers that count. The consumers just want their car and their cooker and their cheap fuel, they're sheep. We must influence those in power, the people that profit from the disinterest that the general population seem to be showing in their future. Professor Durf, the pig-headedness of the human race is on a collision course with the laws of physics. An irresistible force is about to meet an immovable object and we will not survive.'

'How long?' asked Durf again.

'I don't know!' the poor little scientist stressed yet again. Durf was being like the usual idiots, the people who acted as if science was a series of definite facts and scientists benign, all-seeing, all-knowing teachers. The truth was that every door that science opened revealed a corridor full of them, all barred and bolted.

This type of blind faith in science probably stems from popular science programmes on the telly when some utter smughead in a polo neck will explain the riddles of existence with a milk bottle, a ping pong ball and a lot of extremely expensive trips to foreign locations.

'It could be a decade or two, it could be tomorrow. I don't know,' continued the frustrated scientist. 'But I think very soon now. Very very soon.' There was real anguish and fear in his usually dispassionate voice. 'When are you people going to *do* something?'

SHOTS IN THE DARK

Of course they were doing something and somebody else was taking a look at it. Or at least taking a look at an eight foot fence with six strands of razor wire running along the top of it. The EcoAction team had been driving cross-country, parallel to the wire for about half an hour and had come to the conclusion that the fence ran right the way around an enormous property, far bigger than the Aboriginal community spread. From where they stood, the glow of the working lights remained far away. There was no way they could discover anything at that distance.

'Oh man, this is beginning to look kind of sinister, you know? Like, this is a big fence just to guard a building site,' commented Walter, voicing their common thoughts.

'It does seem kind of heavy security for a holiday camp,' added CD.

'They ain't building no holiday camp here, mate,' said Mr Culboon. His wife shrieked with laughter, breaking the tension somewhat.

They had all been feeling rather thoughtful and solemn, but then Mrs Culboon always laughed at odd times.

'Of course they ain't you old fool! We knew that the first time the bloke came with his money, ha! Ten grand a head for a dingo's toilet, ha!' Dingos had clearly made a big impression on Mrs Culboon during her time of living at the Bullens Creek community.

'I reckon if he *is* building hotels, this bloody fence is to keep the guests *in*!!' And Mrs Culboon roared anew. She was not a woman who was easily frightened and the atmosphere had not got to her in the way that it had affected all of the others, except Zimmerman. She did not even flinch when they saw the lights of the car racing towards them.

'Oh my, oh lord!' she said cheerily, 'I reckon here comes the entertainments officer to inform us that there will be a dinner dance in the nuclear fall-out shelter.'

Her good humour was infectious and they watched the approaching lights with interest.

The ToyaNiski Bigdick Wankmobile pulled up with its lights on full beam, pointed straight at them. Its occupants stayed inside, someone spoke through a megaphone.

'Who are you and what do you want?' The voice was that of a man who liked playing at being a policeman.

Zimmerman did not like the vulnerability of the situation, the truck had not positioned itself in a friendly way. They were blinded, and exposed. 'Rachel and CD go right, Culboons go left,' he said quietly. 'Walter stay in the light and talk to them.'

Zimmerman knew that if they all deserted the light, whoever was in the truck would be spooked and who knew how they'd react. By keeping someone in the light Zimm had left their interrogators with a clear course of action.

'Stay in the light, all of you!' the amplified voice barked.

'Get into the darkness,' Zimmerman urged, and they all did, leaving Walter alone and blinking.

'Hey man, what's with all this giving orders scene, you know?' he asked sounding a little hurt. 'I mean, if like a bunch of peaceable people such as me and my compadres, can't even take in a moonlit drive without, well, being blinded and shouted at. Eventually we have to ask ourselves the vital question, like, what is the point? No, but really, I'm serious, I mean, what *is* the point?' Walter clearly felt he had put his case quite clearly.

'Everybody get back in the light, this is private property, you're all trespassers, we want to know why,' the voice insisted.

'No man, no way . . . *that* is private property, Fort Knox in there, this here's the desert and it belongs to the stars,' said Walter.

'You are almost three miles inside Moorcock/Ark Leisure Properties, this fence is just a dingo obstruction. You are all coming with us.' The voice was getting harder, more threatening. This was partly because its owner and his companion were peering about wondering where the hell the others had gone. They soon found out about one of them.

'Dingos!' shrieked Mrs Culboon. 'An eight foot fence for dingos, ha, ha, ha. Bionic dingos, maybe, with jet packs and pogo sticks and trampolines!!' The voice rang out of the darkness with delighted sarcasm. 'What do you reckon, mate? That the dogs have been rooting the kangaroos? That's the only way they're going to get over that fence. Unless, of course, they got some ropes and grappling hooks and stuff.' Mrs Culboon clearly felt that she had hit a rich vein of humour here and intended to milk it. 'Yeah, and after they've done that mate, they can mount a Dingo expedition to have a go at Everest or something, ha, ha, ha! . . .'

'Shut up you old bag!!' the voice was shaky now. 'Get in the light all of you or we shoot the guy with the beard!!'

This was a big surprise. Everyone knew that something was going on and that the people behind the lights were not just going to wave them on their way. But nobody had expected the stakes to rise quite so quickly.

'Jesus,' said a surprised Walter. 'This dude says he's going to kill me. I mean, man, that is just totally unnecessary.'

'We don't like boongs and we don't like hippies!' the megaphone crackled – 'boong' being an extremely rude word for Aboriginals. 'And you're on Moorcock property, so get in the fucking light.' To everyone's astonishment a shot rang out and a spurt of sand burst up at Walter's feet. Instinctively Rachel, CD and the Culboons moved back into the glare of the truck's headlamp.

'Now come on, mate, this is ridiculous,' said Mr Culboon. 'You can't shoot someone for trespassing, there wasn't even a warning sign.'

'Yeah! What's your man scared of?' shouted Mrs Culboon, the jolly sarcasm still heavily present in her tone. Mrs Culboon had lived over half a century in the lucky country, the country that her ancestors had first come to forty thousand years before. It had been half a century of abuse. In her life she had been confronted by bullying racist white men with guns more often than she could remember. Of course, it still scared her, but she had learnt to walk tall. Besides, she,

237

like the others, did not actually believe that the man would
shoot Walter.

'What's his problem?' she laughed. 'Does he think we're
going to order too much room service in his hotels!! Ha, ha!
Raid the mini-bars? Christ almighty lord, what goes on here?
If the porters carry guns, I wouldn't want to meet the manager.'

'It does seem a bit over the top,' added CD. 'I mean,
what's going on . . .'

'Where's the other one?' the voice shouted back, 'the one
with the beard! Get in the light or we shoot!!'

The man's tone was becoming distinctly threatening. CD
for one was beginning to take it seriously. He stepped forward.

'Look, come on, don't be silly, we'll just get back in our car
and –'

The man doing the shouting was not the one doing the
shooting. The trigger happy one was in the passenger seat, his
pistol arm hanging out of the passenger window. Zimmerman
was watching it with interest from his position crouched
against the passenger door.

Zimmerman was back in the jungle, the danger of the
situation clearing away the debris of the years. He was
wondering if the fellow was left-handed or not. If he was, then
Zimmerman could perhaps afford to let him loose off a few
more warning shots, which was clearly the only option
available to the man. Unless he actually was going to shoot
Walter, which Zimm considered unlikely. But, if the man was
right-handed, then he was taking a big risk firing with his left.
It was possible that if Zimmerman hung around too long, one
of his companions would catch an unfortunate stray . . .

'Dreadful accident . . . compensation . . . apologies all
round, but they *were* trespassing and Abos were involved.'

Zimmerman did not need to be a cynic to believe that
Moorcock was in thick with the local fuzz, especially since
Zimm had actually heard Moorcock talking to the chief. All in
all he reckoned it was time to finish the business and get out.

He broke the unfortunate man's arm and took the gun. Both guards were too surprised at the sight of the bearded apparition rearing up at them to say much. Zimm pointed the gun into the cab and spoke quietly to the others.

'Go get in the car everyone. It's time we had a beer and clearly this hotel isn't open for business yet.'

They did as he told them. CD and Rachel were amazed. This new gag cracking, arm breaking Zimmerman was a revelation to them. Even Mrs Colboon felt there was nothing more to say.

'Give me your gun man,' said Zimm to the driver.

'Oh now come on,' the driver replied, sounding a lot less coppish now he wasn't using a megaphone. 'Don't you think maybe this has gone far enough? Why don't you and your friends just get on out, don't come back and we'll just forget about everything.'

'Give me your gun man.' Zimmerman's tone did not change but now it was accompanied by the whimpering of the other guard whose arm was beginning to come out of shock.

'He broke my fucking arm!' he sobbed, 'give him the gun. He broke my fucking arm like a twig.'

The driver drew his pistol slowly and handed it over. Then Zimmerman made a search of the truck.

'Who were you expecting?' he asked, eyeing the extensive armoury, 'the Black Wizard of Thargon at the head of the Great Troll army?'

Luckily Zimmerman did not appear to expect an answer to this. He just shouldered two automatic rifles, a rifle with an infra-red telescopic sight and six stun grenades.

Then he shot out two of the tyres plus the radiator. 'Tear out the radio,' he said, looking in through the cab window. 'There isn't anything but shit in the charts these days anyway.'

'Oh come on, Mister, we're 20 K from base, you broke my mate's arm. They won't come looking for us till morning.'

'You trying to tell me you don't have to call in?' asked Zimmerman.

'We don't, honest, mate,' said the driver.

'Yeah, and I'm a teapot called Erika,' replied Zimm, presumably to show that he was dubious as to the driver's claim. 'I guess if that bastard Moorcock's got you goons, there's just kind of a small chance he's going to have a chopper. Which, if I leave you your rig, will be up my arse in about fifteen minutes.'

CD, standing by the car, debated briefly with himself whether to say something witty about not being prejudiced and that a chopper up the arse was fine between consenting adults using a condom. Wisely he decided that Zimm's mood was too volatile to risk interrupting him and he would save the gag for later.

Zimmerman shot the radio out of the dashboard with a burst of automatic fire, so sudden and so close that both men had unfortunate accidents. Which was a shame because, as it happened, the security set-up being very new, they were not supposed to report back and hence would not be missed until morning, meaning that they would have to spend the whole night, quite literally, in the shit.

Zimmerman loaded the ironmongery into the back of the Culboons' pick-up and suggested that they drove home.

'Maybe we should press on,' suggested CD, 'I mean, we're past the guards after all.'

'Yeah, I thought about it,' Zimmerman replied, 'but we'd never get the wheels through and it's 20 K into the middle. There and back that's quite a hike.'

'Well,' said Walter, 'I guess we should go home, smoke a little doobie and really try and concentrate.'

And on this contradiction in terms, they drove home.

CONSPIRACY THEORIES

Ever since discovering that there definitely was some form of covert co-operation between the world's richest men, Chrissy had been casting desperately about, trying to find the vaguest hint as to what that co-operation might be. After all, it is not illegal for a large group of people to go out to dinner together. It might be boring if you get sat at the wrong end of the table, next to the wrong people. It might be annoying if you got lumbered trying to divide up the bill. Even more annoying if it is decided to just split the bill equally and you *know* that you only had a starter and that you didn't drink because you were driving. It might be all those things, but it is not illegal.

The tiny scraps of information that she did manage to pick up, simply added to the confusion. Using the information contained in Linda's final letter to her, she had been able to follow up one or two of the purchases that her target personalities had made during the first hours of the crash. But this had only made her more confused. For instance, the last thing that Slampacker had bought was a vast quantity of dried food, whilst Nagasyu was involved heavily in the jumble sale sell-off of the West European Space Group.

WESG had collapsed with the concentration of the satellite market, immediately following the crash. It had been hugely wealthy but only in the long-term. Being an entirely civil organization it had been able to concentrate purely on the commercial development of space, whilst both NASA and the Soviets had a huge military commitment. Unfortunately, the whole thing had been financed on credit, selling launch space for pay-loads that would not take flight for half a decade. With the whole sale cancelling most of these contracts, WESG found itself suddenly bankrupt. As it became apparent that the world was entering a decade of low consumer spending ability, all the new TV channels, private phone links, and mass satellite communication stuff had to be shelved. Nobody rents another TV channel when the cupboard's bare.

The Stark Consortium had been aware that this would happen and had jumped in early to asset-strip the agency. This had been the last major move that Chrissy had been able to observe, after that the transactions dried up. Unbeknownst to her, the reason for this was that Durf was now centralizing the preparations in order to speed things up. Obviously neither Durf, nor his assorted buyers, were in Linda's original computer program, so their dealings went unobserved.

But none the less, the few snippets she did uncover were enough to scare her even more deeply than she had been before. Chrissy was a good financial journalist, she understood money flow, she had even read parts of *Capital*. Of course, she did not agree with most of the social conclusions that Marx drew. She knew that the yuppies would do for themselves with cocaine, long before the dictatorship of the proletariat had time to inevitably succeed the dictatorship of the bourgeoisie. She didn't even know who the proletariat were anymore. On the other hand, she had always thought that there might be something in Marx's idea that war was an inevitable part of the money cycle. Money needed war. And somebody very rich was buying rockets. The time had come to seek advice.

A LACK OF INTELLIGENCE

'That is the most preposterous lot of crap I have heard in all my years with the Agency,' CIA man Toole admonished, 'and I was the guy who wanted to poison Idi Amin by putting arsenic in his mistress's bidet.'

Chrissy had not really known what to expect, but going to Toole was the only thing she could remotely think of to do.

She supposed that maybe she had hoped that he would check the door and then inform her that the CIA were already on the case and that she could forget about it. Of course, Chrissy had no illusions about the extent of the CIA's knowledge about anything. Like all intelligence agencies, they knew what they stumbled on, unfortunately they could never believe what they stumbled on because it could be a plant, so they spent all day getting headaches, trying to double-think an opponent they were not sure existed.

But what could Chrissy do? Who could she turn to?

'I know it looks sort of weak but come on, Toole, we've known each other a long time. You're the only agency man I'd talk to. You know I'm not one to start at shadows.'

'Well, sure, but all this capitalist conspiracy stuff is pretty questionable you know, Chrissy,' Toole replied. 'I mean, maybe you should take it to the other side. It's kind of more their game you know. Our lot *like* capitalism, that's what we're here to defend. If there *is* anything in this, which of course there isn't, it is definitely a KGB brief, or maybe the Cubans. I can make a couple of calls if you want.'

'I'm not talking about capital *ism*, I'm talking about capital *ists*, a small group of them, who may be trying to screw the rest of us. Look, you have got to agree that I have the evidence that they were together and you've also got to agree that that is real strange. I mean *real* strange. Now what is the world financial situation at the moment?'

'It's in crisis, Chrissy, even the Agency can read the papers.'

'That's right, there is a world financial crisis. Decades of buying a new Hi-fi when you get bored with the record that's on it, has peaked. The credit boom is crashing about our ears. At any other time in history there'd probably be a war. That's what Marx said. The very nature of the system is growth, expansion and profit and the only way to keep that spiral moving upwards is to blow it apart with a war every now and then. Recreate demand, stimulate production, destroy old products, etc., etc. But it hasn't happened has it? In terms of major power against major power, there has never been a longer period of peace in history. Marx didn't know about nuclear weapons, he didn't know that the very next century after his, people would get scared of war, so the war he predicted hasn't happened, which leaves the world market in crisis . . .'

Toole interrupted her.

'Chrissy, are you suggesting that a group of well-known and respected businessmen are fixing to start their own war in order to recreate a market for their goods, because they're all good Marxists and he's told them how to keep capitalism on course?'

'I don't know,' Chrissy replied, angrily, 'it's just a suggestion. You try and explain what's going on here. My friend was murdered . . .'

'You think,' corrected Toole.

'She was murdered, whilst close to uncovering some kind of bizarre alliance between top money-biz fat cats. I pick up on the research and find that not only are they buying rocket fuel, but also half the West European Space Group . . .'

'Along with about a million other things, Chrissy,' Toole butted in again. 'Look, I'll do one thing for you and that is all. I'll call London and see if they know anything more about your friend's murder.'

Chrissy's knuckles were white with frustration. Toole adopted a kinder note.

'If you want my honest opinion, I'll tell you. I think you're probably on to something here. I agree that there are certain aspects that look a little strange, but no way in a billion years is this Marx business stuff cutting any ice with me, or anybody else. You're going to have to do a whole lot better theory-wise than that.'

'I haven't got any other damn theories!' Chrissy shouted. 'I have no idea what is going on!'

They parted; she to go and get a drink; he to make the one call that he had promised to make.

He was linked with an MI5 man called Carre. He knew him

pretty well and reckoned there was a good chance that he wasn't working for the Russians.

KEEPING A SECRET

Secret Services are a bit of a puzzle really. In the light of the various unsavoury discoveries made about them since the war, it is becoming extremely difficult to find any satisfactory reason for why they exist at all.

It now seems fairly clear that for most of the time since the Second World War, the KGB have completely penetrated and totally compromised British Intelligence. And what good has it done them. They have not, as known, invaded Britain, or blown up any of Her Majesty's shipyards. They seem to have made no real profit out of their astonishing coup whatsoever. In fact, in the history of Britain, the audacious Russian penetration of our cloak and dagger boys will probably be deemed to have done little or no real damage at all, except perhaps to the egos of a few ex-public schoolboys. It has, on the other hand, sold an awful lot of novels. If the Soviets had thought to penetrate the West's publishing houses at the same time that they were penetrating its espionage organizations, they might today have all the hard currency that they so desperately need.

Of late the CIA has got the publishing bug and it almost seems that operatives are writing their memoirs before completing their first mission; with the result of blowing the gaff on past and present colleagues. The whole concept of espionage is so totally riddled with doubt and betrayal that the suspicion cannot be avoided that the entire charade is an utter waste of money.

Except of course it isn't, because the real purpose of national secret services is not to spy on foreigners but to spy on the people that pay for the thing in the first place; the population of the country in question. This is almost certainly the main job of the KGB and, if recently published memoirs are to be believed, is also the principal concern of MI5. The next

John Le Carré novel should be about Smiley trying to penetrate a bunch of vegetarian members of CND in Islington.

THE GATHERING STORM

Chrissy went home more frustrated than ever, wishing that her friend, Linda, had never come up with her observations in the first place. She passed a news stand.

One of the placards announced that the heat in the southern hemisphere was now so severe that the rise in the sea level, due to the meltdown in Antarctica, was now a day to day reality. Coastal towns would soon no longer be safe and the whole of Egypt and Bangladesh were directly threatened. In the early eighties, scientists around the globe had predicted that within forty years the human race would face the most drastic climatic changes since civilization began. It was all happening much sooner than anybody had expected.

But Chrissy could not get worked up about it, she liked warm weather. She saw the second placard, it read:

DOUBLE EURO-NUKE TERROR; FRENCH REACTOR BLOWS; BRIT SUB FLOUNDERS.

Chrissy bought a paper and learnt of the dreadful events that had happened on the previous day. She could not help but smile. If the world wasn't careful it looked as if all her worries about money and the machinations of the world's billionaires would be entirely academic since there would no longer be any life on the planet to worry about.

WARMING GLOW

The submarine in question, HMS *Dogged Endurance*, had hit trouble in a huge and unseasonal sea. The swell had been massive and Captain McEntoe had never seen the like before.

'It's those damn Americans mucking about with the weather,' he remarked, sucking on his pipe.

But it wasn't. It was just the sort of storm that only comes very occasionally and nobody had really minded until the seas began to fill up with nuclear hardware which, once fractured, could poison extremely large areas for thousands of years.

HMS *Dogged Endurance* had been trying to leave harbour at its secret(ish) base in North Scotland when the weather had hit it and, despite its enormous power, the boat found itself drifting towards the rocks that formed the natural harbour. Three tugs had been called out immediately and had actually managed to get a rope onto the wallowing sub. However, to no avail and the side of the ship was breached on the fierce, craggy and soon-to-become extremely radioactive rocks of Scotland.

The weapons were not compromised but the small nuclear reactor, which powered *Dogged Endurance*, was. Within a matter of hours the major European frozen food companies were on the phones trying to get into the Pacific fish market.

The French power station was a much bigger disaster although, since the two incidents were only eight hundred miles apart, their effects became indistinguishable.

After the Chernobyl disaster the world was assured that with modern safety standards such terrible events were unlikely to happen again to a power station, even once in a thousand years. This, of course, was very little comfort because with the present proliferation of nuclear power it will not be long before there are a thousand nuclear power stations; which statistically suggests that one will go pop every year.

The disaster that Chrissy read about in New York made a large section of central France uninhabitable. Besides this, it cast a fall-out cloud that made all meat and vegetables, within a radius of five hundred miles, inedible. The argument for this form of power in the first place had been that it was cheap and clean. Of course, the cost of clearing up the appalling mess of this one disaster was uncomputable, and, with cancers running through many a generation, pretty open-ended.

247

Toole went back to his office at the CIA New York station and phoned Carre in London.

Toole didn't like Carre. Carre was a boring snob and because he worked for MI5 he was obsessed with the idea that everybody would presume that he was gay. He therefore felt the need to continually pepper his conversation with sexual banter to demonstrate just what a clean knobbed heterosexual he was.

'Hi Carre, it's Toole. Still getting plenty?'

'Christ, *unbelievable*, I mean just *unbelievable*. I am getting so much pussy at the moment. I don't know what it is, but really, *unbelievable* . . .' Carre talked without moving his lips, in what he believed was a languid, public school drawl. An accent that only Prince Charles can carry off, and even he, only just . . .

'I mean, honestly, I don't think there are any poofs left in the firm these days. We all get *so much pussy*! especially me.'

'Glad to hear it, bud. Hey listen, could you do something for me?'

'Maybe. Thought you Yanks could pull your own birds,' said Carre in a manner calculated to imply the guarded response of a cool, keen brain; but in fact implying, and implying clearly, that he was a fatuous git. Except in wartime, working for the secret service must be a particularly soul destroying occupation. It is such a useless job. You can never know if you've got anything right; and even if you did you're not allowed to tell anyone. This is probably why secret civil servants have always invented fantasy lives for themselves; because their real ones are so dull. Carre hadn't even done this with any flair. After all, pretending to get laid a lot is scarcely an original pose. The other thing he did was to sit in clubs full of other young men pretending to be old, saying things like, 'Listen, if Hitler had gone to Eton he'd have made a bloody good minister of agriculture.'

Toole was aware of what a git Carre was, but Carre, being a

slime and a toady, knew things, so he was the quickest way to laying Chrissy's story to rest.

'Listen,' said Toole, 'someone's turned up a shot that I reckon is as long as they come, but I promised her I'd run it past your people. She has a major money conspiracy theory going round the death of a hack on the *Financial Telegraph*, called Linda Reeve. My source is convinced the girl was murdered because she was on the tail of some fat cats.'

'What's your source's name and what's her theory?' Carre blurted out. Had he really been the cool hand he liked to think he was, he would have affected disinterest. Toole was very surprised indeed, clearly he had hit something.

'Oh Christ, some mashed potatoes about corporate Armageddon,' he mumbled cheerfully and evasively. 'What about the Reeve girl?'

'No, what about your source, who is it?' Carrè insisted.

Toole was astonished. Obviously there was a case to answer to after all, at the very least about Linda Reeve's death. He reminded himself to apologize to Chrissy.

'Never you mind about my source. What's going on, Carre?'

'Nothing that I know of,' Carre said, finally managing to introduce a casual note into his voice. 'You know me, always interested in totty . . . I recall the case. The girl was killed and the police asked us to look at it. It was a very professional burglary you see, they were surprised that whoever did it murdered the girl . . .'

'Surely that would have gone to Special Branch . . . if that. More like local CID I'd have thought.' Toole, of course, did not believe Carre. There was one rule above all others in espionage: the cops hated the spies. Cops never took kindly to getting their investigations taken away from them and would certainly never have voluntarily handed over a murder to MI5 – no matter how suspicious.

'Well, for some reason or other they gave it to us,' Carre said, unconvincingly. 'We drew a blank. I just wondered if you had anything, that was all.'

Toole could get nothing further out of Carre, who started trying to talk about totty again. When Toole put the phone down he was at a complete loss about what to do. He had this list of vaguely suspicious, but entirely legal, financial transactions, and a girl with an utterly absurd theory about corporate global manipulation. He had been all set to forget about the whole thing after one call, and now the Brit had as good as confirmed the basis of Chrissy's theory; i.e. that Linda Reeve's death was suspicious. That gave a tiny touch of credibility to the rest of Chrissy's wild thinking. And what were the British doing? Certainly they knew something about this journalist's death. Poor Toole was now as confused as Chrissy. He too shared with her the same pangs of fear.

Not for long though, as it turned out, because within two hours Toole was dead. His nemesis had appeared in the shape of the head of the C I A West European operation. A very big fish indeed, he had never come to see Toole before and when he entered – without knocking – Toole sprang respectfully to his feet.

'Just been talking to London, Toole. You've stumbled on a big one. This Linda Reeve business, how did you get onto it?'

Toole explained about Chrissy Kelly; hoping like hell that he had not trodden on any major leaguer's toes.

'And that's all?' the big man asked, and was assured that it was. Then he pulled the gun with the silencer, bade Toole raise his hands, put the gun to Toole's mouth, shot him and placed the gun in Toole's lifeless hands – Toole had wondered when his boss entered the room why he was wearing gloves.

Nobody knew why Toole had killed himself. The body had been discovered by the head of the West European operation, who had gone over to question Toole about unauthorised conversations with dubious British agents who were known to boast openly about indiscreet sexual adventures. Maybe, people speculated, that was why Toole killed himself . . . Lacking any real motivating force in their lives, sex was a spur that secret service types always found tempting to fix on to. People whispered about Toole, pointing out that he had killed himself after talking to a man called Carre at MI5 – which everyone knew had been a den of queers since 1946. What's more, it seemed that this Carre was fixated by demeaning and smutty talk about women – which CIA analysts claimed was probably a denial of his deeper and very different desires. Poor old Carre, the most terrible thing he could imagine happened: his CIA file got marked down as possible subversive homosexual.

Actually Toole died because both Carre and the big American Head of West European operations worked for Stark; although they had no idea of the real nature of their employment. They both presumed that they were simply involved in industrial espionage. Very rich men gave them orders and they carried them out. Carre had been instructed to keep an eye on the Reeve murder – in fact he had recruited a fellow who did it. Hence, he reported his conversation with Toole to Professor Durf's people. They, in turn, asked their top CIA insider to find out what Toole knew, and then kill him. That was it. Five grand to Carre, a hundred grand to the American; money well spent, and the two men returned to their day jobs. Chrissy's address was then faxed to a reliable New York operative.

ON THE RUN

During the few short hours that this was going on, Chrissy had continued to chew over any bit of information about financial dealings that she could get her hands on. There wasn't much because the depression was biting deeper and deeper. It had taken grip with astonishing speed. The world seemed to have just shrugged its shoulders and admitted defeat. Maybe it was the weather. One article did catch Chrissy's eye. It told how the lucky country was attempting to shrug off the slump more quickly than anyone. Apparently, that brave and individualistic trouble-shooter, Silvester Moorcock, was not taking financial stagnation lying down. Chrissy jumped as she read Sly's name . . . The article informed her that he had created a boom town in Western Australia by staggering everyone and starting the construction of a huge leisure complex in the desert. Further to this, it had just emerged that he had gone into co-operation with fellow Aussie Ocker Tyron, who was handling the shipping in of the enormous quantity of material and equipment required to build such a massive scheme from scratch.

Chrissy wondered . . .

Obviously no way were the world's financiers going to unite to build a Kangaroo theme park. And, of course, the amount of money that had been syphoned out of the system, both before and during the crash, would have built Disneyland on the Moon . . . but it was something. It was the only significant financial activity to emerge since the crash and it involved at least two of the figures on Linda's original list . . . She was nervous about bothering Toole again, especially with something even less concrete than what she had already given him, but she had to do something with her time. She had given up everything to pursue this investigation. And Toole had said that he would make a call for her . . .

She picked up the phone. It was a Donald Duck shaped phone which Chrissy had bought because, since all news is bad news, she figured she might as well get it from a cheery source. Cheering up this call was going to need more than a plastic duck . . .

'Toole's dead,' said Donald, smiling hugely under his little sailor's hat. The CIA had seen no reason for secrecy and hence informed Chrissy that Toole was dead, having taken his own life. It happened quite a lot in his business.

Chrissy was utterly terrified. She had been speaking to Toole only a few hours previously, there was absolutely no way on earth that he was suicidal. He must have met the same fate that Linda had. But, so quickly. Chrissy could not believe it; they had done it so quickly.

Clearly she had to get away immediately, far away. But where? How? It is difficult to formulate a plan when, all of a sudden, you realize that within minutes somebody may try to kill you. She tried to think as she ran about her apartment stuffing passport and credit cards into a bag; a few clothes, her notes. Her eyes fell on the newspaper she had been reading. West Australia was the single remaining avenue of investigation that remained to Chrissy; it was a long shot but she had to go somewhere. There was a ring at the door. Chrissy froze. It could be nothing; on the other hand, it could be her executioner.

Chrissy's apartment was on the third floor, as she rushed down the fire escape she could hear the sound of her front door being smashed down. There was a cab rank at the corner of the street. Chrissy jumped in the first one.

'JFK airport,' she said.

'Yeah, yeah. Everybody wants to go to the airport,' said the cabby. 'No one stays home no more. Mind you, in this neighbourhood, who can blame them? Blacks, spicks, I ain't prejudiced, no way, but they're so dirty, and the mugging and all . . .'

Even in her desperate state Chrissy realized that she was faced with the classic cab dilemma: do you risk the

253

unpleasantness of telling the guy to stuff it? or do you bite your lip and make non-committal grunts. Normally Chrissy, like most people, would not have had the energy to speak up but she was in a reckless mood. 'Listen, mister,' she said, 'I'm Jewish myself so just can the racist shit, OK?'

'You're so right, Lady,' the cabbie replied. 'The Jews are the worst, Christ, they should have stayed in Israel. Maybe Hitler had the right idea. Like I say, I ain't prejudiced, but I do hate Jews.'

Chrissy gave up and tried to plan her escape.

She had just about enough cash for the cab. After that, plastic was her only currency and so it would not be possible to travel under a false name. Chrissy was already beginning to imagine her adversaries as totally omniscient, godlike in their power and penetration – which of course they were. She would have to use her American Diners Card though and hope that it would not be traced, otherwise she would certainly share Linda's and Toole's fate.

How alone she felt in that cab on the way to JFK. She knew something; and she knew nothing, and the driver was a bastard. She had no one to turn to, and even if she had, she would not have done so since contact with her appeared to be the kiss of death. That was the real isolation, she was on the run and as long as she remained alive she would not be able to contact family or friends. She had the plague, the black spot, she was a leper and an untouchable.

WAITING AND WONDERING

She got into the airport without incident or at least without being killed, because of course her present situation was one extended incident. Having stood in a Stars and Stripes Airline queue she got to a tickets and inquiries person just as she realized that she didn't really know where she wanted to go. She presumed, correctly, that Bullens Creek would not be a destination covered by an international airline.

'Yes, how may I help you, my name is Sandy, thank you for

flying with Stars and Stripes, we will be pleased to assist you in any way we can, have a nice day.' The girl in the uniform smiled so wide it was demonic; the parched over-tanned skin, the bones sticking out of the half-starved face, and the smile, a row of gleaming tombstone teeth in a blood red mouth. To Chrissy, struggling to contain her terror, the Stars and Stripes lady was like death itself; a skull in a pretty little uniform. In actual effect she was just a quite good looking woman of thirty-eight, making the major mistake of trying to look like a very good looking woman of twenty-one.

'Pardon,' stammered Chrissy.

The Stars and Stripes lady gave her the shorter version of official Stars and Stripes consumer friendly approach. 'My name is Sandy, how may I help you?'

Chrissy's mind was blank.

'Uhm ... Oh God ... Sandy, have you ever heard of a place called Bullens Creek?'

'Oh, now, yes I do recall, I'm sure I do ...'

'Great, one ticket please, one way,' said Chrissy, relief flooding over her.

'Well, I believe it's in Texas, now you would want our domestic –'

'It's somewhere in Western Australia!' shouted Chrissy, expecting, every second, a man in a slouch hat to come and shoot her. 'I want to go somewhere in Western Australia.'

'Well I'm sorry, Madam,' said Sandy, switching to the official Stars and Stripes 'now I hope you're not going to cause a scene' voice. 'But you'll have to be a little more specific than that.'

Chrissy's mind was a blank.

'Listen, I've forgotten. What's the capital of Western Australia? Come on, that's where I want to go.'

'Madam, I'm not at all sure you know where you want to go.' The voice was now pure 'if you're a nut I'm calling a cop'.

'Perth!!' blurted Chrissy, with blessed relief. 'I want a ticket to Perth.'

*

As it turned out, Stars and Stripes only covered the eastern states of Australia and Chrissy was forced to join another queue at the National Australia desk.

She discovered that the first available flight was still eighteen hours away. On inquiry she also discovered that it was unlikely to be full. This was important. She wanted to buy the ticket at the last possible minute, eighteen hours would give them plenty of time to trace her credit card transaction and stop her boarding the plane. The same logic meant that she had to presume that they would be waiting for her at the other end, but Chrissy could only take things one step at a time.

She bought a hat and some dark glasses and sat for fifteen and a half terrible hours in a coffee bar, eating the occasional Danish pastry – which is catering speak for a lump of dough and a blob of sugar and is about as Danish as Tandoori chicken.

Chrissy hoped that they had not thought to check out the cab drivers.

A BIT OF LUCK

'Smallish, dark complexion, in a hurry?' Durf's thug was asking Chrissy's ex-driver.

'Hey, hey, hey, what is this, the third degree?' the driver replied. 'Sure I picked up a dame, but I just drive them, OK? I don't feel the need to commit them to memory.'

'Come on! It's only been an hour, think! Was it a Jewish woman?' the thug added.

'No way, pal, you got the wrong cab, the dame *hated* Jews. She told me.'

THEORIZING

As Chrissy sat, she pondered again, as she had done so often before, what could possibly be the cause of the unholy alliance that she was now quite certain she had uncovered. The swift dispatch of Toole proved to her beyond all doubt that she was on to something very big indeed.

What were they up to? And whatever it was, were they doing it at Bullens Creek? And even if they were and she discovered it, what could she do? Chrissy was quite certain that she would be dead very soon whatever happened.

There were lots of policemen about. How she longed to fling herself on the protection of one, but protection from what? A dinner party in Los Angeles months before? Maybe another one in Singapore? Linda died in a burglary, Toole killed himself. The best she could hope for would be to be locked up as a lunatic. Besides, she had no reason to believe that she could trust the police, her adversaries' tentacles seemed to be everywhere, her CIA liaison had lasted a matter of hours.

No, there was no doubt about it, she was alone, alone and mystified; starting at shadows and expecting every waitress to stab her with a poisoned plastic fork.

Chrissy tried to hypothesize what advantages the world's biggest producers could gain by starting some kind of war. It felt distinctly foolish even to be considering the possibility, but what else could she work on?

Collecting her thoughts, Chrissy made a concerted effort to dedramatize the situation; to come up with a slightly less catastrophic theory to fit the information that she had. After all, the murders meant nothing, people killed for money, it didn't mean that they were trying to change world history.

Putting aside the strange purchases that some of the people who had been at the LA dinner party had made since the crash, it seemed possible to Chrissy that they might be trying to set up some kind of illegal investment bank to buy out or out-produce competition and create some kind of hybrid giant multinational; a world super-company without a nationality. If this were the case, secrecy would obviously be essential because it would, of course, ride rough-shod over trade and monopoly legislation worldwide. Besides this, it would take the competition out of capitalism; it would be a kind of communism for billionaires. Try as she might, Chrissy could not bring herself to see much in this theory. And there was the rocket fuel and the guidance systems ... Australia ... were they going to hold the Japanese to ransom? Blow them up? The Japanese dominated so completely in almost all the new industries, their removal would be a huge new profit stimulus to everyone else. But she knew there were Japanese businessmen at the Los Angeles dinner ... Of course that didn't necessarily matter, capital knew no patriotism; that was for workers, to keep them working. Chrissy had lost count of the number of millionaires who lived in tax exile, or had even changed citizenship in order to get over local investment laws. That famous citizen of the world, Rupert Murdoch – a man who owns newspapers that preach arch patriotic xenophobia in their individual countries – had taken US citizenship with the drop of a hat in order to penetrate the US media.

Chrissy's head was spinning, she could no longer get bombs off her mind. Maybe it was the apocalyptic nature of the newspapers she bought in her long long wait. The French power station disaster dominated for the day but the sea-level thing was still big news. It was getting higher and what's more, the floating scum slick had reappeared. That one wasn't going away either, the record high temperatures of the previous Northern summer had wiped out half the US cereal crop and now it looked like European agriculture was going to be contaminated as far as the wheat bowl in the Ukraine for years to come. What arable land remained in the world was going to have to be farmed more intensely; which would mean more chemical fertilizers; which meant more nutrients getting swept into the sea, thus feeding the microscopic algae, who multiply into the floating glob and suffocate the sea. There was a huge picture in one of the papers of the mid-Atlantic, and poking out of the slime that covered it were the fins and tails and noses of a huge school of dead dolphins. The caption noted that under the slime were literally millions of dead fish and various sea creatures.

It being such a long wait, Chrissy finally got around to

buying the English papers that were stocked at the airport. She was relieved to discover that The Princess of Wales had been shopping and that lovely Mandy, seventeen, thought feminists were silly killjoys and she was flattered if men admired her body.

Contemplating the accumulating natural disasters, Chrissy again found herself wondering whether the sick old world would last long enough for whoever it was, to do whatever it was, they were going to do. But that was silly. 'They' would think of something and the world would be OK – 'they' of course were scientists. At that moment, all over the world, scientists were waking up and wondering what they were going to do. They were looking at a snowball. It seemed like only yesterday that they had held that snowball in their fists; they could crush it, shape it, control it. They turned away for a minute and suddenly the fucker was the size of a house, hurtling towards them, too big to hold and too big to control.

But Chrissy herself had more pressing problems to occupy her mind as the hours crawled by in the coffee lounge at JFK. Maybe they would try to hold the world to ransom; maybe Slampacker was going to demand of the world that they either ate more of his Chicken Slammers or he would nuke them?

What with trying to study every approaching face to see if it looked like an assassin, by the time Chrissy got up from the hard plastic chair to finally go and buy her ticket, her head hurt almost as much as her backside.

BACK IN BULLENS

As Chrissy sat, scared out of her wits, high up in the upper atmosphere, Zimmerman was also preparing to make the trip to Bullens Creek airport. He had to pick up his delivery of comics. Zimmerman was a total comic nut, and he had expended quite a large portion of his meagre resources ensuring that his regular supply followed him up to Bullens.

'Get my comic books tomorrow, I love it when I get my books,' he said as they sat around at the Culboons' house the afternoon after they got back from their exciting trip out to Moorcock's fence.

'Zimm,' said Rachel in disbelief, 'you've just done a whole Superman thing yourself, you took care of those guys as if it was a film, and you're thinking about your comics!'

'That's the whole point, Rachel,' replied Zimmerman. 'I can forget things with my comic books, you know, relax. Kind of lose myself in them, you know?'

The others understood fully. Zimm was, in many ways, a wonderful person, but he was also definitely weird, weird and intimidating. The others sometimes found it rather disconcerting just being around Zimmerman. He actually had to live with himself; it was scarcely surprising that he occasionally wanted to lose himself.

'I dig my comics,' Zimmerman continued. Like all adult comic readers he felt the need to do a big number about it not being childish. 'There's a lot more in them than you think, right? They're really wry, you know, cynical. Like, man, you know, the Phantom and Judge Dread are kind of philosophers.'

Zimm was very big for the whole sub-gothic justice fantasy

thing. He played a nationwide game, favoured by hippies and also science students who didn't like rugby, called Dungeons and Dragons. In the game you go through various semi-guided adventures, playing a character that you have invented yourself. Most of the farties who played the game assumed immensely macho characters calling themselves things like Wotan Skulcrusher, Spearman the Axe Bringer and Goblin Trollthrash. They imagined themselves as Thor-like figures, straight out of Tolkien. Zimm's character, on the other hand, was a tiny stooping old wizard; a gentle, peaceful wizard who knew nothing of pain or death; a wizard whose greatest joy was to invent ever more beautiful types of flowers for the children to pick – but a wizard who happened to have an enormous dick and a scrotum that he had to drag behind him on a trolley.

Everybody got their own thing out of the game.

Anyway, on the subject of his comics, Zimmerman was adamant: 'Whatever we do next it will have to be when I get back from the airport man. I've got to have my comics, you know?'

'Well, take your time, Zimmerman mate,' Mr Culboon commented drily. 'I can't see us coming up with our next move for a while. I mean, what the hell do we do?'

Rachel was very wound up, as was CD. Getting shot at in the darkness was a new experience for them both. The Culboons were more relaxed, it had happened to them before, although not in quite a while. For Zimm, of course, it was like old times, in fact for years he hadn't been able to sleep at night unless Walter popped his head around the door occasionally and shouted 'bang'. Walter himself, like CD and Rachel, had never experienced being shot at but he remarked afterwards that he had been surprised at how lacking in heaviness the whole situation had been. Zimmerman assured him that it was worse when you got hit.

Rachel's frustration was growing.

'We've certainly got to do *something*,' she exploded. 'I mean, Christ, if we needed proof that something was going on, we've got it. You don't guard innocent projects with gunmen. What is that bastard Moorcock up to?'

'*Those* bastards, Tyron's in on this too remember,' said CD, secretly wanting to remind Rachel that it was his detective work that had brought them this far.

'And we don't know who else besides.'

'Oh, man, like it's obvious like, what we've got to do, you know?' said Walter in what, for him, was an urgent manner.

It was like a snail trying to dial 999.

'Either one, or all of us people, has got to get over that wire and take a look, you know? But seeing as some of us are not exactly built like commandoes, maybe just Zimmerman should go.'

'I'm bloody going,' said Rachel, 'this is where it starts to get exciting.'

This was too much for Mrs Culboon, who shrieked good-naturedly. 'Oh, darling, if you get excited being shot at and beaten up, just come and live with us Abs for a while, love.'

'Whatever we do, we should leave it at least forty-eight hours,' said Zimm. 'They're sure to be on their guard for a while, but after that I reckon they'll become cool and think we were just a casual hassle.'

Walter looked at Zimm with awe and affection. 'Man, you are becoming so straight and together that I will have to buy you a tie and get you a job in a bank,' he said.

SURVIVAL OF THE STRAIGHTEST

Walter was right, they had all noticed it. Zimmerman was becoming very together indeed. Certainly he did it in his own very untogether way but, none the less, he was a changed man.

Zimmerman had a theory about staying alive and being alive. He had developed his theory during combat and it was a theory shared by many of his colleagues. Life for a soldier in any war is pretty gruesome to say the least; in Vietnam it was worse because no one in the Australian or US Armies had the faintest idea for what or for whom they were fighting. Whereas their opponents knew exactly what they were fighting for; their country and their families, and had been doing so for thirty years. Faced with this unpleasant imbalance in job motivation, the best thing any allied soldier could do really was to try and relax about it. Unfortunately, if you happen to be spending month after month sat in a sweltering swamp, getting eaten alive by insects and shot to bits by highly motivated and extremely skilled guerilla soldiers, relaxing is easier said than done. One of the quickest and easiest ways to get around this problem was to escape the real world in a false, drug induced reality: i.e., get out of your brain.

Unfortunately, soldiers who are staring at the trees claiming that the colours are dancing and that Jesus is a can of corned beef, don't tend to live very long. Saying 'hey man you're beautiful' at approaching Vietcong cut no ice with them at all, they shot you whether you found them attractive or not. Hence it was absolutely essential to be ready to be straight, or at least functional, when there was danger about. Zimmerman learnt to take his recreation when it was safe to do so and to put up with reality when he needed to be able to rely on himself.

Now although Zimm was never again to be the chemical dustbin he had been when he truly did live in hell (in fact after Vietnam he had given up everything but the odd toot on a bong), the basis of his theory had stayed with Zimmerman ever since. Life was mainly a bummer, so it was best to keep your head somewhere else; invent your own more palatable reality. For Zimm this needed to be nothing more complex than a glass of home-brew, a little grass and a good comic. It didn't matter how often he had read it.

None the less, he never forgot what he had learnt in war: the time to get it together was when there was trouble. Now there was clearly trouble and Zimmerman had returned to earth to meet it.

NO CHOICE

'Listen,' said CD, who was getting nervous. He didn't really like the idea of heroics but if Rachel was going, he was going. 'Maybe we should do some research in the town, ask the workers, that sort of thing?'

'I tried all morning, man,' answered Walter. 'Like, most of them stay behind the wire, half of them don't even speak English and they're all paid serious money, man, you know, top whack. You ask them once, they say they're building a hotel; you ask them twice, they tell you to fuck off.'

It was clear to all of them that the only way they were going to find out anything more about the great mystery that they had stumbled upon, was to take another look.

CD wished he'd fallen in love with a coward.

HUNTED

⭐

As Chrissy's National Australian jumbo began its descent into Perth International, she knew for sure that they would be waiting for her, having doubtless traced her destination through her use of a credit card. Chrissy knew also that if she walked out into them they would kill her. And yet, somehow, she had to get past them and over to the internal airport to pick up and pay for her ticket to Bullens, which she had reserved in a false name at JFK.

She presumed that she was safe enough through passport control and that the danger would appear after customs. She could not lose her passport because they would simply turn her around and put her on a plane back to the USA. Chrissy thanked her lucky stars that as a journo she travelled constantly and had an Australian multiple entrance visa in her passport that was good for another year. But it was no good being allowed in so that they could carry her straight out again in a box. She needed a plan. Luckily for Chrissy, she was a journo, and journos are born schemers and natural liars.

After some thought she got up and walked down the aisle. She asked everybody the same thing:

'Excuse me, I have a salt and sugar deficiency, if you've finished would you mind awfully . . .?'

It was such a strange request that people just concurred instantly and handed over the little plastic envelopes. Then Chrissy disappeared to the toilet. She did not re-emerge until the stewardess knocked on the door to inform her that the plane was landing.

After clearing passport control, Chrissy prepared herself carefully to go through customs. She put on her dark glasses, she wet her brow, and she lit up a cigarette . . . then she ran through green. If the plan had failed she intended to trip and allow the bag to burst open, she had already opened it and held it closed with her fingers. As it happened, there was no need because, as she'd hoped, the sight of a sweating, smoking girl trying to run through green with fear in her eyes, fear which of course was very real, was enough to make a young customs officer take a punt on her.

Of course, when she opened her bag and he idly sifted through it, he thought all his Christmasses had come at once because there was the salt and the sugar taped up in a sheet of clear plastic that had once been a bath hat.

The discreet looking murderer stood waiting, as person after person emerged from the US flight, many being immediately and noisily scooped up by tearful families. He could not see Chrissy. He waited and waited, but he could not see her. He waited until long after another flight had flooded the arrivals hall with still more happy huggers, and still there was no Chrissy.

SALT RUNNING

This, of course, was because she was in a customs lock-up.

'What's this,' they had asked.

'Salt and sugar,' she replied. The last thing she wanted was to be delayed for ever for deceiving the police. She wanted a nice two or three hours while they tried to figure her out.

'Why's it wrapped up like drugs?'

'Is it? That's the way I like my salt and sugar.'

'Mixed up?'

'You never heard of sweet and sour?'

The customs people were a little surprised at her coolness so, instead of whisking her away, they had a look at the package that the young officer had plucked so triumphantly from Chrissy's bag.

'It's salt and sugar,' said the lad.

'Get the Prof' to have a look at it, every grain,' said his boss. After about an hour they decided that what they had found was salt and sugar.

'All right, Miss, what's your game? Trying to make it look like you had a bagful of smack, are you a sicko or what?' The officer was exasperated and disappointed; he didn't like Chrissy at all; he didn't understand her, but he knew that he didn't like her.

'Listen, Buster!' snapped Chrissy, who was beginning to feel that it was time to leave. 'This is Australia, right, not the Soviet Union. So, I got a bagful of condiments? What is that, a federal case? You saying you can't bring salt into this country any more? Is that it? Get this, Mister, if you're so damn paranoid you see drugs wherever you look that's your problem, OK? See an analyst, personally I'm outta here.'

'No you aren't, Miss, you aren't out of here by a long shot.' The officer was very puzzled. Puzzled and annoyed. He could see only two explanations for the taped up plastic bag they had found. Either this woman was a weirdo, or he was being subjected to an incredibly elaborate double bluff. The latter was certainly possible. Any drug-runner ran the risk of being stopped and searched by customs, in which case, obviously there was a good chance their goods would be discovered. Perhaps this woman had conceived the audacious plan of leaving something so confusing on display that by the time it had been fully investigated, and found to be perplexingly innocent, no one would think of searching further.

'Fine toothcomb job, boys,' he spat the words at Chrissy. 'Unpick every fucking stitch in her jumper. Wanda, bung her on the slab.'

CLEAN GLOVES AND WARM TONGS

And so it was that poor Chrissy took a short break out from being chased across the world by shadowy murderers, in order to have an Australian customs officer stuff a long probe up her important little places. No one is at their freshest after a twenty-hour flight, especially in the terrifying circumstances that Chrissy had endured, so the job wasn't much fun for Wanda either. But she was a philosophical woman and had resigned herself to making the best of what had definitely turned out to be a slightly less glamorous job than she had expected. Probing the bottoms of hippies and wicked old grannies was not absorbing detective work, but she put a brave face on it.

'Togs off,' she shouted in a forced jolly manner, like a games mistress on a cold morning pretending she enjoys her job.

'Laddered your panty hose, dear? Yes, I know,' she said, answering her own question. 'I'm a socks girl myself, put my thumb through just one too many gussets I'm afraid.'

Wanda was a strongly innocent choice of person for the job of extracting deadly substances from the internal body cavities of international villains. On the other hand, she would have been a difficult person to bribe.

'Oh I do envy you skinny girls, lucky things. Honestly, if I haven't got a couple of girders in the old boulder holders, I'm polishing my shoes, honestly I am. . . . Come on, dear, up on the slab, the cat's been on the bum bit, so that should be warm enough anyway. Now then, legs in the stirrups.'

Wanda was not rough at the job but a strip search is still an unpleasant and undignified palaver, made even more frustrating for Chrissy by the fact that she had gone through the same thing with her gyno' only a couple of weeks before. Her distaste must have shown and it hurt Wanda a little. After all, in her job, maintaining a sense of professional pride is pretty much all you've got to hang on to.

'Clean gloves and warm tongs,' she would always tell the new girls, 'even an international trader in death deserves that.'

'Cheer up now, Christine – hope you don't mind if I use first names. I always think it's a bit silly to try and be formal with a person when you've got your hands stuffed where the sun don't shine, eh? So, smile-up girl, smile-up, soon be over, eh?'

But Chrissy could not smile up, she just happened to be one of those strange people who absolutely hate lying on their backs with their legs strapped in the air, and some total stranger peering up their fanny. Some people just have these strange little prejudices.

Finally it was over and Chrissy bade Wanda goodbye. Unlike the officer who had ordered the search, Wanda was very pleased that Chrissy was clean. She always found it so embarrassing when she drew out some horrid damp package, like a magician producing a rabbit from a hat, and being forced to inform some spread-eagled, naked old sad act that they would shortly be starting five to ten in the slammer.

As Chrissy took her leave she felt some comment was in order – their relationship though brief had been intimate.

'Well, goodbye, Wanda,' she said, and then after a moment's hesitation, 'for what it's worth, I think you do a bloody rotten job very well indeed.'

Wanda was very touched. Chrissy was the very, very first satisfied customer she had ever had. Her day was definitely made.

'Thanks old stick,' she said and marched off to water her plants.

TURNING TO CRIME

Chrissy was let out of the Customs office without a stain on her character which was more than could be said for her togs, as Wanda would have called them. She had now been on the run, in abject terror, for about forty hours and was getting a bit whiffy. But she was still alive and what's more, she was not required to go back the way she had come and go out through the green channel. As she was unceremoniously ejected through a small door about a hundred metres along the terminal floor, she allowed herself a quick glance towards the arrivals point . . . Sure enough, there was a large, impatient looking man in an anorak, despite the heat, standing forlornly hoping that he would be able to kill someone off the next flight.

She took a taxi to Perth Internal terminal. Australia being such a huge place, most internal flights are still transcontinental, and hence they get their own airport. Chrissy walked as calmly as she could up to the Southern Cross Airline desk and inquired after the ticket to Bullens Creek that she had reserved for a friend under the name of Robbins.

'Why certainly, I'll just see if I can help you in that way, my name is Charlene and I'll be pleased to offer any assistance, thank you for choosing Southern Cross as your internal carrier.' Charlene was an Australian girl, but the American communication disease is infectious.

'Why yes, here is the ticket, now if I can just take a credit card imprint.' Chrissy handed over her card.

But, during Chrissy's long flight, some unseen hand had been at work and Charlene was embarrassed to have to inform Chrissy that the computer had blocked her card. What's more, Charlene regretted to have to inform Chrissy that she had been requested to inform American Diners of the time and location of the attempted transaction . . .

Chrissy mumbled that it was the third time this week and she had been assured that the mix-up had been dealt with and disappeared into the crowd. Chrissy had to think quickly, which in a way was lucky because had she had more time to ponder, she would surely have despaired at the hopelessness of her position. She was being hounded by the most powerful people in the world; people who knew, and controlled, everything.

Supposing she did get to Bullens Creek? And what if the secret did lie there? What would she do? She was going to be killed very shortly anyway, there was not a lot of point in running.

However, Chrissy had made a plan, a plan to get to Bullens Creek and for want of anything better to do, she determined to stick to it. And so, imbued with the fatalism of somebody who basically considers herself as good as dead, she decided to steal somebody's wallet.

This decision required a lot of courage. Because, even in her perilous position, the thought of being caught as a common thief and marched away in shame through a crowd of embarrassed people still held a real dread for her.

But, in fact, that scenario was an unlikely one because Chrissy came up with a brilliant idea. This was partly because fear lends wings to the imagination, and partly because the lack of individualism which the modern world of global finance imposes on us is not confined to the horrors of Slampacker burgers. The rich are equally susceptible to being told who they are.

BADGE OF RANK

Chrissy's plan formed the moment she saw the contents of the rich lady's bag, carelessly placed on the floor beside her as she sat reading the sort of novel that would never have been invented if it wasn't for the Wright Brothers. Inside the bag was a Cartige card wallet. There could be no mistake about that, the distinctive dyed grey crocodile skin with pink edges, the gold-plated corner strengtheners. This was the Cartige logo and identity, jealously protected in courts across the world.

Why this jealousy? The reason is that the wallet was no more attractive than a wallet costing a tenth as much, this is why the distinctive livery is so important. That livery, protected in court from imitation, guarantees that anything carrying it costs a hell of a lot.

These identification uniform 'accessories' are literally nothing more than a personal advert proclaiming one's wealth. A small key-ring, or bill clip carrying the logo of a perfume company, can cost easily two hundred pounds. There seems to be no reason for this inflation, other than that it represents an international visual snob code. It would be cheaper, and no less ostentatious, to simply stamp one's income on one's forehead. At least that had been the gist of Chrissy's thoughts the previous Christmas, when Farty Frank, a commodity broker of her acquaintance, had given her a Cartige card wallet in the obvious hope that she would be impressed.

'It's genuine Cartige, you know,' he had said; meaning that whatever its genuine aesthetic value and whatever its genuine practical value, it certainly genuinely cost a lot.

Chrissy did not really like carrying a financial badge of rank but it was certainly a very nice looking wallet, worth at least thirty of the three hundred bucks it had cost, and so, despite brushing off Farty Frank pretty sharpish, she had carried her cards in the Cartige wallet ever since. In honour of his memory, Farty Frank got a starring role in the scheme that his gift made possible.

THE HIT

'Frank!!' Chrissy shouted, 'Frank, Frank, I'm here,' she scuttled across the terminal as the five Franks in the crowded room turned their heads. Chrissy pushed her way through the people, making as much noise as she possibly could. 'Wait, Wait, I'm here!!!'

This time the carefully pre-opened bag was required, and worked perfectly. It was almost empty, but what contents there were scattered over and into the rich lady's gaping bag. Chrissy played it half-apologetic, half furious. After all the mythical Frank was disappearing and the lady's bag had been in a gangway.

She had to get down first and, as deftly as she could, whipped the lady's wallet, overcoming a momentary paranoia that she was in fact stealing back her own one. Obviously and instantly the rich lady's suspicions were aroused.

'Hey, get your hands out of my bag will ya!'

Chrissy instantly backed off.

'OK, OK, sorry, but I'm in the process of missing my fiancé in from Detroit. It's just the lipstick, the gold compact and the address book . . .'

The rich lady had now assured herself that a Cartige wallet was still in her bag and happily handed over the other items, pleased to meet another American.

'The men you gotta chase are the only ones worth having, dear, go for it.'

Chrissy thanked her and rushed off with a surge of confidence. Not only had she effected rather a neat lift, but also she had covered herself. If the lady discovered the switch, Chrissy could, of course, claim that it had been a genuine mix-up, and take back her own cards with feigned relief. Her only chance of discovery would be if she was caught using the cards and she intended to get that obstacle out of the way immediately.

Watching the rich woman carefully from across the terminal, Chrissy allowed herself only five practises at the signature on the back of the American Diners card. Luckily it was an erratic scrawl which Chrissy, being a journalist, had no trouble at all in emulating.

No more than three minutes after the theft, Chrissy presented herself back at the Southern Cross desk, being careful to choose a different queue to the one Charlene stood at the front of.

Having paid for the ticket, Chrissy returned to the rich woman and explained the mix-up. Not only was Chrissy an honest person who did not wish upon anyone the hassle of having to cancel all their cards, but also she did not need the police after her as well. Obviously the ticket to Bullens would eventually show up on the rich woman's statement but she did not look like the sort of person who kept their transparents and checked them off each month. On her first shot Chrissy had committed the perfect crime.

The rich lady laughed at the confusion.

'Well now, these darn Cart-ee-*jay* things are meant to be so exclusive and here they are falling over each other. Thank you, dear.'

Chrissy was about to leave.

'By the way, did you catch Frank?'

'Frank?'

'That's right, dear,' the lady laughed, 'love 'em and forget 'em. I have three times.'

LUCK RUNNING OUT

The flight left forty minutes later and Chrissy got on it without mishap. She ordered a beer and tried to collect her thoughts.

She had to presume that despite having slipped past the thug at customs, her adversaries must now know that she was in Australia because Charlene would have reported her trying to use her credit card. On the other hand, she had actually bought her ticket to Bullens Creek with a different card, so with any luck they would take a while to find out where she had gone to after leaving Charlene.

This time though, luck was against her. The poor stooge who had so unsuccessfully staked out the international arrivals had rushed straight over to internal the moment he got the word and was now interviewing Charlene.

'She wanted to pick up a ticket to Bullens Creek, but of course I wouldn't give it to her. If my computer says "hold" I hold.'

Having learnt that a plane for Bullens had just left and that yes, a woman closely resembling his sister had been on it, the stooge rang his boss. That boss then rang his boss, and very quickly the message reached Durf's inner team.

Durf's inner team nearly shat themselves. How on earth could this woman, Christine Kelly, have worked it out! She was going to Bullens Creek, the very epicentre of everything. It was shocking how close they had come to a total breach of security. One thing was certain, this time Chrissy was going to be met at the airport

AIRPORT RESCUE

RECEPTION COMMITTEE

The incoming Southern Cross flight from Perth was going to be a little late and so Zimmerman had nothing to do but hang out in the sweaty, humid, horrible arrivals shed until his comics arrived.

Bullens Creek strip had changed beyond recognition since the day that Sly had first flown in and given his speech. The old arrivals and departures hut was now just a store room. To replace it, a large pre-fabricated building had been thrown up and beside it, a car park full of ex-military air traffic control equipment. This sleepy little place that had once received two flights a day, was now taking eight an hour – almost all freight – and that number was scheduled to double within a month. They had extended the original runway and were building three more much larger ones. Being in the middle of the desert there was no space problem, and already Bullens Creek airport was beginning to resemble a thriving little metropolis all of its own.

None the less, despite the crowds and the hustle and bustle in the huge shed, Zimmerman spotted the four men in sports jackets immediately. 'Pigs or gooks,' he thought to himself without much interest.

It was the overplayed casualness of the unpleasant looking little group that was so transparent to Zimmerman. No collection of people who are all waiting for the same thing are capable of holding a natural conversation. Even if the thing they are waiting for is only a taxi. No matter how communicative an evening has been, no matter how smoothly

275

the conversation has flowed, once both parties know that there could be a taxi at the door any minute, the conversation inevitably becomes stilted. And it is the same when you are waiting for women you have been told to take alive at all costs. Of course, Zimmerman did not know that that was what they were waiting for, but he knew they were waiting for something, and he presumed that whatever it was they were up to no good.

However, Zimmerman decided to ignore them. After all, he and his companions were onto something very big and the last thing he wanted to do was start drawing attention to himself. The men were probably waiting for an atom bomb or something to take behind the wire; but there was nothing that Zimmerman could do about it for the time being. Anyway, Zimmerman decided, if he was going to get shot at some point, which he reckoned was a pretty fair bet, he wanted to have a read of what happened to the Phantom and Judge Dread first.

To die with an easy mind is one thing; to die in the knowledge that the Phantom is still bound to the croc' with live snakes and the Judge appears to have inexplicably turned his back upon justice and made a pact with evil, is another.

FORSAKEN

As with all flights, when the Perth plane came in, the people got off first. Zimmerman knew that it would be at least ten minutes before the baggage and freight would be taken off and that he would have to wait. He was interested to see that the four men stirred restlessly though. So, it was a person they were waiting for, Zimm deduced. Reception committee or execution squad? Zimm guessed, by the look of them and the bulges in their shoulders, that someone was in for a nasty touch-down.

People began to flow through the arrivals door. The thugs soon spotted their quarry, they moved as one man. The quarry, a woman, spotted them a moment later. There was clearly nothing that she could do. Zimm watched her, his blood quickening. She had a nice face but it was dull with terror. She seemed to be visibly sagging with exhaustion and the desperation of her condition. For Zimm, whose regular prescriptions from Doctor Goodtime had got him into the habit of visualizing things that were not there, she seemed to be disintegrating before his very eyes. It was as if her will to live was physically dripping out of her and collecting in a puddle at her feet.

Zimm felt absolutely awful. He had been a cornered animal himself and he knew that facing a gang of murderous foes, by whom you were totally outnumbered, was absolutely horrid. As the four goons surrounded her, Zimm knew that the Phantom would not have hesitated. He knew that the Phantom would, regardless of personal risk and the natural reluctance one feels to making a scene in a crowded airport, have *done* something. Dodging bullets and armed only with a luggage trolley and stand-up ashtray the Phantom would have sorted it out. Even the fact that he was at present in Central Africa tied to a croc' with live snakes would not have stopped him saving that girl. Zimmerman longed to get stuck in.

It was not fear that held him back – although taking on four armed thugs was fairly high on Zimmerman's list of things he didn't like doing – it was the wider situation. This new, together, danger tackling Zimmerman could see that he was involved in something potentially much bigger than the fate of just one person, no matter how nice a face she had. He mustn't compromise his Eco-mission . . . None of the others would get over the wire without him, and he would be no good dead, or in jail.

Oh well, he would have to leave the poor girl to her fate. Zimmerman knew that his treasured super-hero comics were going to make hollow reading after he had failed to save a damsel in distress.

TERMINAL TERMINA?

'Don't make any sudden moves or noises, Ms Kelly,' said the lead thug. 'From what you already know of us, I presume that you can guess that we own this town. There is no one here to help you.'

Chrissy knew that he was right, suddenly she nearly fainted with exhaustion. The flight from her apartment with the door being smashed behind her seemed a century away; and now it was over, she was caught and was going to die, probably never even knowing what it had all been about.

'OK, kill me,' she said quietly.

'Please don't be so silly and melodramatic, Ms Kelly?' the thug said with the same smile as if he were greeting an old friend. 'We want you to come with us, that is all, to answer a few questions.'

Of course, reasoned Chrissy, they would need to know if she had told anyone of her suspicions besides Toole; if she had left any notes. Oh well, she was going to stay alive an hour or two longer. It didn't matter, she felt dead.

'Come along, then, Christine, we will show you to your car.' The four men closed around her. She stepped out of the puddle of her will to live and surrendered to her captors. As they led her out she began to weep quietly and copiously.

A KNIGHT IN SHINY TROUSERS

It was not the spirit of the Phantom that forced Zimmerman to act, although he didn't take much persuasion. He decided to intervene on the girl's behalf because as the men turned around to lead her out he recognized one of the men they had encountered at the wire two nights previously. Not the one whose arm he had broken, the other one. This was proof that whoever the girl was, she was an enemy of whatever it was that lay behind the wire; possibly a much better informed enemy than Zimm and his companions were. Maybe she could shed light in the darkness. Anyway, it did not matter, he now knew she was definitely a comrade in arms and therefore Zimm could not desert her. That was one of the rules of war; you looked out for your brothers, or, in this case, sister.

Still, tough situation.

There were four of them, obviously armed and, Zimm had no doubt, virtually immune from prosecution in this little town that had become an outpost of the Moorcock empire. Besides this, he guessed their transport would be waiting just outside in the car park and once they were in that they were out of Zimmerman's reach.

Pausing only to grab his comics, which fortuitously slipped onto the carousel at that moment, Zimmerman sprinted out to the car park in order to get ahead of them. Four men surrounding a prisoner move fairly slowly and Zimmerman, of course, moved extremely quickly, and so he was out in the car park before Chrissy's tears had even begun to flow.

Anyone looking at him, knowing his intentions, would have thought Zimmerman a strange sort of saviour in his ancient shiny loon pants and his sweaty singlet. Which just goes to show that you should never judge a book by its cover or, for that matter, a knight by his trousers. After all, Superman wears red knickers, blue tights and knee-high booties.

MEANWHILE EVERYBODY WAS GETTING CANCER

CD had accompanied Zimmerman to the airport but had elected to stay in the car. It was a beautiful day, the top was down and he was happy to soak up the rays rather than hang around in a crowded non-air-conditioned shed. Had he known a little more about the state of the ozone layer he might have felt a little differently and bolted for the shade, no matter how hot and sweaty it was.

Oh sure, CD, like everybody in the world, especially Australians, was aware that the layer was under pressure and that without it the sun might give you skin cancer. But it was so difficult to believe it. The sun looked the same as it had always done; it felt just as good; it had the same revitalizing powers it had always had and it still made all the girls look mega-sauce.

The problem with the ozone layer is it is such a tiny, thin, gossamer layer, like a sheet of very soft loo paper. The difference being that with loo paper, one notices its absence immediately, because you're staggering about with your trousers around your ankles looking for an old magazine to use instead. With the ozone layer you don't even notice it's gone. Not, that is, until they're hacking the malignant melanomas off you.

ZIMM PICKS UP A GIRL

So CD sat in the car, in the car park, contentedly having his skin cells turned cancerous by the photo-power of the sun, wondering why Zimmerman, who was normally so cool and laid back; who normally motivated himself about the place in a manner that CD felt was rather reminiscent of his own street-cool lope (it wasn't), was sprinting towards him at such an astonishing speed. He was about to comment, but Zimmerman's manner cut him sort.

'Listen, get the engine running, and put it in gear, I've got to get a girl, OK, man? Now, once she's in the wheels, burn man, burn OK? Don't look back, don't stop on red, don't pick up hitch-hikers. Get her home, then dump the wheels. Dig?'

CD was about to protest, he understood Zimmerman's sexual frustrations, he sympathized with it, after all, he was not exactly getting any action himself, but he could not be part of abduction, no way. Zimmerman would simply have to take more cold showers.

Unfortunately CD was not in a position to say anything because Zimm was sprinting back towards the terminal building.

CD turned on the engine and put the car into first. Despite his reservations one's tendency with Zimmerman – especially this new, dynamic and, being honest, violent Zimmerman — was to do what he said.

Zimm arrived back just as the little party of thugs was emerging from the shed with their prey, in fact he nearly blundered into them. Under the circumstances there was little he could do other than confront them right there and then.

'Excuse me, Miss, but do you want to go with these men?' he said.

Chrissy did not reply, she already had Toole's death on her conscience, she did not want another. The leader of the group pushed Zimm and he took a step back.

'She's crying because she's glad to be home. Now piss off.'

'Shit man, if you cry like that coming to a dump like Bullens, you have low expectations in life, real low expectations,' said Zimm, sizing up the opposition. 'Imagine if she ever got to Disneyland, her head would just totally explode.'

The fellow in charge was about to punch Zimm out of the way when one of his companions spoke up.

'Mr Rourke, this is the bastard who broke Pete's arm, I think maybe we should take him too.'

'This guy did it?' said Mr Rourke. 'Now you said the man who did Pete was the hardest fellah you ever did encounter. Fact is, I reckon you said there was six of him. Now are you trying to tell me that this little scruffy piece of hippy shit here took you and Pete to the cleaners?'

Pete's hapless companion was spared further embarrassment because at this point Zimm reckoned that the four blokes were about as distracted as they were ever going to be. He drove his fist full into the face of Mr Rourke, knuckling his eyes and breaking his nose. Following through in fact, almost as part of the same movement, he brought up his right boot between the other front man's legs. He used all of his considerable force, wishing to be absolutely sure that with his first two blows he would halve the odds properly. In fact, he probably overdid it, cracking the man's pelvic bone, but it was a long time since Zimm had had bollocks himself and he had forgotten just how little force is required to be effective.

Nit-picking aside, Zimmerman was doing extremely well; the fight had been in progress for only just one second, and his second victim was already crumpling up. Chrissy was now guarded only from behind. Zimm pulled her forward.

'Across the car park,' he spoke urgently but without alarm, 'Red '66 FC Holden . . .'

He pushed her behind him and hurled himself at the other two guards, crashing both to the ground, one with each hand.

'Go!' he shouted, thanking heaven that Rachel had had the foresight to own a highly distinctive car.

As a journo, Chrissy had long since learnt to take her luck where she found it. She ran into the car park and glanced around wildly. Holden is the indigenous Australian car manufacturer and, being an American, Chrissy had no idea what the classic '66 FC looked like. On the other hand, there was clearly only one old car hanging out in that boom town car park. What's more, it was red, its engine was running and there was a strange, funny little man in sunglasses waving at her.

CD had watched the whole incident with fear and awe. Zimmerman had definitely been hiding his light under a bushel, and a ten foot, lead-lined concrete bushel at that. Zimm's despatch of the front two guys had been awesome. CD now understood that Zimmerman's motives must be honourable and that he wished CD to help him save a person in distress. He shouted and waved, and whilst Zimmerman wrestled with the two remaining thugs, Chrissy rushed across the car park and jumped in beside CD.

Pausing only to momentarily slightly adjust his shades and say, 'Hi, I'm CD and I will be your driver on this trip,' he headed for the exit at speed. He had never been involved in anything remotely as exciting as this before and he grabbed his opportunity to get the pose just right.

'Who the hell was that guy?' asked Chrissy, who was a pretty cool customer herself and had already regained her composure. 'Oh him,' said CD casually, 'yeah, he's one of the team.' It was magnificent posing. But then CD blew it by saying, 'and me, I am as well and what's more, he's my mate, yeah really, he's my mate, I know him.'

WORLD OPPOSITION TO
STARK UNITES

Everybody was beginning to be really scared now.

Zimmerman had still not returned. It had been two and a half hours since CD had sneaked Chrissy back to the Culboons' place, having first left the Holden well out of town. That meant a good four hours since the incident at the airport, and Zimmerman had not returned. What's more, the long wait had left plenty of time for Chrissy to explain her recent history. A history of murder; a history that included things like the CIA; a history that hinted at unseen and incomprehensibly colossal power – no wonder they were worried. Walter considered suggesting that they all try to centre themselves, in order to avoid becoming uptight. Unfortunately, under the circumstances, uptightness would only have been avoided by a full frontal lobotomy.

CD had enjoyed it at first. 'This is Chrissy,' he had announced dramatically. 'Zimmerman and I rescued her at the airport. One of the guys who was at the wire last night and three others were trying to take her away.'

The Culboons were hospitable souls and Chrissy was soon sat on the sofa with a beer and a vegamite sandwich. Walter asked her what the problem had been at the airport.

'They were going to kill me,' said Chrissy, with firm conviction. 'They had tracked me from the States, and they were going to kill me.'

'Are you sure man?' asked Walter. 'I mean, that is a very heavy presumption, "kill" is a kind of terminal word, you know? Maybe they were just going to scare you a bit.'

'They were definitely going to kill me,' replied Chrissy.

'Why?' asked Rachel spotting the most fruitful line of questioning.

'Because they think I know something about what they're up to.'

'And do you?' asked Rachel, anxious not to let Walter start.

'No,' Chrissy said and then added, 'do you?'

'Do we what?' asked Rachel.

'Know anything about what they're up to.'

'What who are up to?'

'I don't know.'

There was a pause as everyone realized that the situation was getting confusing.

'Now look here,' Mrs Culboon said, making everybody look. 'It seems that this lady has had trouble with the same bastards as shot at us last night. Now I don't know what that means in the city, but out here in the country it means you got a mate till proved otherwise. So, if Mr Culboon would be so good as to pay another visit to the refrigerator, perhaps we can exchange notes. Yes, I reckon that's about what we should do.'

They all had a beer and Walter explained to Chrissy the scant details of their progress to Bullens Creek.

'What you have to dig here, Chrissy, is that we are like environment orientated, you know? Like, we stand up for the earth, so when we found out that major fat cat breadheads were forcing people off their land for no apparent reason –'

'By whom you mean Silvester Moorcock and Ocker Tyron, is that right?'

'Dig! Nail on the head time, right,' said Walter, amazed. 'Wow, that is uncanny man, I mean that is *weird!* Did you do that with telepathy or what? Is it a ley line thing? Like, how did you know that those two cats were doing stuff out here?'

'I read it in the newspaper,' replied Chrissy.

Walter was even more impressed.

'Man that is so *together!* That is *clear thinking* lady! Why didn't we think of that?'

'Well it's only become financial news in the last few days,' said Chrissy. 'This damn crash and depression thing has made any development into a story. Especially when it's a leisure complex. I guess you people have been onto this for longer than that?'

'True enough,' said Walter. 'I mean when our man CD here sussed the connection and we became hip to just how much trouble these dudes were going to, just in order to get hold of a bit of territory that weren't worth shit. Like, we thought we'd have a look . . .'

Rachel decided to take over at this point because, as always, it looked like it was going to take Walter a long time to say anything. She explained to Chrissy about the Nazi attack that had made them suspicious; about Aristos, and Moorcock denying his involvement with Tyron. She explained everything they knew, which was, of course, almost nothing, except that they had smelt rocket fuel and that security was strangely too tight for a hotel complex.

In return Chrissy explained the long and terrifying sequence of events that had led her to Bullens Creek airport and near death.

When she had finished there was near stunned silence. Even Mrs Culboon was lost for words, for a moment. Then inevitably she laughed.

'Well, Jes-us this is rich don't you think, Mr Culboon! Here's us thinking we're uncovering a bit of illegal mining or something and it turns out there is a full-on global conspiracy going on right where we used to shower and shit.'

It never crossed any of their minds to doubt the seriousness of Chrissy's conclusions, they accepted absolutely that Linda and Toole had been murdered and that only Zimmerman had saved Chrissy from the same fate. And where was Zimmerman?

PRISONER OF STARK

Where Zimmerman was, was tied to a chair in a Portacabin on the Stark construction site. He faced both Sly and Tyron, neither of whom appeared inclined to be friendly. They had been extremely badly shaken by Zimm's little party at the airport, especially when, after a telephone consultation with Durf, they realized that they had lost the journalist. A journalist who had already tried to alert the CIA to their activities and who knew all about the murder of Linda Reeve.

'Temporarily lost,' asserted Ocker Tyron, who was pacing about the room in the manner made popular by British actors playing Nazi officers in fifties films.

Tyron and Sly had not been having an easy morning in the first place. They had been in the middle of a fairly epic row when security had come through with the bad news.

THE PROBLEMS AND THE ETHICS OF
PREPARING FOR DOMESDAY

'Listen, Tyron, you're talking and acting like the stupid big-headed wanker that you are,' Sly had snapped, making, it has to be said, very little effort at a conciliatory manner.

'Rome wasn't built in a day and a whole new world wasn't either,' he continued. 'I am preparing the site as quickly as is humanly possible and your coming up here and throwing your weight around is not going to speed anything up.'

But Tyron had his own problems, certainly enough of them to make anyone act like a stupid big-headed wanker, even if they were not naturally predisposed to do so, which Tyron was.

'You want to know what I've got in my garage, Moorcock?' he shouted. 'I'll tell you. I've got seven enormous boxes which contain the components of a processing plant that will extract water from perma-frost to a geo-depth of one kilometre. There is no room for my fucking cars . . .'

Sly could not believe it, he had hundreds of men working around the clock on a construction project the speed and size of which defied imagination – and this idiot was talking about cars!

'Listen, I have stuff to do, OK?' Sly said. 'If you want to talk junk, go to one of your stupid mother's dumb jumble sales.'

Tyron's lid came off, he was not about to have his mother's name taken in vain by anyone.

'You leave my mother out of this or I'll bust your fucking head, Moorcock,' he said in his best boardroom manner.

'Sure, I'll leave her out of it,' said Sly, adding viciously, 'after all, that's what you'll be doing when the shit hits the fan. Isn't that right? Bye bye Mumsy.'

Sly had hit a very major nerve. Like all members of the Stark consortium, Sly included, Tyron had spent not a little time in the past few months pondering the subject of life and death; and more importantly on whom should he confer the former and to whom should he leave the latter. One thing was for sure, as Sly had shrewdly guessed, Mumsy was fucked. Tyron declined to discuss his mother further and returned to the subject of his garage.

'Listen I'm here to discuss distribution, or more importantly, the lack of it. The reason my garage contains a space-age artesian well, is because I have managed to completely cover a four hundred acre site with stuff that you are supposed to be taking delivery of and installing! I have a two hundred grand Ferrari standing in the street for Christ's sake! The birds are crapping on a two hundred grand Ferrari! My wife has to park by the public pavement. You have got my wife walking the streets, Moorcock!'

Before Sly had a moment to argue that the Domesday Group's predictions were now so fore-shortened and the demands of Stark so urgent that he was being asked to perform a near impossible task, the phone rang and they were informed of the screw up at the airport. They had lost the girl, but had captured her rescuer and had him held in the Security cabin.

Sly had hoped to lose Tyron before trying to deal with this new crisis, but to no avail. Tyron had nothing to do and was a born interferer; he was one of those people who are incapable of believing that anyone else could possibly do anything as well as he. Had he visited Van Gogh in his studio Tyron would have simply itched to grab the brush and say, 'Oh for God's sake let *me* do it'. One of the reasons Tyron had had no kids was that he could not believe that something which he so manifestly could not do was worth doing.

And so they both boarded a helicopter for the short flight across the construction site in order to go and interview their captive. Actually they could have driven the distance more conveniently but years of incredible riches had led them both to always instinctively take the most expensive option in any situation.

TRAPPED IN THE LION'S PORTACABIN

On entering the room they dismissed the guards who had been standing nervously around a severely trussed and bound Zimmerman ever since his arrival. The guards hadn't known who he was, or what he wanted, but they knew him to be dangerous. He had, after all, hospitalized three of their colleagues (if you included Pete with the broken arm) and it had taken the armed intervention of the Bullens Creek Police to bring him in. This long-hair with the slightly greying beard was the hardest case that any of the cocky little security figures had ever come across and when Sly summarily dismissed them they were more than happy to get him off their hands.

'Out! All of you. The Colonel will keep an eye on the prisoner,' Sly shouted – not because he was a natural shouter, he wasn't really, but they were, after all in the middle of an enormous building site cushioned from it only by a flimsy Portacabin. The noise was fairly horrendous.

'Colonel' Du Pont was the head of on-site security. His rank was self-conferred and was a commission in the world army of arrogant macho pricks. He was an unpleasant, officious bully of a man. He had taken up bullying as a profession partly because of his nose – it was a whopper, made gross by the pitted scars of countless failed experiments in plastic surgery. The terrible complex of impotent, bitter rage that his conk gave him had made Du Pont take up bullying for a living.

He had a large staff of lesser thugs – with lesser noses – but he was the only goon to have been indoctrinated into Stark. The brave new future that Stark would create was to be self-regulating. The last thing those involved wanted was anyone bringing along a private army.

Du Pont stood behind Zimmerman whilst Sly addressed him and Tyron paced about.

Zimmerman was gashed, bruised and bound but he did not in any way cut a sad figure. There was a latent strength and dignity about this cornered animal that made him appear like a rather noble early Christian martyr or something similar – until he opened his mouth that is.

'Oh man, I mean, what is the point, for sure, you know, I mean what *is* the point right? Like, all this tying up stuff and bashing in the face scene is a very long way from being cool, you dig? I mean, sure I know I totalled a couple of your guys and like, I'm sorry, but you know? I mean they were hassling the chick right? Like four goons hassling a chick is –'

'Shut the fuck up, you stupid fool,' barked Sly, who was very disturbed indeed to find that the mysterious hippy was the same one who had eaten his burger at Facefull's revolting restaurant. Was there some kind of shadowy conspiracy on their tail? Hippies? Financial journalists? Beautiful girls, what the hell was going on?

'Who sent you? Who pays you? Who are you and how long have you been working with that girl you saved?' said Sly, trying not to appear scared in front of Tyron.

Zimmerman saw no reason or profit in lying.

'I just met the chick at the airport, right. I don't work for anyone, no one pays me, I'm just a concerned dude, right? You know, social responsibility, dig?'

In fact neither Sly nor Tyron dug very clearly. Of course they both knew the term 'social responsibility' but it held very little meaning for either of them.

'It's like we told you at that chicken shit burger disaster area,' continued Zimmerman; who despite his disadvantaged position, still felt that the onus of explanation lay with him.

'We're green terrorists. Ever since we heard you sicking those Nazis on our Ab' friends, we've been wondering what goes down.'

Sly shot an angry glance at Tyron, who came as close as he was capable to coming of blushing – which wasn't very close.

'What *does* go down here, by the way?' asked Zimmerman curiously.

'Like I told you, you interfering bastard, we're building hotels. Now where are your –' Sly was nervous and angry, but not half as much as he was about to become.

'Oh come *on* man, I mean like, for sure, you know? I mean, do I look like I've had my brains removed man? Do I look like some kind of space case, lobotomized air-head man?' Zimmerman asked.

It was a stupid question.

'Yes,' interjected Tyron. 'Now what do you know?'

'I know you ain't building nothing but trouble here, man, big trouble. Like you got it all pretty covered man but the chopper your goons brought me from Bullens in was close to the ground, like real low man. Man, I was with the fighting forty-third in 'Nam for five years. I know a launch site when I see one, and I seen a big one man! One mother-of-a-fucking enormous launch site. Silos, towers, you got it all! That's the first time I ever heard of a hotel with enough fire-power to take out the whole of South-East Asia.'

Sly and Tyron stared at the apparition in the chair as if their nemesis had just risen up out of the floor and stuffed a pie in their face. Sly nearly shot him dead there and then.

Of course Zimmerman was aware that by exposing so much of what he knew and what he had guessed, he was basically asking to be killed. But he reasoned correctly that whatever it was they were planning, he was in far too deep for them to trust him alive anyway. Therefore his best bet was to make himself appear dangerous. That way, they would be all the more anxious to find his companions and hence be forced to keep him alive to help them.

'Where are the others, the ones who were with you last night on the wire?' Sly asked, confirming Zimmerman's theory.

'There were no others, man,' he replied, 'your goons were so shit scared, I reckon they just must have multiplied me up a few times.'

'Don't crap me, mate!' Sly shouted, making each word sound like an individual and very special threat. 'Or I'll have your bollocks,' he added, making, in Zimmerman's case, no threat at all.

'I doubt it, man,' said Zimm, 'you'd have to go back to 'Nam for a start and then you'd have to find the right tree, OK? Which would be incredibly difficult, and even then man, like even if you did all that, I really don't think they'll still be there.'

Sly didn't follow any of this and so decided to get back to the interrogation. 'There were four of you at the restaurant; you, the other hippy, the pratt in shades and a girl. The one who came prying around, asking questions.'

Tyron stared at Sly angrily.

'Questions?' he barked, 'I thought you said that nobody had been asking questions? I specifically asked you if anybody had been asking questions and you said that nobody had . . .'

'Yeah, well, if you hadn't got your useless pig of a brother to drag in a bunch of incompetent Nazis then nobody would have been asking any questions in the first place, would they?'

'That's not the point, Moorcock. I specifically asked you —'

'Guys, guys, guys, guys, guys, guys, *guys*,' Zimmerman pleaded. 'You know, you two really have to talk this thing out. You have a definite confrontation problem. You need to discuss your frustrations about each other honestly in the presence of a disinterested third party. But excuse me if I don't volunteer. Like, these ropes are cutting into me so can we maybe put the family row on ice for a while, right? You know?'

Tyron strode across the room and punched the defenceless Zimmerman in the face.

'Tell us where your friends are right now!'

'Leave that kind of thing out of it, all right Tyron. We're not savages,' Sly admonished.

'Maybe we are, maybe we aren't,' Tyron replied, nursing his grazed knuckles. 'But this is a fight for survival, either way; the law of the jungle, and it seems that there are people out there who may know plenty. We need to find out who they are.'

'Well I ain't going to tell you, man! Like you know, I'm a peaceable soul but I don't reckon I'd tell you fellahs if your car was on fire. So fuck off!' Clearly lines were being drawn in this discussion and Tyron and Zimmerman stood pretty resolutely on different sides. Tyron was about to hit Zimmerman again. Sly asked him to step outside for a moment.

SUCCESS BY A NOSE

Zimmerman was left alone with Colonel Du Pont.

'My name is Colonel Du Pont,' said Colonel Du Pont, who was also acting like a Nazi officer in a film. 'Now you will please tell me the names and whereabouts of your fellow conspirators. Or . . .' and there was a tiny pause for maximum effect — which was minimal effect on Zimmerman because anyone who had spent fifteen years living with Walter was used to pauses. 'Or . . . I shall be obliged to inflict upon you pain beyond belief. Beyond your wildest dreams . . .'

Whether or not Du Pont would have been capable of this is a moot point. After all, a man who has seen his own testicles hanging from a tree knows a fair bit about pain. Plus, somebody who had done as many different and dangerous drugs as Zimmerman would, in his time, have had some pretty wild dreams.

Anyway, Zimm was left with no time to debate this point with Du Pont, because unexpectedly a plan of action presented itself.

Du Pont had been making a pretty major issue out of strutting and posturing in front of Zimmerman. This was because recently most of his time had been spent working out guard rosters and he was relishing the chance to pretend that he really was in the Gestapo. To this end, at the end of his little promise about pain, Du Pont had thrust his face to within an inch of the bound Zimmerman's. He did this because he felt it was intimidating and impressive. It gave him the opportunity to spit his words directly into Zimm's face, and hence gain for them the maximum effect.

This had been his mistake, for in a sudden and wholly surprising move (to both of them) Zimm had pushed his own face forward and grabbed Du Pont's substantial nose firmly between his teeth. Understandably Du Pont was rather shocked, momentarily too shocked to utter, a fact which gave Zimmerman a chance to speak (with difficulty) a few well chosen words.

'Listen, creep mother-fucker!' he spoke up Du Pont's nose. 'I'm gonna bite it off I swear. I truly swear by the Lord I'll bite it off if you squeak man, if you squeak at all.'

Zimmerman was not an easy man to follow at the best of times, and speaking with a nose in his mouth obviously did not make his speech patterns any clearer. However, Du Pont could not help but be impressed by the extremely threatening tone Zimm was employing.

'I swear I will bite it off if you squeak man!' Zimm reiterated. To demonstrate his point he bit hard and Du Pont could feel the skin break and the bone and cartilage creak. It may not seem the most awesome threat in the world, 'don't move or I'll bite your nose off', but in fact, if one thinks about it, as Du Pont was being forced to do, it's actually a pretty heavy deal. The pain and disfigurement would be considerable to say the least.

Du Pont made an effort, he was after all a security officer. His hand moved to the pistol hanging at his side. Instantly Zimmerman twisted his head right down to the left, nearly breaking Du Pont's neck but keeping an ever firmer grip on his honker.

'Don't fuck with me, man,' Zimmerman spat and Du Pont could feel Zimm's saliva running down over his upper lip, adding nausea to the list of Du Pont's ailments. 'Now don't *fuck* with me!' mad Zimm repeated. And with horrible force spun his head from his left shoulder right over to his right shoulder, and then back again, taking Du Pont's nose, head and indeed whole body with him. Inevitably the nose broke and Du Pont nearly fainted with pain. Zimm spoke quickly.

'It's broke but you still got it! Man, you make a squeak I swear I'll be crapping it out with what's left of my breakfast! Now you untie me, man, you untie me or else I'll bite off your nose and suck out your eyes!!!'

Mad Zimmerman was an intimidating force indeed when he was being mad. In fact what with Zimm's unusual speech impediment, and the considerable noise coming from the building site, Du Pont was not really following the finer points of Zimm's monologue. But it was quite clear to him what Zimm must want, and how best to end the terrible pain.

Du Pont's salt tears ran into Zimm's mouth as Du Pont reached behind Zimm in a strange embrace and fumbled blindly with the knots. They came away and Zimmerman's arms were free. He took Du Pont's gun and released his nose, spitting as he did it and grabbing a quick gargle from the jug on the table – these are, after all, paranoid times.

DAVID AND GOLIATH

The old biblical story of David and Goliath, in which we are reliably informed a plucky young lad bested a great big bully, is a story fraught with moral contradictions. The principal contradiction being that David only achieved his famous victory by means of superior weapons technology. His use of a sling shot (an early version of the Stinger, the Exocet and the Cruise) allowed him to floor Goliath before the big fellow even got close. The moral weight traditionally ascribed to David's victory establishes a fairly dangerous precedent. For instance, when a mere handful of British Empire troops were able to slaughter thousands of their spear-carrying opponents by means of the Gatling Gun, was it a David and Goliath situation? When a few hundred USAF flyers attempted to 'bomb Cambodia back into the Stone Age' were they plucky little Davids using wit and cunning to overcome the Goliath that was the population of Cambodia? In fact Goliath was no Goliath at all but a pathetic, muscle-bound Neanderthal throwback. An elephant charging a bazooka.

Now *if* in that bible story, David, a small boy in a loincloth – which is the biblical version of wandering around in your underpants – had been facing a Goliath who was a multi-headed, multinational monster, richer and more powerful than any other force on earth. A monster bent on committing craven and wicked acts in the final seconds before the domesday clock strikes twelve and the dark midnight of ecological oblivion cloaks all life on earth. If that had been what David had been up against, the trick with the sling shot might have cut a little more ice.

DAVID

As Zimmerman hopped it out of the window, his friends, old and new, were hopping it out of the Culboons' place. It was beginning to seem to Chrissy as if she had been scampering about in terror all her life.

They had decided that after Zimm had been missing for five hours, they would take a calculated risk. They would ring the police.

'After all,' Rachel had said, 'maybe he just got busted, I mean arrested . . .' Even in this moment of crisis Rachel fiercely resisted the slow, insidious encroachment that Walter's language was making on her brain. 'It would have been a pretty serious disturbance up at the airport. Perhaps he's just sitting in a cell waiting to get done for disturbing the peace.'

'Listen, Rachel, I'm telling you,' insisted Chrissy, 'the guys Zimmerman was mixing it with run the world. When they have a problem they are not going to call the local cops.'

'Maybe he's in hospital,' suggested CD.

'Sure. Propped up in bed with a bunch of flowers signed love from the world's billionaires,' said Chrissy to Mrs Culboon's laughter. 'They've got him, I'm telling you, they've got him.'

'Well, if they have got him,' said Mr Culboon, sucking on his pipe, 'they're going to be coming after us pretty soon. I reckon Zimm won't tell them nothing but we can't lie low for ever.'

'They know us blacks were involved,' added Mrs Culboon. 'Why there ain't no more than fifty of us in the town, won't take them long to get here.'

'Exactly,' said Mr Culboon, 'we have to fuck off mates. Somewhere to think.' It was at this point that they decided to ring the police.

'I mean, man, if they're going to get on us anyway, we might as well at least check that nobody knows where he is,' said Walter. 'You know he could be dead or dying or . . . or maybe he just had a little victory celebration after the fight and got done for tooting on a doobie.'

Unfortunately Chrissy was right. The police denied all knowledge of the airport incident, which meant for sure that Zimm was being held by the shadowy mega-corporation. Also it meant that the police were bought ... 'And it means that that call you've just made, Mr Culboon,' said Chrissy, 'is being traced as we speak.'

'OK let's split,' said Walter.

And so it was that the entire world opposition to the Stark Consortium was splitting at once. Zimmerman was climbing out of the window of Du Pont's office. Rachel, CD, Walter, the Culboons and Chrissy were running out of the back door of the Culboons' house. They loaded up the old station wagon with what food they could, also some spare clothes and the guns and grenades that Zimmerman had taken from the guards at the perimeter fence, and drove out of town.

GOLIATH

Tyron and Sly stood in the burning sun on the steps of Du Pont's Portacabin, shouting to make themselves heard above the noise. Although as it happens they probably would have both been shouting anyway because they were so furious with each other.

Sly strongly objected to Tyron's interfering and his casual violence. Tyron objected to what he saw as a lack of urgency in Sly's manner. After all, there appeared to be a situation developing where it was possible that a carefully orchestrated plan of infiltration was being carried out against them. Who could tell how far it had got already.

'We have absolutely no idea how big this thing is,' Tyron yelled, 'maybe it's the Russians! Those Kremlin Ayotollahs would give their balls for a piece of what we have going here!'

'For God's sake, Tyron, don't be such a dickhead!' Sly shouted back. All around them the roar of Stark's ghastly creation seemed to swell to match their mood. 'We've run a full background make on the KGB, the OKVD, the ABC and XY fucking Z for all I know!' Sly continued. 'Nothing. Nobody, has a hint of what's going on here. We have an eye in every intelligence agency there is. We pay for half of them for Christ's sake! Durf's on the case, he says there isn't a major criminal, government or military establishment that we aren't monitoring. We are too big to touch.'

'So who's running Rambo in there?' Tyron jerked his thumb towards the door of the Portacabin.

'No one's running him! I'm telling you, Tyron. I've met them, they're kids and ageing hippies; greenies. They have not got the faintest idea what's going on. They're just troublemakers taking a long punt on a short idea because of your stupid Nazi pogrom. Even this journalist from the States doesn't know what she's discovered. We have that from the report on what she told Toole. There is absolutely no reason to panic, and certainly no reason to go around slapping hippies.'

'Know nothing!' shouted Tyron, 'know nothing!! Christ that damn hippy I just slapped had identified the world's six biggest rocket silos! How much does he have to know?'

'Yes, well he's in our hands isn't he? All we have to do is to try to persuade him to tell us where his friends are and then we'll have all of them, won't we? And let's try to do it peacefully, eh?'

They re-entered the office to find Du Pont's prostrate form stretched out on the floor looking like the victim of some terrible sexual liaison . . .

'Oh man, we went all the way, just about bit off each other's noses and everything.'

Whatever had happened, the prisoner was gone.

COUNCIL OF WAR

The little EcoAction team got out of the Culboon's nice new house about ten minutes ahead of the horrible criminal squad who broke in and took the place to pieces, finding nothing but a note left by Mrs Culboon saying:

Dear Bad Fellahs, fuck you. PS could you leave the back door slightly ajar for the cat.

As it happened, by the time the leader of the search squad was presented with this note by a subordinate, the back door had already been reduced to match-wood.

Mr and Mrs Culboon knew a little place that they called their holiday home. It was about thirty kilometres in the opposite direction from the construction site; a tiny cave squeezed into the side of one of the piss-poor little hills that ringed the Bullens Creek area.

Quite a few Aboriginals, especially country ones, set a great deal of store by meditation, or dreaming, or just sitting staring into space, depending on individual mood, and the little cave in the hills was where the Culboons did their bit of drifting.

'Reckon we've sat here dreaming and peaceful many a time, haven't we, Mr Culboon?' said Mrs Culboon.

'Reckon so,' replied her husband with a tinge of sadness.

'It'll make a nice change to sit here shitting ourselves in terror instead,' she shrieked, and everybody laughed with her.

'OK, you know, man,' said Walter calling things to order. 'It is time to assemble our thoughts; it is time to get it together man; it is time to make some kind of plan, dig?'

Of course they all dug very well.

'The problem as I see it, you know? Right? Is that it is comparatively easy to dig the plan that we have to make a plan. It is less simple to dig the actual plan. I mean in order to do that, we have to *have* a plan, which we don't. Dig?'

'Of course we don't,' said Rachel, 'but we haven't had a plan from the beginning, have we? We've just followed our noses. And that's all we can do now. It's obvious that we have to help Zimmerman. We have to find a way through that wire and help him.'

'I'm really sorry to be so negative,' Chrissy replied, 'but from my experience of these people, my guardian angel will be beyond hope by now. The guys he took on are more than a police force, or an army, or a government even. They're money, dirty money, they are everything and they own everything, and that, I'm afraid, includes Mr Zimmerman.'

'They don't own Zimmerman, lady,' said Walter. 'He's not a part of their world, he doesn't even live on it. He got in a space rocket and left the minute he got back from 'Nam.'

'Anyway,' Rachel asked slightly resentfully, 'what do you suggest we do then?'

Rachel could not avoid thinking that things hadn't been so bleak before Chrissy had turned up.

'I don't know,' said Chrissy. 'I just don't know. We still don't have a clue of what it is we're really up against. Even if there was someone in authority that we could trust, we actually have nothing whatsoever to tell them. I suppose you're right, Rachel, we will have to go in. On the million to one chance that instead of getting our butts shot off, we discover what they are up to.'

'Hey, Chrissy, you should curb it with the blind optimism,' CD said. 'We don't want to jinx ourselves.'

Mrs Culboon, of course, laughed. Nobody else did much.

'Well, you know, I guess we should not, like, *all* get down on it, right?' said Walter. 'Because, like, if Chrissy is right and whoever goes over that fence comes out dead, I for one would like to think that maybe somebody was left around to like try and tell the tale, and also feed the Culboons' cat. I'm serious you know? I see no reason why like the cat should have to collect the bummer that we have walked into.'

'If somebody's going to try and eventually alert some form of authority,' said Rachel, 'it should be Chrissy. She's got a real job and credit cards and everything. What are the rest of us? Just a bunch of no-goods. Chrissy should stay.'

Chrissy had, in the previous forty-eight hours, lied and robbed her way across the world, in the process of cheating death many times. Suddenly she felt very tired.

'Sounds good to me,' she said. 'I ain't the volunteering kind.'

'That's right,' said Mrs Culboon, 'Chrissy's taken most of
the shit so far, and she's best qualified to speak up for our
corpses. She should stay here. I guess she's used up a heap of
luck, what with stealing and pretending to smuggle drugs.'
Mrs Culboon laughed. She had greatly enjoyed Chrissy's
account of her adventures, told during the futile wait for Zimmerman.

'I think Mr and Mrs Culboon should stay too, you know?'
Walter said. 'Mr Culboon's head man of a community. A lot
of liberal politico's dig that sort of thing and they're the only
ones who are going to listen to anything as weird as what
we've got.'

'*Mr* Culboon's head man, I'm not,' said Mrs Culboon. 'I'm
sticking with you, Walter. Shit, I want to know what the hell
they're doing to our old homestead.'

And so it was decided. Walter, Rachel, CD and Mrs
Culboon would try to get inside the wire with the twin aims of
trying to find Zimmerman, and of trying to find out what was
going on. Meanwhile, Chrissy and Mr Culboon would remain
holed up at the holiday home.

Mr Culboon went to the back of the station-wagon and
unloaded the guns. 'You know how to use these things?' he
asked the four newly commissioned commandos. 'Because
I've shot various rifles in my time,' he continued and,
shouldering one of the semi-automatic rifles, loosed off a
couple of rounds. He was knocked off his feet by the kick-
back.

'Yes, just as I thought,' he said. 'It's much the same but
you have to hold it a bit more firmly.'

TAKING COVER

The years slipped away from Zimmerman. It was the early
seventies again and he was just the same as he had been then,
except of course that he didn't grow his bollocks back. But,
apart from that, he was the same: a cunning, ruthless, hunted
man, scared and exhilarated at the same time. He lay on the

roof of the Portacabin, prostrate along the guttering, listening to the furious altercation below him.

'We should have shot the bastard!!' yelled Tyron. 'We should certainly shoot you!' he added, glaring at the unfortunate Du Pont who looked a sorry sight with his huge conk turned almost sideways.

'I just hope it rains Du Pont,' Tyron continued, 'because the way the guy left that trunk of yours, you're going to drown.'

'Leave him alone. Do you want to have to indoctrine a new security chief into Stark? What happened to Du Pont could have happened to anyone.' Even Du Pont, who was grateful for Sly's spirited defence, had to privately concede that this was pushing it a bit. The chances of getting your nose half bitten off by a securely bound hippy seemed pretty slim.

'Look, he can't have gone far,' declared Sly nervously, 'and he can't get out of the compound. The whole thing's covered by cameras, and it's open country all the way to the wire. We've got fifteen choppers for Christ sake, he can't move.'

Zimmerman had actually already presumed all this for himself, which of course was why he hadn't attempted to move. It was fairly audacious of him to stay on top of the Portacabin, but a calculated risk. A favourite method of hiding in the jungle had simply been to stand stock still and pretend to be a tree. Any searcher will look under hedges and behind rocks; few will study the open spaces very carefully, or, for that matter, the roofs of the prisons from which a person is supposed to be fleeing for his or her life. This was the reason that Zimmerman elected to stay where he was.

'Du Pont,' snapped Sly, 'I want every man on this, and I want more brought in. At the moment he is a maximum of half a kilometre away; a minimum of a few yards.'

Zimmerman went slightly cold. This bastard was a bit too clever for his liking.

'Get on it, take the place apart, fanning out from around this Portacabin,' Sly continued. And Zimmerman hoped that Du Pont would not take this to mean upwards as well as outwards.

If he survived the next fifteen minutes, Zimmerman reckoned he was safe. He then resolved to stay exactly where he was for quite a while, long enough for them to become worried and confused. Long enough for them to begin to wonder whether he had got out after all.

Fifteen minutes later Du Pont, Tyron and Sly were gone. Zimmerman smiled to himself. He was in the shadow of the heating flue and considered it extremely unlikely that he would be spotted from the air. He was pretty safe for the time being. He curled up in the gutter with his *Phantom* comic. He had plenty of time and he intended to luxuriate over every page; digging all of the pictures in detail. Quite often there were little jokes and bits of drama in the drawings that it was easy to miss if you skimmed through. What's more, after the Phantom, he also had two new *Judge Dreads*, he reckoned it could be a pretty good day. All he hoped was that CD had got the woman away and that they all had the sense to stay put.

THE BRIGHT LIGHTS OF A DARK INTENT

Zimmerman of course hoped in vain. For as the sun set, in all its blazing desert glory, and as the billions of volts of Moorcock lighting came on, almost eclipsing it, the little EcoAction commando unit moved out.

The first major clash of the titans was at hand, for the two armies were approaching each other. Du Pont's men, dogs, trucks and helicopters were heading for the wire from within, spreading ever outwards, looking for Zimmerman.

Meanwhile, from the opposite direction, outside the wire, the resistance forces were rushing to their fate; a huge peace freak, a lovesick dickhead, a born again environmentalist and a middle-aged woman with a degree in sarcasm. The last of these was driving and she was having some difficulty, because they had elected to travel without lights in an effort to sneak up on their quarry.

'That'll fox 'em right enough,' said Mrs Culboon, pursuing

her preferred line of humour. 'If we turn the lights off they'll *never* see us. After all, they only rule the world.'

Progress was being rendered more than unusually difficult by the weaving, flickering lights on the horizon. The distant sky was a blaze of eerie, unnatural colour. This turned the pitted, wind shaped desert floor into a mass of treacherous shadows, any one of which could be deep enough to snap a twenty-five-year-old axle. Even more disconcerting was that occasionally one of the shadows turned out to weigh ten stone and be capable of jumping sixteen feet. It was a tense situation, Rachel's car was a soft top and they had visions of being joined from above by a kangaroo.

'There just isn't room back here,' CD said, 'it will have to sit in the front on your lap, Walter.'

They abandoned the car about a kilometre from the perimeter wire and, carrying their guns and a set of wire clippers, began to slowly approach the scene of what they realized could be their destruction. They recalled all too vividly the trigger-happy encounter on their previous visit to the wire. This time there would be no Zimmerman to miraculously save them. In fact, it seemed, there was a good chance that Zimmerman was already dead. The things they had learnt from the new comrade, Chrissy, had been shocking and fearful. Billionaires plotting together; ruthlessly slaughtering anyone who got on their trail. They crept up to the brightly lit wire with an almost fatalistic detachment.

'Oh *man*!' whispered Walter, pointing. 'Closed circuit TV in the desert! These people are unnecessarily paranoid.'

He had spotted a camera mounted high on a pole. It was turning slowly towards them. That was it, he, CD and Rachel thought. The moment it focussed on them the game was up.

'The thing probably has a death ray fitted as standard,' Walter whined.

Mrs Culboon raised the night-sighted rifle that she was carrying and destroyed the camera with a single shot. There was a surprised silence – silence that is, apart from the humming din emanating from the centre of the construction site.

'Well done, Mrs Culboon,' said CD after a pause, 'I was thinking of doing that myself.'

'Hey, Mrs Culboon, I was never hip to the fact that you could shoot,' said Walter, excited and impressed.

'Mr Culboon hates the fact that I can out shoot him every time so I try not to rub it in,' Mrs Culboon laughed modestly. And there was momentary elation at their minor victory until Rachel reintroduced a touch of realism.

'I reckon pretty soon somebody will be beginning to wonder why a screen's gone dark and start thinking about looking into it,' she reminded everybody. 'So I think we should make the most of our small advantage.'

'Dig,' said Walter.

They cut the wire, which was not electrified. This had been a deliberate decision on Sly's part, the last thing he wanted was a load of barbecued kangaroos drawing the unwelcome attention of animal lovers.

For a moment the scared little group stood on the outside, staring at the hole that they had made. Then, with hearts beating nineteen-to-the-dozen, and bowels struggling to maintain some semblance of control over the situation, they climbed through.

At first they had it very easy. They walked for an hour, covering maybe four kilometres and did not see one truck, one guard or one helicopter. Of course they didn't realize it but this was because the security people were not worrying about intruders that night. In fact, nobody had even noticed the dead camera that Mrs Culboon had destroyed. They were all looking for Zimmerman, every single one of them. The four intrepid Eco-commandos had not yet reached the exapanding area covered by the search, but they soon would.

'Well, you know, man,' said Walter, lazily rolling a cigarette as he sauntered along, his hunched lope growing looser and more relaxed with every step. 'I guess maybe the chick Chrissy has lived too long in the US of A. I guess maybe, like a few Yankees I've met, her paranoia dial is set to double ape-shit. I make this observation because we have been strolling in the lion's den so to speak for the space of five whole cigarettes now and, as I hope you have noticed, we are by no means dead.'

'Yeah,' added CD. 'You know, if I'd known that terrorist infiltration was going to be as easy as this I would have taken it up long ago. Don't you think, Rachel, I mean, we could have skipped all those peace bazaars and stuff and just strolled into the White House and kidnapped the President.'

'Listen you two idiots,' Rachel snapped, causing CD to shiver with frustrated urgings. Such was his monumental desire for a passionate encounter with Rachel that CD relished any display of emotion towards him on her part, even when it was derogatory. He would have got a hard on if she'd tattooed 'what a wanker' on his forehead while he was asleep.

'I love it when you're bitching,' he observed irritatingly.

'Colin *please* try to be less pathetic,' said Rachel, causing tense little sparks of suppressed sauciness to pitter patter up and down CD's trousers. 'You're both being pathetic,' she continued. 'We haven't done anything yet, we haven't found anything out, we haven't rescued Zimmerman, in fact we haven't started. Still being alive is the absolute minimum we could have achieved. So don't be so bloody smug.'

'Ha ha, I reckon Rachel told you boys,' said Mrs Culboon, and even with the ever present industrial roar in the distance her voice could still shatter granite. 'Here's you two congratulating yourselves like we've saved the world and all we've done is take a walk under the stars.'

'All I'm saying, man, is that maybe the people we're up against are not such a terminal bummer as we had imagined, dig? All I'm saying,' insisted Walter, 'is that maybe these people aren't as big as they'd like to think they are, maybe they ain't so tough and all powerful, and maybe we're a match for them. Is that so dumb?'

And Walter's question was answered because shortly after he had made this monumentally optimistic observation, they came to the edge of a small ridge in the land and the full and majestic scale of their opponent was revealed to them in all its roaring, burning, terrible beauty.

They had been climbing very gently since crossing the wire and were now crossing the little undulating hills which had once ringed the Culboons' quiet, dingy existence and now ringed the central axis of the Stark conspiracy. From where they now stood, the desert floor swept down into a very shallow valley, a valley which was in fact really little more than a dip in the vast, flat desert.

In the middle of this place, a place of ancient peace; a place which had slept almost undisturbed since the waters of prehistory subsided: a place untouched by human hand, save for those few souls who had scratched out a meagre living on its barren surface. In the midst of all this, boring deep and spreading wide, lay the Stark construction site. Hissing, steaming and glaring into the still desert night.

It wasn't that the area covered was particularly huge, it was more the intensity of the activity that struck the little group of conspirators dumb. Stretched out below them were six burning bright areas of weaving lights and towering cranes – or at least they seemed like cranes, perhaps they were towers of some kind. These hellish patches on the desert floor were arranged not in a circle but in an asymmetric, almost haphazard way, like great fluorescent lilies spread across a pond. From each of these six places came constant blasts and explosions; first an eerie silent flash and then, moments later, a dull crump that could be felt deep in the belly. The exploding lilies were connected by snakes of orange light, along which travelled other lights, some white, some red. Above it all hovered helicopters throwing their own beams downwards in a seemingly futile effort to add to the orgy of illumination. All light soon blended and was lost in the great and terrible glow. A glow that had a strange, translucent quality, induced by the clouds of dust and steam that were constantly being thrust upwards into the shuddering air.

It was like Hell's kitchen on the day that all seven deadly sins had come to dinner and the Devil was trying to do a complex Taiwanese banquet that he'd never attempted before. In silence they began to descend down the long, shallow, featureless slope. It took a lot to shut up CD and Mrs Culboon, but for once neither of them had anything to say. They were all thinking much the same thing; which was that any group of people who could organize the Devil's kitchen that they were now approaching, could probably handle four ecologically concerned individuals.

'Still think that Chrissy's paranoid, Walter?' said Rachel.

A moment later the little group finally met up with the outer limits of the expanding search for Zimmerman. The phoney war was over. It all seemed to happen at once. Above the general roar, the gutteral rat-a-tat-tat of a helicopter emerged as a single and definitive sound; and it was getting louder. Soon they could see it, in the distance, its search-lights scanning the ground below.

'Take cover!!' snapped Rachel.

'Where?' replied Walter, and he had a point.

THE GREAT SANDY DESERT

The Great Sandy Desert of Western Australia is not known for its prominent features. If it were, perhaps it might have had a slightly more interesting name. It might have been called 'The great, sandy and with lots of interesting little nooks and crannies and rocks and caves and great places to hide in Desert.'

But it wasn't called that because there are virtually no nooks, crannies, rocks or caves. All there is, across 99 per cent of its surface, is space and sand. It is a great and sandy desert. Never was a place more aptly named.

BATTLE AND CAPTURE

The four frightened fugitives stared around them looking for somewhere to hide and there was nowhere. Or at least there was nowhere that they could see. Had Zimmerman been with them he would have calmly told them to crouch stock still and think like a bush, or lie flat along one of the tiny creases of land caused by the soft desert wind.

'Stillness is the essence of camouflage,' he would have told them, 'it is very difficult to pick out something that doesn't move.'

That is what Zimmerman would have told them had he been there, but of course he wasn't. And so his four friends ran around in circles flapping their arms in panic shouting, 'What the fuck are we going to do!! What the fuck are we going to do!!'

There was literally nowhere to run to. The chopper was approaching fast, making great sweeping arcs with its horrifyingly powerful search-light, covering hundreds of square metres of flat, featureless terrain and subjecting it to careful scrutiny.

Suddenly, for the four terrified commandos on the ground, it was day, bright bright day as they were swathed in the harsh light. Their shadows stretched out like deep black ditches behind them. They stared, blinking into the beam, frozen into momentary petrification. Four skittles waiting to be knocked down.

Then CD had a thought.

'Scatter! I'm going to take out the light!!' he shouted, and raising the automatic weapon to his shoulder, squeezed the trigger.

Considering that CD had never fired any form of gun before, and that he was starting out on a state-of-the-art machine gun that could have cut the front off a house, it wasn't a bad effort. He missed the light but he was very close. As it happened, he hit the fuel tank, causing the helicopter to burst into a horrifyingly brilliant fireball.

The machines that Stark employed were police-designed craft, hence they were not armoured. Contrary to what cop shows would have us believe, most police helicopters are used for traffic surveillance and it takes a pretty vicious contra-flow system to provoke the average motorist to dig out an automatic rifle.

The instant inferno hung in the air with its spinning blades hurling burning debris into the night. Strangely, and rather eerily, the search-light which emanated from the helicopter's nose cone, remained on, although it no longer bobbed and weaved about. For a little while nothing further happened. The helicopter burnt in the sky and the four figures on the ground remained motionless, transfixed by what they had done, still casting their long black shadows in the light that shone from the dead aircraft. Then it crashed to the ground with the sort of noise that only a burning helicopter crashing into the ground can make, and gloom descended once more.

Still the four of them did not move. They just stood, trying to get their heads around the enormity of developments. The stakes had suddenly got a very great deal higher. Now they were killers, murderers. CD was vaguely surprised to note that the old cliché that 'it didn't seem real' was true. It didn't.

'You should have let me do it, CD,' said Mrs Culboon. 'I'm the one who can shoot, remember?'

'I forgot,' said CD lamely.

'You had to do something,' said Rachel, her voice hard. 'It was us or them.'

'We *hope* it was us or them,' corrected Walter. 'Man, all I can say is that this whole situation had better be as serious as the paranoid Yank chick says it is, because if that chopper was just patrolling a building site we're going to prison for ever.'

The terrible thing that had happened seemed to have driven the memory of their recent and stunning sight of the construction site from his mind.

'Oh come *on*,' shouted Rachel, 'we *know* it's serious, for God's sake, Walter, they were shooting at *you* the other night with these very guns. They've taken Zimmerman and the police claim there wasn't even a fight at the airport. And anyway Walter, what the fuck is that!! A retirement village!' She pointed down towards the site. Now that the burning helicopter had ceased to light up the sky, the construction site had regained something of its awesome brilliance.

'Chrissy has *got* to be right,' Rachel urged. 'Something

utterly terrible is going on and CD was absolutely right to do what he did.'

'Well, right or wrong, we're in the shit now,' said Mrs Culboon, 'so I say we press on as fast as we can and get away from that cemetery over there.' She pointed at the wreck of the helicopter and CD wished that she had chosen a different phrase. He did not know how many people it took to crew a small helicopter, but however many it was, that was how many people he had killed.

They began to run; Mrs Culboon, as the slowest, setting the pace. They ran towards the glow of the building site, each pondering their own confused thoughts. They did not know what they were running towards, what they would find, or what they would do when they found it. They were just running away from a burning helicopter full of dead men.

As it happened, what they were running towards was, in their case, even worse than a burning helicopter full of dead men; it was a not burning helicopter full of live men. Men who did not take kindly to the sort of shock that CD had just given them. On the whole, people take jobs in private security firms in order to throw their weight about, not in order to get shot out of the sky.

After a minute CD, Rachel, Walter and Mrs Culboon stopped running. They could hear the helicopter coming, they could see the headlamps of the trucks and jeeps which were also hurtling across the sand towards them. There was absolutely nowhere to hide.

Mrs Culboon cocked her rifle.

'Oh man,' said Walter wearily, 'I think we've done enough of that, you know? I mean, we are in a no-win situation here, you dig? Like, they are going to get us for definite, no way can we fight them all so I think maybe it would be wrong to just kill people for no reason, even if they are the bastards who are after us.'

As it happened Mrs Culboon had not really wanted to fight. She was just thinking of trying to defend her friends; acting instinctively that was all. None of them wanted to fight, they all wanted to go home to their mothers and be tucked up in bed with warm milk and vegamite soldiers. But they couldn't, they would have to face the music.

'Drop the weapons,' a voice barked.

They dropped them and with a fair degree of unnecessary force, were bound and thrown in the back of a truck.

Mrs Culboon and Walter lived on the fringes of society, this was not for either of them their first experience of brutality and danger. They didn't like it but they recognized it. For CD and Rachel, it was unknown territory, and hence utterly terrifying. All people who live in well-ordered societies harbour a secret dread of what would happen if order was removed. If suddenly they found themselves in a brutal human jungle without the protection of the social rules on which we all rely. It was happening to CD and Rachel. It seemed to them, lying face down in the back of a three ton lorry, that they were beyond action and beyond help.

CD would have given anything to see a copper. It wouldn't have mattered how young or arrogant; seventeen-years-old and a face like a plate of rhubarb and custard, CD wouldn't have minded. But there's never one there when you want one.

IMPRISONMENT AND
INTERROGATION

THE CENTRE OF CREATION

Sly and Tyron were in the project control building when they got the news regarding the capture of four intruders. At first Sly thought that this might wrap the problem up. If necessary they would simply hold the fugitives until after Domesday.

Unfortunately, he quickly discovered, to his extreme frustration, the original fugitive, the highly dangerous nose-biting hippy had not been recaptured.

For the first time Sly began to feel a twinge of doubt about the whole bloody business in which he was involved. These little human intrusions on their vast and inhuman project made him vaguely aware of how small he was himself. That, coupled with the continuing and irritating presence of Ocker Tyron, a genuinely small man, despite his size, made Sly feel uncomfortably impotent in the midst of all his power.

The project control building was a depressing place in which to experience doubt and humility, containing, as it did, an awe inspiring array of high-tech equipment, most of which was going blip blip blip in what seemed to Sly to be an unnecessarily irritating manner. The stuff had been assembled by Nagasyu at various collation points all over the Far East and so efficient had his administration been that when all the gear arrived, there was little more to do than to plug it in. Incredibly it had even had a plug on it.

The whole thing certainly looked cool; a quarter of an acre

of chrome, plastic, glass and brushed stainless steel, all bleeping, spinning and flashing. Almost as complex as the dashboard on a BMW. Yard after yard of console covered in monitors and buttons, walls of tapes, sometimes spinning one way, then, no doubt for some reason, spinning another. It was an exhilarating and terrifying sight. And so it should have been. There was, after all, only slightly less equipment in the room than it takes to record a Pink Floyd album.

Twenty-five or so white-coated technicians bustled about flicking switches and looking intelligent. Tyron had been impressed, despite himself.

'Now all it needs is something to shoot,' he had said.

'What's your hurry, mate! Anyone would think you're looking forward to this bloody awful thing . . . this . . .' Sly searched for a word, '. . . Apocalypse. Christ Almighty, let's enjoy what time is left.'

'I just don't want any fuck-ups when the time is right, we're only going to get one chance at this, Moorcock, one chance at life or death, right! I want us to be ready.'

In fact in a strange way Ocker Tyron was looking forward to it. Utterly horrible though the prospect was, its hugeness still gave him a strange exhilaration. He had had the power of life and death over virtually everybody in his life for so many years that Tyron was definitely a hard man to thrill. Stark, however, made his very trousers tingle. Despite its irreversible horror, Tyron still felt a pretty considerable buzz at the prospect of playing God, even if it was a multi-headed corporate God. He relished the prospect of being one of the chosen ones, one of those chosen to survive. Besides this, there was the eerie potency he felt about his part in choosing who should die. In a way it's not surprising he was a little excited, it is quite something to be a father of creation. Only God had made a world before.

MINOR IRRITATIONS

Tyron's delicious little fantasies were cut short when one of

316

Du Pont's security men entered and announced the capture of the prisoners. Suddenly Sly found himself wondering about the girl.

'Look, Ocker,' said Sly. 'I can handle this, all right? Why don't you just sod off back to Perth, eh? It's just a minor irritation, some hippies who think we're destroying precious natural flora. I'll talk to them.'

The security man knew he had a chance to make a big impact and he grabbed it.

'They shot down a helicopter,' he said.

There was a pretty stunned silence, apart from all the blipping going on that is.

'Shot *down* a fucking *helicopter*!' said Tyron incredulously. 'What the hell is going on? Christ first a guy disarms our security chief with his teeth, then one of our choppers get shot down.'

'Look, will you cool it, Tyron,' said Sly, not really knowing what to say. 'We have to think.'

'Too fucking right, mate!' Someone's found out what we're up to and they want in. This is only the beginning.' Tyron was pretty badly shaken. It always gives a person cause for thought when he's just been having a God fantasy and somebody shoots down his helicopter.

'Don't be stupid,' Sly replied. 'These people are just dumb meddlers. It's an ecological thing, we know that from the hippy who bit Du Pont.' Sly was still thinking about the girl. 'Mind you, they certainly know how to meddle . . . We won't tell Durf about this, or the others, it's not necessary. I intend to deal with this situation right now.'

FANCYING THE ENEMY

Sly could not kid himself, he was pleased to see her. There was no doubt about it. As he walked towards the room where the captives were being kept he had been hoping that she would be there and when it turned out that she was, he was pleased.

This was an entirely new experience for Sly. Occasionally in the past he had developed 'things' about girls, but never on so short an acquaintance and certainly never with such immediate force. After all, he knew nothing about the girl apart from the fact that she seemed to be firmly against absolutely everything that he stood for. There was no getting round it though, he was pleased to see her. She seemed even more pretty than when they had met in his office. Action and adventure had lent a highly attractive flush to her cheek and her eyes sparkled with defiance and fear. She was also firmly tied to a chair, which was something that normally took Sly ages to persuade his girlfriends to put up with.

QUESTION AND ANSWER

Sly pulled himself together. This was a time for masterly self-assurance. He stood before the sorry gang of renegades and addressed them with what he hoped would be an icy and intimidating tone.

'What in the name of fuck do you think you're doing?' he blurted.

Walter looked at him defiantly.

'Trying to find out what you're up to, man,' he said. 'Just like last time, you know, like, still trying to suss out what goes down.'

'What goes *down*, you filthy bastard,' shouted Tyron, 'is one of *my* helicopters!!'

Sly tried to calm himself. They couldn't both stand there screaming at a bunch of hippies. It was so unreal. Here he was, a colossus in the world of power and money and he was standing shouting and screaming at a Carlton drop-out. That's the trouble with spending all your time on the twenty fifth floor, when you come down there's a hell of a bump.

'Why are you so interested in what I'm doing?' he asked.

'We, we won't know that until we find out what it is, will we man?' replied Walter. 'But we have a pretty good idea that whatever it is, it's heavy. Now where's my man Zimmerman?

If you've harmed him I swear ... I swear, I'll lay some *very* bad Karma on your head. Dig?'

Walter's three comrades felt slightly embarrassed at this. Having Walter lay some very bad Karma on your head sounded something akin to being savaged by Bambi.

Sly did not even realize that he had been threatened.

'Who are you talking about?' he asked.

'My man Zimmerman, a kind of hippy dude, he ate your hamburger at Facefulls.'

Sly was about to add that since then he had eaten his security chief's nose as well, but he decided to be more circumspect. 'We have him safe, don't trouble about that,' Sly lied.

'You'd better start worrying about yourselves,' Tyron chipped in. 'Now what the fuck do you know? All of it, everything. What do you know and where's the Yank bitch? Come on, out with it. Now!!'

There was a sullen silence.

Tyron grabbed a gun from one of the guards and pointed it at them. Sly tensed up and watched Tyron carefully.

'You answer me right now or you're dead, you hear,' Tyron barked. 'I don't suppose there'll be anybody much mourning any of you, we'll just leave you for the dingos. Now come on, answer me.'

Walter's reply was a shrewd one.

'You ain't going to shoot us man. No way,' he said. 'Because you don't know what we know and ... and ... you don't know what the Yank chick knows. And you don't know who we've told ... and you don't know, uhm ...' Walter seemed about to flag, but then he got his second wind, he always did love to bullshit, '... and you don't know how many of us are out there. Yeah, that's right, you have no idea of the hugeness of our network, yeah, you have no concept of its almost cosmic enormity. You don't know how many heavily armed and totally dedicated hippies are out there just waiting to come in here and ... and ...' endless late nights watching American cop shows came to his aid, '... come in here and cream your arse, yeah, that's it, cream your arse . . . and uhm . . . expose all the things that we know to the world.' He finished and then added 'man' as a kind of full stop.

It was a good performance. CD nearly spoilt it by applauding. Luckily his hands were tied behind his back. Unfortunately for Walter, Sly was not stupid, he simply smiled and said, 'Oh yeah, if you're all so heavily armed mate, how come you came in carrying only the guns you pinched off us in the first place?'

There was a pause.

'Uhm . . . irony, man,' said Walter. 'Yeah, that's it, we have a keen sense of irony.'

'These people don't know shit,' said Sly, 'they're shooting in the dark.'

'And bringing down helicopters,' added Du Pont, who saw no reason why he should be the only person to feel a dickhead that day.

Tyron was not satisfied with Sly's confidence.

'I agree there's no way they can know much,' he said, 'but we have to find out what little it is. Besides that, we've got to find the American girl. Du Pont, can you make them talk?'

'Of course I can make them talk,' said Du Pont and his tone was not pleasant, especially if you happened to be his prisoner.

'Now, what the hell do you two think you're talking about?' Sly shouted. In a way he was going through a similar learning process to that which CD and the others were going through. They had never been involved in gun battles before and he had never heard colleagues casually hint at torturing total strangers. It was being brought home to all of them just how high the stakes were getting.

'What I am talking about,' Tyron shouted back, 'is the Stark project and the countless billions that we have all invested in our future. I have no intention of letting a few adventurous idiots like this ruin everything. Ruin the biggest thing in the world . . .'

There was a moment's embarrassed silence as everybody

realized that Tyron had been about to reveal all. He turned to the four captives. 'Now you can either tell us peaceably what you know, or Colonel Du Pont here can force it out of you. What do you know?'

'We don't know shit, man. But you sure are making it all sound interesting,' said Walter. 'Why don't you tell us?'

'Right, Du Pont, which will be easiest?' said Tyron.

'The kid in glasses maybe, or the girl,' he replied.

'No!' barked Sly.

Mrs Culboon decided to have her say. 'Listen! My friend's telling the truth, we don't know nothing about your big stuff and your damn future. We're here because I got beaten up on my own land by racists and that's all we know. And if you don't tell us no more, then we'll still know nothing, and you can let us go.'

'That's right,' said Sly and Rachel thought he was acting extremely reasonably considering that they had shot down his helicopter.

'Like fuck they don't know anything,' asserted Tyron, heating up. 'They have to know where the Yank is, maybe even where this hippy Zimmerman fellah got to.'

'Oh yeah? Thought you said you had him safe,' taunted CD.

Tyron turned towards him with a look like granite. 'Get on with it, Du Pont,' he said.

'Stay exactly where you are Du Pont,' Sly countered. 'Tyron, can we have a private word please?'

He ushered Tyron out of the room leaving Du Pont to guard the prisoners. Despite the fact that this time he had four guards with him, Du Pont was careful to keep his nose out of reach.

ORIGINAL SIN

Outside the room there was yet another tense altercation between Sly and Tyron.

'For God's sake, Tyron, you were about to have those people tortured!' said a rather disturbed Sly.

'I still am, mate, if it's necessary,' Tyron replied.

And of course Sly could see his point. They had no way of knowing what these irritating people knew, and who, if anyone, they had told it to. Besides this there was the much bigger problem of the American journalist still being at large, they really did need to find her. On the other hand to discard any civilized behaviour so quickly, right at the very beginning of the great plan, did not bode at all well for the future. After all, the whole point of the Stark project was to reshape civilization and give it a new start; a fresh chance. Stark was to be a phoenix rising out of the dead ashes of a failed and disgraced civilization. If they started this way, they were bound to fail again. It was almost as if Sly was looking the Original Sin in the eye.

LOVE FINDS A WAY

Of course, Sly did not consider all these thoughts so coherently in the few seconds that elapsed before he replied to Tyron. Mainly he was thinking about Rachel. His natural repugnance to Tyron's casual acceptance of brutality as a viable course of action was multiplied *ad infinitum* by the thought that he intended to practise it upon the girl Rachel. He really did seem to have gone soft on her.

'Listen,' Sly replied, 'I agree that the situation is touchy. But don't forget that nothing we're doing here is actually illegal. Totally shithouse morals-wise, perhaps, but not actually illegal. They can't possibly have anything on us yet and if the American does try to make a move, well, let's face it, we've got her. We control the police, the phones, the transport, the credit. We control everything.'

'Yes I know, but they've still got this far,' replied Tyron.

'Look, just give me a day or two to sort this situation out my way, all right? Leave them alone for the time being, eh? I mean, the minute anyone makes a move anywhere in the world, let alone in Bullens Creek, Durf will know. So what's the problem? Let me talk to them, I'll find out what they've got and it will be nothing.'

Sly had already decided on the course of action he must take.

He and Tyron re-entered the room.

'Don't worry,' Sly said. 'We're not going to hurt you. I will simply be questioning you one at a time. You first.' He pointed at Rachel and motioned a guard to untie her and lead her out.

It nearly broke CD's heart to see Rachel thus contemptuously ordered about. Luckily he was securely bound and so was not forced to try and do something about it. Better a broken heart than a broken neck.

THE SWORD OF DAMOCLĒS

While CD's heart was breaking in northern WA, not too far away, just off the coast, near a place called Shark Bay, something else was breaking, something that was going to make a broken heart seem small beer and even a broken neck a minor inconvenience.

SHARK BAY

The early Aussies, as was their unerring habit, had named Shark Bay after the sharks which were the bay's most prominent feature; apart from water of course. Undeniably the most prominent feature of all in the bay was water and so for a while there was a strong movement amongst those tough, hard bitten and laconic men and women, to call it 'Waterlogged Bay'.

The more sophisticated souls countered that if you started calling bays 'Waterlogged Bay' because they were waterlogged, then all bays would have the same name and it would be impossible to tell the buggers apart. And they got called a bunch of poofs for their pains.

'If you can have a Great Sandy Desert, a Snowy Mountains and a Southern Sea, you can have a Waterlogged Bay,' the laconics claimed.

'But there's only *one* of those things,' pleaded the more sophisticated souls, 'there are loads of bays.'

In the end, the logic of this statement had been grudgingly accepted and so it was decided to name the bay after its most prominent feature apart from water.

Somebody suggested that the fact that it was a bay was a

pretty major feature, but 'BAY BAY' had been rejected as sounding too childish. 'Horizon BAY' had been considered for a while, it was a pretty name, but was eventually thought to have the same problem as 'water'; i.e., that it could describe any bay (as could 'wave' and 'tide').

Eventually, after a fellow called Jim had come home from a fishing trip minus a leg, having been gored by a shark, it had been decided to call the bay 'Shark Bay' and to call Jim, 'One-Legged Jim'. There had been a small group of poetic, erudite individuals who had lobbied hard for 'Bay of the Bitten Jim' but they were told to fuck off back to Sydney where their type were tolerated.

And so Shark Bay it became, because there were sharks in it.

Not everyone was happy of course. One-Legged Jim, for instance, was monumentally pissed off, but this wasn't because of the name business. He was unhappy because he had been horribly mutilated and now he only had one leg. Jim's pragmatic, no bullshit attitude to life was much admired by all.

Some of the citizens of Carnarvorn, the town on the northern tip of the bay, had wanted to call it Carnarvorn Bay and wandered around for weeks muttering under their breath that there were sharks in every bloody bay in Australia. None the less, Shark Bay it had stayed for a hundred and fifty years until the the thread broke on the Sword of Damoclēs and rendered life for a shark in Shark Bay utterly impossible.

THE SWORD

As the Domesday Group had constantly made clear to Stark over the years the ecological cause and effect syndromes which they had isolated as The Swords of Damoclēs were very different indeed from those which were categorized under the Avalanche Effect.

The actual story of Damoclēs and his monarch Dionysius is of no relevance here, except, that is, for the punch line, which left Damoclēs sitting at dinner beneath a naked sword suspended from the ceiling by a single thread. The moral of the legend being that a person's situation in life is always chancy. Another moral might have been that if you find yourself at dinner with a sword hanging over your head, move seats.

And that was exactly the point made by the Domesday Group. Ecologically, the difference between avalanches and Swords of Damoclēs was that with avalanches you didn't know about them until they fell on you; but Swords of Damoclēs were slightly less serious because the danger was there for all to see, and hence it was possible to do something about it. A typical example of the Swords that Domesday regularly put before Stark were the so called Leper Ships; ships so loaded with appallingly toxic chemicals that no country would let them enter their ports. Alone and virtually stateless, they roam the seas searching for a place to disgorge their vile load.

'One of them's going to sink one of these days,' the Domesday Group would say.

At Shark Bay the thread broke.

THE *ATARIA C42*

If Captain Robertson on his North Sea shit sludger thought he had a tough job, he should have tried carting the real crap around like poor old Captain Popplewell had to.

Captain Popplewell, the master of the Liberian registered *Ataria C42*, had three years of hell then died. It started when his ship was chartered by a company called Dispo Holdings, who wished him to ship a few barrels of ash and sludge to a toxic-waste disposal company in Britain – a country with a world reputation for taking on other peoples' shit. Whilst at sea a scandal burst revealing the true nature of the load which turned out to be a horrifying cocktail of chemical and heavy metal poisons. A mix of aluminium, arsenic, barium, cadmium, lead and mercury, so potent that no port in the world would take it.

At first Captain Popplewell was instructed to do what so many others had done before when faced with a cargo that cannot be offloaded. He was told to dump it in the Third World. For years, contrary to every legal and moral objection, Africa has been used as a dustbin for the impossibly toxic residue of the life-styles of the West.

Unfortunately for the *Ataria C42*, her cargo had become somewhat notorious and environmental activists were on to her – hence even Third World ports were barred to the ship. It was bitter gall indeed for Captain Popplewell to see other Leper Ships successfully slipping in and dumping their terrible loads and having wild leper ship parties, whilst he was forced to skulk about in mid-ocean like the pariah he was. Of course, he and the ship's owners turned to the company that had chartered them, but, as happens too often in these situations, they had gone into liquidation. In fact Dispo Holdings might be said to have pulled off a brilliant business coup in the same way that Sly did by destroying healthy businesses with his corporate raids. Dispo had accepted a contract to dispose of large quantities of appallingly toxic waste. They had performed their duties by chartering a ship and putting the waste on the ship. When it proved impossible for the ship to find anywhere to sail to, Dispo had gone into liquidation. Brilliant.

Sly's attitude would probably have been that business is a tough game; dog-eat-dog, and you had to admire their audacity.

THE FIRST OF MANY

During the three years that the *Ataria C42* drifted about, occasionally being allowed to take on more fuel or food, the seas became crowded with lepers. Slowly, as people began to wake up to the appalling danger of this stuff, fewer and fewer were prepared to even consider trying to deal with it. Unfortunately, the poisons still got made and so more and more ships found themselves floating about, sitting on enough poison to wipe out an ocean. These were the Swords of Damoclēs.

Just as CD was crying over Rachel, crying over the sort of small, human things that make life worth living, the sword fell for the *Ataria C42*. In a terrible storm just west of Shark Bay, the ship ruptured and fifty-five thousand gallons of the choicest contents of Pandora's Box flowed into the Indian Ocean, and hence into all the seas of the world.

RACHEL AND SLY

'Why are you doing this?' Sly asked bluntly, once he and Rachel were installed in the lounge room of his private quarters and he had poured out a couple of gin and tonics.

'Doing what?' replied Rachel, wondering hard how to play the situation.

'Pursuing me and my business. Don't you have anything better to do?' he asked.

'We're concerned citizens. You're the sort of person who will have bribed and bought out all the usual restraining influences so it's up to people like us to keep an eye on you,' Rachel replied.

'And what is it that you think I'm doing that is so very wrong?' asked Sly.

'Well, shipping in high-grade missile fuel disguised as petrol, for a start.' Rachel was gratified to note that Sly was extremely taken aback by this bald statement. She realized that in making it she had removed a card from her sleeve and placed it on the table, but there seemed little point in concealing her knowledge. After all, he could not tell from it what else she knew. Rachel felt that Walter had been right, if inept, in his efforts to convince Moorcock that he was up against a formidable force. Rachel did not know whether her life was in danger or not, but she thought that if it was, Moorcock would be less likely to do away with her if it seemed likely that there would be others to follow on and avenge her.

'What do you know about the rocket fuel?' asked Sly.

'I don't intend to answer any more of your questions. Let me and my friends go, or you'll be sorry.'

Rachel was well aware that this statement had a credibility

reading of zero but she didn't have anything else to say. She had absolutely no idea of how to handle the situation for the best and so had decided to shut up. She needn't have worried, Sly was going to be doing most of the talking. For a moment he sat staring at her across the room. She was sitting cross legged on the sofa, holding her glass defensively, like a shield. She looked great.

Sly was preparing to throw caution to the wind.

CRUSH

Not everybody falls in love as impulsively as Sly had done. For some, love grows; it slowly dawns on them. One day they might think 'mmm nice bum' and leave it at that. Later, perhaps at the office party, whilst casually chatting, they discover a mutual interest in religious music. After that, dinner and a movie just seem like a logical step . . .

'No way is it serious, I don't even know if we get on, actually.'

A massively disappointing first shag serves to cement a mutual sympathy and finally, about a decade later, comes the, 'You know, I don't know, but I think I might be in love with you, what do you think? Or is that stupid, I mean, if it is, forget it?'

But not everybody is so cautious.

Once, whilst driving along a country highway late at night, Sly had caught a seven foot Red Kangaroo in his head-lights and, seconds later, had slammed into it full across the 'roo bars at a highly illegal hundred and forty kilometres. This is how some people fall in love. Sly had always wondered how the 'roo must have felt. Now he knew.

The reason so many 'roos get spread across bonnets is because they have an instinctive fascination for light sources. Unfortunately for them, when they get caught in head-lamps, they stop dead still and stare straight into the light; oblivious of the consequences; entirely captured by the magic of the beams. Sly was just the same, except of course that he didn't have a huge long tail and a pouch with a baby in it. He was mesmerized by Rachel's light.

It can happen. Especially to a man like Sly whose life-style meant that his experience of real people – straight, unaffected people – was minimal. Coupled with all this was the fact that Sly wanted to fall in love. For the first time in his life he was desperate to find someone, and quickly. He fancied Rachel; he thought her different and interesting; she was in the right place at the right time. Sly, a man used to making decisions, decided to fall in love. Of course at the time, Sly would probably have denied that the emotions he was nurturing were anything like that intense. He would have admitted to lust; he might even have conceded an objective interest in her strange personality, but he would not have admitted that he was falling for her.

None the less, he was.

SMALL TALK

'What did that long-haired guy who talks through a time warp call your group?' Sly asked, breaking the silence.

'EcoAction,' replied Rachel defiantly.

'And what's that supposed to signify then,' Sly asked with a slightly mocking tone.

'It's supposed to signify, *mate*,' said Rachel, bridling at his attitude, 'that if something isn't done soon, the world is going to die, that's what. It will die, you arrogant, smug, complacent . . . rich bastard.' Rachel was, of course, a born again Eco-freak; a convert, and in any system of belief it is the converts who are the real zealots. If there was one thing that Rachel couldn't handle it was people taking the piss out of the stuff she was into.

'You're wrong,' said Sly quietly. 'The earth isn't going to die unless you stop it.'

'Oh yeah well you would say that wouldn't you,' Rachel sneered. 'You've got a vested interest in carrying on fucking it up.'

'You're wrong,' continued Sly, 'because it's going to die anyway. It's virtually dead already, and there is absolutely nothing that you or I or anyone else can do about it. The earth is going to die.'

'Well that's a bit sodding cheerful I must say,' said Rachel, sarcastically. But none the less she was shaken by the cold certainty in his voice.

Sly gulped down his gin and tonic, poured himself another, even stiffer, and decided to go for it.

'Rachel,' he said, 'do you know the story of Adam and Eve?'

He stopped himself, realizing that he was about to embark on the most monumentally naff tack he could possibly take. He decided to start again. 'Forget that,' he said. 'Hot isn't it? Let's talk about the greenhouse effect.'

COMMUNICATION
BREAKDOWN

By morning Tyron was getting impatient. He had never much liked the idea of waiting for the miraculous Moorcock powers of persuasion to convince the captives to divulge all that they knew. Now Tyron felt that his cynicism had been amply justified since many hours had passed and he had not heard a thing from Sly. He felt, as he did about everything in life, that he would probably do a much better job of interrogation himself. Besides, it was very difficult to sit still and do nothing, it was so bloody hot for a start. The night had brought a little relief but now it was morning again and he felt like he was sitting in a grill pan. It was definitely the worst summer Tyron could remember. The whole world seemed to be having it at once. He'd heard that there was no skiing at all in the USA and you had to be an eagle to try it even in the Alps.

Everything was getting so depressingly hellish. Everything seemed to be stinking and rotten. You couldn't trust the water any more because unseasonal flooding had contaminated the supplies. What's more, there were millions more bugs than usual, probably because of all the rank water that was lying around, steaming up into the clouds and then pissing down again almost immediately in torrential poisoned deluges. It was hot and horrible, and now besides that, Tyron had this smelly crew of blacks and hippies to deal with.

There was still no sign of the fugitive Zimmerman. Tyron was forced to accept the possibility that he was now outside the wire. Even more reason then for discovering where it was that this irritating little group had based themselves and hence where Zimmerman would be heading. Tyron decided to have a go at the prisoners.

POWERS OF PERSUASION

Mindful of the time honoured techniques of interrogation, where it is considered important to establish both a hard option and a soft option, he decided that his first approach would be to exercise his charm.

Unfortunately, Ocker Tyron possessed all the charm of a job at Kentucky Fried Chicken and so he had little chance of getting very far. Tyron was a shouter. He was under the impression that it was possible to persuade people that you had almost instantaneously become their bosom buddy simply by assuming a kind of rugged, good-humoured *bonhomie*. He had learnt to communicate at the 'Adverts for Furniture Warehouse School of Sincerity'. A place in which the sad figures who own carpet and furniture warehouses, or second-hand TV emporiums are taught to star in their own television adverts. Desperate, desperate men in loud, slightly comical sports jackets, standing superimposed in front of a photograph of their place of business, shouting at the camera, possibly playing on a slight speech impediment, to single them out as individuals.

'Why pay those *fancy* prices!!! Get the family down to BudgetPriceMart! Bring the *kids*. If *you* can find *anything* cheaper, Honest Bob'll *refund ya! OK!!*'

These people are under the impression that a rough and ready display of overblown pig-ignorant philistinism will somehow endear them to the general public as straight talking, good blokes. In fact, everybody wonders why this stupid wanker keeps shouting at them.

Ocker Tyron had himself, in his early days, appeared in one or two of his own ads. He had been trying to shift a warehouse full of dodgy nylon 'fur' coats and had appeared on TV with a bevvy of West Australian lovelies, all wearing the 'fur' coats, and nothing else.

334

'Tyron's bargains,' he had screamed at the camera, at the top of his voice. 'These terrific, low budget, family, fur substitute, luxury style winter warmer, garment, casual wear designer durables are so like the real fox, sable and mink, retailing at thousands of dollars . . . Ha ha, you'll think they're going to bite ya!!!!!'

And then had come the obligatory sting, where Tyron put his arm around a lovely, and there was a taped lion roar, cut to freeze-frame close up of Tyron's honest, comically shocked face.

Tyron's mum ended up giving all the coats to a Methodist mission. But he did not learn his lesson and Tyron still shouted when he was trying to be ingratiating and convincing.

IRON HAND AND VELVET GLOVE

'Aw, come on guys,' Ocker roared at CD and Walter with a big smile – he ignored Mrs Culboon. 'Just tell us what you know and you can piss off. No hard feelings, wadaya say?' He held a cup of water to CD's lips.

'We don't know anything, mate. We were coming to find out,' he replied, with a fair degree of honesty.

'Now look here,' Tyron continued, 'I reckon you and I see eye to eye. Similar breed, straight talking if you follow me. I guess we're just a couple of OK West Australian blokes. Am I right?'

'Well not really,' CD replied politely. 'I'm British.'

'Well, even better,' said Tyron, delighted. 'You can't get more Aussie than that. After all, the poms were the very first Australians.'

'Ha bloody ha mate,' snorted Mrs Culboon contemptuously.

'A Stone Age fucking culture is not what I call being Australian,' snapped Tyron. 'I call it dumb. Christ you lot had the place for forty thousand years, you never even invented cricket, ha ha ha!' Tyron had more in common with Gordon Gordon than he would have liked to think.

'Listen you,' said Mrs Culboon, 'we don't know nothing and we ain't done nothing, and that's the truth I reckon.'

'You shot down one of my helicopters, Mrs,' said Tyron.

'Look, that was a very heavy trip for us, too, you know,' Walter chipped in with a hint of reproach in his voice. 'Each of us is trying to come to terms with it in their own private space, and I have to say that it would help if you didn't keep dragging it up all the time.'

'Anyway, mate,' added Mrs Culboon, 'I reckon he would have shot us. Oh yes, I reckon he would, that's for sure. What should we have done? Stood there in the light and said come on and shoot us? Ha! I don't reckon so . . .'

'Shut the boong up,' snapped Tyron; and Du Pont stuffed a rag in her mouth.

'Hey listen, man!' protested Walter. 'Like, can we keep the heaviness down, OK? I mean can we just cool the heaviness. You know heaviness never solved anything right, like.'

'Right!' shouted Tyron, giving up on the charm-school effort and making his decision to break his deal with Sly and get rough. 'What do you know? How many more of you are there? And where are Zimmerman and the American journalist?'

His tone was very threatening and there was a sullen silence – from Walter and CD that is. Mrs Culboon was grunting unintelligibly through the rag. Which just goes to show what a small barrier to communication a lack of language can be, because it was quite clear to everyone that Mrs Culboon was saying, 'Get the fuck this rag out of my mouth.'

Tyron was about to turn up the heat on the proceedings considerably when his three hostages were granted a last minute reprieve. A messenger arrived to announce that Professor Durf had arrived and would be obliged if he could see Tyron urgently.

TO BE OFFERED THE WORLD

In the long hours of the night, whilst Tyron had lain cursing the heat and slapping the bugs, Sly had indoctrinated Rachel into Stark.

It had been a shocker, no doubt about that. Certainly the most surprising thing anybody had ever told her; more astonishing even than her youthful discovery that Daddy had a seed which he put in Mummy's tummy because they loved each other very much.

VANISHING POINT

First of all Sly had given Rachel a run-down of the apocalyptical doom scenario that he had first been fully made a party to at the dinner in Los Angeles. He explained the theory of the approaching vanishing point. 'The world does not know the half, a quarter even, of the shit it is in, Rachel. All your wildest fears; your conspiracy paranoias; your worst predictions about the state of the world, it's already happened ten times over. Words cannot describe the vandalism that has been perpetrated on this planet.'

Rachel did not know where this could be leading to. The last thing she had expected Sly to be was a green activist. He continued in the same dry tones.

'There are virtually no forests left. There are no longer any effective atmospheric barriers. Soon there will be no polar ice-caps. Coupled with this, every single thing on this planet has been subjected, to a greater or lesser extent, to toxification. It is a fact that nothing on earth can be said to be clean. Not one drop of water, not one gulp of air, not one mouthful of food. It is all irreversibly filthy. Without the forests, deserts will very soon take over the majority of land remaining above sea-level. Which will not be much because once the ice has melted all low lying land will be submerged under a filthy sea.'

Sly always did love to hold the floor and on this occasion he was particularly anxious to make an impression on his audience. He assumed an almost schoolmasterly air, pacing about with his hands behind his back. He near as damn it put on an English accent, which is how the Australian advertising industry implies weightiness. If they want to impress upon people that a particular box of cereals has dignity, they get a pom actor to do the voice-over. Sly was trying to sound weighty.

'The degradation of the soil through salination, chemical imbalance and intense over-farming is set to make almost all agriculture untenable worldwide. When that happens, billions of people are going to turn on each other in starving fury. If it hasn't already died of skin cancer or toxic shock, the human race will commit bloody self-murder . . .'

This was one of Durf's phrases and Sly felt it sounded rather good. He continued, 'This combination of various ecological disasters, any one of which alone could see us off, we call the Vanishing Point and we are satisfied that it will occur within the next two or three years. It is a straw that broke the camel's back situation really. Things will stagger on just about getting by, until one day a crack appears that shatters the entire structure and everything comes tumbling down at once.'

Sly spoke of the end of everything without any great emotion. Of course he had been living with the facts and the figures for many months, but he was still pretty cool about it.

The reason he was so cool was, of course, that he knew that it wasn't *quite* the end of everything.

WASTED TIME

'Oh come on, this is out of it,' said Rachel, understandably shocked. 'I'm sure something can be done.'

338

'Something *could* have been done a long time ago but we didn't do it, did we chum?' said Sly.

'Who's we?' asked Rachel, wondering why the hell Sly was going on about ecology. Surely he wasn't hoping that somehow he could persuade her that her principles were futile and hence she should leave whatever evil stuff he was up to alone?

'Well everybody, of course,' said Sly in answer to her question. 'But mainly myself and the other big players. Ever since the first industrial revolution when James Watt boiled a kettle and invented acid rain, or whatever the hell happened, the natural, life-forming parameters of our world have been like an hour glass, getting thinner and thinner. The question being, would we squeeze past the middle and break on through to the other side. Now, if we had acted earlier, when it first got obvious that we were really screwing up home sweet home, then maybe it would have been OK and we could have started looking after the old world and the chances of life on earth might have expanded again. But we didn't do it did we? We opted for instant profit and comfort; beer and skittles at the expense of the whole of future history. Anyway, now the gap in the glass is plugged, it's a vanishing point, there isn't a way through any more.'

'So how can you be sure?' demanded Rachel.

'Rachel, it's happening, now, we don't need to speculate, the facts are all around us. All you have to do is make a little graph of the deterioration in the various life forces; the toxic overload being forced into the air; the food; the very dirt we walk on! Expand the curves just a brief moment into the future and you have complete Eco-breakdown.'

GUILT AND REDEMPTION

Understandably Rachel was extremely shaken by his conviction, and, of course, rather scared.

'What was that about you and the other big players then?' she asked. 'Who are you?'

'The super-rich; those of us who own the means of production; the people who make everything that fucks everything up. Now listen, don't get me wrong. I ain't absolving the little guys from guilt, they bought the stuff we made, they wanted the stupid little things that we swapped the planet for. Nobody objected. A quick look at the litter on the Carlton beaches makes me pretty doubtful that things would be much different if "the people" had been in control ... But it's still mainly my fault, mine and my colleagues. I mean, is the man who buys pornography as guilty as the man who makes it and sells it? I reckon not, after all, the poor wanker on the receiving end would not have thought to even want it if it wasn't stuffed under his nose.'

Sly was enjoying getting all this off his chest. He had kept his own counsel for so long that it was an immense relief to talk about it, wallow in his guilt. Especially to Rachel, a greeno who he had developed such a desire for. He was like the adulterer who confesses all to his faithful wife in order to absolve his own guilt; laying it on the least deserving recipient. This was confession and absolution for Sly, he needed it. And, of course, he would pay Rachel back for her patience a billion fold. After all, he had the whole of creation to offer her.

'You know I was once the major backer for the development of a kind of instant French fry in a tube,' Sly said, continuing his strange confession. 'What you did was heated up some oil in a frying pan and pumped the tube into the fat, out came a chemically expanded string of reconstituted potato. *Voila!* No need for deep-fat chip pans and peeling spuds and all that. What's more, it was terrific fun, you could have chips as long or short as you liked them. You could have them in whirls, tie them in knots, write messages with them. As crap products go this one was actually kind of nice.'

'Sounds good, I'd have bought it, once, just to see what it was like,' said Rachel, fascinated to find out what all this was leading to.

'Yeah, a lot of people did. We only put it out in the States but it made a packet. I was real sorry when we had to take it off the market,' said Sly.

Rachel did not ask why he had to take it off the market, reckoning that he was going to tell her anyway, which of course he did.

'Damn thing finally got banned. It was a kind of aerosol, see. The potato mixture was expanded by Chlorofluorocarbons, CFCs, you know the ozone eaters.'

'I'm an environmental commando, Mr Moorcock,' said Rachel, wishing to assert herself but actually sounding pretty dumb, 'Of course I know what a Chlorofluorocarbon is.'

'Yeah well I knew too, right from when I started marketing the stuff. It didn't stop me backing an aerosol that made chips though. What's more, I used every damn bit of political clout I had to lobby the politicos to stop them legislating against CFCs.'

'Well you're a bastard, aren't you?' said Rachel.

'Well, I suppose I am. It didn't seem that way at the time but I suppose I was and I suppose I still am, because I *knew* what that damn can was doing to the sky and yet I still put it on the shelves. People trust things on shelves, they think if there was anything wrong the government would do something. I mean, let's face it, nobody asked for an aerosol that sprayed chips . . .'

Rachel was getting tired now.

'Look, what the hell is going on?' she snapped suddenly, 'what are you doing here? What's all this shit about the end of the world? And what do you want with me? Come on, give me an answer . . . or . . .' There is nothing more demeaning than getting half-way through a threat and realizing that you don't have a punch line.

It was all right though, Sly had one of his own.

WELCOME TO STARK

'Welcome to the Stark project, Rachel. I've told you that the world is dying. It is, believe me, it really is. But, the vanishing point isn't total. One grain of sand is going to slip through – I and my colleagues are getting out. This construction area is to be the launch site for the Star Arks, a small fleet of rockets that will carry us away and with us everything we need to start again, to build a new world. This, if you like, is the dawn of creation. Genesis.'

Necessarily there was a pause, Sly's statement was not the sort to which there is a stock answer. Eventually Rachel said:

'Well, Darth Vador, this is fascinating, but don't you think it's the sort of fantasy you should have had when you were six?'

'We're going to the moon, Rachel, and from there we will watch the earth die.' Obviously Sly was aware that it was all going to sound a bit far-fetched, so he set about trying to make it convincing. 'It's over twenty years since the Americans landed on the moon, isn't it?' Sly continued. 'Haven't heard much about it since, have we? Not a squeak really. All that huge effort, a whole generation ago, and then nothing. Why do you think that is, Rachel?'

'I'm sure you'll tell me,' said Rachel wearily. It was clear that whatever else this loony intended he wasn't in a mood to let her go.

'We bought it,' said Sly, and Rachel was surprised. Sly was pleased he had finally solicited something other than disbelief or contempt.

'You bought the moon?' she asked.

'Not me,' said Sly, 'I was only fifteen at the time. I've only been a party to the Stark project for a few months. But the then members of the consortium bought it. The US government had stuck a flag in it, just the way the British once stuck a flag in Australia, and like the British the Yanks thought that meant they owned it. Well, there wasn't much they could do with it at the time, the whole project had been a prestige affair anyway, so we made them an offer, and they sold it to us, along with all the research, technology and hardware that had gone into getting to it in the first place.'

Sly could see that he had given Rachel real cause for thought. It had, after all, been a whole generation since the moon shots, and it was true that nobody had been back since.

'The original reasons given were potential mineral research and all that,' Sly continued. 'Which was partly true as well. In those days the super-rich still thought that earth's Vanishing Point could be avoided and that the moon would just become another place to make money. Since then the situation has changed a lot. The importance of a bolthole like the moon has become rather clear.'

'Bolthole!!' exclaimed Rachel. 'Don't be ridiculous, you can't live on the moon. There's no air and ... and ... well there's nothing, no food, no ... Oh God I don't even know why I'm talking to you. The whole thing is just bloody ridiculous.'

'You've got no idea what we can and cannot do, Rachel,' said Sly glaring at her and trying to be tough and commanding. 'The richest people in the world have been working on this for nearly three decades. Think about it, three decades *before* the moon shot they had only just developed a jet engine. What do you think we can achieve so long after?'

'I don't know, but whatever it is it can't possibly be a viable alternative to slogging it out on earth, however bad things get,' protested Rachel, amazed at herself that she was even discussing it.

'I keep telling you!!' said Sly, for the first time slightly losing his cool. 'Don't kid yourself, the earth's illness is not like a normal disease that you just presume one day "they'll" come up with a cure for. There is no cure, it's dying, all our research is conclusive, we *have* to try and get out, however unpleasant or difficult the prospect. Don't you see?'

'No, it's insane, you're mad, this is all ridiculous. I don't even know why I'm talking to you ...' said Rachel, also losing her cool. Sly pressed on.

'For fifteen years now we have been blasting off the necessary equipment, leaving it floating up in space ready for us to reclaim, should the need arise. The orbit of the moon is one vast warehouse of spinning hardware: 65 per cent of the hundreds of commercial satellite launches that have taken place over the years haven't carried communications satellites at all. They've carried dead weight of hardware, everything from food to frozen sperm. Thousands of tonnes of it has built up and it's all been left, spinning around the earth or the moon, all armed with little booster rockets, waiting for the time when we will fire them down onto the moon's surface. And that time is almost upon us. Come on, I'll show you something,' said Sly.

He grabbed Rachel by the hand, which was the first time they had ever touched, and led her to the door.

NOAH'S WORKSHOP

It is very difficult to take in something really impressive. This is probably a good thing because if the mind was truly capable of comprehending the magnificence of, say, a great cathedral, or the strangeness of most fish, we would probably all go mad.

Certainly Rachel had considerable trouble getting her head around the creation that Sly was so spaciously showing off for her benefit. She felt as she had used to feel at school when faced with Shakespeare; she knew it was huge stuff and she could sort of see why, but the truth was it still failed to penetrate in a genuinely moving manner.

First Sly showed Rachel one of the biggest holes in the ground she had ever seen, a massive concrete chasm, filled with tiny figures working on things in it.

'I reckon some of those guys must be beginning to think it's a strange kind of hotel they're building,' said Sly. 'Still, fuck 'em, they're getting paid more than they could ever have dreamed of, and they're all foreign anyway. So fuck 'em. I don't guess anyone's going to be over anxious to rock the boat and lose a job like this, especially with the depression we've got going right now. What do you think of it?' said Sly turning to Rachel with a degree of proprietorial pride.

'What is it?' she asked, not really wanting to hear.

'It is one of the six largest launch silos in the world,' said Sly, 'the other five are all within three miles of here . . .'

They stared over the edge together in silence, then Sly mused, 'and the Lord said, make it a fuck of a lot of cubits tall, and a fuck of a lot of cubits wide,' getting biblical for a minute.

They drove in Sly's Jeep to one of many warehouses. Sly

showed her four huge, silvery rolls of a kind of gossamer thin metallic mesh. 'Three hundred and fifty miles of solar cells, woven into a flexible fibre,' Sly said. 'This will be part of the payload of one of the three unmanned launches which will blast simultaneously with the Star Arks . . .'

And even in all the strangeness of her situation, Rachel found herself snapping . . . 'Unstaffed.'

'Yes, sorry, unstaffed. Hopefully our new world won't be a sexist one,' Sly continued in the sort of tone Hitler must have used when he was guaranteeing Czechoslovak neutrality.

'Everything we need is already up there but the consortium has always reserved one final set of launches to allow for improved technology. Obviously, at the last minute we want to take the very best the world has to offer. These solar cells make the ones we sent up five years ago obsolete. They'll provide the power of four nuclear plants, and no chance of pollution you see.'

'That's nice,' said Rachel, for want of anything better.

Sly continued, 'The idea is that with the human launch we establish a kind of camp which will be supplied entirely artificially, from what we take with us on the blast. This is why the silos are so big, there's a lot to take. It'll be a bit cramped, but we'll live in the camp while we concentrate on building a self-sufficient world . . .'

As they walked through the warehouse, Sly felt obliged to confess some doubts. 'It all *sounds* all right. I suppose it might work, it might not. Quite exciting really. These solar sheets will simply be flown up and left spinning in the moon's orbit with the rest of the junk until we are ready to boost them in. The estimate is approximately five years. Everything will stay in orbit until we are ready to bring it in. There's even a micro-film library floating up there. Wonder when we'll need that, not for ages I suppose. Bet it's all Keynes and Adam Smith anyway. That's the trouble with setting off with a bunch of bankers . . . Apparently we're taking with us from earth enough of everything for five years. After that we're on our own. But I'm told our only real job will be to create a viable atmosphere, after that all else will follow on . . .'

'Just create it, eh?' said Rachel.

'Yes, it will be done with plants, photosynthesis, all that biology business, the plants will use the available carbon dioxide and the sunlight to create oxygen. The water comes from under the surface.'

Rachel's mind was reeling, as Sly had intended that it should. He knew how she felt, he had felt exactly the same way when the whole terrible, enormous, cowardly, craven project had been put to him.

'There are seventy-five members in the Consortium,' said Sly, adding casually, 'each can take a partner. Then there is a scientific and work team of fifty who have been indoctrinated into Stark. They will also be allowed a partner, but one who will be required to have some medical or scientific skill. All told, there will be two hundred and fifty individuals in the Arks. A decade from now they will be all that is left of the human race. But we are taking a lot of frozen embryos. I suppose if the water runs out we can always drink them.' This was a joke but not one that Rachel appreciated.

'We're also taking a lot of animal foetuses all frozen in suspended animation. Same principle as Noah really, but a bit more high tech. And obviously we aren't taking the nasties. No cockroaches for instance, although what's the betting a couple of the bastards manage to sneak into the ship.'

They wandered into another warehouse.

'See that,' said Sly, pointing at a box that on opening appeared to contain an ice-making machine. 'That's a kind of filter. It can get the horrid bits out of sweat and piss and all that, so you can drink it again. Apparently a very large percentage of the water that we will require we actually take up in our own bodies, clever eh?'

Rachel believed him. She could not believe that she believed him, but she did.

'You know that if the world finds out that, having made a pretty substantial contribution to the mess we're all in, you're all pissing off, well there's probably going to be a fair degree of protest,' said Rachel.

'Yes, we know that,' Sly replied.

'I mean they'll probably all march up here and tear you limb from limb and torch the whole disgusting dump,' Rachel continued.

'I don't think so, Rachel,' said Sly. 'I reckon they'll come up here, all right, but they'll be trying to get on the Arks, mass panic. Billions of people trying to be one of the two hundred and fifty. But if people did find out, I doubt they would believe it, you didn't until you saw it and I'm not about to show it to anybody else. But no one will know. Between us the members of the Stark Group own far too much of all the newspapers and TV and radio stations in the world, Soviets excluded of course, but we just ignore them and they just ignore us. Imagine if the Chairman of the Central Committee of the Politburo or whatever it is, tried to tell the world that good old Tex Slampacker, who has done so much for little children in hospital, was going to fuck off and leave them all to Eco-doom. Nobody would believe him would they?'

Rachel asked the question she'd been meaning to ask for some time.

'Why have you showed me?' she said.

Rachel was not at all a vain person but she had guessed his answer. 'Because, Rachel, I want to take you with me,' Sly said.

A HELL OF A DATE

Well, of course, Rachel had been propositioned before, she had some small experience of chat-up lines that went beyond a casual 'what about it?' She had been promised meals, asked on holiday, CD had even offered to devote what remained of his life to making her happy. But no one had ever offered to save her from a dying planet. No man had ever asked her to go with him to the moon and stay there. And of course, if what Moorcock said was true, then nobody had ever offered to save her life before. The whole situation was one that would confuse anybody.

'Why me? Haven't you got a girlfriend, a wife?' she asked.

'No,' said Sly. 'I have no one to take and I want to take you.'

'To the moon?'

'To the moon.'

'You do realize,' said Rachel, 'that this is tantamount to asking me to marry you?'

'Of course,' replied Sly.

'And you've known me for about five minutes?' she continued.

'Look,' said Sly, 'I have no one to take, all right, no one I would even dream of considering. I liked you the first moment I saw you, the whole situation's insane anyway. I'm acting on instinct.'

Rachel said she'd think about it.

TIME RUNS OUT

The next morning Durf arrived and Sly, like Tyron, was asked to kindly join him in the project control room. He brought bad news.

HANGING ON THE END OF A CHAIN

'Gentlemen, I have received predictions from the Domesday Group which have convinced me that Vanishing Point is upon us. I have alerted principal Stark shareholders to proceed to this location forthwith. Once enough have arrived for us to be quorate, I shall propose immediate departure, suggesting that we deploy the eight day count-down procedure as agreed in Helsinki.'

Sly and Tyron just stared at him. There isn't a lot one can say to a man who has just told you that you are emigrating to the moon in eight days. Perhaps sensing the need for small-talk Durf added, 'Personally I wouldn't eat that crabmeat sandwich.'

Sly and Tyron stared at him again. In fact, they just carried on staring at him since they hadn't stopped from the first time. There was a plate of sandwiches on the desk. They had come with the coffee, Tyron had absentmindedly picked one up.

'I am reliably informed,' said Durf, 'that the long feared T T O has occurred in a food layer stretching from micro-organisms right up to simple animals.'

Eight days? Sandwiches? T T O? Sly, at last, found his feet. 'Durf, what the fuck are you talking about, you patronizing, one-eyed, South African bastard.'

Sly's attitude did not surprise Durf. After all, he was a patronizing, one-eyed, South African bastard.

'What is the long feared T T O and what is the problem with the sandwiches?' asked Sly, deciding that things would probably move faster if he was less confrontational.

'T T O, is Total Toxic Overload and it is the point at which a species becomes so compromised by toxic waste that it becomes a liability to the food chain. Unfortunately, only man is capable of recognizing this problem and isolating the offenders . . .'

Only Durf could have called a polluted microbe an offender.

'If we are told that a tuna has been contaminated with mercury, then we do not eat it. But all other creatures who include tuna in their diet will, of course, continue to eat it, and hence become compromised themselves.'

Durf had the politicians' habit of sanitizing unpleasant things by refusing to describe them properly. Hence 'polluted' became 'compromised' and, no doubt, 'polluted to death' would be 'terminally compromised'.

Durf continued his description of the terminally compromised food chain. 'Each creature is poisoned by its diet and then itself becomes the poisoned diet of a superior creature. In this manner the poisons gather momentum on their way up to the top of the food chain where sits man. Man eats everything from simple crustaceans to highly evolved mammals, hence it is fair to say that we consume the accumulated pollution of all other species.'

The sandwich fell from Tyron's limp grasp. It lay on the floor, poised and vicious, like a scorpion, primed and ready to kill.

'Well, that's great isn't it?' said Tyron.

'Now that the entire base of the food chains have achieved, or will soon achieve, T T O . . .' Durf spoke as if the base of the food chain should get a prize for this, '. . . we can assume that within a single season, all animal food on earth will be poisoned and entirely inedible. This, combined with the world crop failures, which are now a regular feature of our greenhouse summers, means . . .'

'It really is all over,' Sly spoke slowly, like a person just waking up and trying to remember where they are.

'There can be no doubt about it,' said Durf. 'The nuclear pollution in the Northern Hemisphere has forced a far greater reliance on food from southern seas. With the wreck yesterday of the toxic waste ship, *Ataria C42*, off Shark Bay, that source, already massively strained, collapses altogether. There is virtually nothing left to eat on earth. We have polluted all of it. This is why I am calling in the shareholders. With their permission we will start the eight day count-down.'

'Well you've got my permission, let's bugger off while we still can,' said Tyron.

'But the rockets are only just in place,' said Sly. 'We can't possibly be ready?'

'We *have* to be ready, Mr Moorcock,' Durf insisted, 'otherwise we go with what we have. Nagasyu is only a few hours sail from the west coast with the remaining hardware. I have every confidence in him. We *will* achieve what is necessary.'

'And then I suppose we walk on water for an encore,' Sly found Durf's manner irritating, 'although with the shit that's in it these days, we probably could walk on water.'

'It is not a question of miracles, Mr Moorcock, but careful planning. Planning that commenced considerably before your own indoctrination into Stark,' said Durf, who sometimes forgot that he was an employee. 'The only problem that seriously concerns me is that of the American journalist. My men have not so far located her in or around Bullens Creek. I am confident that she knows nothing and has no means of alerting people, even if she had something to say –'

'So what's the problem then?'

'There *is* no problem. It is just that the world is about to realize it is dying. Even the suspicion that there is an escape route might cause the more volatile to investigate. There is no room on Stark for panic-stricken hordes. The chances of information leakage are at present small but then again so are the microbes at the bottom of the food chain and look at the damage they have wrought. It would certainly be preferable if we could locate the American.'

'Locate' of course being Durf-speak for kill.

POWERS OF PERSUASION

Neither Sly nor Tyron had mentioned to Durf that they held all but one of the journalist's friends who, one presumed, must hold the key to her whereabouts. Sly had kept quiet because he was concerned for Rachel, and Tyron because he was determined to sort the situation out himself. He would make them talk, he would find the American and everything could proceed as planned.

Therefore, while Sly returned to his quarters to tell Rachel that the moment had come and that she'd better decide, Tyron collected Du Pont and returned to his prisoners.

ADMINISTRATIVE METHODS

The prisoners had now spent nearly an entire night tied up on chairs and were looking pretty bedraggled – which in Walter's case meant exactly the same as usual. However, Tyron was disappointed to discover that their long hours of discomfort had made them no more co-operative. With only eight days left, Tyron determined to dispense with the charm idea altogether and get straight down to business.

He ordered Du Pont to do his stuff.

Du Pont had the guards drag CD, still bound to a chair, into the middle of the room.

'Guys, guys, guys,' said CD, trying to lighten the tone a little. 'Really this is so medieval, surely there is a better way. I mean, we just don't *do* this sort of thing any more.'

'On the contrary,' said Du Pont, who loved saying things like 'on the contrary' to helpless prisoners. It ranked up there with phrases like 'that was very foolish' and 'please do not underestimate me, Mr Bond'. Despite his bandaged nose, Du Pont was feeling particularly tough and hard. 'Torture is more prevalent today as an accepted part of the armoury of the busy administrator than it has ever been,' continued Du Pont.

CD watched in cold horror as Du Pont opened his small suitcase and took from it, amongst other things, a kind of wire sponge, rather like an enormous pan scrubber. CD wondered if he was to be flayed alive with a huge scouring pad.

'I'll tell you a good way of torturing people,' CD babbled. 'Water! It's a sure fire one, water! That's right, the Chinese water torture. What you do is you drip water on a person's head . . . Ugh! It's just horrible! I mean, it drives people into agony and insanity through the sort of maddening inevitability of it. Why don't you do that one to me? Go on, drip water on my head, phew! I bet I wouldn't be able to take that one.'

But it was a futile effort. CD was relying on the old war movie cliché that the worst tortures are not physical, but ingeniously psychological. Well doubtless you end up with less mess on the carpet, but if one were to ask the average victim whether, given the choice, they would opt to be irritated by water, or have five billion volts shot through their nipples, that person might just choose to learn to live with the splish, splish, splish.

CD was not to be given such an option. It was to be straight physical intimidation for him. He realized he had been wrong with the flaying theory when Du Pont put on thick rubber gloves and attached two jump leads to the wire wool. The leads ran back into a variable transformer, which was, in its turn, plugged into the wall.

'Look, man, please, I mean, you know!' said Walter. He was a hard man but what was going on would have upset a horny sadist in a party mood. 'Look, this is ridiculous, I mean, please.'

'Just tell us where the Yank bitch is,' barked Tyron, using the word 'bitch' in order to enter into the spirit of the occasion.

CD was thinking hard. To disclose the location of the Culboons' holiday home, where Chrissy was waiting, would almost certainly mean her death. On the other hand, he had no illusions as to what his performance would be under torture. He was faced with what must be the classic dilemma in such circumstances. Why not give in immediately? Since the chances are almost certain that you're going to capitulate in the end, should one not simply collapse in the first place and save oneself a great deal of unnecessary unpleasantness.

CD had considered lying of course, saying something along the lines of, 'The Yank bitch is holed up in the old quarry'. But he knew it would be pointless, his interrogators knew that Chrissy was either in or around Bullens Creek. A helicopter could check out any story in less than fifteen minutes, and then no doubt it would be a bigger sponge and longer jump leads.

Du Pont instructed one of the guards to pour a jug of water over CD. The guard had to fill it, because it was the same jug that Zimmerman had gargled with the previous morning as a health precaution after biting into Du Pont's nose.

They soaked CD down, but he was under no illusions that he was to be subjected to Chinese water torture.

WARTIME MEMORIES

On the roof Zimmerman wondered how long he could afford to give it before he made a move. He did not particularly wish to make a move. He was, after all, pretty heavily outnumbered and a day and a night hiding on top of a roof in the searing greenhouse heat had made him wilt a little. But he would have to do something. Through a tiny crack in the guttering he could see the steel-grey sponge and he recalled the last time he had encountered such a device.

The Vietnam war had been an unpleasant one even considering the high standards of horror set by modern conflicts. Both sides paid scant regard to the Geneva Convention. Zimmerman had himself taken part in Napalming civilians although he had never committed the private cruelties of rape and pillage that were so common. On the other hand, he had himself been subjected to inhuman cruelties by the other side. The Vietcong had caught him on a forward reconnaissance, and had, with the aid of the battery from a crashed US helicopter gunship, subjected him to electric shock treatment in order to discover where the rest of his Yankee unit were. In vain had Zimmerman protested that he was Australian, they were not interested.

Zimmerman had been almost as mad at the time as he later became and so he was able to withstand the torment for the ten minutes he underwent it. That is until a low-level bombing raid mercifully dispersed the party. On the other hand, he was aware that he would not have lasted much longer. It hurt.

SHOCK TREATMENT

CD's whole body convulsed. Despite the fact that he was tied to a chair, he managed to jump about six feet in the air. He screamed. Walter screamed. Mrs Culboon bit her rag grimly.

The world will never know how much CD could have taken, although he himself later admitted with disarming honesty that as the water dispersed the shock across his whole body, he knew that he could have taken absolutely no more whatsoever. But, before anyone had a chance to find out if this was the case, Zimmerman sailed back in through the window out of which he had made his exit so many hours before.

Everyone was shocked at this sudden apparition. It was Tyron's second shock within a few seconds. He had not really imagined that the disgusting Du Pont would actually start torturing anybody for real. Even Tyron balked a bit at that. He had presumed that the whole purpose of the torture threats had been to scare the prisoners into submission. Oh sure, a punch or two maybe, but not this. Tyron was a businessman, and this wasn't his business. He was quite capable of ordering death and beatings at long distance, and had done so in the case of Linda Reeve, but this close up horror was too near the knuckle by half.

Du Pont had rather shocked himself as it happened, he was just a little git really and for all his bluster he had never had the chance to properly do something like this before. Zimmerman had been surprised too. He never thought Du Pont would do it. He thought, like Tyron, that the whole thing was bluster and intimidation. That was why he had let CD take the first shot, he hadn't believed that it would happen. Of course, now that it had, he was forced to act.

Of course, the person most shocked of all was CD, but that was because he had just had about a million volts up him.

When he heard CD scream, Zimmerman realized that his only allies were speed and surprise, hence the entry had to be good. He flipped over onto his back, gripped the guttering, kicked hard, throwing his legs over his body, off the edge of the roof and swinging down in through the open window.

'Zimm!!' shouted a delighted Walter, 'Oh man . . .' He was about to add that Zimmerman's sudden appearance just had to be one of the very finest trips since the Beatles released 'Pepper', but there simply wasn't time.

'Freeze!' said Zimmerman, brandishing the gun that he had taken from Du Pont.

At least he would have been brandishing it if he hadn't accidentally left it on the roof. All he was actually brandishing at the surprised guards was fingers. Luckily he realized his mistake before anyone else did and he was able to grab the gun of the guard standing nearest. Zimm did not even have to hit him, the guard just let go. This is the sort of effect that you can get if you start a fight by flying in unexpectedly through the window.

'Right,' said Zimmerman, 'I'll start again. Freeze!!'

CONTEMPLATING
TREACHERY

HORROR MOVIES

The previous night, after Rachel had told Sly that she would think about his unusual chat up line, he had very considerately left her with what he hoped would be sufficient evidence to bring her around to his way of thinking.

The evidence was in the form of a video film and it made your average horror movie look like something intended for Granny and the wee ones. Any Hollywood producer worth his salt who had chanced to see Sly's video, would have quickly realized that all the stuff about monsters exploding out of people's stomachs and small girls being raped by the devil, was totally out of the window. Once you've been chilled and thrilled by the story of the Sandoz Chemical Plant screwing up the Rhine or the slow death of the Baikal Lake, it no longer seems particularly worrying that a group of teenagers on a holiday camp get cut to bits with chainsaws because they're too stupid not to go down to the old boat shed.

The Sandoz and Baikal stories were just two of the many that were touched upon in the videos that Rachel watched with increasing despair. It opened with the bleak announcement that it was a top secret preparation to be viewed by members of the Stark consortium only. Sly was still in the room when this message came on . . .

'I'm not a member of the Stark consortium,' Rachel protested.

'Once you've watched that you will be,' smiled Sly and left her to it.

The show opened with a smart-alec looking fellow in an eye patch, addressing the camera. Professor Durf announced that the time had come to leave. That the long feared moment of truth was finally upon the Stark consortium.

'I can think of no better illustration to underline the urgency of our situation than to suggest that were God to attempt to take out an insurance policy on the world, he would not be able to afford the premiums.'

This was Durf's little joke. He had decided to kick-off with a gag just to show that, despite things being in a terrible state, he at least could maintain his suave intellectual detachment.

'What an arrogant creep,' thought Rachel.

Durf followed his little gag with a warning against a false sense of security engendered by current political cant.

'Of late, certain politicians have been attempting to play the green card in their grubby scramble for public support. Believe me, such tokenism is entirely cynical. The situation can never be reversed whilst market forces remain superior to political will. The politicians have always left us alone, and they *will* always leave us alone, because we pay the piper, and we call the tune.'

Much of what followed Rachel already knew something about, but the sheer weight of current catastrophe certainly took her by surprise. It could not have been a more unmitigated tale of gloom and impotent despair if it had been written by Dostoyevsky.

It started on a fairly light note, briefly detailing the world's smaller disasters, like the 1986 Sandoz Chemical leak in Switzerland. This minor incident, which at the time was entirely overshadowed by the World Cup, concerned the accidental discharge of thirty tonnes of toxic waste into the Rhine. Of course, thirty tonnes doesn't sound that much – the lead singers of heavy metal bands can sometimes weigh as much as that – but the seriousness of a toxic leak depends entirely on how toxic the leak is. Well, in the case of Sandoz, the words 'very, very' spring to mind, and then spring out again as being scarcely adequate. And then spring back again for the want of a better alternative. Put it this way, if the universe is very, very, big, then the Sandoz leak was very, very toxic. That thirty tonnes leaked from one factory, into one river, swept through France, Germany and Holland and killed every single living organism in its path.

The catalogue of disaster unfolded before Rachel. She learnt of the Baikal. Situated in the Soviet Union it is the world's largest lake. The Russian people harbour a love for it of huge and mystical proportions, which is rather apt because the lake is itself of huge and mystical proportions, being a kilometre and a half deep and containing, according to some, 20 per cent of the world's fresh water. 'Fresh' of course being a loose description for something that is being filled with shit and industrial waste.

Everything that Sly had attempted to impress upon Rachel unfolded before her on the TV. The message was always the same. The myriad destruction in every single area of the natural world must soon provoke a total breakdown. The time had come to bugger off.

Rachel's head was numb. It couldn't have been more numb if she'd woken up in the middle of the night to discover that she'd been sleeping on it in an awkward position ... So this was the way the world was to end. Not with a bang, not with a whimper, but with retching nausea as the teeming billions struggled for their final gulps of food and air before sinking for ever into the stench, filth, disease and slime that would certainly be our final environment in the huge rubbish dump and toilet that we have created out of Paradise.

LORDS OF CREATION

Professor Durf was speaking again ...

'As you all know, as principal creators of the world's wealth – the one human creation, I am happy to say, that remains untainted and unpolluted – we have known for many years now that were human activity to continue unchecked it would and must lead to oblivion. We declined to interfere though, believing social engineering to be immoral. We all hoped, of course, that market forces would produce a solution; that ecologically responsible activity would somehow become profitable. As we know, it hasn't and that is just too bad. We had a duty to progress, to make money and create wealth, that was our bounden mission. If the earth had to die in the defence of a free market economy, then it is a noble death.'

Rachel glanced around for a bucket, this man was the human equivalent of sticking two fingers down your neck.

'Now is the time to look to the future,' the televised Durf continued. 'Now is the time to board the "Starks", the Star Arks. It is fitting that you, the world's richest men, should lead the human race to fresh fields and pastures new. For in the time of the first Ark the people worshipped God and hence, Noah, the most pious of men, was chosen to survive the flood and shape the future. In modern times people worship money, Money God in that it has been deified and can clearly be said to rule our lives. Hence, as I say, it is fitting that you, the super-rich, those who have worshipped money with a diligence and conviction far above the faith of lesser men, that you should board the Star Arks and carry our faith to a new civilization beyond the flood, on the moon.'

A DIFFICULT OFFER TO REFUSE

Clearly Rachel's moral dilemma was a considerable one. Such was the depth of her concentration that she scarcely noticed the thunder in the sky which signalled the arrival of Nagasyu's final deliveries.

On the one hand she was disgusted. It was worse than the time she had inadvertently seen someone pick their nose and eat it. These repulsive people, having made a very large contribution to screwing up the world, now intended to slink off and leave everybody literally in the shit. Rachel would no more wish to associate with this type of human slug than she would voluntarily set up home in a nest of game-show hosts ... And yet ... and yet.

One thing was certain, Rachel no longer doubted the Vanishing Point scenario. Everybody was going to die, and die pretty unpleasantly at that. Except of course, not everybody. There was, it seemed, a flight out, and because a man with the hots for her had got a couple of tickets, she was being offered salvation.

She played the situation around and around in her mind. Strangely she was not over-exercised about the imminent end of earth. Despite the fact that she believed in it now, it still seemed like a story. What Rachel was wrestling with was simply the moral dilemma. The choice between a pointless act of suicidal courage and an act of pragmatic self-preservation. It was clear that no useful purpose could be served by her staying and she flattered herself that she deserved to live as much, if not more, than some bimbo that Moorcock might choose to take if she declined to go. The morals of the situation were by no means cut and dried. Rachel was no more guilty than anyone else, it wasn't her fault that we killed the world.

She kept on thinking. Wondering what she would do; wondering where her friends were; wondering what she thought about Sly.

And so the long night wore on, the last night before the Stark count-down began.

In the morning Sly returned from his meeting with Durf and Tyron where he had discovered TTO and the fatal sandwich. It was decision time.

THE TABLES TURN

GETTING TIED UP IN KNOTS

Covering his erstwhile captors with one hand, Zimmerman cut his comrades' bindings.

'Man, I've been hanging out on that roof for twenty-four hours,' he remarked, 'I don't recommend that kind of shit to anybody.'

'Zen is the only way to deal with trips like that, Zimmerman,' said Walter. 'I guess you must have found your centre and relaxed into a meditative balance.'

'I killed two lizards and ate them,' replied Zimm.

Walter agreed that this was one way of passing the time and that everybody had to do their own thing.

By now Zimm had released all three prisoners. He dragged a chair into the corner of the room and stood on it, this gave him the optimum available field of fire with which to cover operations while the others used their bindings to tie up Tyron, Du Pont and the guards.

This done, Zimmerman inspected the knots. 'CD, man, this is a double bow,' he protested.

'It's the only one I know Zimm, it works fine on shoes,' said CD who had not really recovered from his interrogation and still looked like you could have run a three bar electric fire off him.

Zimmerman attempted to explain the art of knot tying to CD, taking the two ends of the rope and creating a complicated system of loops and bows. 'This is a knot, man. You have to make a tunnel, then the train goes through the tunnel, right? Then these two ends here are the people OK?

And you put them perpendicular to the train and wind the track round them, right? Then you gather up the slack right, that's the uhm . . .'

'Station buffet?' enquired CD.

'Well, no man, I don't think so, but I guess we can call it that, because actually, rules are just mind control,' said Zimmerman who, it must be remembered, was only lucid when he absolutely had to be. 'You gather up the station buffet . . . stuff it into the train . . . Oh yeah, that's right, it's the *coal*, not the station buffet, it's coal, right . . . you stuff the coal into the train, and pull the train back through the tunnel, man, then you jerk the signal tight and dig, the dude will *never* escape.'

As Zimmerman said this the knot fell apart and the two ends of cord fell to the floor.

'Maybe you forgot the driver, man,' suggested Walter. 'When I was in the boy scouts I remember there was always a driver.'

'You were in the *boy scouts* man!' said Zimmerman, surprised.

'Well, yeah, like for a week,' replied Walter defensively, 'until I discovered it was just fascistic social engineering. Anyway, man, what's your beef? You were a fucking Marine Commando.'

'Oh yeah, Walter, that's right, dwell on the past,' said Zimmerman.

Mrs Culboon tried to restore order. 'I can do knots,' said Mrs Culboon. 'I'll tie them up.'

'Hey, listen lady, I can do knots, right?' said Zimmerman in an offended tone. 'I mean, knots are one of my big things.'

'Ha!' said Mrs Culboon. And even mad Zimmerman had to admit that she had a point.

'Look, be sensible,' protested Tyron, 'you can't possibly get away, it's many miles to the wire, there are guards and cameras everywhere. And even if you did get through, where will you go then? We own Bullens Creek, lock, stock and barrel, and everywhere else for that matter. You're in the middle of a desert, what can you possibly achieve?'

'Oh yeah, that's right, bring us down,' said Walter. 'Make it all sound totally depressing, why don't you? You have a real attitude problem, Mr Tyron. You have to take a more positive trip. It's just a bio-rhythm thing.'

'Listen,' interjected CD. 'I don't care what there is to face out there. While we were in your care, Mr Tyron, I got plugged into the wall and turned into a light bulb. Personally I'll take my chances.'

'They're all tied up good,' said Mrs Culboon.

FURTHER INTERROGATION

'OK,' said Zimmerman, 'nearly time to go, but first we need a few answers. After all, I reckon that's why we came here in the first place, to find out what's going on . . . So, what is the scene Daddy? What goes down here? Why the rocket fuel? The launch silos? The guns and stuff? Man what *is* this trip?'

There was a sullen silence from Tyron and Du Pont, the guards obviously said nothing because they knew nothing.

'So you ain't going to tell us nothing, then?' continued Zimmerman. Still there was a sullen silence.

'CD would you be so kind as to pass me the electrified wool, please,' said Zimmerman. 'Taking care to hold it by the leads. Dig?'

There was a surprised silence at this turn of events. CD crossed the room and picked up the instrument of torture. It crackled a little and a few tiny sparks flew from it.

Tyron and Du Pont were thinking. Tyron was thinking about guts, honour and not being pushed around. Du Pont was thinking that this was a mad hippy who had recently nearly bitten his nose clean off.

'We're building a colony fleet of rockets to emigrate to the moon because the earth is in rapid and terminal ecological decline,' blurted Du Pont and Tyron gave him a disgusted stare.

The ironic thing was that Du Pont's craven cowardice did him no good at all because obviously nobody believed him.

'You sure do have to hand it to these fellahs,' laughed Mrs Culboon, 'when it comes to thinking up really shitty excuses for what they're up to they are the very best. The moon! I reckon that's even better than the story about building a hotel.'

There was general laughter, and then Zimmerman seemed to snap. 'Now let's have the fucking truth!' he screamed making everybody jump at once. 'Right now!' He grabbed the electric sponge from CD and held it so that its edge was a millimetre away from the whimpering Du Pont's face.

'It's own medicine time, man!!' Zimmerman's eyes were wild and fearful. The veins on his hands stood out firm as he gripped the clamps of the jump leads. 'You're gonna *burn* man, you are gonna fucking burn!!!!'

Walter had no cause to love Du Pont, even less so did CD, but they both felt that Zimmerman was becoming somewhat alarming.

'Hey, Zimm baby, this is your man, Walter . . . Listen you have to cool it, you know? I mean, we cannot start torturing people, because like, in many ways that puts us on the same level as them, right? Which kind of begs the question, what are we fighting for?'

'Yeah,' CD chimed in, 'he who sups with the devil should use a long spoon and all that.'

'Give him a tickle with it, the bastard deserves it,' said Mrs Culboon, representing the hawks, so to speak.

Zimmerman just went wild. He screamed that everybody – and he meant everybody – should shut the fuck up. And whilst Walter mumbled something about hurting a guy's feelings, Zimm hurled what was left in the jug of water at the wall, then he dragged the electric wool back and forth across it, in huge sweeps, causing great showers of sparks to burst further from it.

'We have no *time* man!!!' he shouted, 'We have no time for chicken shit liberals!!!'

Had a psychiatrist popped his head around the door at that moment and taken a peek at Zimmerman, he would have instructed his secretary to cancel all calls for the next decade because he had a big job on.

'We have been shot at! Imprisoned! Sexually abused!' This last one was a surprise to everybody, but Zimmerman was employing the degree of dramatic license traditionally afforded to the psychotically insane. 'My main lady, Mrs Culboon, has been hassled by Hitlerheads,' he continued, pausing only to kick Tyron in the chest so that the chair which he was tied to toppled over backwards. 'And I want to know *why* man!! I want to be hip to what is going *down* here! And *this* dude!!' He flung a fist across Du Pont's face '. . . is going to lay it on me! Man, he is going to divulge the whole vibe, or the lights are gonna dim all over Australia, because he will be soaking up most of the national grid!!'

Zimmerman spat on the wire to make it crackle. 'Now – lay – it – on – me – man!!' And he punctuated each word by sweeping the mesh at arms length in front of a weeping Du Pont, missing him by a hair's breadth – and a thin hair at that, not the thick, coarse, lush kind, but the sort that comes from a person that you always think is going bald, even if they aren't.

Du Pont was, understandably, terrified and also rather confused. All this dig, dude, hip and vibe talk was new to him. He had spent the sixties as an administrator at a Swiss finishing school.

'What does he want?' Du Pont pleaded through his tears.

CD jumped in. 'He wants to know what you're building here, and please tell him quick.'

'I swear you'll fry, man, I swear!!' added Zimmerman un-necessarily.

Du Pont nearly had a heart attack.

'I've told you,' he bawled, his cheeks wet, 'we're building a colony fleet of rockets to emigrate to the moon because the earth is in rapid and terminal ecological decline. It's true, please believe me, it's true.'

'Like fuck it is,' said Zimmerman suddenly calming down and turning off the electricity at the wall. 'But you're a brave bastard, man, that's for sure. I took you to the edge, nothing left to do after that but fry you and I'm no pig. I'll leave that to you.'

The tension in the room relaxed somewhat.

'Well you certainly had me fooled, mate,' said CD, 'I really thought you'd gone completely mad for a minute there.'

'I did go completely mad,' said Zimmerman, 'but I'm completely mad anyway, so it doesn't make any difference.'

'You should have given it to one of them,' said Mrs Culboon, 'now they know you won't do it, none of them will talk and maybe we'll never know.'

'If you want to do it, Mrs Culboon, be my guest,' Zimmerman offered her the jump leads but she declined.

'I ain't the damn loony Vietnam hero,' she said. 'You are, Zimmerman. It's your job to do any electrocuting that needs to be done.'

'Well, I'm not going to. So let's get out of there,' he replied.

'Hang on, hang on, what are we going to do about Rachel,' protested CD. And suddenly CD's mind flooded with horrible fears and suspicions. What the hell had that man Moorcock taken her off for?

DECISION TIME

Sly knocked on the door of his quarters. He had not seen Rachel since the previous night when he had shown her around the launch site, and left her with the videos to consider his proposal.

She was standing at the window when he entered, watching the intense activity which the impending commencement of departure count-down had made all the more intense.

'Those are the rockets, the Star Arks,' he said, 'we've started preparing them for lift off.'

'Really? I thought you were putting in some new plumbing,' replied Rachel, who may have been seeing too much of Mrs Culboon.

'We're going real soon. Probably in eight days. Apparently the food chains are collapsing, it's Russian Roulette every time you have a sandwich,' said Sly ignoring her sarcasm. 'Better make up your mind, Rachel, there's only going to be one trip. Those who go, will be gone for ever, those who stay will stay for ever. The only difference being that those who go will still be breathing.'

'Breathing bottled air in a tiny cage.' Rachel was trying to protest but knew that she was wavering.

'Don't knock it, I expect it will be welcome enough when that's all there is. Besides,' Sly continued, 'that will only be for a year or two, slowly but surely we shall expand the cage and with that will come a less artificial environment, with oxygen from plants rather than bottles.'

'But you can't just go . . . can you?' Again she felt herself assailed by doubt.

'Well, I'm assured we can,' said Sly, 'I suppose maybe it'll

370

screw up, but as I hope you have now accepted, the alternative is certain death. I know it sounds cowardly, I suppose it is, but at least somebody will be getting out. Would you rather we went out and picked up a couple of hundred hippies and dropouts? Would that be a better, more moral thing to do?'

WHO DO YOU LOVE?

'Look,' said Rachel, getting down to the main point. 'Why me? I mean a new life on another planet is a lot to offer a girl you hardly know.'

'Who would you take?' asked Sly.

'What do you mean?' replied Rachel.

'Exactly what I say, who would you take?' he continued. 'You're not particularly attached, you have to take someone, or else you'll be all alone in space, so who?'

'Well . . .' said Rachel with hesitation.

'Not so easy, is it? Sure, at first you think that there must be someone. You think, after all, I'm very fond of any number of people. But that's not enough is it? If, despite knowing them well, you're only fond of them and not in love with them, then there's a reason for that. Sides of their personalities that you can avoid on earth, you couldn't get away from when you're drinking out of the same bottle of air. So, for a single, essentially lonely man, there is no clear choice, in fact there is no choice at all, I simply don't know anyone I love enough to take . . . In fact I'll go further, despite being fond of quite a few women, I love them so insufficiently that I *actively* don't want to take them . . .'

'And me?' asked Rachel, seizing the obvious line of questioning like an ace lawyer.

'Well, I don't know that I love you, but I certainly fancy the knickers off you, besides you're a spunky type . . . Now I'm a clear-headed enough bloke, I've fallen for girls before, it could all be over in a week, but you see I don't *know* that, do I? Maybe these feelings will last for ever, that's the difference, you see. With all the other girls that I care anything for at all, I *know* I know that I will never love them. With you I have a chance. That's why I want you to come with me. Until you busted your way into my life, frankly, I had no idea of what I was going to do . . .'

'Well, I must say you certainly have some terrific root lines. Live with me because I might not end up hating you . . .' replied Rachel.

'But that's not what I'm offering, that's not the reason you should come with me. The reason you should come with me is because that way you'll stay alive and what's more, it's the only way . . . Listen I'm not going to try and jump on top of you the moment we blast off . . .'

'Well thanks,' said Rachel, dryly.

'I'm just saying that, well with a bit of understanding, we might be able to build something together . . .'

'Please spare me the hearts and flowers, Mr Moorcock.'

'Look, don't take the piss out of me, girl! Because this is not a piss taking situation! I'm offering you life for Christ's sake.'

'All right, all right!' Rachel snapped, 'you've been living with this for a long time you know. It's still fairly new to me.'

She sat down, stood up, wandered around a bit, trying not to think about her family and the people she knew . . . they were all so far away.

'Well . . .' she said, and looked at Sly for a long time. He was certainly quite tasty. What's more he'd been straight with her about his emotional end of it. He didn't seem quite the bastard he had before. And after all, *somebody* had to survive the Vanishing Point.

'Well . . .' she said again . . .

BETRAYAL

Sly's conversation with Rachel had taken place whilst Zimmerman had been going mad and threatening Du Pont with electrification.

When Rachel had thought a bit more, she and Sly made their way over to the complex of security cabins. They entered just as Zimmerman and his little party were gingerly emerging from the room containing the bound and furious figures of Tyron, Du Pont and the guards. For a moment the two groups stood at either end of the corridor, very surprised to see each other – CD was ecstatic.

'Rachel!' he shouted, 'you're back, you look fantastic, no really, fantastic. It's OK, don't worry, we've escaped! God you look great.'

'Keep it quiet kid,' said Zimmerman, pointing his gun at Sly. 'Thanks for bringing our comrade back, man, if she's been hurt you're going to suffer for it. You OK, Rachel?'

'Umm, yeah, great,' said Rachel rather nervously. 'Listen, Zimm . . .'

'Then what are we doing hanging about?' replied Zimm, 'we'll just tie-up the fat cat here and we'll all be on our way.'

'Zimm,' said Rachel more firmly. 'It's not going to be like that, I need to talk to you all.'

'Rachel, for Christ's sake, we have to split,' said Walter.

'No really,' said Rachel. 'I need to talk to you.'

Zimmerman gave her a puzzled frown, then he waved his gun towards the open door of an empty room. As quietly as possible, they all hurried in.

'Uhm, Colin,' said Rachel. 'Mrs Culboon, Walter, Zimm.

This is Silvester.' She looked slightly nervous, on edge, all sorts of terrible thoughts entered CD's head . . .

'What have they done to you, Rachel?' he shouted. 'What's he done to you, I swear I'll . . .'

'Oh do shut up, Colin, we don't have much time. I've found out what we wanted to know.'

CD nearly had an apoplexy.

'How! How did you find out, what did he make you do!!'

'Shut *up*, Colin, I'm telling you . . .'

And she went on briefly to outline the things she had learnt. She did the best she could to convince them of the true facts about the earth's condition, explaining that most of the terrible evidence had long been suppressed in order not to interrupt commerce. She described some of the things that she had seen on the video, and some of the things that Sly had told her. She spoke passionately, but of course, they were very sceptical, she had been herself. It is extremely difficult to convince people that their world is in a hopeless condition and virtually dead.

She explained a few of the details of Stark which sounded even more far-fetched. It wasn't until the end of her little speech that she managed to impress on the four sceptical listeners that she at least certainly believed every word that she was saying.

'I'm going,' she said, 'I'm going with Silvester. He offered me a place and I accepted.'

Obviously it was a shock. Walter was the first to speak.

'Man, you have got to be crazy?' he said inadequately. 'With this dude? With this bread-head? What about all your . . . all your *stuff*, man, the things you believe in. I mean the whole Eco-trip . . .'

'It's got nothing to do with the things I believe in,' said Rachel not very convincingly. 'I still believe all the same things . . . this is simply a matter of life and death, that's all. My principles won't be any use to me dead will they! I'm sorry, but if you get the chance you might as well choose life . . . You're going to die . . . I'm telling you, you are, and I think given my opportunity you'd make the same decision . . . Yes you would, you fucking well would. It's easy to say you wouldn't because you don't have the choice to make, but you would . . .'

CD found himself crying.

Sly tried to help her out.

'She's right you know,' he said, 'any one of you would jump at the chance, if you had it. But you haven't, so shut up and listen.'

'I'm not listening to you, you . . . prick!' shouted CD.

'Colin, if that's your attitude, just shut up, all right!' Rachel shouted back. 'And that goes for all of you! Silvester and I have made an understanding. He's my . . . friend. So if that's your attitude, any of you, just insulting him, well screw you! I only came down here because I made releasing you lot a condition.' There were many tears starting in Rachel's eyes.

'We don't need any favours girl,' said Mrs Culboon, 'this fellah's giving you stuff, and he gets what you've got in return, right? Well, there's a word for that kind of woman where I come from, and it isn't a pretty one.'

'All right, you watch your mouth,' shouted Sly, 'right now! You start watching your mouth.'

'You telling me what to do? Ha!' said Mrs Culboon, who loved saying, 'ha'. 'I got a gun this time, Mister, and you ain't. So this is what it feels like to be a boong, OK!'

She poked Sly in the ribs with her rifle. Walter decided it was time to pour oil on troubled waters.

'Hey, come on everybody, be cool. Please can we just be cool? You know it's still a free world, right? even if it is dying. A chick can hang out with whatever dude she pleases and for whatever reason you know man? I think that's in the American Constitution or something. Like what I'm interested in Rachel, is your prior implication that you might be able to help us get out. Is that for real?'

'We don't need any help, Walter, we've being doing just fine on our own,' said CD.

'Oh yeah, kid?' Zimmerman was in a lucid mood, 'well

certainly *we've* being doing OK so far, but may I remind you that we are still in the centre of the pig-pen and I reckon two hippies, a middle-aged black woman and a guy who won't take off his sunglasses are not necessarily guaranteed a safe passage out of here.'

CD had not taken off his shades since the mission began, not even at night, possibly this was how he had come to shoot down the helicopter.

'Can you help us get to the wire?' Zimmerman asked Rachel.

'Of course. We'll be gone very soon,' said Rachel. 'There's nothing you can do to stop it and anyway, I can't be involved if you lot are all locked up like animals. I've told Silvester that he has to let you go.'

'I won't go!! I'm staying here, I can't leave Rachel with that . . . that . . .!' About five minutes later CD would think of a magnificent and perfect insult but for the time being his mind was blank. Zimmerman gave him little time to think.

'Shut up, man,' said Zimmerman, 'if we can split, we will split.'

'Stop telling me to shut up,' shouted CD even louder, but it was clear that everybody thought that he should shut up.

'I have security passes here, they should get you through if you're careful,' said Sly.

'Hey, uhm, forgive me if I appear cynical man,' said Walter, 'but, like, why should you do this thing for us?'

'I can't see a problem with letting you lot go,' replied Sly. 'After all, what we're engaged in is not actually illegal. We were always more concerned about the panic that we would spark if what we were up to was known. There's no time left for you to even convince the people of Bullens Creek, let alone anyone else. We own most of the papers, we own most of the TV, we'll be gone in a matter of days. What can you do? Anyway, Rachel wants it –' He looked at Rachel.

'How very fucking touching,' observed CD bitterly.

Rachel tried once more to convince them that she really had no choice. It was difficult of course because it rather meant rubbing in the hopelessness of her friends' own situation. After all, her argument for picking up on Sly's offer was the absolute certainty that the world was dying.

She soon gave up and took her leave without a word, Sly followed her. Zimmerman considered detaining them, but could see no point, they had been given the passes, there was no reason for Moorcock to come after them. Anyway, it was still difficult to see Rachel as one of the enemy.

FURTHER DIVISIONS

'Mrs Culboon,' said Zimmerman, 'we have to find our way back to the wire where I'm presuming you have wheels. This is your patch, you'd better lead.'

'Hey, it wasn't a rocket launching site when I lived here,' Mrs Culboon protested, 'things have changed.'

And so they had. Already the consequences of the proposed eight-day count-down were being felt, the whole site was alive with thunder and light.

'Well, I know it's tough, Mrs Culboon,' said Zimmerman, 'but you have to try and guide us, we need to get out and to consider this. It's like an incredibly heavy conspiracy that we have uncovered here and we have to consider it very carefully.'

'We have to do something about Rachel,' insisted CD desperately.

'That woman's doing just fine by herself, boy,' said Mrs Culboon. 'You'd better start thinking about your own problems.'

'We can't just leave her!' CD protested. 'I mean he's probably brainwashed her or something.'

'Listen man, I know you are hot for the chick,' said Walter, trying to be soothing, but failing utterly, 'but you have to curb your urgings you know? Like put the lid on the whole passion thing, turn down the sex heat until we have a plan.'

CD bridled.

'It has absolutely nothing to do with a passion/sex heat thing,' said CD sniffily. 'I will have you know, Walter, that my emotions and intentions towards Rachel are entirely honourable.'

'Ha!' barked Mrs Culboon, who could be as irritating as anybody when she wanted to. 'Boy, I reckon your tongue's been hanging out so far for that woman I'm surprised you don't have cleaner shoes.' And she laughed long and loud. Discretion was not a major part of Mrs Culboon's nature and despite the fact that they were trudging through the enemy camp she could not keep her voice down. Luckily people were far too busy to notice.

CD was surprised, he had thought that he'd been discreet about his obsession. Of course, he had confided in the guys, but he could not recall sharing the secrets of his heart with old Mrs Culboon.

'How did you know?' he asked in all innocence.

'Listen son, when a fellah eats up a girl with every look and follows her around the room like his eyeballs were attached to her legs with string,' Mrs Culboon explained, 'I guess he ain't paying a casual interest in her.'

CD blushed to be so transparent. Then Zimmerman lost patience.

'Oh man, I mean, what is the point, no, like for real, you know? What is the point? Like I have to lay some information on you people right? We are in heavy shit here, you know? But are we doing a little hurrying? No way, man! Is there a degree of urgency in our actions? Is there fuck! No like there's just a whole lot of hanging out and chatting about sex, a subject incidentally, right, that *some* of us find like a drag and irrelevant, OK? I mean just what *is* the *point*! I rescue you all from death by electrocution and . . .'

'Zimm, you're getting hung up, man, you have to deal with it . . .' Walter, like Zimmerman, was anxious to move things along. They were, after all, still in the midst of the enemy camp and, despite their security passes, by no means out of danger. He for one had no desire to find himself back in a chair facing the electric wool.

'We really do have to split.'

And so with Mrs Culboon as a very nervous guide, they set off to make their way out of Hell's kitchen. She did think about trying to make a route by the stars but was forced to discard the idea as it was still daylight.

LEARNER DRIVER

The little EcoAction team were not the only people to be trying to get out of the compound that morning. There was a constant roar as trucks carried off workers whose tasks were now finished. There was much whooping and hollering from the happy ex-employees of Stark as they headed for Bullens Creek airport. They were all suddenly very rich, having received upwards of a year's salary for a couple of months' work. Stark had paid well for fourteen hour days with no questions asked and now they were laying off the workforce, giving them the sort of severance pay normally reserved for loyal employees of fifty years standing.

'Maybe,' suggested Mrs Culboon, 'we should try and hitch a ride out on one of these trucks because even if I can find the route, it's going to be a hell of a walk.'

'I've got a better idea,' said Zimmerman.

A couple of hundred metres or so from where they stood was the source of Zimmerman's idea, a heli-pad, on which stood four helicopters.

'You think we should steal a chopper?' asked CD, momentarily forgetting his misery over Rachel in this new excitement.

'I don't really accept the term "steal",' replied Zimmerman. 'I mean, in the greater scheme of things, like that helicopter is as much ours as it is anybody's.'

'You should have studied law, man,' said Walter. 'You'd blow the average wig-head away.'

Zimmerman began to lead the little group towards the helicopters, strolling casually, as if he was off to the shops.

'Take it easy everyone,' he suggested, 'it is important to be inconspicuous . . . C D, what goes down?'

It looked like CD was going down. He had adopted a sort

of crouched, low lope, dodging about behind parked cars and piles of equipment, scurrying from one thing to another.

'We're trying to steal a helicopter, Zimm,' said CD reprovingly, 'don't you think maybe we should take some cover?'

They were having to shout to make themselves heard, they were close to the heli-pad and one of the machines was ticking over noisily.

'Hey listen, CD, I didn't expect the SAS you know? But you are a definite liability,' shouted Zimmerman. 'Did you take lessons in looking suspicious, or is this a natural talent? I mean if you lope around like that, you might as well hang a sign around your neck saying "I shouldn't be here, please shoot me". The art of camouflage is to blend in, man, be inconspicuous.'

There was a pause.

'What?' shouted CD.

Zimmerman gave up, reflecting that despite the impracticality of CD's approach, it was probably better karma if everybody did their own thing. And anyway, there were no rights and wrongs in life, only different ways of being.

They walked along together, both pursuing entirely contradictory methods of disguise. Zimmerman, strolling with confidence and brazenly nodding greetings at passers by. CD crouched low, dodging about, occasionally jumping behind piles of equipment to emerge moments later glancing furtively over his shoulder with his collar turned up. Zimmerman made a mental note to ask CD why he felt that turning up his collar made a man about to steal a helicopter less easy to spot.

Of course, Zimmerman never did enquire, because for him, making a mental note was about as reliable a memory-jogger as writing condensation in the window.

The four of them strolled onto the pad and a great big man with a leather jacket and a gun asked them who they were. Zimmerman grunted and waved the pass that Sly had given him. This seemed to satisfy his macho challenger, who, if he thought them a pretty strange crew, decided to let it go. Live and let live was the guard's philosophy. He believed that everyone should be different, that was what made the world go around. In fact, under the leather belts and buckles and bullets, he himself was wearing white silk panties. Why should he worry because some bloke doesn't comb his beard, no reason to start a war. Private security attracts all sorts of types. Wearing a crash helmet for a living is, after all, a fairly weird job in itself.

There was an engineer working on the craft that had its engine running. Zimmerman approached him.

'This bird work good?' he asked.

'Sure, just fixed it up myself,' the man replied.

'Good, we're taking it.' Zimmerman did not even need to use his pass. The whole Stark operation had come together so quickly that everyone was a stranger to everyone else. What's more, none of the people employed in security had the faintest idea what it was that they were supposed to be guarding. The helicopter engineer accepted the arrival of the four weird looking strangers with the same fatalism that he greeted his enormous pay packet. He didn't know what it was about, but he certainly wasn't going to start rocking any boats.

They squeezed into the machine. It was a tight fit because it was clearly really only designed to take three, which meant it would have been tight for Walter on his own. CD grimaced, it had been one of these same craft that he had shot at, he could imagine the men screaming and writhing desperately in the tiny space as they burnt to death.

'I must say, Zimmerman,' said Mrs Culboon, sitting in Walter's lap, 'I must say, there doesn't seem much that you can't do mate. All this fighting, and shooting and stuff and now knowing how to fly a helicopter. Yep, I reckon you're a pretty spunky all-rounder and no mistake.'

Having delivered this magnificent compliment she settled herself as comfortably as she could on top of Walter.

'I don't know how to fly a helicopter,' said Zimmerman, waggling the stick and punching buttons.

'Ha ha!' shrieked Mrs Culboon, 'and I reckon you're quite a card with it, ain't that so mates?'

She twisted around, soliciting Walter's agreement for her sentiments, but Walter knew Zimmerman better.

'You say you can't fly this thing man?' he asked nervously as Zimmerman experimented with the levers under his seat.

'I didn't say I couldn't, I just said I didn't know how to,' Zimm replied.

'Oh yeah? Well like, what the fuck is that supposed to mean?' asked Walter, not unreasonably.

'Well, there's a difference you know? Like I might be able to guess.' With that Zimm must have pushed a particularly significant button, or pulled on an unusually sensitive knob, because the whole craft screamed and shuddered and rattled and vibrated so that the poor occupants could scarcely focus on each other. Fortunately it resolutely refused to leave the ground.

'I think maybe the anchor is out or something,' shouted Zimmerman. 'I mean we have plenty of power here, but no rising-up scene, is going down.' The others could not hear him, they could not even hear themselves think. Had they been able to they would probably have heard themselves thinking, 'Get the fuck out of the helicopter'. However, before this idea had a chance to percolate through the shuddering and the noise and penetrate into their rattling brains, an alternative course of action presented itself. The engineer whom Zimmerman had addressed before, came charging out of a nearby hangar to see who was making a purée of his chopper's gear box. He rushed up to Zimmerman's window and began frantically banging on it, jumping up and down, mouthing obscenities and generally employing body language to express distress.

Zimmerman opened the window – probably the only function in the whole helicopter that he was capable of working. He hung his elbow out and turned his head slightly. He looked for all the world like he'd just parked his '57 Chevvy down by the boardwalk and was preparing to eye the chicks, catch some rays and take it nice and easy. The fact he was sitting in the middle of what was beginning to resemble a mini-earthquake, had yet to dent his sang-froid.

'Yeah?' he mouthed at the frantic engineer.

The engineer leaned in through the window and flipped the controls about a bit; here a knob, there a lever. The machine spluttered and the juddering mercifully calmed itself, the noise dropped to something just below ear bleeding, and the vibrations no longer threatened to actually remove teeth.

CD, Walter and Mrs Culboon breathed a sigh of relief. Now it was merely intolerable, before it had been like a disco.

'Don't you know how to fly a chopper, Mister!!' shouted the angry engineer.

'Nope,' confided Zimm with disarming honesty. 'Do you?'

'Well of course I do,' the man screamed, 'but that's not the point. What I want to know is . . .'

He stopped there, not because he had suddenly lost his thirst for knowledge but because Zimmerman was pointing a gun at him.

'Get in,' Zimm said.

'Don't be absurd, look what the hell is going on . . . There isn't any room.'

But a glance at Zimmerman's expression convinced the engineer that it was time to make room. With resignation he squeezed in and sat on Zimmerman's lap.

'Ha ha!' laughed Mrs Culboon, mightily relieved that Zimmerman had relinquished the controls. 'Take us towards Bullens Creek, cab driver, and no racist anecdotes.'

BIRDS EYE VIEW OF GENESIS

They soared above it all. Above Tyron and Moorcock and the ghastly betrayal in which they were both involved. They soared above Rachel too. CD stared desperately downwards, in the absurd hope that he might be able to spot her amongst all the trucks and construction and scurrying figures. Under normal circumstances, the thrill of his first ever ride in a helicopter would have driven all other considerations from his mind, but this was different. Already he didn't care, he only cared about Rachel, despite the fact that she had betrayed them. Except he could not think of her in those terms, not as a betrayer, as a Judas. He knew that however weak-willed she had shown herself, he would always forgive her. In the midst of these fine emotions, it was bitter gall indeed for CD to know that Rachel almost certainly didn't give a flying bugger whether he forgave her or not.

Mrs Culboon and Walter had no such romantic distractions to block their view of the fascinating scene beneath them. Five rockets were already in place, towering out of their silos and jutting up towards the helicopter. The rockets were supported by the spindly latticework towers that the previous night Walter and Mrs Culboon had taken for cranes. The final rocket was still awaiting installation. It lay on its colossal transport, like a designer biro, silver and white shining in the terrible burning sun. It bore the legend 'Star Ark' and beneath that a stylized representation of the moon. Even at this desperate moment, the grey figures of Stark, whose lives had been ruled by obsessive marketing, had not been able to resist the temptation to imbue their final product with a logo, designer graphics and a corporate image.

With the exception of the final rocket that had not yet been stood on its end, the Stark edifice was pretty much complete. It was an awe-inspiring sight.

'This really is vaguely out of sight,' said Walter.

'Sure is,' said their pilot, 'weirdest hotels I ever saw. Still, I guess the kids will like them and it'll certainly bring a lot of money into the state.'

It's quite difficult for an astonished silence to fall upon a group of people who are bursting out of an over-stuffed and roaring helicopter, especially when the group includes such gregarious individuals as CD and Mrs Culboon. None the less, an astonished silence is what descended in reaction to the pilot's statement.

Walter recovered first.

'Uhm, listen, forgive me man, but you do not need to be Dan Dare to work out that those are rockets down there,' he said.

'Rocket shaped hotels,' replied the man.

Silence returned; a silence sufficiently imbued with awe to deaden the tumultuous thwaka thwaka of the blades spinning above them.

'Rocket shaped *hotels*?' inquired Walter.

'Sure,' said the pilot cheerfully, who did not seem to mind being abducted. 'I guess it's some kind of theme park, you know, like Disney. Reckon kids could get pretty excited about sleeping in a rocket. Yeah, it sure will bring a heap of money into the state.'

A FINE STATE

It is a strange feature of federated countries like the United States or Australia that there is often even more pig ignorant xenophobic tunnel vision regarding the rivalry between states than there is in the area of national patriotism. It is common to hear some brain-dead tub of lard politico, running for office, whose principal argument for being elected is that he was born in the same state as those whom he seeks to lead. The fact that his qualifications for being a leader of men extend no further than the fact that he is human, is less relevant than where his mother happened to drop him.

'Intellectually he may be a vegetable but at least he's a vegetable from Texas' which of course makes him superior to an Einstein figure from any other state.

Likewise, in the field of economics, more can be excused if it can be proved to be of benefit to the state than would be acceptable if it were the business of the entire nation ...

'Slavery is clearly a grey area and certainly there must be a proper regulating body. None the less, it provides work and more than that *it will bring money into the state*.'

It is this parochial patriotism that explains Sly's early popularity despite his selfish and destructive business practices. He may have been a bastard but he was a *West*

Australian bastard. People would have liked to see any of those poofters in Sydney or Melbourne produce an entrepreneur with half his ability to create misery and unhappiness.

TOUCH-DOWN

None the less, localized xenophobia notwithstanding, it was still a deep shock to all in the helicopter, excluding the pilot of course, to discover that people were still happy to swallow the leisure story.

'Yeah, I heard there'll be planetariums and stuff and weightlessness and everything, I guess the parents'll love it as much as the kids.'

They had crossed the site now and were heading for the wire. Walter seized the opportunity to try a little control experiment.

'Yeah well, that's shit man,' he said, trying to sound sincere, 'there ain't going to be no hotels, and there ain't going to be no money for WA. Those are real rockets man! The world's dying and the fat cats are splitting.'

But of course it was no use, the man just laughed and said that he had guessed that his abductors were weird, but they were really *weird*.

Walter gave up. Zimmerman asked Mrs Culboon to point to where they had left the wheels.

The helicopter put down with a bump and the squashed occupants burst out. As they unloaded the weaponry that they had taken plus that which was in the helicopter, the pilot spoke up rather nervously.

'Hey, listen you people, I want to thank you,' said the pilot, whose name, it turned out, was Eugene.

They were all a bit surprised at this, they had after all abducted him at gunpoint which hardly seemed like grounds for gratitude. None the less, Eugene seemed quite happy. In fact he had been surprisingly cheerful throughout the whole experience.

'It's just that I've never flown before,' Eugene explained.

This was worse than Zimmerman, at least he had admitted that he didn't know how to fly before they took off. Mrs Culboon, Walter, and CD all shouted in their own shocked and individual ways that Eugene had said he could fly.

'I can fly,' protested Eugene, 'and I did didn't I? We're here aren't we? Of course I can fly. But I'm just a mechanic,' he added bitterly.

'*Just* a mechanic, ha!! I'd like to know how long they'd stay in the air without us mechanics. But do we get any thanks? Do we hell . . . Excuse my language Ma'am,' he directed this at Mrs Culboon.

'I don't give a fuck what you say, Eugene,' she replied.

'They just strut around and insult you,' continued Eugene, who had clearly hit a pet subject, 'they say it's not clean enough or it's missing on a cylinder when you *know* that it's as sweet as a nut and it's just that the big-headed twerps can't fly properly. But will they give you a go? *No way* ha! They just –'

'Yeah, OK Eugene, we get it,' said Zimmerman.

'They just tell you it takes training and that you have to have a degree. Oh yeah? Well I've been trained mate, yes, in the school of life, I've got a degree in hard knocks.'

'Yeah, fine, Eugene . . .' Zimmerman interrupted again.

'They always say that we don't have a class thing in this country, but we *do*, we're worse than the pom's. *I* couldn't train as a pilot, oh no, not poncey enough, I had to be a mechanic because *my* dad was only a door-to-door trouser sales-man . . .'

'Eugene! Shut the fuck up!!!' screamed Zimmerman.

'No, but really, I mean, really, you don't have to be a daddy's boy to . . .'

They left him and headed for the car.

'So, what next?' Mrs Culboon asked as she drove them all towards the holiday home. 'I can't think of a single thing we can do.'

'Well all that stuff we discovered,' protested CD, 'the launch silos and everything. I mean it must be illegal . . .'

'Hey man, it's a wicked world you know?' said Walter. 'Like, if a couple of bread-heads want to dig holes, they can.'

'And that's just the point isn't it?' whined Zimmerman. 'The whole system of values is just *so screwed*. Like they bust me for having maybe one tiny toot on a mild and tension relieving doobie for my own personal private use. The world gets protected from me lying on the carpet for twelve hours giggling and then eating fifteen Mars Bars. I get hassled by the pigs for destroying nothing more than what's left of my own brain, man, and you're saying that some freaked out, off-the-planet world domination mind-fuck can launch rockets to the moon and everything is cool?'

'I'm just saying, man, that a dude can dig a hole. OK? I mean –'

'Oh shut up will you fellahs?' said Mrs Culboon. 'First Eugene, now you, going on and on, I'd rather listen to a didgereedoo, and that's saying something.'

They drove on in silence feeling awful about everything.

COUNCIL OF WAR

Mr Culboon and Chrissy were very relieved to see their friends again. It had been both a wearisome and a frightening wait in the parched desert with the temperature some five degrees hotter than usual. The physical discomfort had been complemented by a fair degree of the mental kind. It is a strange and disconcerting experience to sit in what should have been the still of the desert while Hades appears to be under construction not far away. They were very relieved that whatever happened next, at least the waiting was over. After the initial greetings, Mr Culboon noticed that not the whole party was present.

'Where's Rachel?' he asked.

'She's gone over to them, man, and for kind of a depressing reason,' answered Walter.

'Who is them?' asked Chrissy, eager to discover at last the nature of the beast she had been stalking.

And so between them Walter, CD and Mrs Culboon explained all that they had learnt. Chrissy was completely astonished by their extraordinary story; it far outdistanced any of the possible scenarios that she had conjured up herself to explain what was going on. In comparison to trying to recreate the story of the Ark, the idea of holding the world to nuclear ransom seemed fairly mild.

'You are saying that they are convinced that there is no hope for the world. It really is dying?' asked Chrissy.

'Yeah, and they're splitting man. The rats are leaving the sinking ship,' said Walter.

'Well we have to try and stop them!' Chrissy replied.

'Oh yeah, how?' enquired Walter, 'and also for that matter,

why? Who gives a fuck? Let them go. If I have to die I don't need pigs like that at the funeral.'

'And what about Rachel?' snapped CD who died a little every time he thought of Rachel's decision. 'Is she a pig?'

'She had a chance, she made her choice,' said Walter. 'I have no problem with that. Personally I wouldn't have decided to go. Like, for me, eternity with a bunch of bread-heads would not be a viable option.'

THE GREEN EYED MONSTER

CD was at the end of his emotional tether, suddenly he found himself so hemmed in by unhappiness that it left him gasping for breath. He lit a cigarette without even trying to look cool. He was too far gone even to manage to construct some romantic fantasy out of the character of betrayed friends. An emotion had burrowed its way into his stomach and his soul, an emotion of such intensity that no matter how many times it washed over him, he remained surprised at its strength. He had become a jealous guy.

On the trip back to the cave, CD had tried to persuade himself that the anger and frustration, and deep deep sickness that he felt to his stomach, were to do with *whom* Rachel had chosen. He told himself that it was the fact that it was Moorcock that really hurt, the fact that she had defected to the very world which she and he had been trying to fight. This, he tried to believe, was the root of his despair, and an understandable and righteous root it would have been.

But it was not the case, this was not why CD felt the way he did. He would have felt the same way if Rachel had opted to go with St Francis of Assisi or the Mahatma Gandhi. CD was not seething over some betrayed principle. He was not sinking into chasmic despair because of the discovery that Rachel had feet of clay. He was in the state he was in through pure, unadulterated jealousy. He was discovering that beyond love, beyond unrequited love, perhaps beyond any other passion known to humanity, deep deep in the depths of the turgid, clinging, swamplike pit of despair that lies dormant, within every soul, lurks jealousy. Jealousy, that most demeaning and debilitating of emotions. Jealousy, which doubles the strength of the love upon which it is based but whilst doubling it, warps and perverts it, demeans it, until it is no longer recognizable as the thing of beauty it once was and nothing is left of love but lies, doubts and bitter self-loathing. Jealous love is no more like true love than Mr Hyde was like Dr Jekyll or a stagnant swamp is like a freshwater lake. CD could not be said to be feeling his best.

WHAT NEXT?

Still, if CD was feeling down, at least it kept him from dwelling on the imminent death of the earth, which was the cheerful subject that the others were mulling over.

'I still don't believe their story,' said Mr Culboon. 'The world ain't dying. I reckon they're fixing to kill it, I still reckon they're going to nuke the world and make us all slaves.'

'Oh shut up, you old fool,' said Mrs Culboon. 'You weren't there. I heard it from Rachel. They're fixing to go all right and damn soon.'

'Well for God's sake we have to do something then!' shouted Chrissy. 'I mean we're still alive aren't we? The world isn't dead yet is it? What are we going to do?'

'Well, personally I was thinking of selling my pad,' said Walter, 'scoring the best grade shit I can and smoking my way to hell.'

'Nice,' said Zimmerman. But Chrissy did not think so.

'Look, these people must know something, they must know a hell of a lot if they've made the decision they have. Maybe they know something that could help!' Chrissy almost pleaded.

'Listen, Chrissy, it's exactly what they do know that's made them make the decision they have. I mean, these guys have everything, they're not likely to give it up unless they have no choice. I mean that's why Rachel made the decision she did,' said Walter.

Chrissy was astonished at his fatalism but of course she had not heard what he had heard, and she wasn't a hippy . . .

'It *can't* be too late,' she continued. 'Nobody's even tried to stop the rot yet. But I'll tell you something, if the world knew that men like nice old Slampacker's hamburgers were doing this terrible thing, then they might wake up. We might still be able to patch things up on earth. This whole terrible plan could be the very motivation people need to get their act together!'

'I think Chrissy has a point,' said Mrs Culboon, 'and also there's another thing. If that bastard Moorcock is right, and it really is the very end of everything. And what goes up in those rockets really is going to be all that's left of the human race . . . Well I reckon I'd die easier if I thought some decent folks were watching down on us from on high, instead of a bunch of men, selfish, grasping . . .' she was, for once, lost for words '. . . I'll tell you one thing, I bet no black people have tickets on that flight at present.'

But she had struck a chord. CD spoke up, he was anxious that they should decide to do something, he could not stand just sitting around feeling the way he did. His guts were so heavy he felt that he was in danger of sinking into the ground.

'Mrs Culboon's right,' he said, 'I mean if we could stop them, I don't know, get them arrested or something . . . then somebody else could escape instead . . .'

'Like who?' asked Mr Culboon.

'Well, I don't know, they could have a competition. Artists or something, I don't know. . .'

'Man all you'll see is another set of fat cats standing in line,' said Zimmerman cynically. 'Politicians, soldiers, all that shit.'

'I'm telling you, the thing to do is to *stop* the thing altogether,' pleaded Chrissy, '. . . use it as a shrine, a monument, something to galvanize the human race into action . . . Christ even if we all have to go back to living in shacks and being penniless there must be a way to stop the rot.'

'What do you mean, go back?' asked Mrs Culboon, her humour returning.

'Besides that,' added Chrissy, 'if anything is to be done to save the world we may actually need these people.'

'Oh yeah, like a freak needs a drug squad,' said Zimmerman. 'I mean, shit Chrissy, these people have fucked absolutely everything right up. What the hell do we need them for?'

'Look,' said Chrissy, trying to martial her thoughts and not to sound patronizing, 'it is possible, in fact it is pretty likely, that only those who have the power to destroy things so effectively have the power to create . . . The way the world is run, the way things get done, are incredibly complex . . . The means of production are owned by individuals; the raw materials of change are owned by individuals . . .'

'Oh come on man,' interjected Walter, 'don't give me any of that commie shit, like that's all the same trip man you know? Like two sides of the same coin, "if you go carrying pictures of Chairman Mao, you ain't gonna make it with anyone anyhow",' he said, quoting from the classics.

'Listen meat-head,' said Chrissy, whose long wait had not improved her temper, 'it's got nothing to do with commie shit, I'm a Roosevelt Democrat like my daddy before me, OK? I am talking economics,' she continued. 'If these bastards actually think that time is so short for the earth that they're leaving, well then hell, time must be that short, right? . . .'

'Now I reckon we'd better listen to this here Yanky woman, yes I do,' said Mrs Culboon. 'After all, we got to do something that's for sure, and I guess she's thinking a whole lot clearer than the rest of us sun-fried bunch of no hopers. Ain't that right, Mr Culboon?'

'You speak for yourself, woman,' replied Mr Culboon. 'I'm as sharp today as I ever was.'

'Which is sharp as shit I reckon, old man,' replied Mrs Culboon, 'and that's blunt. Go on, Chrissy. What's the plan?'

'I don't have a plan, godammit, I just know,' said Chrissy, 'that these people represent a workable economic structure within which things get done. A structure which, in an emergency, could react quickly. It may be a shithouse structure but it's there, it's in place, it's controlled and it takes orders. Now, if every damn boss in the world high-tails it, there will be complete economic chaos . . .'

'As opposed to what we have now,' interjected Walter, cynically.

'Listen buster,' said Chrissy – who had never said buster before in her life. 'What we have now is a controlled slump, a cycle dip, it just means poor people starve, that's all, it ain't anarchy . . . Now if most of the damn bosses suddenly disappear *at once* it could be months, maybe years, before new chains of command emerge within their empires. There will be power struggles, court-room battles. For a while at least it will be almost impossible to shift money about, utilize assets, mobilize equipment, *make a decision*!! . . . Don't you see? I understand money, nothing will get done! And it's those few months that may mean life or death for the earth. We have to stop them leaving and force them to help save the world.'

'*If* it ain't dead already, lady,' said Zimmerman.

'OK that's it, fuck you,' said Chrissy getting up. 'I don't know about you lazy bastards but back in New York City where I come from we like to put up a fight,' she added, lapsing briefly into parochial xenophobia. 'You don't lie down till you're dead, and even then you bite their damn ankles. I don't know what I'm going to do, but I'm going to do something. See you, hippies, I'm going to save the world. You Culboons coming, CD?'

CD wasn't actually listening but the Culboons were about to agree when Walter interjected.

'Hey hey hey, Lady. You like . . . well . . . you certainly know how to hurt a guy, you know?'

'Yeah,' added Zimmerman. 'Just because we're indulging in a moment's negative vibe does not mean that we are off the team, it's just a ying and yang thing, OK, balance, that's all.'

'So you're prepared to try and do something then?' asked Chrissy rather suspiciously.

'Of course we are, man,' said Walter. 'Hey listen. I have to tell you something. Ego is a bad thing, and pride comes before a fall, but I have to tell you man, that while you have spent your life tapping out shit about bread for the papers, me and Zimm here have saved a couple of two hundred ton whales, right?'

'And what's more, it spoke to us,' added Zimm, 'and told us of its life beneath the deep, within the whale nation.'

'Yeah, well, that was Zimm's interpretation,' said Walter, 'and as such it was valid, but some other people on the team thought they were just going eep eep eeeep.'

The brief schism over, discussion recommenced on the problem at hand.

'OK Chrissy,' said Walter, 'like what do you suggest? These cats have had us hiding out and running every time we so much as breathe. Man they chased you all around the world. You'd be dead right now if it wasn't for crazy Zimm. By the looks of it, they're fixing to split real soon. What do you suggest we do? How in fuck, man, do we stop them blasting off, so's we can like use them and their fat cat bread-head corporation to tell the world that it's dying?'

'I don't know,' said Chrissy quietly.

There was a pause.

THE RATS GATHER AROUND
THE LIFE BOAT

The count-down had begun. There were no objections. The consensus was that if the foul deed had to be done, then it would be better if it were done quickly. The terminal, global decline was now visibly apparent everywhere. From the alternately parched and steaming earth, to the gloomy haze of pollution that hung high above them; a haze that made the intense heat dirty and sticky, like wearing a filthy old wool blanket in the blazing sun. The Leper Ships floated on the suffocated sea, the dolphins struggled in the nylon nets. The maple forests withered where they stood, the iguanas felt the rumble of the dozers. The sewage slid out of the sludge ships and the salt bubbled up through the ground. Durf's talk of TTO in the food chain was not really necessary to convince the terrified old men. Each day as their factories belched out poison, they lived in abject fear at the possibility of an avalanche factor developing and scuppering the whole thing. Every day that they hesitated, something could go wrong . . .

Besides the imminent possibility of Stark being thwarted by a natural phenomenon, the other reason for immediate departure was that with everything now ready, things could only go wrong in human terms. Discovery, government intervention, mass rioting, theft, played heavily upon Durf's mind. The majority of the security had been laid off along with the construction workers. Obviously Durf had had no desire for there to be a large group of heavily armed men around, at the point at which it became clear what was going on. The prospect of a couple of hundred gun-toting thugs, trying to force their way onto the absolute last train out of the ghost town, did not attract him. However, it had meant that Durf was forced to take the calculated risk that the last few days the Consortium spent on earth would be comparatively unprotected. Even a mob from Bullens Creek would probably be capable of ruining everything.

The news that Tyron had lost the captives and been discovered hours later trussed and bound along with his security chief, had been a shock. Sly had asserted that there was absolutely nothing these people could do in practical terms (except destroy helicopters). None the less, it was most disquieting.

Anyway, all things considered, no one had debated the fact that it was time to move, and the count-down had begun even before Zimm had commandeered the helicopter.

The far-flung and disparate members of the Stark Conspiracy – people who wielded such huge power and influence on their societies – were simply told to get up, take one piece of hand luggage, collect their partners and leave their entire lives for ever.

ADAMS AND EVES

Obviously the 'partner' business was fraught with indecision and embarrassment. There were those of course, indeed a surprising number, who had decided to take their spouses.

Since the whole project was a self-financed, self help group, rather than some noble scheme to perpetuate the human race, youth and fertility were not required. The object of the exercise was personal preservation, pure and simple, so people could take whom they liked. Anyway, the future had been taken care of in pre-packed and frozen form. Actually some of the crusty old couples, exhausted by a lifetime of hatred, violence and naked greed were rather looking forward to spending their old age peacefully on the moon, bringing up little test-tube space children.

These were the lucky ones, the people who had been able to

make their decisions early and hence also their preparations; sharing the whole thing with their wives or boyfriends – eight of the conspirators being gay – and in three cases, husbands. There were only three female Stark conspirators – the upper echelons of international capitalism being still very much a male domain. The richest woman in the world, the Queen of Britain, had not been approached. It had been considered that on the whole she was likely to prefer to go down with the ship, and would probably have blown the gaff. Besides, it was one thing Sly selling off his brewing interests to raise his contribution, but alarm bells really would have started ringing if Balmoral had suddenly appeared on the market.

EVE WITH A STAPLE IN HER STOMACH

For the adulterers the process of departure was not so smooth. Ocker Tyron, for instance, had definitely decided not to take Dixie. Unfortunately he had also raised her suspicions. Obviously she did not suspect that he was about to leave her behind on a dying planet to face ecological oblivion alone. But she did suspect that he might be putting together a little illicit rumpy pumpy – which of course he was.

Tyron was playing a very dark hand; lying to his wife, and lying to the rumpy pumpy. He had not told the *Playboy* centrefold what it was he was taking her to the desert for. He could not trust her discretion. He had merely told her that it was a big adventure and a big surprise. Now she found herself stuck in the middle of a baking desert, with very few amenities indeed, amidst an ever-growing group of people she did not know, most of whom were in late middle-age. Understandably she wanted to know what the big surprise was going to be. But Tyron wasn't there to tell her, he was back in Perth, about to leave his house for the last time, trying to deal with Dixie.

He was trying to grab a toothbrush whilst she was lying on a machine which wobbled her fat about . . .

'It's not right that a girl should have to go so long without her man,' Dixie whined. 'What's going on, Ocker? Come on out with it.'

'Business,' said Ocker, 'now shut your face.'

His mother had followed Ocker into his and Dixie's private bathroom – something which she felt perfectly at ease in doing. She leapt at the chance to have a shot at Dixie.

'If you can't keep a man in the marital home, Dixie,' she spat, 'it's no good complaining to him when he's gone.'

'This isn't a marital home!!' shouted Dixie wobbling away, 'it's a damn old peoples' home!! Run for the exclusive benefit of one resident!! And this is Ocker's and my *private* en suite!'

'I know that, Dixie dear, but he doesn't have private things from his mother. Good Lord, I've seen a lot more than his bathroom in my time.'

Dixie, thighs flapping away, biting her lip with fury, turned to Ocker for support. But he was gone, they heard the door slam . . .

'Ocker!! Ocker!!' shrieked Dixie, jumping off the wobbler and running to the stairs, 'don't you dare just walk out like that . . .' But he was already in the car and could not hear her.

She went downstairs in fury, followed by her mother-in-law. There was a moment's silence. Then she noticed a blank space on Ocker's desk.

'He's taken his picture,' she said slowly, '. . . the picture of his school team, that's his favourite thing . . . He doesn't even let the maid dust it . . . Why would he pack that in an overnight bag?'

Dixie Tyron and old Mrs Tyron looked at each other, for a moment united in shared fear and suspicion.

'Ocker!!' Dixie shrieked, running to the window. But the car was at the end of the drive already. She sank back into her chair.

A picture of her had always stood beside the team picture on Ocker's desk.

'I notice he left your picture,' said Mrs Tyron. Their moment of solidarity shattered

FROZEN FOOD ON A
HOT NIGHT

On day minus eight and day minus seven, Sly found himself with plenty to do. The three remaining rockets had to be erected in their silos, and then all six had to be loaded and made ready for blast off.

Time seemed almost as stodgy and untraversable as the weather in those final, baking days. It was almost as if it had to be waded through, like a swamp. As Sly stood watching the rocket-moving transport crawl along at its top speed of three miles an hour, he felt as if the actual moment was destined to never actually arrive and that they would all be locked in the process of last minute preparation for ever.

'Don't rush it, it's nearly a vintage machine, Mr Moorcock,' Nagasyu had remarked, commenting on the fact that the transporter had been purchased from NASA nearly twenty years earlier and was actually the same rocket-mover that had brought the Apollo moon shot, Saturn V, to its pad. Nagasyu considered this a good omen.

Stark had purchased the thing in the late seventies and held it in storage ever since. They had got it for peanuts because the American love affair with space was over and, with its budgets cut, NASA had no need for such machines. They moved into shuttle research and the concept of a re-usable rocket. Stark, of course, did not have the same problems since they were only taking a one way trip.

BREAD AND LASAGNE

On the fifth night before the blast off, Sly visited Rachel. They had not seen each other since shortly after leaving Zimmerman et al in the security complex. Rachel had spent her time walking about the site, making an effort to take it all in, talking to whom she could and trying to understand and come to terms with the enormity of the thing that she was involved in.

Now it was evening and Rachel stood alone in the same room that Sly had first brought her to, watching for the fifth to last time as the hazy red furnace that used to be the sun sank through the sweaty, gaseous quagmire that used to be the sky.

Rachel was, by nature, of a fairly buoyant personality, but standing alone amongst strangers, watching the world die, would depress anyone. When Sly strode in she was pleased to see him.

'So, shall we have that dinner then?' he asked.

'What dinner?' Rachel replied.

'The one I asked you to about a century ago.'

Sly was astonished to discover that he was nervous. This was a very new sensation for him. Normally he didn't care enough for the women he found himself alone with to be ill at ease in their presence. What's more, their acquiescence was so utterly guaranteed that there was never any question of fear of rejection. This time things were as different as they could be. He did care what Rachel thought of him and he was by no means certain that she desired him in the same way he did her. He had, after all, persuaded her to hang around with him by telling her that she would die a reeking, steaming, panic-stricken death if she didn't. Many a girl might have responded to a chat-up line like that.

'Don't mind. Why not,' replied Rachel, regarding the dinner.

And so Sly prepared it. Peripheral Stark personnel had been cut to a minimum and there were no cooks or serving staff in those last days. Each cabin had a microwave and a huge stock of frozen food . . .

'Pretty shithouse tucker, I'm afraid,' said Sly, bunging a couple of lasagnes in the oven, 'still guess it's kind of better than what we can expect for the next few years, until the greenhouses get going and the frozen foetuses turn into lamb chops.'

Actually, as far as Rachel was concerned, the food she had eaten since joining Stark had been superb. Compared to toast and vegamite, which was what she normally had for supper, gourmet frozen lasagne was a pretty good feast. She didn't say though, Sly liked to talk and Rachel liked to let him.

'One thing about them,' he said as the oven went ping, 'this stuff was packaged a good three years ago, I own the factory actually. No Total Toxic Overload in this. Christ, Durf's got me so spooked on the food chain business I look at the sell-by date and hope the damn thing's *past* it.'

They drank some wine and ate the lasagne, no bread, the last thing you want to risk before embarking on a trip to the moon is food poisoning . . .

'I guess the shits would be pretty unpleasant if you're stuck in a space-suit,' Sly said, and he laughed.

MOULDY OLD DOUGH

It wasn't that the grain itself was massively toxic, but the intense heat and humidity (caused by the flooding, caused by the deforestation), had created an atmosphere that had been a perfect breeding environment for all sorts of microscopic organisms. Therefore, what crop had grown in that last, famine-struck summer of Stark, was mouldier than the washing up in a student residence. Unfortunately, because it was all that there was, it still got ground into bread and, what's more, because there was so little of it, the stuff actually doubled in price. Mouldy bread was one of the few healthy items on the stricken stock market . . .

'Get into food,' the arrogant twenty-one-year-olds in bow

ties and pink glasses had said to each other.

'Food is very big right now.'

TOO GUILTY TO PARTY

As he attacked his lasagne, Sly pondered the contradictions of life.

'Funny to think that I own bakeries that are making bread that I'm too scared to eat, and yet the same stuff is turning in a straight 200 per cent profit and curving skywards. Not that major profit strikes are any use to me now. Still, it's funny,' he was in a philosophical mood.

'Please, Silvester,' said Rachel, 'try not to be such a ruthless pig. I'm trying to persuade myself that I don't dislike you.'

'Well, it *is* weird,' he replied defensively. Sly had not realized he was being a ruthless pig, nor had he been spoken to by a woman this cool in years. Not surprisingly he found it exciting. 'That bakery was my first ever corporate takeover. I only kept the bread bit, sold the rest off and now the bread's poisoned, and more profitable than it's ever been. I call that weird. Don't you call that weird?'

If Rachel was a different experience for Sly, well the opposite was also the case. Rachel had never met a man with so little remorse, so little guilt, he simply did not bother to anguish over the terrible repercussions of his horrible life. This sublime peace of mind was entirely alien to Rachel. Those like her, who aspire to a social conscience, spend their lives consumed with guilt. They can never take full pleasure out of the nice things that come their way because they cannot escape the gnawing conviction that their happiness is *unfair*.

Sly, on the other hand, knew that life isn't fair, and what's more, the bastard didn't seem to mind. It was a new experience for Rachel, who generally hung around with worried liberals like herself, to be talking to someone who could make a statement like the one Sly had made about the bread, without feeling the need to conclude it by adding, 'I mean, God I *know* it's terrible, but I really don't know what I can *do* about it, you know? I mean it's so *difficult*.'

It wasn't that Rachel condoned his callousness, nor did she wish that she could emulate it (not much anyway). It was just strangely refreshing to be talking to a person who had conquered the guilt that oppresses us all. Perhaps this is why rogues are such popular figures of fiction; they have the ability to be bastards and not worry about it – they give us a chance to escape the ever oppressive conscience.

THE MOON SHINES BRIGHTER

Anyway, for whatever reason, Rachel decided to go to bed with Sly. He was pretty despicable but also exciting, like a Dirty Harry movie. Rachel had always had a penchant for big, strong men. The perfect combination for her would have been new man politics combined with a macho man body. In this case she was prepared to settle for the latter on its own. It had, after all, been quite a long time for Rachel, she was a pretty choosy girl. Also the condoms she carried in her bag were in danger of slipping past their sell-by date. Going without gets frustrating in the end.

The last thing Rachel expected with a man like Sly was that they would have to go through the lengthy and gruelling familiar rigmarole of coffee and more coffee and edging towards each other that precedes most first bonks. But to her amazement, they did.

Sly could not be his usual, forceful, demanding self with Rachel, he found her too confusing, worrying even. Rachel was also inhibited because despite her politics she had never been one for making the first move. It still sounded weird to Rachel, a woman asking a man to go to bed; she knew it shouldn't but it did. Language and convention remain great barriers to enlightenment.

And so, with the earth on the brink of extinction, and the conspiracy of cowardice and betrayal lumbering towards its thunderous climax, Rachel and Sly nervously chatted, drank more coffee, played some music, drank even more coffee and finally got close enough to go for it. It was more like two students at the end of term rather than two conspirators at the end of the world.

Well the moon held no more fears for Sly, suddenly it shone bright and friendly in the sky because now he knew how he wanted to spend his time on it. He wanted to spend his time rooting Rachel. It had been a revelation! Sly hadn't really liked sex up until that point. Now he loved it. Suddenly he felt as if he had been completely wasting his time since his balls dropped. He realized that all the sex he had had in the past had just been elaborate wanking; he had finally discovered the real thing. This was not the case for Rachel of course. She had enjoyed it, certainly, but that was all. Not being obsessed with power and money she had not found it necessary to put in a sixteen-hour day, seven days a week all her life, acquiring things that she could not possibly use, therefore, despite being many years younger than Sly she had found much more time in her life to develop satisfactory relationships.

But Sly was ecstatic; and as he lay there in the dark wondering whether Rachel fancied another bash and if so could he coax a magnificent third erection out of his frankly startled penis, and deciding that he probably could if Rachel helped – he was looking forward to going to the moon.

SPREADING THE WORD, PAYING THE PRICE

Chrissy's plan was to try to drum up sufficient media outrage in order to force either the authorities or the mob to intervene against Stark. Clearly she had a major problem in this situation, and that was that no one was likely to believe her story in a million years. Chrissy didn't know that she only had a week in which to act, but she could guess that however long she had, it wasn't very long.

It had been decided during the Council of War at the holiday home, that Chrissy would do her best to provoke press interest and that Mr Culboon and Walter would have a bash at alerting pressure groups and sympathetic politicos. This fairly hopeless and frankly embarrassing task was further complicated by the fact that they believed that the moment they showed themselves in public they would either be captured or killed. What's more, they carried the uncomfortable responsibility that if they did manage to bring anyone into the situation, they would be putting that person in great danger too.

However, in the two or three days following the helicopter flight, it looked as if their consciences at least would remain clear. They were unlikely to be putting anybody in danger, because trying to alert total strangers to an utterly fantastic situation, whilst remaining anonymous, proved beyond any of their persuasive powers.

Chrissy, Walter and Mr Culboon had travelled back to Perth in Rachel's Holden.

'I feel that we have a right to requisition our erstwhile

comrade's wheels to the cause. This hog is now a peace tank,' Walter had said.

It was, however, a peace tank which did not like being thrashed along red-hot highways by terrified renegades. It took nearly two days to get back to Perth.

They planned to operate out of telephone boxes, fearing that if they happened to contact anybody who was in the pay of Stark, the call could be traced. As it happened, what with Durf at the launch site and all the conspirators heading towards it at full speed, the omniscient power of Stark had been much reduced. But Chrissy did not know this and even if she had, the experiences of the previous few weeks would still have led her to be very very careful.

COMMUNICATION BREAKDOWN

Feeding in money that they could ill afford, Walter tried first. He phoned the office of the only member of the state parliament who had been elected on a no nukes platform.

'Listen, uhm, I have to speak to Ms Grant, OK?' Walter asserted. And, feeling the need to underline the urgency of the situation he added, 'You have to get the chick on the line, right now, I mean, like yesterday or the lid comes off. Dig? I mean the lid comes *off*. And that is off with a double 'F' right? I am talking the Fucking lid comes off, OK? You seeing where I'm coming from sister? Well you'd better because unless you get the main lady blowing in my ear pronto, we ain't *going* anywhere. I am talking about being *dead* lady. Dead with a capital 'F' . . .'

Inevitably Walter was asked his business. This rather surprised him. He had not thought that the groovier type of politician would go in for all that bureaucracy crap.

'Lady, can we please leave the mind control until we have the leisure to enjoy it?' he asked. 'You know, just put Big Brother back in his box. Because what I have to lay on the boss is very very very heavy. Right? It's something that she needs to know . . .'

The communication breakdown was unavoidable. Walter could not say who he was, and also he would prefer not to state his business except to Ms Grant personally . . .

Eventually, having been told three times to put it in writing and it would be dealt with he shouted, 'Listen, up at Bullens Creek they're fixing to blast off, man! The earth's dying and they're splitting!' The phone went dead.

After his first attempt, Walter was relegated to selling off his few possessions to acquire dollar bits for the phone. Sadly, Chrissy and Mr Culboon fared no better than he had.

They both tried many times, many different people and did it much more articulately than Walter had done, but the results were the same. Two days went by, Chrissy's finger ached from punching the phone. They seemed to have tried every media outlet and free-thinker in Australia. With no money, no time and no one to turn to, all three realized in a great wave of desperation that the chances of alerting the world were about zero. Walter was just thinking of suggesting that maybe they should try using the small ads and perhaps even put up some cards in newsagents windows, when they got a break.

It wasn't international, it wasn't even national, it was just a local TV news programme going out around Perth, but it was all they had and they had no choice but to go for it. The risks involved were horrible because the company insisted on a personal appearance. They said they could not possibly lend the credibility of their programme to rumour, hearsay and uncorroborated stories. This was most unfortunate because the three conspirators knew that whoever went on the television would be putting their head above the trench in no uncertain manner. None the less, they had to go for it. After all, they, like the world, had nothing to lose.

Mr Culboon and Walter felt that they should all face the music together, but Chrissy was insistent. There was no point them all risking their lives, she would go alone.

'Well, I reckon maybe you're right,' said Mr Culboon, 'you sure got the style Chrissy. I reckon there's plenty out there wouldn't want to listen to some old black fellah whining about his land. And as for Walter . . .' Mr Culboon simply shrugged his shoulders and exhaled.

As Chrissy got into her taxi she could still hear Walter trying to get to the bottom of this gesture.

'So what was with the shrug man . . . I mean maybe I'm being paranoid here, but well, it struck me as being dismissive.'

DEATH WARRANT

On arrival at the studio, Chrissy was met by a researcher who led her straight to make-up for the ubiquitous 'touch of powder, just to take the shine off'. The show was going out live and it wasn't at all long to air.

'We were *so* pleased that you could come at such short notice,' the researcher, whose name, like many researchers, was Jan, had said over her shoulder as they wound their way through the long corridors adorned with huge glossy photographs of newsreaders, weather men and stuffed cuddly Emus.

'We were well and truly *stuck* for an item when the wombat died, just tearing out our hair. Your story was a gift from heaven.'

Chrissy couldn't help thinking that this was a very strange way to view the profession of journalism, even at a local level, but there was no time to pursue her doubts. After five meaningless dabs with the powder pad they were led into the studio.

A shiny, very tanned man wearing a suit that was both trendy and conservative at the same time, sat reading the news. He looked like a footballer who had been invited to open a disco. Chrissy felt that local newsreaders always looked like footballers who had been invited to open a disco, or, if they were girls, aerobics instructors at a wedding. It was not going to be easy to make this work.

Chrissy was very tense. This was her one chance to make

410

her story public. It *had* to be good. Chrissy was convinced that the only way to construct an even remotely effective last ditch defence of the earth was for those who controlled the financial infra-structure to stay in place, at least for the time being. She had one chance to force a public reaction against Stark, and hence an intervention against the launches. One chance, she would give it all she had, even if she was signing her own death warrant.

As Jan and the floor manager sat her down in the interview chair opposite the tanned man in the footballer suit, Chrissy felt a tremendous sense of purpose; she had a rendezvous with destiny and she intended to pitch her story like no story had ever been pitched before.

The suit and the tan were winding up.

'. . . motorists are strongly advised to avoid that intersection until further notice,' said the newsreader and Chrissy knew by the way camera two swung around to face her that the moment of reckoning had arrived.

'And now it's time to brush away all the doubts and cares because news doesn't have to be all bad, there's always someone about to put a smile on all our faces. Yes, it's time for our Daily Daft Dingo, a look at the sillier side of life. Now we had said yesterday that we were going to bring you William, the wombat who can say 'Western Australia, pure Aussie' but unfortunately William's caught a little cold and won't be with us today. But fear ye not! We have another and even sillier Daft Dingo to chat to, not a wombat, but a lovely lady from the good old US of A . . .'

The bowels of the Daft Dingo, or Chrissy as she was known to her friends, were dissolving beneath her.

'. . . this super silly has a theory, get this, that the new Moorcock Tyron Leisure Centre up at Bullens Creek is, in fact, a rocket launch site. Ha ha. And that the world is so polluted that Sly and Ocker are going to blast off and leave . . . ha ha! As if anyone would ever want to leave WA, the greatest state in the world – the state of excitement. I mean sure, things are a touch hot and stinky right now . . .'

Chrissy did her best.

She tried to sound learned and convincing, consumed though she was with anguish and embarrassment, she explained the story of Stark, her confidence which had already been shattered, wilting further with every word she uttered.

Public ridicule is a strange thing; being right makes it no easier to bear.

'But surely, Chrissy,' laughed the interviewer, 'the explanation that it's a space-age theme park would seem a little more likely than the concept of Star Arks . . .?

Chrissy kept trying, and the interviewer kept laughing . . .

'Sure, we realize everything's a little strange at present; the economy, the weather, agriculture . . . but I hardly think a couple of true Aussies like Sly and Tyron are going to run away from their problems, do you?'

Chrissy shouted in her shame, which of course made her look even more of a dickhead than before . . .

'Please stop laughing, godammit, the world is dying. These terrible people are trying to get out while they can,' she pleaded. 'We have to *do* something.'

But the studio laughed, and the viewers laughed. The only people who did not laugh were Durf, who was in the mission control room at Bullens, reaching for the phone, and Dixie and Mrs Tyron who were putting two and two together in stunned disbelief.

WARRANT PRESENTED

Chrissy ran out of the TV building, burning with frustration and shame, the cruel laughter of the bastard presenter ringing in her ears. She could not get out of the place quick enough, which was a bit of luck for her as it happened because Stark still had claws enough to deal with people who went on TV to blow the gaff.

Two minutes after she left, Durf's henchmen arrived at the studio. Moments later they were taking fresh orders from Durf over the phone.

'Find out from the television company where they are staying . . .'

Chrissy ordered the cabbie to drive around for a while, she wanted to collect her thoughts, come to terms with the failure and humiliation.

'You want to sightsee in an area like this?' said the cabbie. 'The whole place has been ruined by Asians, Vietnamese running drugs and killing each other, boongs getting pissed on the pavement . . .'

Chrissy did not even hear him. It was half an hour before she finally had the cab pull into King Edward the Seventh Empire Terrace, the home of Walter and Zimmerman, where Rachel had first visited them a few months previously. Then it had been dead of night, now it was bright searing sunlight; then it had been silent and peaceful, now the air rang with the harsh cracks of gunfire and the desperate screams of men.

Durf's killers had been trying to hold Walter and Mr Culboon quietly until the girl came back but whether in some desperate effort to warn Chrissy, or simply because they knew that their time was up anyway, they had tried to make a break for it.

Walter moved first, a frenzied, scrambling rush past his captors to the door. Unfortunately for Walter, these men were not quality, they did not know their work. It would have been easy for them to detain Walter but instead they shot him. Moreover, they shot him with machine guns. His huge body was lifted up by the force of it and danced for a moment in the air like a marionette, as he was perforated with bullets. When the endless split seconds of mayhem and smoke were over, Walter fell to the floor approaching extinction at last.

Mr Culboon, seeing how the land lay, charged the window. He almost made it. The thugs were still contemplating the soggy mess, above which the soul of Walter was beginning to hover in peace. Their attention was distracted. Middle-aged as he was, Mr Culboon launched himself through the glass and landed, rolling in the uncleared jungle that surrounded the house; a jungle which was, if anything, thicker and more inpenetrable than when Rachel had encountered it. The weeds and the brambles closed in on Mr Culboon like a net. If Zimm and Walter had a lawnmower about a decade earlier, Mr Culboon might have made it to Chrissy's cab. Instead he fell victim to Walter's lifelong belief in non-interference with the natural environment, which translated loosely as a lifelong hatred of gardening. From Walter's dash to Mr Culboon's ensnarement, was a matter of a few short moments, although time, of course, is a relative and a subjective concept. For Mr Culboon this tiny period represented all the time in the universe. For it was the rest of his life.

Chrissy's car was still approaching, she was staring wildly out of the window. Mr Culboon saw her as he struggled with the tropical brambles and uttered his last words on earth. 'Get out Chrissy, Walter's dead, get the fuck . . .'

As with Walter, the point blank range leant tremendous power to the bursts of fire that tore through poor Mr Culboon. He too was lifted up with the force, but he did not dance in the air, he was immediately jerked down again. Zimm and Walter's garden did not give up so easily and seemed to grip Mr Culboon ever more firmly with each successive burst of fire. Even after his death, Mr Culboon's body still strained to escape into the air, shooting forward, propelled by the bullets, only to be dragged back by the jealous tentacles and twine.

'Get out of here,' screamed Chrissy at the driver. An unnecessary command, since by the time she made it her car was already a block away. Having got thus far, it screeched to a halt.

'Out,' shouted the terrified cab driver.

'But . . .' mumbled the equally terrified Chrissy.

'Just get out. Now, get out, please get out,' the driver was nearly hysterical. Chrissy tried to collect her wits . . .

'You have to take me somewhere where I can hire a car . . . Please.'

But the driver did not hear the 'please'. He had jumped out of the car and rushed around to Chrissy's door. He tore it open and dragged Chrissy out onto the pavement. 'It's nothing to do with me,' he shouted, 'I don't need it, I don't want it, I work hard. Get out, get out, get out.' The driver was blithering, Chrissy was already out; she was spread-eagled on the pavement. He rushed back around the cab, jumped in and drove off, leaving Chrissy sobbing, her head in the gutter.

LOVE AND WAR

Mrs Culboon and CD were sitting alone in the holiday home when Chrissy returned. There had been nothing for them to do so they had simply had to stay put. Zimmerman, who it seemed had mysterious plans of his own, had brought them some food but then disappeared. That had been two days before and they hadn't seen him since. Not surprisingly they were pleased to see Chrissy when she turned up. She had managed to acquire a hire car on the strength of some hocked earrings. It was now way overdue, but nothing seemed to matter much now anyway.

She told her story.

When it was finished, there was nothing anyone could think of to say. CD was crying, Mrs Culboon sat stoney-faced, Chrissy who had driven non-stop for about sixteen hours in order to bring this terrible news, sat chewing her lip.

How lonely could three people be? In the case of CD, Chrissy and Mrs Culboon, the answer was very. Chrissy was ten thousand miles from her home and friends, Mrs Culboon's husband was dead, CD had lost Rachel to Mr Culboon's murderers, Walter was dead. The scale of their sadness and their defeat was incomprehensible. Set against it, the death of the earth seemed a comparatively simple thing to assimilate. They sat in silence, the noise from Stark had gone now, save for intermittent murmurs. The silence of the grave descended upon them in the sweltering desert. It was as if they all believed that they would simply remain where they sat until they died. Perhaps they would have done had not Zimmerman returned.

They heard the padding first, rhythmic thudding that

managed to sound both hard and soft at the same time, as if somebody wearing a boxing glove was punching the ground very hard. It was getting closer, and sounding stranger and more ominous. It reminded Mrs Culboon of something but she could not remember what. CD wondered about taking up a rifle and putting up some semblance of self-defence, but then he wondered what the point would be, and decided that there wasn't one. Then Mrs Culboon remembered what the noise sounded like, it sounded like a camel. Shortly after which, she heard it snort and decided that it was a camel.

BATTLE CAMEL

From behind the rocks that formed the cave rode Zimmerman resplendently perched atop a great ship of the desert, like an Australian Lawrence, burnt by the sun, cloaked in white and swathed in weaponry. He made an impressive figure.

'I've been speaking to some of the workers they laid off,' he said, without bothering to greet them. 'The shit is definitely about to hit the fan. We have to make our move.'

'I think we've made enough moves,' Chrissy said dully. 'Walter and Mr Culboon are dead.'

Zimmerman sat on his camel in silence, his expression did not change. It was as if he hadn't heard.

'That's why we have to do something, I reckon,' said Mrs Culboon, her face still like granite and her voice flat as the Great Sandy Desert. 'What move did you have in mind, Zimmerman?'

For a moment Zimmerman continued his silence, then he seemed to return from wherever it was that he had been. 'Gotta fight, I guess,' he said quietly.

'Oh Zimmerman,' Chrissy's voice was so tired and dull. 'How can we fight them?'

'Got to fight them,' he said and the camel snorted. 'Isn't a question of how, we've got to do it.' He still hadn't mentioned the death of his friend.

'Walter's dead,' Chrissy repeated.

417

'This has nothing to do with Walter, lady,' said Zimmerman. 'He's doing his thing some place else. We fight for whoever's left. That's the way we always did it back when the sharp end was sharp. Remember the dead, sure, but defend the living.'

Something had been bothering CD. At first he couldn't place it, then he remembered. He knew what it was he wanted to ask.

'What's the story with the camel?' he said.

'I found her,' answered Zimm.

'You found a camel? Where have you been, Arabia?'

'They have camels in Oz. They brought them over before they knew about Toyotas,' asserted Zimm without changing his tone. 'Some are wild, some are tame. Walter here was wild, but now she's tame. I had to punch her in the mouth one time but camels don't mind. She's gonna see a heap worse than that before she gets much older.'

'Walter?' asked CD.

'Yeah, her name was Sai Wan after a girl I once knew, but now it's Walter. I can call her Walter Culboon if you'd like that, Mrs Culboon?'

'Not particularly,' said Mrs Culboon, 'although it's a nice thought.'

'Actually I'd like to,' said Zimmerman. 'Mr Culboon was a brother too, you know?'

'OK, whatever.'

Zimmerman sat on the ridge, on top of Walter Culboon the camel. He towered above the other three, almost black against the sun. He was clearly mad. This was why the others could handle the conversation. The world was mad, Zimmerman blended in. If he had been straight he would have been a freak. The world was about to die and Walter and Mr Culboon had gone before and now they had both come back as the same camel, and Zimmerman was sitting on them. Chrissy, who had seen a man shot to pieces and then driven for sixteen hours in temperatures that would have defrosted a frozen elephant in time for supper, felt dizzy.

'Where's my man lay?' asked Mrs Culboon when the silence was finished.

'Yesterday he was in Zimmerman's back garden ...' Chrissy could not bring herself to say 'Walter's as well'. Camels didn't have gardens. 'I guess they must have moved him by now.'

'Hmmph,' said Mrs Culboon. 'Reckon the police are pretty used to getting rid of dead blacks.'

'It's morning now,' said Zimmerman. 'We'll hit 'em an hour before dawn tomorrow.'

'On a camel?' asked CD who was staying closest to reality. Wherever that was. It was a new experience for CD to be the most together member of the team. Maybe Chrissy sensed this, she pulled herself back from the place she was drifting in and blinked the salty sweat out of her eyes.

'Yeah,' she said, 'won't they laugh at the camel?'

'The camel can cover very rough ground at great speed,' said Zimmerman. 'It is incredibly hardy and has a very unfazeable personality.'

If Walter Culboon realized how highly she was being spoken of, she did not show it. She chewed and shuffled about a bit. Perhaps Zimmerman knew what he was talking about, she certainly did not seem fazed.

'It is a stealthy beast,' continued Zimmerman in his quiet drawl, 'with soft, padded feet and is ideal for approaching an enemy in silence.'

Perhaps Zimmerman should have added that she had great timing, for this was the moment that Walter Culboon chose to let rip with an unfeasibly camelish bottom burp that rent the air in twain. It barked its way around the desert for a good eight seconds and rolled down into the little hollow in which the other three were sitting, leaving them knee deep in a primeval fug which made even the air of the summer of Stark seem vaguely alpine. Nobody was cruel enough to say anything, but even Zimmerman could work out what they were thinking.

'Now I know, like, that you're thinking that the farting

situation kind of contradicts the stealth and silence thesis,' he said, his voice showing some emotion for the first time since he had appeared. 'But like, I suggest you put yourself in the position of a security guard, right? Who, whilst doing his security guarding thing, hears a camel blowing off in the still of the desert night. Like, does that guard think to himself, oh wow, bummer, the avenging hand of EcoAction is upon me? Or does he think that a camel has blown off . . . or maybe a lonely kangaroo?'

Nobody had the faintest idea what to say to this and so Zimmerman explained his battle plan.

A MOMENT OF DOUBT

As Zimmerman talked of battle, listing his resources – which consisted of four people, a station wagon, a hire car and a truck; as his companions listened, becoming, in the process, almost as flatulent as Walter Culboon the camel, the fifth night of the count-down approached. On the following morning there would be three days left.

The eight day period had been defined for purely practical reasons. Durf was in a position to trigger the remote launch procedure at any point. The time had been decided upon in order to ensure that all members of the consortium would have time to withdraw from their lives in an orderly fashion, without provoking comment, pick up their partners and make their way to Bullens Creek.

In fact by the fifth night, most of the conspirators had arrived. They were all acutely aware that if they missed this particular bus there would not be another one along in a minute.

Rachel and Sly lay together sweating in the heat. Sly's work was done, there was nothing left to do but root, eat frozen lasagnes and shower about every thirty minutes.

'We could root in the shower and save time,' said Sly through the darkness.

'Save time for what?' Rachel's voice replied.

'We only have three days left.'

This provoked a silence that even Walter Culboon would have felt embarrassed to intrude upon.

'Oh God, Silvester, let's not go,' said Rachel, 'please let's not go. Come back with me to Carlo, we can eat ice-cream at Fernandez.'

'Rachel,' said Sly, and he held her hand, 'I'm saving your life, I'm saving your life because I love you. Don't you want that?'

'Yes I want it,' said Rachel, and she did want it.

ORDER OF BATTLE

During the previous afternoon, Zimmerman had done a little scouting on Walter Culboon. He had brought back encouraging news.

'Man, things are definitely no longer so tight,' he said. 'I reckon they're fixing to split and they don't want no bully boys around to put two and two together and try to hitch a ride.'

'There's no one left to fight?' asked CD, for whom, it must be remembered, hope sprang eternal.

'Shit man, a whole lot more than we could ever handle,' answered Zimm, 'but at least it ain't no army no more. The security seems to be situated in an outer ring about 15 kilometres from the epicentre,' Zimm continued. Being about to enter combat he had become lucid once again, if, in a rather manic kind of way. 'I reckon they're keeping the thugs away from the business end. They got a truck with a bunch of guys about every seven kilometres in a ring around the base. I got the glasses on Du Pont one time, I sure hope we get that bastard . . . Now,' said Zimm, getting to the point, 'we have to get past this ring to get right in and destroy the rockets, OK?'

'Hey listen, bud,' said Chrissy, 'I may not be General Custer but I guess that I can figure out that we ain't gonna knock 'em out by going back to Perth.'

'*Listen*, soldier!' hissed Zimm. 'This is combat preparation, and in combat preparation you state the obvious because that way everybody knows the *same* obvious, and you'd better pray your brothers and sisters do know the same obvious because when *your* arse is on the line, your cover needs to have his gun pointing in the same direction as you're going.'

'All right already, so make me do some push ups.'

Zimmerman ignored this and continued. 'Obviously they have to have some form of mission control and our job is to get in there and fuck it right up. OK, just fuck it straight to hell, just fuck that mother like the pig that swallowed a hand grenade . . .'

'Zimmerman, please, just tell us what we have to do.' Mrs Culboon paused and then added a second 'please'. She, like the others had accepted that today was not a real day and that her ordinary life was still going on somewhere else. None the less Zimmerman, on full throttle, was taking freak tolerance too far.

Somewhere in the depths of Zimmerman's hat support structure, Mrs Culboon's tone hit a chord. He calmed down.

'I was psyching my head, it's important to psyche my head. Don't you feel that you should psyche your heads?' he asked.

'My head is psyched,' replied Chrissy.

'Me too,' said CD, and it was clear that Mrs Culboon felt the same way.

'OK, cool,' said Zimmerman. 'I'll psyche my head on my own after the briefing. Everyone must do their own thing and find their own astral plane to die in. I like mine angry.'

'Zimm,' said Chrissy, 'tell us what we have to do.'

Reality returned. In as much as their situation would allow it to, that is.

'OK,' said Zimm. 'Now we have to hit the control centre, which means getting past the security ring. Now they have trip-wires and cameras and electronic beams running between the guard concentrations so there is no way we can slip through, like, discreetly. Unless, of course, they aren't looking and listening. What I propose is that you cats attack our chosen guardpost directly from the front, creating a diversion, and while that's going on I'll slip through further up the line and then come around and attack them from behind, OK?'

'How many guards in each of the concentrations, Zimmerman?' asked Chrissy, not wishing to hear the answer.

'Twelve,' he replied, 'but they're lightly armed and we have the element of surprise.'

'We sure are going to surprise them arriving on a camel,' said Mrs Culboon, cracking her first joke since she had heard of the death of her husband. She remained in a daze over the tragedy. Not in as much of a daze as Zimmerman was in about Walter's death, but then Zimm had started out way ahead of Mrs Culboon in the daze stakes. Mrs Culboon was reserving the full burden of her grief for another occasion, should one arise, when she would have the time and the peace to assemble her ruptured emotions and take stock of her loss. For the present she knew that the battle in which Mr Culboon had fallen was far from over, and that it was a time for courage and good humour, not mawkish introspection. Mrs Culboon had seen and felt suffering before. That was why she had cracked the gag about the camel.

'They aren't going to see the camel until it's too late, Mrs Culboon,' said Zimmerman. 'Because of the diversion, right? What you have to do is this. At a specific time . . . you know, a time that is the same for all of us, right? A time, right, that we have all dug together . . .'

'Yes, Zimmerman, at the same time,' said Chrissy.

'You got it soldier, well done,' said Zimmerman. 'At that time, you three hit our chosen troop concentration full on from the front with whatever we've got. Now so relentless will be your withering barrage,' said Zimm, whose words were growing with his stature, 'so pulverizing will be your symphony of death, man, that those cats out there are going to be under the impression that the whole Australian Defence Force has forgotten about the Japs and is coming at them all at once, right?'

The others merely stared.

'And while their attention is diverted with saying things like "oh fuck what are we gonna do" and shitting themselves and stuff like that. But mainly while they are looking outwards at you, I'll cross the wire on Walter Culboon and knock them out from behind. You dig?'

They nodded. Despite the extravagance of Zimm's description there was no doubt his plan appeared feasible. Three people shooting in the dark could certainly make enough noise to distract a company of twelve. After all, Zimmerman only wanted them to get the guards' attention. He was going to kill them, it seemed.

'When they're down,' Zimmerman concluded, 'you come through in the station wagon and we burn for the middle. If we can't crack them, I'll head in on Walter Culboon and try to do it alone.'

EVE OF BATTLE

They spent the first part of the night before the battle cleaning and checking the weaponry. Zimmerman took them through the reloading and firing procedures of the pistols, the rifles, the automatic weapons and the grenades. There was only one shoulder-held launcher, so this he kept for himself.

Around two, Zimm declared that they knew enough. There is only so much about the science of armour that can be taken in at once, besides which, according to Zimmerman's plan, the other three were only expected to cause a huge distraction and draw the enemy fire. Zimm himself would do the precision killings.

For the hours preceding the strike, each sat alone with his or her thoughts. Occasionally Zimm would stand upon the ridge beside Walter Culboon and stare out towards the field of battle and the target beyond, psyching his head.

'I still can't quite see how it came to this,' said Mrs Culboon, 'the four of us defending the whole world. But I want you all to know that I'm proud to be a part of it, and proud to be alongside you all.'

424

It was a nice thing to say. For a moment CD wondered why Walter did not say something nice back on behalf of everybody, he normally did that sort of thing very well. Then he remembered that Walter was dead. CD went back to thinking about Rachel and what honeyed words and stirring arguments he might employ to bring her back to them once the battle was won. Who could tell? he thought, hope springing, as always, eternal. Maybe she'd be so ashamed of herself she'd let him sauce her there and then, under the big desert sky, as a penance. Yes! that was it, this was his big chance.

BATTLE

'OK let's go,' said Zimm in the low, almost hissing murmur that he had adopted ever since he had turned into Clint Eastwood. 'We got just one shot at saving the world.'

The hours of waiting had embittered Mrs Culboon.

'And avenging our dead,' replied Mrs Culboon. 'Most of me is doing this for my husband.'

Each had their ghosts to bury. If any of the combatants fell, they would be in good company. Mr Culboon, Walter, Linda Reeve, Toole ... Rachel. CD certainly harboured the most searing sense of mission. The others had only lost the dead; he had lost the living. He was going in to save Rachel from a fate worse than death, he would do anything to stop the launch and give her a chance to come to her senses.

They shouldered their arms and whilst Zimmerman mounted Walter Culboon, the other three got into the station wagon. They had decided on using the station wagon only, being shot was going to be bad enough, there was no sense having to pay for a damaged hire car as well.

'Now don't forget,' Zimm said, 'don't try and take 'em, that's my job. Just draw their fire, I'll be coming up behind them.'

The proposed target was very clear, a truck and two search-lights, men hanging around, some making a desultory attempt at being guards, others just crashed out on the ground. There were two camp-fires and a number of lamps run off a little generator by the light of which some of the men were playing cards.

'Well they certainly have gone to a lot of trouble to pick themselves out as targets, haven't they,' said Chrissy.

'It's nearly time,' said CD who had been earnestly studying the luminous dials on his watch.

They began to crawl closer. As they did so, they spread out, to about fifty metres apart. When they started shooting it was essential that the enemy believed themselves to be facing a formidable opponent. Zimm had told them to vary their weapons every few bursts, even to fire with both hands – it didn't matter what at since they were only the diversion.

CD fired first. From somewhere to Mrs Culboon's right she heard the crackle of automatic fire. Almost simultaneously she opened up, as did Chrissy to her left.

'Make it look like they've got a fucking army in front of them,' Zimmerman had said. 'Just party down man, whoop, holler and make it big.'

CD was the best at it, he was throwing grenades vaguely towards where the light had been, shouting at the top of his voice quotes from all the war movies that had got him through so many endless Sunday afternoons.

'Steady there,' he screamed. 'Dress from the right. Up periscope. We're all scared kid. Charge. Take cover. Banzai.'

It is unlikely anybody ever heard him but the explosions he was lobbing certainly had their effect, even if they were falling about sixty yards short. All the lights went out in the security encampment and it began to return fire. They seemed to be doing it in as haphazard a way as EcoAction, and of course they were, because three people make extremely small targets in a great big desert and the guards firmly believed themselves to be facing a much larger enemy.

Once Zimmerman heard the return of fire he figured that they were about as abstracted as they would ever be and spurred Walter Culboon on towards the cameras and electronic sensors of the security perimeter.

AN ARMY APPROACHES

The battle had been going for less than a minute when Durf made his decision. What could he do? He had no idea what was attacking him, but if it was anything bigger than a handful they were in trouble, and it sounded a lot bigger.

'Whatever you do hold them where they are,' he barked down the phone at the officer in the field. 'A ten thousand dollar bonus to each man; they must not get through.'

A few minutes later Durf was addressing a very shaken final Stark Summit Meeting.

A MERC' AND A CHEVVY APPROACH

As Zimmmerman and Walter Culboon galloped towards the perimeter he was astonished to be passed by two cars, a Mercedes and a Chevrolet, about a hundred metres to his right. Zimm wondered if this was the long delayed effects of some unwisely taken hallucinogenic. But it couldn't be, he had been straight for donkeys years. Zimm was a pretty laid back guy at times but there was no way his body worked that slowly. As Zimm charged along he decided that the cars must be real but there was no point worrying about them.

A TRUCK AND THE CAMEL

Zimm galloped across a wide diagonal sweep of desert floor in order to place himself behind the scene of the battle. His friends were still kicking up as much racket as they could but it would clearly not be long before the guards cottoned on to the fact that very little was happening. Speed was of the essence. Zimmerman had to get to the enemy and hit them while they were still confused.

The security guards had retreated to the comparative safety of a sand dune from where they were vaguely popping bullets out towards the source of their discomfort. As Zimm cantered up behind them he heard a commanding voice ring out. A depressingly commanding voice, the last thing Zimm needed in the enemy camp was somebody who knew their job. Unfortunately that was exactly what he had got.

'Hold your fire!!' he shouted raggedly, for his men were scarcely crack troops. He was obeyed.

The result was slightly embarrassing really. A quarter of an hour before when CD, Chrissy and Mrs Culboon had opened fire, their collective mayhem had seemed quite convincing and impressive, coming as it did out of the eerie stillness of the night. Since then the company had been joined by the noise of twelve men firing back and the noise had been terrible. Now that the defenders had stopped shooting and the three Eco-attackers' fire was left to itself again, it no longer sounded impressive, in fact it sounded pathetic. It sounded like exactly what it was, which wasn't much.

The commanding voice rang out again.

'Christ, there's fuck all out there. This ain't no army, it's kids or yobs or something. I want three men, we'll clean 'em up in the armoured truck.'

If the commanding officer had thought to radio his conclusions back to Durf the outcome of the night might have been very different. However, he didn't because he suddenly had other things to think about. This being that his armoured truck was now a blazing fireball and clearly not about to clean up anybody, at least not until they had put it out.

Zimmerman, on hearing the commander's aggravating grasp of the situation, had decided immediately to go onto the offensive. He started his campaign by shooting a shoulder-launched anti-tank shell into the security truck. This, Zimmerman had intended to be only the beginning, unfortunately after this he lost control of events.

MAN OVER CAMEL

When Zimmerman had first met Walter Culboon, he had based their relationship on a combination of brute force and superior will. Having stalked her at a dried up water-hole (the

428

same one at which her distant ancestor had killed the explorer Bullen), Zimm wrestled her to the ground and punched her in the face. After this Zimmerman had tried to establish some form of psychic bond between them. He had talked long and hard into her ear; he had developed eye contact and applied his small knowledge of hypnotism to the situation. His will had unquestionably triumphed over the camel's and Walter Culboon had decided to do what she was told.

Zimmerman flattered himself that this was because the camel recognized a fellow wild beast when she saw one; another creature who knew the terror of the hunted.

'I'm more camel than I am man, man' Zimm had assured the camel as he twisted its neck upon the ground as one would a steer, 'except for the hump and stuff obviously. But like inside we are the same.'

Actually Walter Culboon had not recognized a soul mate, but she had recognized trouble. Her finely attuned animal survival instincts had alerted her immediately to the fact that she was in the presence of an unstable wild bastard. The fact that he had jumped her from behind, throttled her to the ground, punched her in the face and then appeared to be trying to make friends, did nothing to dampen this impression. This was why she had decided to do what she was told.

The present situation, however, had forced Walter Culboon to revise her decision, the bloke on her back might be an unstable weirdo with a fist like a 'roos tail, but he did not explode in a twenty foot mushroom of burning oil. The truck had, and the camel didn't like it. Gunfire and explosions were out as far as Walter Culboon was concerned and so she decided to run like fuck.

Unfortunately she was facing the wrong way because Zimmerman had been approaching the enemy from behind. He now found himself careering back towards his friends, all his efforts at penetrating Stark in vain.

'Hey listen, I thought we were a team,' protested Zimmerman as they careered across the desert back towards the others. 'At least run the other way Walter Culboon,' he pleaded, 'we have to save the world here.'

But it was no use. Walter Culboon had made up her mind, she wanted out. Obviously when the other three saw Zimm careering towards them out of the dawn on his camel, they stopped firing, therefore, quite suddenly, through the actions of one camel, peace descended again upon the desert. Hearing this, Walter Culboon responded at last to Zimm's frenzied pullings and pleadings and stopped running. By now Zimm was about another hundred metres past Mrs Culboon heading towards the holiday home. He turned Walter Culboon around and headed back to regroup.

In the sand dune the apparition of a wild figure on a camel appearing from nowhere and blowing up their truck had left the security forces in thoughtful and subdued mood.

'Shall I radio back a report, sir?' said the radio operator.

'What, and tell them that we got beaten by a man on a camel? No way. Turn the damn thing off, this needs thinking about.'

THE END AND THE
BEGINNING

RACHEL

All Rachel's plans were completely thrown. The careful scenario that she had been plotting for almost a week was as knackered as the ozone layer. They had been awoken shortly before dawn by the sound of intense gunfire and a series of explosions out towards the security perimeter. Sly jumped out of bed, unlocked his desk and brought out a machine pistol. He put it beside him and began to dress hurriedly. The phone rang, it was Durf. When they had finished speaking Sly slammed down the phone, told Rachel that everything was all right, that he would be back shortly, and rushed out of the room.

Rachel sat, wondering what on earth could be going on out at the perimeter; wondering what it meant to her and her plans, wondering what she was going to do right now.

She did not have long to wonder, for much more quickly than she had expected Sly rushed back in, breathless and fantastically excited.

'This is it! This is fucking *it*!! We're leaving early,' he blurted.

'What do you mean?' said Rachel, very scared. 'We can't. What's going on?'

'Trouble out on the wire,' said Sly pulling out their pre-packed flight packs. 'Looks like something's coming at us . . . seem to have a hell of a lot of fire-power too, heard some vague talk about camels. Those are the new Soviet hand-held

431

armour piercers. Could be anything from ten men to a bloody army! Durf thinks it's big. Anyway, whether it is or not, we aren't hanging around to find out. There's only five members not arrived yet and it's been decided to leave them . . . This is it, darling! We're going, we are fucking *going*!! Off to a new world. In forty-five minutes we will be in fucking *space*!!'

Sly was breathless with excitement. He was shaking as he took the bags to the door. Who wouldn't have been? The world was an itchy, steaming, rotting pigsty and he was off with his best girl to the pure, cool cleanliness of space. Except he wasn't.

He turned at the doorway to urge Rachel on.

For a moment she felt a terrible regret, not doubt, but real regret. It would, after all, have been a very big adventure.

She had walked across to the desk and snatched up Sly's gun. Now he was looking down it, the elation frozen on his face.

Rachel hated it, she had not wished to confront Sly, she liked him too much for that. Their passion had been a genuine one. Her plan all along had been to wait until the morning of the launch, perhaps even as the ships were loading, before making her move. She had intended to claim a desire for one last private walk upon earth. Then she would have made her way to the mission control room which by then would be functioning on remote, and hence be empty of staff. Once there she had intended to kick it, unplug it, throw chairs at it, basically carry out any method of disabling the controls that sprang to mind at the time. Having done what she could and, presuming that nobody had shot her, Rachel then intended to make her way out into the desert and try to find her friends.

The basis of this plan had formed the moment that Sly had made his proposal. She had seen instantly that here was a chance to transform herself from hunted nuisance to privileged insider; she had known at once that no such opportunity would ever emerge again to stop Stark. And stop it she must, that she knew.

Rachel's instincts had reached the same conclusion as

Chrissy's logic. She could guess that if the world was to stand a chance, which surely it must, if only a tiny one, then those in control, those with power and influence, must be forced to take some responsibility for that which they had helped to create. It was obvious to Rachel that the fastest way to motivate the world was to make Stark admit to its vile plans and then be forced to use their colossal resources to help try and deal with the awful situation instead of running away from it. Therefore, from the first moment that she had been indoctrinated into Stark, she had resolved to use the unique position that her sauciness had presented her with to abort the launch.

However, she had not expected to be confronted by Sly, intent on rushing her straight into a ship and she had not expected to feel that she was betraying him.

'What the fuck are you doing, Rachel?' demanded Sly staring at the gun in disbelief.

'Stopping the launch, Silvester. I'm sorry but nobody's leaving. We're going to the mission control room. Lead the way.'

Of course he protested, but she cut him short.

'Shut up! I don't want to hear. I tried to persuade you to give it up, I said let's stay, you and me, but you're such a selfish bastard, you wouldn't do it. We're going to the control room, lead the way.'

Sly was astonished, it was twenty years since anyone had spoken to him in that manner. Actually he was rather hurt. They left the room in silence.

THE MERC' THE CHEVVY
AND THE CENTREFOLD

Outside, as Durf and the rest of the technical team began to marshal the bleary-eyed and rather terrified conspirators towards the transports that would take them to their rockets, two cars screamed to a halt in the pre-dawn half-light.

Tyron was in the process of trying to persuade his centrefold, whose name was Suki, to put on her flight suit when he saw the cars. Understandably Suki was beginning to wonder what was going on. This did not look like the jolly, supersonic ride she had been promised, it looked like something much more serious . . . When Dixie Tyron got out of the first car, she reckoned she was right . . .

Despite her enormous sunglasses, Dixie seemed to be able to take in the whole scene at once. She spotted Tyron immediately and stormed towards him. Suki was terrified, she was well aware that the position of 'bit on the side' held very few rights or privileges once the wife turned up. Dixie was certainly an intimidating sight, appearing out of the shimmering heat, a cloud of silver-blond hair, tightly bound body thrust forward as if two invisible strings were attached to her nipples and were being wound in by some distant winch. Her blood-red mouth seemed to snarl crimson venom at Suki. It was as if she had eaten one or two of Ocker's playthings already that morning and would be happy to devour a third as an early lunch.

Scuttling after her was Mrs Tyron. She emerged from the second car which had been chasing Dixie all the way from Bullens, waving a birth certificate.

'I'm your mother, Ocker!' she cried. 'I'm your mother . . . sixteen hours of pain . . . I refused all drugs, I wanted to experience your birth in all its beauty . . .'

Dixie pushed Suki roughly out of the way.

'Excuse *me*!' said Suki who had her pride after all.

'Listen, cow, one word! Just *one word*,' said Dixie, pointing a talon that looked like it should have been scooping fluff out of the devil's belly button, 'and the next man fondling your scrawny body will be the police mortician . . .'

Durf tried to interject, he could still hear gunfire out at the perimeter and was desperate to hurry.

'Ladies, please, I must insist –' he got no further.

'You zip up too, Mister,' said Dixie, brandishing a second talon, 'or you'll lose the other eye . . . Hullo Ocker love.' She

434

turned to Ocker with a voice that nearly warped the rockets, 'I think you forgot to tell me that we were going on a trip!'

'Sixteen hours of pain, Ocker, I refused all drugs! Your own mother, Ocker!' Mrs Tyron butted in, 'I must just not have found your note . . . where did you leave it, darling?'

Dixie turned on her mother-in-law in fury.

'Look! For the last time will you bugger off and leave me alone with the man I love, you ancient stinking old cow.'

'Man she loves! Hark at the fat pig,' countered Mrs Tyron. 'I don't notice that young delivery boy who always seems to take two hours to drop off the dry cleaning around here.'

'You damn snake, you skunk, you . . .'

Cow, pig, snake, skunk, it was indeed ironic that Dixie and Mrs Tyron should be trying so hard to get onto the Arks because between them they seemed to represent most of the animal kingdom.

Just as Ocker was feeling that the situation could get no worse, Aristos emerged from his mother's car.

'Hi guys,' he said addressing the assorted millionaires and their partners who were standing about in a rather bemused fashion. 'Ciao Ocker,' he said, turning to Ocker. 'Been trying to get me? Sorry, I've had the girls hold all calls for days, meetings, meetings. Even turned off the carphones. I've got two now, you know, in the same car, different numbers. It's *such* a godsend, don't know how I managed. Hey Ocker,' Aristos had noticed Suki, 'fo-o-oxy chick, and how! wow! woof woof!!!'

'Yes, she *is* a pretty thing, Ocker,' said Mrs Tyron with great malice straight at Dixie, 'just your type – slim. Tell us her name, why don't you?'

The etiquette of the situation was not easy for Ocker.

'Uhm yeah, this is . . .'

But Suki saved him the trouble, she had had enough.

'Don't bother, Ocker,' she said, 'when I have affairs, I sort of prefer it when the fellah doesn't bring his whole family along . . . Call me in Sydney.' She turned and walked towards the little red jeep that Ocker had provided for her amusement during the week they had spent in the desert. Ocker watched her fabulous bottom swaying away from him.

'Suki, wait!' he shouted.

'Ocker!!' shouted Dixie and Mrs Tyron in unison, and Ocker's courage deserted him. Even at this moment of destiny, he could not exorcize the lying hypocritical relationships that had been the one constant element in his life for three decades.

Suki got in her car and drove off towards Bullens. It wasn't until about forty minutes later when her rear view mirror suddenly filled with the flame and smoke of burning clouds that Suki realized that she might have had a luckier escape than avoiding being punched by Dixie.

The whole embarrassing scene had only taken a few minutes, but Dixie could see that the people around her were getting restive and that there was a man with an eye patch who was clearly anxious to move things along.

'Right,' said Dixie, icy calm in her eyes. 'Clearly my husband has made a *mistake* uhm . . .'

'Durf, Madam, Professor Durf,' Durf replied.

'But the mistake has gone, and I'm here now,' she put her arm through Tyron's forcefully, 'where are we sitting?'

This was too much for Mrs Tyron who kicked Dixie. Pushing Aristos forward she announced, 'I'm his mother, he's taking his proper family . . .'

Before Tyron could speak, Durf, desperate to get moving, interjected. 'We are having a shortfall of five Stark members, there will be no problem accommodating all of you,' he said.

Tyron could have killed him.

He was heading for the moon to be a part of the phoenix human race, rising out of the polluted ashes of its dead self. However, he was to be accompanied by his wife, his mother and Aris-fucking-stos. Ocker Tyron could scarcely believe this appalling turn of events.

As they awaited their final instructions his family huddled close around him, fearful that he would yet find a way of deserting them. But he had none.

The site was eerily empty. All non-indoctrinated personnel were either on the perimeter or had been dismissed altogether. The actual conspirators were now milling about at the transporters awaiting the final trip out to the rocket silos which lay a few kilometres further on into the desert. Only Sly and Rachel were at large.

'Please, Rachel, darling ... uhm, love boat, honey bunch ... For Christ's sake they'll be gone soon,' he pleaded, 'we'll miss the fucking boat ... Look we've *got* to go, there's nothing left here on earth but hell ...'

'Nobody's going anywhere, so shut up. We're going to destroy the control centre,' Rachel replied. 'Your bloody friends can damn well try and save the world not run away from it.'

'But it *can't* be saved,' Sly was desperate now. 'Do you think if I really thought there was a chance I'd be going? God Almighty, Rachel, why the hell would I?'

Even though Rachel was behind him, Sly could feel a moment of tension and doubt descend upon her.

Just then, far away, on the perimeter, Zimmerman blew up the armoured truck. Sly knew that this was as distracted as Rachel was ever likely to get. He had to take his chance. He was fighting for his life, and hers. Besides, he didn't think she'd shoot him.

She didn't. Rachel never knew if she would have done, he was too quick for her. In the split second of distraction following Zimm's blast, Sly swung around and grappled with her for the gun. In an instant, the tables had turned.

'Right, we're going to get in the fucking rocket,' said Sly viciously.

'You maybe. I've told you, I'm not going.'

Sly knew how little time he had. For a whole five minutes he tried to reason with Rachel, again explaining why the whole thing had to happen whether they liked it or not, telling her he loved her, but Rachel was adamant, she would not leave.

Then, the final thirty minute count-down started. Zimmerman's blast had also spooked Durf. He tried calling up the perimeter on the radio, but it had gone silent. Durf had no idea what the problem was and he had no wish to wait around to find out. He hit the button that activated the actual launch procedure.

Inside the control room, outside which stood Sly and Rachel, a tape began to turn.

'Attention, attention,' the pre-programmed NASA equipment boomed. 'Clear launch site, final count-down commencing, minus thirty minutes and counting,' continued the long-since recorded voice.

Sly grabbed Rachel roughly.

'Listen you bitch, if you ain't coming you picked a fine time to tell me. So *I'm* telling *you*! You are coming. I'm not going up there alone, without a companion, a woman, how can I? I wouldn't be a man in the moon, I'd be a fucking nothing in the moon! You put me in this position, you're what I've got and I'm taking you now. Move!'

'*I'm not going*,' screamed Rachel through her tears.

'You are! Now move!' replied Sly, brandishing the gun, 'or else I swear I will knock you out and *carry* you onto the fucking rocket. Can't you see girl!! Can't you see! How could I go without you? . . . don't even think about it, you're coming.' Rachel realized that unconscious she would be done for sure. She had to concentrate, there were after all thirty minutes left. Slowly, she turned, and got back into the car for the drive to the assembly point where Sly intended to force her, if necessary, onto the last transport out to the rockets.

VOICE ACROSS THE SAND

Out on the perimeter Zimm had just managed to tempt Walter Culboon back to where Mrs Culboon crouched in the desert. CD and Chrissy had assembled too. Having seen Zimm's wild and ungainly charge away from the epicentre they all presumed, rightly, that things had fucked up somewhat and that they had got nowhere.

'Don't blame the camel man,' said Zimmerman, 'it's not the camel's fault.'

Just as the others were about to protest that they had no intention of blaming the camel, they saw a truck from another perimeter post approaching; the one that they had been attacking. Clearly their dash for the centre was now completely cut off. What's more, it was obvious to the meanest intelligence that their enemies were not going to take the indignities inflicted upon them lying down.

EcoAction had exposed itself as the weakened force that it was. Now, yet again, it was they who were the hunted.

'We'll have to pull back,' said Zimmerman, 'but I don't think those guys are going to make it easy for us.'

'We can't pull back,' said CD in panic, 'we haven't got Rachel.'

'Listen, man, will you just stop thinking about sex all the time,' shouted Zimm '. . . I find it just totally insensitive. The chick made her choice man. Now listen, this place is blown. We have to move further up the wire. You people make for the station wagon. I'll cover you, then I'll follow on Walter Culboon.'

Walter Culboon could not speak English but she knew a worrying tone of voice when she heard one. More and more her keen camel instincts with their delicate sensitivity to the biorhythms of life were shouting at her, 'You got a looney on your back!! You got a looney on your back! Buck the bastard into a dune and run like fuck.'

Walter Culboon was about to do exactly this when, like everybody else, she was distracted by the voice across the sands.

For just as Zimmerman was giving his orders, and just as the commander of the security unit that had lost its truck was about to commandeer the second truck, with the intention of 'killing the fucking jerk on the camel'. Just as that morning's biggest earth disaster was about to hit the first editions – flash flooding in Bangladesh put three-quarters of the country under water.

Just then, Durf pushed the button and the count-down started. The voice that Sly and Rachel had heard was clear as day across the desert – it was probably heard in Bullens Creek where, no doubt, they thought that the Moorcock leisure park was installing the sound-track for a new ride.

'Attention attention,' the recorded American voice spoke from the sky. 'Clear launch site, final count-down commencing. Minus thirty minutes and counting.'

Everybody turned and looked. Attackers and defenders alike, turned and stared as one person towards the centre of Stark, all forgetting their differences and the battle which they had been fighting in response to this eerie voice.

In the clear light of the morning, ten, maybe fifteen kilometres away, the six rockets pointed upwards from their silos, supported by the spindly towers. It seemed impossible to comprehend, but the voice was referring to the rockets and it was being serious. The jaws of the security guards dropped lower and lower. The rockets had, after all, only been visible for a few days, and of course, being security guards they had seen it as a matter of professional pride that they had never questioned what it was that they were guarding. Now they had no choice . . .

'Count-down has commenced. Final loading must be carried out immediately. Repeat immediately.'

'Jesus,' whispered Zimmerman. 'They're going to blow all six at once. Shit I guess I'm glad we didn't get any closer man. I mean, we would have been *fried* man! Fried, as old Walter would have said, with a capital 'F'. And that's *fucking* fried.'

Zimmerman gave Walter Culboon a friendly pat, which nearly stunned her.

'Man, if Walter Culboon hadn't gone the wrong way I'd have been riding *into* that man, finding out what it feels like to be a meat pie looking at a microwave.'

'Aren't we safe, then?' asked Chrissy more out of abstract interest than anything else.

'I reckon we're probably safe where we are,' said Zimm, 'but, oh boy, when those mothers blow you're going to see a burning cloud roll across the desert like surf from Hades. It's going to look like they dropped the big one right in our laps.'

Everyone, guards, officers, Eco-terrorists, had turned to stare across the desert at Stark. Mrs Culboon had fished out the high-powered field glasses taken from the helicopter ride and had wandered up to the top of the ridge behind which they had been sheltering. She felt no fear at exposing herself in this way. In a matter of seconds, the whole situation had changed. The launch count-down, floating across the desert, had made them all comrades in wonderment.

She steadied the glasses on a rock and peered.

'Christ,' yelled Mrs Culboon, 'I can see the buggers queueing for seats, there's funny kind of trucks taking them out towards the rockets. Jesus, God, Lord, Almighty, there's that bastard Tyron.'

One by one, they all took a look, as the voice counted off the last thirty minutes to the blast. CD was last to get hold of the glasses. By the time he looked most of the passengers were heading for the rockets. There was only one bus left . . . the departure point was almost empty.

Almost empty that is. He could just make out two figures marching in single file – one of them had a gun.

Month in, month out, CD had studied her walk, he had ogled her legs, stared at her every move and posture. He had devoured the shape of her bottom, tortured himself over the tilt and movement of her breasts. He had longed and ached for every part of her, the way she held her head, the tiny bulge of her tummy that only showed with tight skirts and which she hated but which he desperately wanted to sink his face into. With the unique passion of the unrequited, CD had stored up her every little shape, tilt and movement of use in his private fantasies – to conjure up again when he was alone in his bed.

He had pictured her so many times, there was no way he could mistake her now, even over fifteen kilometres with the binoculars shaking with passionate anger. That was Rachel, and what's more, she was being forced onto a rocket. 'The bastard' he screamed, 'that bastard Moorcock is forcing her! Hang on Rachel, I'm coming!!'

He ran for the station wagon ... Zimmerman saw him and shouted, 'It's too late man!! You won't get half-way there, it's eighteen minutes, you'll fry, you'll burn! CD there is no time!!'

But CD was in the car and away ...

A VICTORY FOR HUMANITY

Moments after CD had thrown down the binoculars, Sly and Rachel arrived at the door of the final transport. Durf was in an agony to be off.

'Come *on*, Mr Moorcock,' he protested.

'Get in,' said Sly brandishing the gun.

'No! Never!' said Rachel. 'It's horrible, I won't go!'

'Please, Rachel,' said Sly quietly.

'Look if the girl won't go voluntarily, knock the silly bitch out,' said a sweating Durf.

'You shut your foul mouth, Durf,' shouted Sly, waving the gun, 'or it'll be you that won't be going.'

'But we have to leave *now*,' pleaded Durf. 'We are only sixteen minutes from ignition ...'

'Rachel, I'll give you the moon!' Sly shouted, turning her towards him, feeling tears start in his eyes – his first tears in decades. 'No girl was ever offered that, please, for God's sake come, I love you.'

'Then stay here with me,' said Rachel quietly, whilst Durf hopped from foot to foot on the step of the transport, desperate to hurry things along, but recognizing also that Sly was armed and in a highly volatile state. Sly no longer even knew Durf was there.

'I can't stay here,' he said, 'everyone's going to die here. A whole race of losers, I can't be a loser ...'

They stared at each other for a moment. Sly thought of

pleading again, but he knew it would be useless. Perhaps that was the reason he loved her, she was strong.

'Mr Moorcock,' shouted Durf, 'we've got to go! Either get this girl on the transport or I'll drag the silly bitch on!'

Durf made to grab Rachel and Sly grabbed him, banging his head against the door of the transport.

'I told you to keep out of it you bastard, and you'd better or I'll kill you, understand? I'm going to get her on!'

'Then you'd better start running,' said a triumphant Durf.

Rachel had grabbed her chance. She was running for the car. The control bunker was only a minute away, she'd be safe in there – obviously it had been built to withstand the blast. She was presuming that Sly would not shoot her in the back. She was hoping that he would follow her. He did neither.

'Rachel!!' he screamed, raising his gun, but what was the point . . .

'Wait here,' he snapped at Durf.

'If you go after her we will have to leave without you,' said Durf icily, his hand on his gun, blood trickling from his injured head, 'The count-down is irreversible, we have no choice.'

Nor did Sly, he couldn't make himself a loser for a girl, he just couldn't do it.

'Rachel,' he shouted to her as she jumped into the car, 'come back you stupid bitch! You'll all be dead in a year . . . You stupid bitch . . .'

But she drove away and Sly and Durf boarded the transport.

'You should have dragged her on,' said Durf, as they tore towards the rockets. 'Now you'll be alone, you will have to wait for one of the frozen embryos to grow up.'

'Just one more word, Durf,' hissed Sly. 'One more fucking word, and I'll snap your scrawny neck in two.'

Everybody seemed to be threatening Durf that day, he wished people would not be so emotional.

Rachel had not a moment to lose. She raced the car back to

the control area, screeched it down the ramp into the underground loading area, jumped out and rushed into the central control room, slamming the lead and concrete doors behind her.

The voice informed her that there were thirteen minutes to go. She considered trying to carry out her plan of destroying the controls, but she had no weapon – where was all the modern furniture? Rachel had presumed the place would be full of glistening steel chairs. The sort of chairs that Sunday supplements inform you are the way furniture is going for the next decade – chairs that ought to come with their own osteopath.

But there were no chairs, just rank upon rank of glistening console going bleep bleep bleep. Rachel would probably not have tried to destroy the place anyway, they were all aboard, she might kill them. Sly was aboard. Rachel collapsed in an orgy of self-recrimination. Because of her lies, Sly would have to face life alone, perhaps for ever more, without a woman. If she had not plotted against him, he would have taken someone, now he was alone. Then again, they were all alone, everyone in the world, just waiting to die.

CHASE

Something in Walter Culboon's instincts urged her to obey Zimmerman. There was such genuine anguish in his tone as he jumped upon her back that she felt able to take courage and head back towards the scene of her previous terrors.

'Shit man, he won't get half-way there, and then man, bang! Poof! CD is part of the greenhouse effect,' Zimm had shouted as he ran towards Walter Culboon.

They charged off together, heading towards Stark in CD's wake, and nearly ran smack into a little jeep picking its way along in the opposite direction. It was driven by a stunning looking girl and had the name 'Suki' written across the sunstrip.

'Don't worry, Walter Culboon,' said Zimmerman, 'it's only another "woman driving across desert in car" hallucination.

I'm having a lot of those today.' Luckily the camel did not think it was a hallucination and swerved to avoid it.

They pressed on after CD. Zimm was armed and ready to fire should the security cordon have tried to stop him, but they had clearly decided that events had got bigger than their brief. Some were staring at the rockets; some were heading towards Bullens in terror. Either way, Zimmerman sailed right through them, as CD had done moments before.

Zimm reckoned he had a chance, CD was not making fantastic headway. The desert floor was extremely uneven and it was not possible to drive quickly, on the other hand he did have a start and Zimm was chasing him on a tired camel.

Over the harsh scrub he thundered in the wake of CD's dust cloud, every step taking them closer to being engulfed in a mega-cloud of burning rocket fuel and white hot fall-out.

CD didn't care, he was hunched manically over the wheel, conscious of only one thing – the need to rescue Rachel.

As the minutes ticked away, Walter Culboon pushed herself to the limit whilst Zimmerman sat astride roaring at CD to stop. 'Why don't you listen you stupid bastard,' he screamed.

The terrible voice of the count-down boomed again across the desert, drowning Zimm's puny efforts, informing all and sundry that they were now eight minutes from ignition, seven . . . now five.

Five minutes to a sextuplet rocket launch and CD was trying to drive into it! Zimm knew that he himself was crazy but he thanked heaven that he wasn't that crazy.

'Stop, you insane arsehole,' he screamed over Walter Culboon's head, as they careered towards oblivion . . .

'Four minutes and fifty seconds,' said the voice.

Then Zimm saw his chance. There was a little hillock ahead, only about ten feet at its peak, but it was the top of a long sand wave that CD would certainly have to traverse if he wanted to head on in.

'I hope the bastard smashes straight into it,' thought Zimm . . . But no, CD's brain was still clear, except of course for the part that was telling him to commit a pointless and suicidal act.

CD turned the car to travel along parallel to the ridge of sand, this gave Zimm his one chance to get ahead.

As the voice informed him that he now had four minutes and forty seconds left to live, Zimm spurred Walter Culboon up to the top of the hillock. He unslung the shoulder-held launcher and attempted to judge the distance between himself and CD, the speed CD was travelling and any likely changes of direction. What he wanted to do was to put a shell in the ground about twenty metres ahead of CD's car. This, Zimm hoped, would stop the car without killing CD, although why he was bothering with the stupid bastard was a mystery to Zimm. His own years of acting like a maniac had not made him any more sympathetic to when other people tried it. There was so little time, Zimm had to force himself to take aim carefully, he knew he would only get the one shot.

Before the smoke had cleared, Zimm had urged Walter Culboon down into it, where, amidst the dust and fumes, they found CD crawling out of the shattered car.

'Dig you stupid dumb pommie bastard,' shouted Zimmerman.

And the voice said, 'four minutes and twenty seconds to ignition.'

'Dig?' asked a dazed CD.

'Dig!' shouted Zimmerman. CD was confused.

'Yeah, uhm, right Zimm, I dig,' he said.

'Dig the ground,' said Zimm, grabbing CD by the neck.

'OK, OK,' spluttered CD, 'I dig the ground, although I don't see what's so great about it.'

'I mean, really dig, actual digging, not the hip word, dig?' shouted Zimm and he frantically started attacking the ground.

'Oh *dig*,' said CD understanding at last.

'Dig,' said Zimm.

Luckily the Culboons' station wagon was equipped with spades, as indeed are many outback station wagons. Zimmerman grabbed a couple.

'I mean man, what is it with you? And what's more, what *is* the point!' moaned Zimm thrusting a spade into CD's hand. 'Like can I just relax and watch the blast? No, not me, not old Zimm, I have to be fucking *in* it!!'

'I'm sorry, Zimm,' said CD.

'Not as sorry as you're going to be if we can't make some cover. You dig a trench for yourself and me, I'll look after Walter Culboon! We stop at minus twenty seconds!!'

CD realized that with the car gone Rachel was now definitely beyond reach and so for three minutes, as the voice counted them towards near certain oblivion, they dug.

Zimmerman was a wild man, he needed to be, trying to make a hole big enough for a camel. But they were at least in a natural hollow with the ridge CD had been trying to drive around between them and the blast. With forty-five seconds to go Zimm stood Walter Culboon, who was wondering what the excitement was about, at the edge of his shallow little trench.

'Sorry, Walter Culboon, but you'll thank me for this . . .'

He chopped the camel in the neck and Walter Culboon fell neatly unconscious into the hole. Even in this moment of extremis, CD could not help noting that being able to lay out a camel with a single blow, really was pretty mega-cool.

Walter Culboon collapsed and in a blur of energy, Zimmerman scraped down debris from the side of the incline on top of her.

'Ignition minus twenty-five seconds and counting,' said the voice.

'OK, get in,' shouted Zimm, and keep your head down, man. It's a shame, we're going to miss the whole scene . . . but I suppose really it's the sort of thing you ought to see stoned anyway.'

They lay down together in the little shallow grave that CD had dug and desperately tried to pull earth in on top of them.

'Leastways they won't have to bury us,' said CD in triumph – he had finally managed to crack a gag during a moment of extreme tension.

'Minus five,' boomed the voice.

'Cover your face, arsehole,' said Zimm.

And as the world seemed to erupt in heat and shuddering noise around him, CD's last thought was to wonder why Zimm should want him to cover his face and arsehole.

A HELL OF AN EXIT

Back on the perimeter, as they listened to the final countdown, Mrs Culboon and Chrissy took shelter behind some rocks. They could see across their former battleground that those security personnel who had remained were doing likewise.

It was a hell of an exit.

Six old style space rockets blasting off in close succession. No sooner had one great tidal wave of burning atmosphere rolled across the desert towards them, when another would start, and then another. And out of this thick, bubbling carpet of shimmering orange heat and black black smoke the rockets rose slowly, almost seeming to hang in the air, reminding Mrs Culboon of the helicopter that CD had brought down, making her half expect these rockets to suddenly lose their fragile momentum and come crashing back down to the ground. But they did not, of course. Stark had been preparing for too long to make any mistakes.

And so Stark flew away.

Slowly the rumbling died down, the streaks of flame began to fade in the sky and they were gone.

HELL ON EARTH AS
IT IS IN HEAVEN

And so it came to pass that the Stark consortium left the earth in their Star Arks. Escaping just in time as the storm of ecological disintegration gathered to become a catastrophic deluge; a great flood of dust, disease, heat and filthy, poisonous water, rising to engulf the billions who had created it.

As had been predicted, the horrifying legacy of all the years of thoughtless vandalism turned in upon its creators, and upon all other forms of life on earth, for whom ignorance was no defence. Wave after wave of pollution washed across the dead and dying dirt. Warm, thick, heavy toxic rain fell from the muddied, burning skies, the acid in every drop bursting out upon what life remained, sad useless weeds, clinging to the shifting sands of the barren, infertile, salty ground.

The seas, swollen and bloated by waters which had remained frozen since before the birth of humankind, rose up to reclaim the earth that had been theirs before the cold had bound them.

The deserts that for so long had been chained and guarded by the great forests leapt forward claiming all the land that the seas did not seem to want. And everywhere along the changing shorelines of our retreating world, was washed up, with every tide, the filth and waste disgorged by the teeming billions day by day. Sand and pebbles became a memory as the shrinking coast grew mountainous, piled high with the live and festering muck which nobody knew where to put any more.

All these things came to be, just as the scientists who served Stark had said they would. Indeed, all these things had already come to haunt the earth long before the rich and powerful finally took their leave. The seas have been rising, the deserts spreading, the stinking piles of rubbish growing, the poison rain falling and the land drying, since before the members of the Stark Conspiracy were born.

THE TRUTH DAWNS

After the Stark blast off, the world very quickly learned the facts of what had happened. At first there had been mystification as the news of the launches swept around the world. Then some bright spark at a local Perth TV studio realized that they had a scoop. Suddenly the Daft Dingo became the hottest news on earth. The tape (with the interviewer's derisive comments edited out) was beamed around the globe.

Chrissy's voice was heard everywhere.

'They have a research team called the Domesday Group, who have proved that the world is dying . . .'

'. . . I've seen the evidence, it's true . . . there doesn't seem to be any hope any more . . . but there *must* be, I mean we're not dead yet, are we . . .'

For those who still doubted, the final proof came the next day with the first broadcast from the Stark fleet; a sombre message, explaining the situation, and almost apologizing for leaving.

'We are sorry,' Durf's voice and image bounced off the world's myriad communication satellites, 'but we knew the truth, the Domesday Group had proved it for us. There is no hope. The Stark Consortium is now the human race. We will do our best to make it work this time.'

Panic and fear swept the earth as daily reports of the departed renegades dominated the media. The world's richest and most powerful producers had gone and left the consumers to their fate. Strangely there was little bitterness, or anger, it was all too hot and hopeless for that. People knew that they were all to blame, not one single person was without guilt. The least anyone had done was to stand idly by. The best that could be said of a person was that they had done no more than close their eyes to the cost of the great global party.

People felt that the cynicism of the Stark departure was no greater than the cynicism with which the riches of the earth had been squandered. The world was dying and the world deserved it. This was the shocked fatalistic attitude of the final generation. If those bastards had bought their way out, it didn't matter any more anyway.

IF ONLY

'If only,' people sighed, 'if only we had *done* something. Acted when we still had time, even just ten years ago,' they said, 'back in the late eighties, the early nineties when there was still time. The signs were all there, why didn't we *do* something.'

But they hadn't, back in '89, '90 and '91, the years when the decisions needed to be taken, nothing had been done. People had listened to the politicians' empty rhetoric at election time but nothing huge, nothing drastic, nothing *real* had actually been done. Too much money was involved, it simply wasn't economical. Nothing had been done and now the reckoning was upon them all.

PARTY TIME

After the blast CD had tried to say 'is it over, Zimm?' but it is rather difficult to speak when you seem to have eaten about half of the Great Sandy Desert.

Spitting and spluttering dust out of his mouth he rose up to find Zimmerman, sitting on the prostrate form of Walter Culboon, rolling a ciggie.

'We have to wait for Walter Culboon to come around man, I reckon I hit her a little hard,' was Zimmerman's reply.

As they waited they saw a car heading out from what had been the launch site. Zimm presumed it was another hallucination and ignored it. For CD, as always, hope sprang eternal, and just this once it was justified in doing so, because it was Rachel.

It is a tribute to CD that the ecstatic relief he found in Rachel's survival, and the discovery that she had remained loyal to the team all along, was only slightly tempered over the next hour or two by the dawning realization that Rachel's experiences had not been sufficiently cathartic to shock her into wanting to sleep with him.

The four of them headed off together, away from the smouldering remnants of Stark, until they found Chrissy and Mrs Culboon. There they said goodbye to Walter Culboon and the remnants of EcoAction (in CD's case, smouldering), headed on back to Bullens Creek. Back to the home that Mr and Mrs Culboon had bought so recently when they had thought their luck was in. Now Mr Culboon was gone and Durf's thugs had smashed most of it up. Anyway the earth was dying. The cat was OK though.

'So what do we do now?' said Chrissy.

'Well, I reckon we should sell the hire car and buy some beer,' said Mrs Culboon.

'I could certainly do with getting a bit pissed,' said Rachel.

'Yeah, but it's not really the time for a party is it?' said CD, thinking of the friends they'd lost and the failure of what they'd tried to do.

'Sure it's the right time,' said Zimmerman, 'it's time to party like there's no tomorrow.'

HELL

And the pioneers of Stark? Their lives were hell.

It was too much for poor Sly. After only one year, on yet another lonely lonely night, he opened a pressure door and allowed himself to float away to heaven. He was glad that Rachel had not come with him. He would not have wished the

452

world that Stark had created on anyone, let alone someone he loved.

He was not the first to crack, and he would not be the last. The frozen embryos were destined never to be brought to life. The problem was not the conditions, it was not the work they had to do, nor even the food – the problem was the company.

The pioneers of Stark hated each other. They had created Hell in Heaven. They had escaped pollution on earth, only to discover that they had carried with them another pollution, a pollution that they could not escape. The pollution in their own souls.